Re-Deal

A Time-Travel Thriller

Re-Deal

A Time-Travel Thriller

by Richard Turner

Re-Deal
by Richard Turner

©2009 Richard Turner
All Rights Reserved

Showdown Creations, Inc.
515 Mission Viejo
San Antonio, TX 78232
210-495-4448
redeal@richardturner52.com
www.richardturner52.com

ISBN-13:
Paperback: 978-0-9819606-0-9
E-Book: 978-0-9819606-1-6

ISBN-10:
Paperback: 0-9819606-0-X
E-Book: 0-9819606-1-8

Cover Artist: Gary Bell

Dedication

Asa Spades, my wonderful son, I have authored this thriller in the event God calls me to a greater journey prior to your growing into a man. Woven within this story are many of my personal life experiences. Through these calamitous encounters, I have discovered a peace that surpasses all perceptions. My most passionate prayers are that you find this same peace.

I also give a special thankful hug and a kiss to my heavenly treasure Kim AKA Miss Guided. I love you so, so very much!

I also offer a special thanks to my editor and friend Lillie Ammann, whose passion for paring words made this book possible.

This document bequeaths to the owner to wit my west Texas ranch of 1562 blocks of 640 acres each with a value of $2.50 per acre

with a land value of $2,500,000.

I also bequeath 50,000 head of my Longhorn steer at $10 per head with a total land and cattle value of $3,000,000.

Lucas McCain
July 12 1882

I, GOVERNOR L. BRADFORD PRINCE,
transfer all my vast land holdings,
and the territory to which I am Governor,
most commonly referred to as
THE TERRITORY OF NEW MEXICO,
which lands extend from Arizona to
the west Texas border.

This document turns over to
JOHN L. CYPHER
all these properties and territory
completely and absolutely with no
restrictions or restraints.

Sincerely,

L. Bradford Prince

L. Bradford Prince, Governor Proprietor

July 12, 1882

Note from the Author

I got the idea for the Poker Championship of the West from the book *Sucker's Progress* by Herbert Asbury. The story of the biggest raise ever risked on a poker pot appears on page 347 of the original 1938 edition of the book.

A high-stake gambler faced off with a rich Texas cattle rancher in what was billed as the Poker Championship of the West at Bowen's Saloon in Santa Fe in the 1880s. The rancher ran out of money and wrote out a deed to his ranch and thousands of head of cattle and added it to the pot, which included more than a hundred thousand dollars in cash. The gambler didn't have the money to raise or call so he held a gun to the head of L. Bradford Prince, the Governor of the New Mexico territory, and forced him to sign over the state. The rancher folded, declaring, "I quit, but just be glad that the Governor of Texas isn't here."

I always wondered what would have happened if the Texas Governor showed up and the rancher had won the territory that became the state of New Mexico.

In *Re-Deal* I have taken artistic license with historical times, places, and characters to weave this thriller. All inconsistencies and discrepancies are mine.

BOOK ONE

CHAPTER ONE

Direct Contact Angel

"Do not forget to entertain strangers, for by doing so some people have entertained angels without knowing it." Hebrews 13:2

Strong hands held Matt down while someone cinched a band tightly around his arm. He felt the biting jab of a needle. His lungs constricted, and he gasped desperately for air. His heart pounded so hard he feared it might explode inside his chest. His head felt fuzzy and heavy, then he crumpled to the floor. His world went black.

As time passed, Matt saw flashes of light and heard loud voices arguing as he slipped in and out of consciousness. He felt himself being lugged across the floor, then lifted into the air. He felt like he was floating. Suddenly, his body landed on something hard. He ached and throbbed all over, and he faded into blackness again.

Matt continued to slip in, then out, in, then out again. He tried to pull himself out of the darkness. He blinked, trying to clear the confusion and make sense of the blur around him.

Someone shook him by the shoulders. "Mr. Matthew McCain, I bet you'd rather answer ta Matthew than Magoo. Am I right?"

As Matt slowly came to, he could hear the voice of a woman, using the loathed nickname Magoo. He opened his eyes to see a strange lady gawking down at him. He slapped the woman's hands from his face and jerked up to a sitting position.

"I can't stand that name! Now get your hands off my eyes!" Matt rubbed his temples. "Oh, man, does my head ever hurt bad."

Although the pounding in his head felt like a sadistic gremlin banging with a sledgehammer, he was relieved to still be alive. What had he done to himself? His fuzzy head surfed through emotions, thoughts, and feelings he didn't have the strength to recognize, sort out, or identify.

"I must be dying, or dead ... or something?"

The woman patted his hand. "I saw what wicked evil the Cyphers did ya."

Matt jerked his hand back. He didn't remember much, but he did remember that Big Lew was determined Matt would manipulate the outcome of his rigged Hold'em game.

"Who are you? What are you here for? Did Big Lew send you to bring me back? If he did, I'm not going!"

"I'm not here ta send you back anywhere. I'm here to help you."

"Help me? Sure you—" Matt stopped in mid-sentence when he realized he could see her face clearly. His eyes went wide with amazement. "Hey, I'm looking at you."

He let a few moments pass as he tried to grab hold of something, anything, that would root him in some reality he could understand. He hadn't seen worth two bits in years, ever since Big Lew's sadistic henchmen had forced him to stare into the direction of the 104-degree blazing-hot sun. He had squeezed his eyes closed, but his attackers spread his eyelids apart, forcing him to stare into the blinding white light. A shadow had passed in front of his eyes— a large magnifying glass! The magnifying glass flashed, and the sun zoomed in and filled his view. The retinas were fried like eggs on a skillet. Ever since that terrible day his burned eyes had been just about useless.

RE-DEAL

"What's going on here?" He looked around in a panic. There was no horizon, no ceiling, only endless space. Matt said in wonder, "I can actually see you clearly, and you're beautiful."

"Why thank ya, Mr. Matt." The woman moved her face closer to his and softly touched him on his cheek. "Yer a sweet talker all right, a real sweet talker. But, of course, ya can now see me. Yer out cold! It just might give yer heart a chance ta catch up with yer stubborn, ornery numbskull."

Matt was struck by a memory. Stubborn, ornery numbskull. Those were his mother's words right before he knocked her down and ran away. He had a hard time dealing with his mother. She was always praying and fretting over him, and when she tried to convince him to stay away from Damen Cypher and his henchman Carlos and Gustavo, Matt just lost it. Now this unknown female was calling him stubborn, ornery numbskull just like his mother.

"Don't talk like that."

"I beg yer pardon," the woman said. "That's about how yer kind mama spoke it. Don't ya reckon?"

Matt turned away and swallowed a sob. He felt guilty for telling his warm, caring mother to go to hell and worse.

"Come on." The woman took his hand. "Push forward, Mr. Matthew. Look at me while ya got the chance."

Matt felt like he was in some kind of no man's land. He didn't know where he was or who this stranger was, but her kindness and beauty impressed him. He turned back toward the lady with a sniff.

The woman smiled. "Remember when ya clamored out ta yer Maker, when they were throwin' ya out like the garbage?"

That's what the floating feeling had been—he had been thrown out of the window of Tom Andrews' apartment. Damen, along with Carlos and another of the Cypher flunkies, had taken him there for a mild pick-me-up. But once there, they made fun of him, demanding he perform some of his cheating moves to entertain them. Tom Andrews even said his great grandfather had been a card mechanic and supposedly was the legendary card cheat, Erdnase. Then instead of giving him the mild pick-me-up he wanted, they had forced a needle in his ...

Matt shook his head, then winced in pain. He wouldn't think about what they had done to him. He remembered calling out for help, maybe even saying, "Oh, God. If it's not too late, please help me!" However, he couldn't understand what this woman meant by "clamored out ta yer Maker."

"It was Damen and them. I said I didn't want it. But they forced it on me."

The woman ran her delicate fingers through his long stringy hair and said, "Mr. Matthew, please let the hogs lie and give yer attention ta me. We got but a small parcel of time here, so we must get started quick."

Matt could hardly believe he could see her pretty face as she spoke. And her clothing—an old-fashioned blue and pink dress and flowery hat—perplexed him. Staring wide-eyed at her, he said, "Yes, yes, ma'am."

"There's a season ta squat still," she explained, "and another for action. Ya grabbed the ear of the Almighty, Mr. Matthew. Now yer future depends on how ya step up and proceed with yer mission." She took his hands in hers. "Now ya better draw yourself together and get ahead of them Cyphers before they whip your kindhearted papa like they done yer wonderful grandpappy, Lucas."

"Oh no!" Matt's stomach flipped with fear. "They'll hurt my dad?"

"Yes, ya got it. Mr. Matthew, they'll torment more than that, and I can't tell ya how far tardy we are in addressin' the situation."

Matt snapped back. "Are you blaming me? It's not my fault! I can't do anything—"

"Mr. Matt, it's okay. Slow down. It does no good ta fatalistically fuss about the past. Ya know the account, how yer great granddaddy was swindled out of it all."

"Not Lucas the Loser again," Matt mumbled. He had spent his whole life suffering for the stupidity of his great grandfather. "Will my family ever be free of the McCain curse? They say he was cheated," Matt scoffed.

"It's history, Mr. Matthew. I have a very pleasant reminiscence of yer wonderful grandfather. Ya know if the human

RE-DEAL

race didn't bear in mind any history, it would be perfectly happy. But, my boy, that's not good. Man should learn from his past."

Matt tried to shake his head clear. His brain started to spin again just from listening to her odd chatter. He realized his family would never be free from the Lucas curse. "Yeah, sure lady, whatever you say."

Lady, thought the angel in human guise. *Ya don't recognize me, but I have a mission. Sir Gabriel himself assigned me, his mirthful heavenly hostess, to put paradise's peace back into the McCain's pitiful, dirt-poor lives. You, Matthew McCain, will vanquish the remorseless Cyphers, their leader Big Lew, and his followers of forsaken fiends.*

She said none of this to her new charge, though. "Mr. Matthew, when I feel blue, I start breathing again. Now, come on, my fine boy. Ya know it in yer heart. Yer good daddy sat sun ta moon teachin' ya their trickery and all about the genuine wild-wild West. I know ya understand from listening ta that wonderful speech ya made so many years prior, that when the Creator scooped up a fist full of that grass-growin' dirt, then blew into it, man is no longer inert soil, Mr. Matthew, so ya can set a high value on who you are."

"How do you know about the speech I gave back in junior high?"

"The Divine Creator made ya'll gifted with ability and comprehension. Why yer explanation of creation was masterful. Ya even reminded folks that oranges are already sliced in the peel."

Matt asked again, "How do you know about that?"

"The Almighty made ya with what it takes to make it better for yourself. I know from listening' to yer God-fearin' Mama, you understand what I'm sayin'."

Matt gave up on getting a straight answer to his question. "All right, lady. I believe you. But I'm only a Loser McCain. You can ask anyone—McCains are all flops. But if I would've been there, before the Lucas curse came on our family, things would've been different. I would never have been so stupid to fall for such a moronic shell game. My dad, who spent years studding with Professor Vernon, one of the greatest card manipulators, taught me how to control the cards. In fact, that tyrant Big Lew says I'm the best card mechanic he's ever seen."

"Oh, please, please, Mr. Matthew. Never exalt yourself. Pride always precedeth a fall. Besides, if ya swindle the money ya win, it's the devil's money, and it ain't worth a plug nickel."

"Well, lady, you don't really have anything to worry about anyway. I'm only a loser from a long line of losers."

"Well, cheating is not the way we're gonna approach the circumstance anyhow. Now the real question is—do ya have true faith in the most excellent Author ya earlier clamored out to?"

Matt was puzzled by the question. In his heart, he really did want to trust God like his mom did. He was so empty inside he thought anything would be better than his miserable life now. He told her with a slow nod, "Of course, I do. I really want to have the faith. But God doesn't care about me. I'm just a worthless Loser McCain."

"Oh no! That's not true. He does care. And I know the answer; it's easy. The Good Book says if ya have a mustard-seed faith, we can turn the tide back, travel outside-of-time, go backward, and reconstruct the past. But first, my boy, we must get ya whole again."

Matt's mind was in another spiral of confusion. Go back? Time? Once more he tried to understand her. But smoke sifted through his mind, obscuring his thinking. He faded away into the empty darkness. *What a weird dream this is*, he thought hazily as the darkness consumed him. Matt watched as this strange, crazy, but very beautiful woman faded to a blur, then disappeared.

CHAPTER TWO

Escape from the Rat-Hole

Matt felt a woman's hands shaking his shoulders. "Mr. Matthew, it's time ta wake up and consume some vittles."

Matt slowly came to. He felt someone helping him up to a sitting position against a washing machine. As he gradually became conscious, he realized he was waking up in a laundry room. Wow. What a bizarre dream. He sluggishly opened his eyes and felt a shock of deep disappointment to discover the damage to his sight was still there. He silently cursed the reality.

What a downer to discover that seeing normally again had been only a dream. Things were still as blurry as they had been before. Matt was sure the aftereffects from the drugs made things seem to move by themselves. Spinning, crawling, like herds of spiders in his shadowy vision. He'd become a bubbling caldron of conflicting thoughts and emotions.

The frightening day at Tom's came back to him. He realized Damen wanted him dead and knew he was lucky to live after that drug concoction. Once and for all he had to get away from that evil clan.

He looked around and felt sick inside, discouraged to realize it had only been a stupid dream that he could see. He had to go back to that embarrassing way of trying to see by looking out of the sides of his eyes. He hated it. People always looked at him like some kind of freak, just because they couldn't tell who he was looking at when he was talking.

Was the beautiful lady with that odd Southern voice just a dream? Had she really been talking about going back in time? His head throbbed and his brain was still fuzzy. He squinted hard to try and get a peek of her. Yes, yes, she was the same woman he'd clearly seen in that curious dream.

"Wow! Lady, I could see! But what did I see?"

The woman moved Matt's hair off his feverish face. "Mr. Matthew McCain, have ya returned ta the land of the here and now?"

"I don't know. Maybe. I think so."

"Just relax a spell. And have faith. Everything's gonna be fine."

Mat thought he could hear a quiet confidence in her voice. "Okay, I'm listening."

"Well," the woman said with a shake of her head. "I suppose the Master has a plan for the skimpy little piece a material He furnished in yer case. But I can only suppose what it might be." She squeezed his skinny, emaciated arm. "My-my-my, yer just flesh on sticks! Yer nothing like yer grandpappy, Lucas McCain."

What did Lucas the Loser have to do with anything? Oh no, he was going to lose it! He fell to the side and ejected the contents of his stomach. He hacked and choked until nothing was left but bile. He muttered, "Sorry, lady ... couldn't hold it. That was really gross." He wiped his mouth on his coat sleeve.

"Emptying that nauseated, sick stomach shoulda made ya feel a little better."

###

Nearby, Juan was running back to the laundry room. He wondered who that weirdly-dressed woman was and what her sudden appearance could mean for him.

He'd been trying to escape from Cypher hell ever since his poor sweet sister had been used by an old man until she was just a shadow of herself, then sent to work in the

RE-DEAL

factories. She had disappeared, and Juan had been following orders as a Cypher drudge as he built up his karate skills and looked for a way out.

He couldn't stop them from shooting Magoo up with heroin and throwing him out the window. After Matt had been tossed through the window, Juan did something he had never done before. He whispered a little prayer. *'Ey Man in the Sky, if Yer up there, then please get us out of this rat-hole.*

They didn't get out of the rat-hole, and now Big Lew blamed him that Matt was missing. Magoo was Cypher's preferred mechanic because the other players never suspected the burnt-eyed dealer could cheat. Juan had to find the missing card man and get him back in time for the big Hold'em game, or he'd be the one that paid.

He'd found Magoo and was trying to bring him round when the weird woman grabbed him from behind, called him by name, and asked him to help her get Matt out of the bushes.

Since he would be the one in trouble if Matt didn't recover in time to deal the game, Juan went along with the weird female and helped drag McCain into the laundry room of the apartment building.

When he asked the woman who she was, she answered, ""I am just another created being who knows yer in trouble if Matthew departs his earthly body. Now tell me, do ya want ta help save him—and yourself?"

"'Ey man, whatever you're saying, I want to do it."

"Then, please, rustle me up some vittles. Somethin' that will stick to the poor boy's ribs."

"Vittles?" Juan frowned. "Are vittles food?"

"That's it. He's lackin' protein, my young friend."

The woman took her tiny purse off her arm, opened it, and removed a shiny coin. She handed it to Juan and said, "Take this for pay. Now, please, pound yer dawgs an hurry!"

"Pound my what?"

"Why, your feet, silly boy. Now go."

The coin felt unusually heavy. Juan looked more closely at it and saw that it was gold with a date of 1882. Overwhelmed, he asked, "Um, this is real gold. Are you sure you want me to spend it?"

"Yes, and ya may keep any change. Now please, hurry!"

He considered keeping the valuable coin and running away from her, the Cyphers, and the rest. Yet, something inside told him to go back and to do exactly what she said.

Juan wondered if this might be some kind of weird answer to his and Magoo's desperate prayers. He'd heard the Man in the Sky worked in mysterious ways. But on second thought, he decided he was a fool to believe anyone or any God would care about a little Mexican peon like him.

Nevertheless, he'd decided to use his own money for the food instead of the old gold piece. He quickly grabbed four burgers and two fries at the local Gag-in-a-Bag. He downed three of the burgers and the two fries as he dashed back.

When Juan returned, Matt was helping the kind woman clean up his mess. His head perked up like a squirrel as the door opened.

Juan ran in and saw Big Lew's favorite dealer awake and sitting up. He was relieved, but not for Big Lew, who was only using this poor guy to make him more money. Juan walked over to the odd-talking woman and handed the bag over to her.

"'Ey man, here's the grub for Loser Magoo."

She took the meal and nodded with a smile. "Thanks, Mr. Juan."

"'Ey man, here's your money." Juan held up her coin. "It was worth more than the food, so I used my own cash."

She took Juan's hands into hers and fastened his fingers around the gold coin. "Honest Juan, you keep it. It's round, so trade it in for some wheels."

Wheels? What the hell was she talking about now?

Juan saw Matt looking around in the weird way he had of looking sideways out of the corners of his eyes. He grabbed the top of a washer and tried to pull himself up to a standing position. However, he was so weak he started to fall.

RE-DEAL

Before he dropped, the woman reached over and caught him. Matt ignored her help, shoved her away, charged in a fury toward his nemesis, and knocked the punk back outside into the grass and the spraying water sprinklers.

Matt's attempt at a yell came out in feeble squeak. "You creep! You tried to kill me! I hate that name Loser Magoo!"

He tackled Juan to the ground. The two blustered and wrestled in the wet grass and dirt. But the younger Juan effortlessly subdued the weak blind boy.

He scoffed, "Yer a tough mother, huh?" He broke loose, shoved Matt away, then dusted himself off. "Whoa, yer macho man, huh? Wimp!"

The woman stepped over to Matt. "Boy, when ya wake up ta a matter, ya sure do let loose." She brushed him off as he tottered, trying to keep his balance. "Look at you, Mr. Matthew McCain. It looks like ya got a heaping case of the drunken staggers. Now, Matthew, this ain't how a McCain does it."

She grabbed Juan with her dainty little hands and pulled him over to Matt. As the weird woman grabbed him, Juan noticed her hands were Herculean in their strength.

"Mr. Matthew, this here's the first friend you've had since yer eyes got burned. He'll help ya save yer pa—Juan bears the name of a great man of God. Now shake and make up."

What the hell is she saying now? I bear the name of a great man of God? I have no name. She must be from outer space or something. But after feeling the strength in her grip, I'm not going to argue.

He reluctantly offered his hand first and said, "Sorry, McCain."

Matt took the proffered hand and said in a voice laced with doubt, "It's okay."

The woman nodded as they shook hands. "Now that's more like it, boys." She removed the burger from the sack and handed it to Matt. "Now, please chow down, Mr. Matt."

Matt had no strength left. He was winded, scared, and cold. That short skirmish took everything out of him. He panted hard as he looked out of the sides of his eyes, groping for her hand. With hands that shook, he took the hamburger, unwrapped it, and buried his teeth into it.

Juan looked at his watch, started to panic, and looked down the street. He knew Damen would be looking to see if he had found Magoo.

"I can tell yer chuck full of anxiety, Mr. Juan. Ya want ta help see what we can do ta untangle this clutter?" the strange woman asked.

"Help?" Juan jeered. "'Ey man, you're just a girl—"

"Why, thank ya, Mr. Juan," she said with a curtsy. "Ya finally noticed that I'm in the semblance of the female side of creation."

"Huh? Female side of what?"

"Why yes," she replied smiling. "Ya called me a girl, not 'Ey man.'"

"Yeah, you're a girl, and Cyphers kill!"

But on the other hand, Juan thought, *there's something special about this woman. And if it's time for me to break free from the Cyphers, maybe she can help.*

"'Ey man, if you think you can do something to help, tell us what."

"Yeah, lady," Matt mumbled. "How? We need help, an army or something, not one little lady."

"Boys, the situation is like this. Sometimes the Almighty assigns someone ta answer yer prayers. Mother Teresa was on assignment, and yer favored with me."

Matt was still trying to keep up with this woman's blather. He asked, "So, you're like a nun?"

The incognito angel nodded pleasantly at the remembrance of her senior celestial associate. "Close enough. My name is Guided."

"Did you say Mrs. Guided?" Juan asked.

"Oh no," she told them with a smile. "I'm not wedded."

Juan snorted, then laughed. "So you're Miss Guided?"

She nodded. "Yeah, choice name, huh? However, my boys, right now the chronometer is runnin', and Mr. Matt needs ta be made whole again. Furthermore, Big Lew means ta go ta work on ya if we don't leave here, fast." The guardian gazed over at Juan. "We need ta help put Humpty Dumpty back ta his prior wholeness. I know where. Let's get! Quick!"

CHAPTER THREE

Miss Guided, Of Course

The woman hustled Matt and Juan to the street. She led the two young men to a blue buggy with a pink interior that coordinated with her dress and hat.

As they drew close Juan's eyes went wide. The sight of the white stallion, seventeen hands high, and colorful buggy with four large, frosty white wheels in the middle of Cypher City stunned him.

He asked, "'Ey man, where in hell did that Barbie-doll stage come from?"

The woman's eyes flashed. "Hell is not its origin," she told them. "Nobody but a half-wit would think this lovely blue coach came from hell. Why does humanity always squawk so freely about places they don't ever want ta be eternally captivated in?"

Juan was set back at the strange rebuke. *Whoa!* he thought. *What did I just step in?* He tried to shake his head clear from her confusing jibber-jabber.

"'Ey, what places are you trying to tell us, man?"

"Yeah," Matt added. "Wh-wh-what places?"

"Why the place called hell, of course!"

"Hell!" Juan was starting to lose it. "What the hell kind of gibberish are you talking now?"

"I'll give a description for ya, Mr. Juan. Hell is the region for the no-good. I'll explain. First, do ya know why it's so blazin' hot in El Paso, Texas?"

I knew I shouldn't have come back, Juan thought in exasperation. *I should have taken the money and kept going.*

He said, "I don't know. Tell us why it's so hot in El Paso."

"It's like this," the smiling woman explained. "The charge to call from El Paso to hell is only two measly bits. Twenty-five cents, a fourth of a buck; you see, it's a local call. That's why it's so blazin' hot. This will cause much weeping, wailing, and gnashing of teeth. Now contemplate residin' in El Paso until the end of time without an umbrella or any Gatorade. That's what hell will be comparable to."

"Oh yeah?" Juan taunted. "What about those who've had their teeth punched out? Can't gnash without teeth."

"No teeth, um." Miss Guided paused for a moment. "Teeth will be provided!"

Once again Juan's head rattled in bewilderment. He was certain this woman was from some foreign place he'd never heard of. He asked, "'Ey man, where are you from and what do you do?"

"Why thank ya for askin'," she answered. "I'm a tongue-tickling tutor who loves to laugh and teach. Oh, and I'm here by means of Texas."

"Yeah, is that right?" Juan said. "What part?"

"What part? Why all of me, of course!"

Matt giggled at the lady's hilarious answer. He repeated, "What part? Why all of me, of course."

I'm not buying this, Juan thought, weary of the verbal eruptions. He pressed further, "'Ey man, have you lived there all your life?"

Miss Guided's blue eyes sparkled with glee. "How could I have lived all my life in Texas? Look, I'm still alive."

Juan shook his head in disbelief. He asked, "Lady, how old are you?"

Her eyes widened. "Why, Mr. Juan, I'm as old as my folks were when they were at my stage of life."

"Huh? Do you have any kids? I'm sure you know women shouldn't have children after thirty-five."

"I'll say—thirty-five kids are enough."

RE-DEAL

That's it, Juan thought, bent on setting her up for a little joke of his own. He raised his eyebrow and asked, "Your name again is?"

She said with a slight curtsy, "I'm Miss Guided, of course!"

Juan elbowed Matt. "'Ey man, I think she's misguided all right!"

"Okay, come on. Hike it on over, boys." She led Matt to the front of the buggy. "Mr. Matt, I'd like ya ta make the acquaintance of my triple-trotter horse, Seraphim. Seraphim, this man is Mr. Matthew McCain, the descendant of the great rancher, Lucas McCain."

Juan, watching the horse's eyes closely, noticed something peculiar. The animal's eyes communicated complete understanding, as if the horse understood everything this strange dame said. Juan watched thunderstruck as Seraphim lifted his muzzle high into the air and brayed a loud welcoming whinny.

Juan wondered if he'd entered the Twilight Zone. The situation was getting more bizarre by the second. Was he dreaming? Or had Tom shot him up with the drugs? This lady was like no one Juan had ever met. Except maybe in a stupid kid's movie like Mary Poppins or something.

He cocked his head, raised an eyebrow, and said, "I've never seen a three-legged horse before. Why doesn't this glue-factory tip over?"

Miss Guided straightened her pink ribbon around her neck and pulled a couple of sugar cubes from her tiny purse. She put them before her horse's mouth and answered, "Seraphim is unorthodox."

Matt staggered close as he tried to see the horse. "Lady, why would you buy a horse with three legs?"

"Why, boys," she answered, "I received a twenty-five-percent discount."

Juan scoffed. "'Ey man, ya got duped. You should've got four legs."

"I didn't get duped. I brought home all four. I keep the fourth leg in the trunk as a spare."

Juan snickered and said to Matt. "She's funny!" Still, he wasn't interested in traveling around in this old relic from a canceled cowboy Western. "Miss, Miss Guided, you don't really expect us to ride around in public in this old buggy from the Big Valley, do ya?"

"Oh, that's an affirmative, Mr. Juan. I expect it. This buggy is a blazer and smooth as melted butter, too."

"Yeah, man?" Juan replied. "Like Damen's Lamborghini, huh?"

He circled the powder blue coach and wondered how the extra large white wheels stayed so clean. He moved around and stopped at the back where there was some kind of a lever.

He asked, "'Ey man, what's this handle for?"

"Oh, that's the trunk. I store Seraphim's fourth leg in there." The woman pointed toward the top. "And there's gear racks up yonder." She stepped to the side, opened the carriage door, and said, "Now the pair of ya, please pile in. Time is tickin'."

CHAPTER FOUR

A Little Visit to Hell

Suddenly, from around the corner came the roar of a loud powerful sports car. Oh no. Now what? Juan feared the worst.

Before they could leave, Damen's Lamborghini screeched up to the cross street and parked. Damen and Carlos squeezed from the vehicle and cut an angle across the grass. Damen Cypher was the great grandson of the clever cheating gambler, John L. Cypher, whose crooked triumph in the big poker showdown with Lucas McCain back in 1882 had spread the power and influence of the Cyphers' nefarious operation around the globe.

Matt heard them coming and thought, *"My dictionary says cypher means a nobody, a nonentity. But Lew Cypher is the total opposite of that — he's the richest, most powerful man in this part of the world, if not the whole world. For sure, he's the most evil.*

The richly-attired Damen, in his mid twenties, smelled of expensive cologne. He smoothed down his brown hair and pierced Matt with his ice-blue eyes. "Hey Magoo, buddy!"

Matt cringed at the hated nickname Damen had given him years ago because, as Damen told everyone who would listen, "The McCain runt crashes into things like the cartoon character Mr. Magoo."

Carlos moved alongside his boss. As Damen Cypher's top henchman, he had a reputation for tormenting his victims, especially Matt. Carlos, who had no last name, was twenty-something but no one knew his year of birth. He wore a pointed Van Dyke beard and long black hair tied back in a ponytail. He grinned as he spoke in his strong Spanish accent. "Wha's up, man?"

Juan cried out, "We're busted!"

"Halt, boys." Miss Guided thrust her flat hand forward like a blue-coated cop. "Can't frolic at the moment."

As Damen and Carlos closed the gap, they found the ground was mushy and getting mushier with every step. Then without warning or explanation, their feet stuck fast. They were stopped cold and couldn't move.

Carlos swore crudely. "What the—? My feet are stuck!"

Damen tried to continue forward, but his feet were likewise circled in strange gummy muck. "What the hell is this?"

Miss Guided walked across the same mucky ground as if it were dry. Carlos's eyes bounced between his boss Damen and the woman scooting his way.

"Hey man, something's not right!" He shook his right arm, causing a hidden knife up his sleeve to secretly slide into his hand.

Miss Guided studied Damen. "Howdy, Damen L. Cypher. I heard ya curse when ya planted yer feet in the bog. Might I suggest ya pay more mind to yer decayed poetry."

"What the hell are you talking about?" Damen snarled. "How do you know my name? Have we met before, freak? What circus train did you bounce from?"

"Well, let me ponder for a moment. Where could our acquaintances have crossed? I don't go abroad by train, only by buggy. I know; have ya ever resided on the moon?"

"What kind of idiot question is that?" He taunted the woman in lascivious, obscene terms. "No, I haven't been to the moon, have you? You freaky strumpet!"

"Why, that's a negative." She shrugged. "I haven't sojourned there neither. I reckon it must have been another pair of folk who met there. Well, Damen L. Cypher, I figure that answers that."

He snapped back, "That didn't answer anything. I hate stupid broads, and if you don't get out of our way, right now, freak," he held up a clenched fist and his eyes bulged "I'm gonna personally send you to the moon!"

RE-DEAL

Miss Guided started to back up toward her blue buggy as she said, "We can't meet with ya for a lunar cheeseburger. Maybe some other time. If you're no longer in need of our fellowship, we got ta pound a hoof and spin a wheel."

Matt stood balancing himself next to her coach with his fingers wrapped around the door handle. He hadn't laughed in years, and he'd never heard anyone talk like her. Even when they were in danger, she was funny!

Carlos was superstitious and knew it was bad luck to be around anyone who smiled a lot. For some reason it always made him nervous and gave him the urge to pee. Nevertheless, his trusty blade was ready. He'd like to decorate the face of this witch before she cast some kind of spell over him.

Juan cried out, "'Ey Miss Guided, the wetback's got a blade!"

The woman asked, "Mr. Carlos, may I see yer pretty little nail file, please?" She held up her hand and glanced at her long, pink fingernails. "Look here. I think I just chipped a nail."

Carlos swung his piece up into her face. It was a stiletto with the blade still retracted inside its case. "This is not a file, you dumb dame. It's a stiletto!" He pressed the button on the grip so the razor sharp blade would shoot out, but to his shock, nothing happened. "Stupid piece of crap! The blade is jammed!"

"Wow! Mr. Carlos, stiletto, immense word. I wasn't surmising ya were bilateral and could speak in English and French."

Damen tried to break free, but his feet remained rooted to the ground. He blared out, "You dumb dame, a stiletto is a spring-loaded deadly knife. Not a stupid, girly nail file! Now get the hell out of our way, duchess, pronto!"

"There's no hell in your way. But if ya like, I might arrange for ya a little visit."

Carlos frantically pressed the button, but still nothing happened. A sudden urge to urinate gripped his loins. Panicking he thought, *Something spooky is going on around here. First my feet stick. Now my skinner is stuck.*

"If I may, let me assist ya, Mr. Carlos." The woman held out her hand. "I can make it work for ya."

For some inexplicable reason, Carlos couldn't counteract the enchantress as she took the knife from his hand. She mashed the knife's marker and a lady's long nail file shot out. She slid the file across her nails and said, "Mr. Carlos, some folk are under the misconception that I file my nails. But now that we have multitasking computers, there is no more filin'. I just fling them into the trash."

She punched the mark and retracted the file. She held the hilt close to Carlos's tight throat. "Thank ya, Mr. Carlos. The craggy edge is gone."

Carlos watched with wide eyes as the weird babe-from-the-past moved close to his neck with the knife. He knew she was gonna push the button shooting the blade right into his windpipe. His mind raced in frantic hysteria. *This spooky dame is gonna gore me!* His whole body froze with fear. His bladder released, and he peed his pants.

"Why, Mr. Carlos, look at yer trousers." Miss Guided glanced away. "Why, my-my-my, I do declare, European. And I had an inkling you were from Mexico."

That last joke completely shattered Matt and Juan's protective shells. They both let loose with roaring laughter. Juan choked, holding his stomach with one hand while pointing at Carlos with the other.

Laughing, he said, "He's pissed all right!"

"He sure is!" Matt agreed as he gasped for air.

"Shut yer ugly face, kid!" Carlos yelped. "Or I'll bust your little neck! That goes for you too, Loser Magoo!"

Miss Guided kept her eyes pinned on Damen and Carlos like a cat keeps its anxious eyes pinned on its prey.

Her voice was soft and steady. "Mr. Juan, I'm gratified ya liked my tease. Now let's get goin' with no dalliance. Please, move like a squirrel and assist Mr. Matt into my buggy. You hop in, too."

Matt was waiting for her command. Even though he was very weak, he quickly turned and opened the coach's door and stepped in. Juan stepped up behind Matt and shoved him

RE-DEAL

onto the seat with his back to the horse. Then Juan jumped in across from McCain. He wasn't sure which was worse—driving in this sissy buggy or facing Damen's wrath.

He called out, "We're in, Miss Guided!"

His face reflecting bewilderment, Damen snapped, "Miss Wacko, are you from Mars?"

As she backed across the green grass toward the boys in the buggy, she gave a dismissive wave. "Oh, don't be ludicrous, Mr. Damen. Mars is borin'. Give me Saturn. I love those rings. They're really pretty."

Damen swung his cold eyes toward Juan and screamed, "Hey, little punk! You leave with this circus act, and you're dog chow!"

Miss Guided stepped into the buggy next to Matt and slammed the door.

Juan looked topside. "'Ey Miss Guided, I know this is probably a stupid question. But who is gonna sit up top and operate this thing?"

"Oh, Mr. Juan, where's yer faith? Seraphim knows the trail." She slung the stiletto out the window toward Damen and called out, "See ya'll next go! Giddy up, Seraphim, away. Dump this borough!"

Sparks flew as the buggy rushed away. Juan thrust his head out the window and made a spitting motion toward Damen. He said with a laugh, "'Ey man, ya need to change your ugly thug's diaper."

Carlos's eyes sparked fury at Juan as the coach spun away. He was gonna kill that little worm. But he was stuck. He lifted his leg, and this time his foot came loose.

He cried, "Hey Damen, I can move now. First she squirts me in the crotch so it looks like I wet. Then she breaks my knife. The witch put a hex on us. She's a sorceress."

"No!" Damen glared as the buggy raced away. "She's an alien. Stop her. Fast!"

They ran to Damen's car and jumped in. But by that time, there was nothing to see. The buggy had disappeared.

"Gone? Already?" Damen asked. "Where did that sissy milk cart go?"

CHAPTER FIVE

Hog-n-Dawgs Ice Cream

As the horse leaped forward, the sudden jolt tossed Matt out of his seat. His stomach vaulted toward his throat. He groaned, still woozy from Damen's hotshot. He felt like he might be sick, and he didn't want to lose it again in front of this beautiful and funny lady. He crawled back into the opposite seat with Juan, facing forward across from the unusual woman.

"'Ey man," Juan said, laughing. "Card dealer you are; coordinated you're not."

The coach unexpectedly stopped cold, and for a second time Matt was hurled back down onto the hard carriage floor.

Miss Guided shook her head, then laughed. "Oh, Mr. Matt, yer exterior color looks like the interior of a cow udder. Are ya preparin' ta recycle yer lunch?"

When has anyone ever seen the inside of a cow's udder? Juan looked back down to his feet where Matt had fallen again. He shook his head and laughed. *What a klutz!*

The woman held the handle and opened the pink door. "Follow me, boys. We're here. Mr. Matt, it's time ta stop snoozing on the floor. We've arrived; let's stir."

"'Ey man," Juan said doubtfully. "How could we be anywhere? We just left. It's been two seconds. Damen will be ready. He'll have Carlos hurt us bad for leaving."

RE-DEAL

"Don't fret, Mr. Juan. We're safe."

Juan still didn't believe her. He looked out the window flap and saw that, in what seemed like only two seconds, the buggy had left the city and was now in the country.

Miss Guided opened her miniature blue bag and pulled out a three-foot metal cane with a sharp hook. She handed the cane to Matt. "Please accept this, Mr. Matt. It'll support ya for gettin' about. It also smarts if ya bash a bone."

Juan watched the long cane come from this weird-talking woman's little four-inch purse. Convinced he knew this trick, he told her, "'Ey man, I can do that. You have one of those telescoping magic canes."

He grabbed the cane and was stunned to find it was a solid aluminum rod with a sharp hook.

He sputtered, "But? But? Guided, Miss Guided. How did you do that? It's solid metal. How did you get this big cane out of that little thing?"

She took the cane back and handed it to Matt. She shoved them onward and answered, "There's a hole in the bag, and I keep it in there. Now, we've work ta do, so let's move on."

Matt took the cane. He was surprised to feel how light but solid it was. She was right. It would hurt bad.

He looked over at the strange woman and said, "Thanks, Miss Guided."

"Come on now, boys. Matt, do you mind if I take your hand and give you a little help? It's a mite bit bumpy with gopher holes out here on the road."

Matt's blood rushed at the feel of her soft hand. "No, not at all." He held the cane in his other hand as he walked beside the woman. "Where is this place?"

"This is my cozy little domicile. It was an abandoned schoolhouse that came up for transaction, so I purchased it. Mr. Matt, we are poised in front of a little hill. It's encircled by wonderful red oaks, and on the top of the hill is my little old one-room schoolhouse." She pointed off to the side of her school. "And over yonder is Seraphim's stable yard."

The schoolhouse was painted red side-slab. Outside, some chickens strolled about, pecking and scratching. Miss Guided let go of Matt's hand and hiked up her skirt, and the young men followed her up the steps toward the door and into the archaic building. Once inside, Matt tipped over a chair and a table, and then ran right into an old pot-bellied stove.

The angel shook her head. "Mr. Matt, would ya please refrain from redecorating my school? Now, please come take a load off yer dawgs and have a seat by this nice warm fire."

She led him over to an old blue school bench in front of a flaming fireplace. Matt sat down, wondering who started the fire.

"This is my school," she told them. "Ya both will be safe here. We're gonna rest a spell, change, then Mr. Matt, tomorrow ya start trainin'. Tonight ya both sleep with Seraphim. Tomorrow we get started. Now make yourselves cozy while I make ya'll some vittles. But first I need ta feed and put Seraphim away."

Juan watched the offbeat lady go out a back door, then he walked over next to Matt and sat down. He stared over at the fire—the flames felt warm, peaceful, and safe. *At least until Big Lew finds us*, he thought.

The door slammed. "I'm back, boys, and ready ta start fixin' something for ya'll ta eat."

Matt was still trying to catch on to Miss Guided's off-kilter accent. "What are ya fixin'?"

"Well, Mr. Matt, I'm gonna fix ya'll one of my fancy new dishes."

Where Juan grew up there were many days he dined in someone else's trash. So whenever there was food, he took it.

He asked eagerly, "And what is this favorite dish?"

"Well, Mr. Juan, for appetizers, I'm gonna whip up an old John the Baptist favorite, live grasshoppers dipped in molasses. And for the main course, I'm preparin' a vat full of varmint soup."

"Varmint soup?" Juan asked wide-eyed. "Did you say varmint soup? What kind of varmints?" He couldn't tell whether the strange lady was serious or just talking weird.

RE-DEAL

"Oh, for my varmint soup I use whatever the dawg lugs in."

Matt began to feel sick again. He turned to Juan and asked, "What did she say?"

"I'm still working on her talk," Juan replied. "All I can imagine is a pot full of board-stiff, Firestone-treaded cats, rabbits, and armadillos."

Matt's stomach was still queasy from the drugs. "And if we skip dinner, is there any dessert?"

Smiling, Miss Guided said, "Oh yes, boys. I'm gonna create somethin' really scrumptious. This morning I heaved a fresh pig and pooch in the freezer."

Juan cocked his head inquisitively and said, "'Ey Magoo—"

Miss Guided gazed into Juan's brown eyes. She shook her head and scolded, "Talk nice now."

"Oh, sorry, McCain. Calling you Magoo is just a bad habit."

Matt was starting to catch on to this funny lady. He could feel a laugh coming their way. He asked, "Lady, what the heck could you possibly make with a frozen pig and pooch?"

"Yeah?" Juan asked. "Besides trouble from the animal rights wackos?"

With a grin, she answered, "I'm makin' some hog-n-dawgs ice cream."

Juan laughed and poked Matt with his elbow. "She's an odd chick!"

For the third time in as many years Matt felt like laughing. This comical woman cracked him up. Maybe he was finally in the company of someone who would help him change his life. And, if she looked like the woman in his dream, he was positively going to like the change.

But on further reflection, Matt remembered he was only a McCain, and a Loser McCain at that. There was no way his situation would ever change. However, at least now he had a new confidant. Juan was in the same miserable predicament he was in. The sickening part was that Matt knew his ancestor Lucas the Loser put Juan there.

Matt sure wished he could at least get rid of the despicable labor camps. But that would never happen. He couldn't do anything against the rich powerful Cyphers. He was just a skinny, burnt-eyed card dealer. A feeling of helplessness overwhelmed him.

Juan had never seen any joy on Matt's face until just now. The guy's week eyes lit up for a moment, but just as quickly filled with sadness and despair. Every Hispanic brother Juan knew despised and hated the McCains, and Juan would never before have considered doing anything for a Lucas the Loser relative. But now if he could do something to help the poor-sighted man maybe for once he'd consider the idea.

Matt and Juan looked at each other and shook their heads. Juan said, "Lady, you got us again."

"Yer on ta me," she said with a snicker. "Ya knew I was just ribbing' ya about the hogs and dogs."

"Yeah." Juan decided the three earlier burgers should get him through the night. "Thanks, lady, for the varmint soup offer. I'm sure it's finger-lickin' good. But, for now, we'll just go crash."

Matt gave another weak laugh.

"Come on, boys," the lady said. "Follow me."

Miss Guided led the lads back to the barn and up to some piles of hay. "Here ya are, boys. Snatch yourself a pile and get some rest. Now please trust me, boys. For a fleeting spell ya can lay yer fears aside." As she closed the barn door, she said, "See ya at sunup."

Juan pondered the strange things that had happened this day. *My life is going to change big time. But,* he wondered, *will it finally be for the better this time? Fat chance of that.*

Exhausted, Matt flopped down onto the hay, at peace for the moment. He wondered, *Who is this woman? And why did she decide to help me? Could it be my frantic prayers?*

He bent and loosened his high-top sneakers. He peeled off his dirty, discolored, jacket and threw it aside. He lay down on the hay, fatigued from the drugs and his strange rescue. Darkness finally crept in, and for the first time in years, Matt McCain fell into a peaceful sleep.

CHAPTER SIX

Those Sick Cyphers

At daybreak the following morning, after a breakfast of biscuits and bacon, the angel and the two men sat around the table skimming the newspaper.

Miss Guided said, "Keep shovelin' in that protein, Mr. Matt. All those years of self-destruction has taken a toll on yer body and mind." She pinched his bony arm. "Mr. Matt, we positively need some bulk on them toothpicks ya call arms, and ya don't make omelets without bustin' several eggs. Learnin' martial fighting facilities will be the solution for those skinny bones. As for yer gray matter in yer shaggy head, I haven't even used half my brains yet, and I'll be delighted ta share my other half with ya."

"Thank you!" Matt yawned. "I think."

"Now, boys, it's a pretty far piece, so we'll get trottin' before sun. I got ta feed, slop, milk, and then we'll tote ourselves on down into town."

Juan was exhausted from the short night and early-bird rising but not too worn to grasp what she said. He asked, "Tote? Does that mean walk?"

"My-my-my," Miss Guided said with a strong shake of her head. "Ya don't understand what I mean by tote. If we weren't so pressed for time, I'd sit ya down and we'd meditate on some books. I'd tutor ya on a study of the three R's."

Matt rubbed his tired bloodshot eyes. "What three R's?"

Her blue eyes twinkled. "Why, readin', ritin', and r-thritis. Those who don't study their literature and Holy Book end up becoming a dawg-catcher, jailbird, or the like."

Arthritis? I don't think that starts with an R. Matt thought with a weak chuckle.

"Hold it! Back up," Juan said. "How far is this little tote?"

"It's not too far. About eight miles, take or give one. Now spark up yourselves a little goose-gumption, boys." She tapped the paper. "Now we'll first visit this Murphy's Butcher Shop and Karate School. Ya'll learn ta beat, chop it up, and eat it. Ya'll also need ta learn how ta blend in."

She pointed to an advertisement: 'Lamb's Players Theater holding auditions.' I called; we have a 10 AM interview." She looked at Juan and asked, "Do ya want ta halt Big Lew Cypher once and for all? Are ya with us? Gonna be tough!"

"Cypher will find us for sure." Juan shook his head. "He'll kill us."

"Yer observance is true. Mr. Cypher and his son strike a fair picture of the most terrible of human society. But have faith. Not at my school, Mr. Juan—here yer safe."

Juan hesitated. "I guess," he finally said. "Okay. Yeah, I've been wanting out for years anyway. Those Cyphers are sick!"

Miss Guided moved to Matt and lifted his chin. "And Mr. Matt, yer mind declares?"

"I'll do anything not to deal anymore and to get my dad free from those evil people! John Cypher stabbed my great gram through the heart with a dagger and then he stole their ranch. I also think they had something to do with burning my eyes. I hate them!"

"That's so sorrowful, Mr. Matt. But in order ta grasp yer desire ta halt that wicked Lew Cypher, ya must first be willin' to overcome yer visual hindrance. It's a hefty obstacle, but not insurmountable, and I know ya have it in ya. Let me tell ya about a legend, about a fellow whose music I love. His name was Beethoven. He was as good as deaf and burdened with constant sorrow. Yet he had a notion and created some of the prettiest symphonies ya'll ever lay an ear too. He would press his ear ta the piano and would bash the chords with such force the vibrations permeated through his head. That's called perseverin', Matt. Now ya got Lucas' blood blastin' through yer veins. Lucas might have fallen for a snooker, but he was faithful. And faithfulness is the most long-term, fruitful thing ya can have.

"Yeah right," Matt said, ashamed of his relative. "How can you know anything about Lucas the Loser?"

"Let me tell you the story," the angel said. It was a hot July day ..."

CHAPTER SEVEN

The Poker Championship of the West

July 12, 1882, Bowen's Palace, Santa Fe, New Mexico

Lucas McCain was a lean man with light hair, a beard, and a deep tan that came from years spent outside working his cattle ranch. Lucas was outfitted in a tailored coat with a tan Stetson, black cowboy boots, pressed pants, and a belt with a gold buckle of engraved cards. The gold fan of cards held two aces and two eights with a nine of diamonds set in the center—the combination called the Dead Man's Hand. The beaten gold buckle had been a gift from his late wife after the killing of his comrade, Wild Bill Hickok.

A uniformed doorman brought an umbrella to shade the wealthy rancher and escorted him up the steps of Bowen's Palace.

Baldheaded George Devol and Buckskin, a rifleman dressed all in leather, watched from inside.

"It's McCain," Devol growled. "Cypher wants him unarmed."

The doors began to close behind Lucas but were stopped by the two thugs. They pinned their gun muzzles to Lucas' head and pushed him backward across the threshold.

Devol glared coldly. "Invitation?" He twitched his bald head toward his accomplice and ordered, "Buckskin, rummage his pockets good."

Lucas kept his hands raised to the sky as the pelt-covered gunman poked his pockets and found his gun.

RE-DEAL

"Don't find no invite," Buckskin said as he removed the weapon.

"Actually," Lucas replied with a deep Texas drawl, "I've been invited."

A middle-aged Mexican lady with warm brown eyes and a gentle smile sidled up to Lucas. Maria Bowen, the beautiful wife of the proprietor, wore a floor-length daisy-yellow dress with a single yellow rose in her long, brown hair.

Maria wrapped her arm around Lucas's arm. "Luke McCain, tastefully late as always."

Lucas grinned with a timid tip of his hat. "And yer lovely as usual."

"Why thank you!" Maria turned to the guard. "I'll take custody of this one, Mr. Devol." She pulled Lucas past Devol and said under her breath, "Careful with that George Devol—he's mean."

George watched McCain and growled at Buckskin, "Watch the door. I'll go tell Cypher that McCain is here and unarmed."

Inside, a lavish party was in progress under the sparkling chandeliers of the richly-appointed room. Luke and Maria strolled past genteel waiters carrying silver trays filled with drinks and food. They moved among the conversation and laughter of cowboys holding drinks and puffing on long cigars.

Lucas looked the place over. "Whooeee! Maria, how'd ya get Jamie ta spend all that money?"

Maria laughed. "The hard part is getting him to spend it on me! So, how's my son? Can't you make that boy write his mama?"

"Raul's doin' great," Lucas answered. "Got his hands full at the governor's mansion."

"Thank you so much for helping Raul get his feet on the ground. Who would have thought he'd end up working for Governor Asa Turner after he ran away to Texas?"

On a sofa off to the side, a smiling woman sat knitting a scarlet-colored scarf. She had blissful blue eyes and beautiful, golden-blonde hair. She wore a traditional tailored dress, and her small bonnet decorated with pink and blue flowers matched her dress and petite purse. People recognized the contented glow that flowed from some kind of an inward assurance, but they didn't realize that the beautiful woman was the direct contact angel, Michala.

Maria smiled fondly and waved to the woman as she passed by. Lucas stopped and stared, surprised to see his son's sweet, funny teacher. The angel in human form stood as she saw her melancholy charge coming her way.

"Miss Michala." Lucas took her hand and asked in an amazed voice, "How in the name a Moses did ya cross that hot prairie? And how did ya do it before me?"

"Well I declare," she answered. "Ya know my triple-trotter is faster than anythin' ya mount. As a matter of speakin', Seraphim will blaze any quarter horse clean off the track."

Lucas looked at her in confusion. "How can that be?"

Michala smiled with her mouth and with her blue eyes. "Confidentially, Mr. McCain, Seraphim trots about on three legs. A quarter horse pogos about town on one."

"Ya never fail ta amaze me." Lucas shook his head in awe. "And my boy, too."

He gave the teacher a peck on the cheek and followed Maria.

"My boy Davy William loves her," Luke said. "Ever since Elizabeth was killed, Miss Michala has been a Godsend. She keeps him laughin'." Lucas looked down at the floor and said to no one in particular, "The merry Miss Michala tries to keep me laughin' too."

As the angel watched her charge move on, she murmured, "My lonely Lucas, you need to lay your ghastly grievance in the hands of our loving Lord."

Maria walked him up some steps toward a knot of people congregated on a higher level in the room. She led him to the bar where her husband Jamie and Bat Masterson were going over their plans.

RE-DEAL

Jamie Bowen, a thin, dapper man, brandished a cigar. Maria placed her hand on Bowen's shoulder and said, "Jamie, Luke is here."

Bowen turned to face Lucas and relaxed. He tossed the last of his cigar into a shiny brass spittoon freckled with globs of tobacco and tar. He grabbed Lucas's hand. "Luke! What did you do, walk?"

"It's a long trail from Texas," Lucas said as he gripped back. He leaned toward Bat Masterson's offered hand. "Good ta see ya again too, Bat."

Bat nodded upstairs.

"Cypher's up there with his team of gunfighters. His days as a murderer and exploiter of cheap labor are numbered. We're going to bust the scalawag once and for all."

"Yeah," Lucas agreed. "Cypher has beat the judicial system for the last time."

"Luke, we grieve with you," Bat said as he warmly placed his hand on Lucas's shoulder. "Even with your personal loss, we're so thankful you decided to accept Cypher's no-limit poker challenge. You're the only one rich enough to raise the 100,000 dollar cash buy-in."

"Thanks, Bat," Luke returned, trying to hide his aching heart. "I've accepted this here challenge as my civic duty. I don't feel sorry for Cypher. He's chosen the devil's path ta destruction. I believe gambling is a foolish risk of one's hard earnings. But three of his kills were in Texas." He left unspoken that one of those kills was his beloved wife Elizabeth.

He visibly tightened.

"That's why I want ta see that evil man finally stopped and destroyed." He turned to Bowen. "I understand Governor Prince has been told our plan and is gonna stand with us."

"That's right," Bowen replied. "The Governor is in town and is gonna watch the game."

###

Upstairs in a private suite, John Cypher waited with his cohorts. He paced the floor, holding a costly pocket watch connected to a long gold chain. The chain was attached to a hand painted vest under an expensive, black frock coat. He was a large, coarse man with threatening coal-black eyes.

A pack of intimidating gamblers and killers worked with John Cypher in this gambling scam. The wheezing gunfighter Doc Holliday scrutinized Cypher as he paced. Next to him sat a gold-and-jewel-bedecked dandy, Eric Andrews. The New Mexico Governor, L. Bradford Prince, rested his obese fanny on the corner of a bed. They were conspiring together on how they were going to wile Lucas McCain into betting his million-acre ranch.

Cypher irritably checked his pocket watch. "Where's that sucker McCain?"

"McCain is here," George Devol cried as he crashed through the doorway.

"Let's go." Devol pointed down to the saloon. "It's time to get started." He turned to the bejeweled card sharp. "Andrews, you watch the money, and I'll go back and guard the door." He faced the governor. "Prince, I don't want you to be seen with us. Wait until we get down, then you come."

Four of the conspirators left the room and sauntered down the steps.

Bat Masterson spotted John Cypher coming down the staircase followed by Andrews, Devol, and Holliday. He nodded his head in the direction of Cypher and said, "Here come Cypher and his mob."

Bowen pulled a chair over and stepped up on it. He drew his Colt 45 and fired twice toward high Heaven. Bowen said, "If I may have your attention please! Gentlemen!" He turned toward his wife and the knitting schoolmarm. "And ladies. I'm Jamie Bowen, and I welcome you to the poker championship of the West!"

The crowd burst into cheers, and Bowen basked in the celebration.

Cypher glared with an evil grin at Lucas McCain.

McCain looked back at the killer with disgust.

RE-DEAL

"I do declare," Bowen went on. "There has never been such an assemblage of the high and mighty, the wild and notorious, as I see here today! There are over a hundred of us, so take your drinks and move back against the north or south walls."

Jamie stepped down from his chair and nodded to his wife. "If I may show my pride and joy, as well as the mother of my son Raul. Maria, my dear, please stand; let these boys see how lucky I am!"

"Thank you, my husband." She pulled to her feet the blue-eyed beauty sitting with her. "Let me introduce Miss Michala. This lovely lady is Lucas McCain's son's teacher from Texas. All you men who say a woman can't beat a man, well, Miss Michala left Texas after Lucas and got here before him."

The noise from the applause and whistles for the two beauties shook the palace's foundation.

"Thanks, my dear."

Bowen fired again, and the crowd settled down. He faced the excited bunch of lustful gamblers and pointed with his pistol.

"Boys, keep your hats on! And beat this, all you cowboys. My son now works for Asa Turner, the governor of the big state of Texas!" He smiled with pride. "Who knows, maybe one day he'll be president."

Then the entire group noticed a low rumble, like the beginning of a high-magnitude earthquake—the sound of Governor Prince trembling his way down the stairs. He shook the banister on every step.

Bowen turned toward the governor and said respectfully, "Please everyone, give due deference to whom these lands belong, His Honor, Governor of the New Mexico Territories, L. Bradford Prince!"

Cypher showed his teeth to the governor as he applauded.

The governor teetered as he stepped down onto the dark wood floor. He made a loud noise like a brick chimney falling. His eyes darted back and forth like a weasel waiting to pounce. He loved to see all these walking wallets.

There were groans and burps as he removed his spectacles and bowed.

Prince said with a drooling smile, "Ya'll welcome to my fine little territory of New Mexico. Please feel free to spend-spend-spend!"

The bartender quickly pushed Bowen's rolling office chair over, and Prince poured himself into it. Everyone could hear the springs groan in the swivel chair as Prince plopped down.

"Thank you, Governor," Bowen said with a nod. He pulled out a long, rich-smelling cigar and held it up for Prince to see. "We shall do that."

He looked over toward Bat. "I'll now turn the game over to the distinguished Bat Masterson, who will set down the rules of play."

As Bowen stepped back he looked over at John Cypher and thought, *Cypher, your hours as a killer and slave master are numbered.*

CHAPTER EIGHT

The Biggest Raise Ever

Masterson approached the table with an air of command. He saluted the crowd with his diamond-studded cane, and the crowd responded with enthusiastic applause. He stepped up behind a green felt poker table, which separated Cypher and McCain, and said to the excited gathering, "Thank you, Jamie! Welcome to this no-limit poker showdown!"

He gestured with his walking stick. "I would now like to introduce our two players. Here on my left we have John Cypher. He set forth the dare that he could whip anyone, even in an above-board game. For this showdown we will hold Cypher to those words."

Cypher pushed his chair back and stood up. He drew back his lips into a twisted smile, exposing a mouth full of jagged teeth. As he tipped back his hat, he exposed bulging ferret eyes that scanned from one side of the saloon to the other.

"Now there is a smile only Lucifer could love," Masterson said with a sneer. He turned away and gestured. "Over here on my right, accepting John Cypher's duel, is Lucas McCain. I've known Luke for many years. His ranch in West Texas is second in size only to Governor Prince's lands. Luke is one of the few gentleman gamblers still alive."

A burst of applause erupted and McCain stood and nodded with a modest smile. Masterson held his arms out straight. "This showdown is for the poker championship of the West."

Loud screams and whistles greeted his announcement.

"But first the rules," Masterson continued. "In this contest, there will be no limit on betting. And at Cypher's insistence, both players are obligated to have the cash or property on hand. No IOU's will be accepted." His eyes were packed with loathing as he looked down at John Cypher.

Masterson scowled at Cypher and then gave a nod to Lucas. "Gentlemen, please be seated. The first shuffle goes to the challenger, Mister Cypher."

They each anted 500 dollars, and Lucas opened the first round of betting.

After about two hours of slow, assiduous play, Cypher grew impatient and resolved to get down to the business at hand. He signaled to the bartender for a fresh deck. Devol had earlier replaced the saloon's decks with ones stacked in Cypher's favor and then resealed them like new.

"This deck has gone soft," Cypher snapped. "Bartender, bring us a fresh unopened pack."

Cypher brought his cheating dexterity into play. He ostentatiously opened the fresh deck and false-shuffled the cards, retaining Devol's stacked deck. Cypher delicately signaled to Devol.

"Cypher's ready to bring my stacked deck into play," Devol explained to Andrews. "McCain will get a strong full house, three bullets and two hooks, and Cypher will get four cowboys. But if everything goes according to our game plan, McCain will fold, Cypher will be the new owner of McCain's ranch, and Prince will be a mountain of worm food." He rubbed his hands together. "And, of course, we'll split the cash." Devol watched as Cypher passed the deck over to McCain for the cut. "Stand back. Time for a little distraction."

Devol jumped up, ran across the casino with a roar, and rammed his granite-hard head into the door. The crowd jumped and squealed as they watched the door crack in two. Cypher picked up the deck and hopped the cut, placing the top stack back on top, keeping the stacked deck.

RE-DEAL

Lucas glanced between Devol and Cypher and suspected some kind of collusion between the two killers.

"Devol, that'll cost you fifty bucks," Bowen protested. "You're to guard the door, not demolish it!"

"Oh, don't get all uppity, Bowen. It's just a small crack."

"Gentlemen! Gentlemen!" Masterson tapped his cane hard on the dark wood floor. "The game, please."

Cypher smiled to himself at Devol's brazen diversion. He picked up the uncut deck and dealt a hand of five-card draw.

Lucas picked up his cards and smiled to himself when he saw three aces and two jacks. He counted off five bills and, showing no emotion or change of demeanor, began the betting. "Let's make this little contest more interestin'. I'll open with five big bills." He tossed 5,000 dollars to the table.

This was the moment Cypher had waited for. He counted off 25,000. "I call your pitiful five and raise you another twenty."

"I don't think you're bluffing," Lucas said, staring as if reading Cypher's mind. "The way you jumped in with that bet, I think you have at least four of a kind."

Lucas suspected that this viper had cheated and knew what his cards were. He decided to throw Cypher a curve ball by breaking up his full house and drawing for the fourth ace. Lucas tossed twenty thousand-dollar bills into the pot.

"Here is yer pint-sized raise." He threw away his two jacks and said, "Give me two cards."

Cypher was so stunned that he almost dropped the deck. No one would be so dim as to break up a pat hand for the scanty chance of drawing something stronger. He reluctantly dealt the two cards.

Lucas asked, "How many cards are ya gonna take?"

"I'm going to draw one card," Cypher answered. He dealt a single card to himself and leaned back in his chair, holding on to the four kings he already had.

Tension sparked in the saloon. Lucas looked at his cards and discovered he had drawn the fourth ace, but he betrayed no emotion. He could hardly keep from grinning when he realized his hand couldn't lose. Because of the way Cypher bet before the draw, Luke knew he couldn't have a royal flush, which meant the best his opponent could possibly have was four kings. With Luke's four aces, there was no possible way his opponent could change the outcome now.

Lucas gathered all his money together. He felt a deep satisfaction as he thought, *And now for the stabbing death of my beautiful wife, John L. Cypher, we're gonna bust ya once and for all and put an end ta yer cheatin', slave tradin', and killin'.*

The breathless quiet suddenly snapped as Lucas shoved the rest of his cash into the center of the table. "I know my cards will crush yer hand. My bet, the rest, seventy-five grand."

"Is that right? Do you like that hand?" Cypher decided to try a little harassment. "McCain, yer nothing but an arrogant four-flusher. You got nothing!" He slapped a stack of bills onto the pot. "I call your bet." Cypher reached into his boot and pulled out the roll of bills he'd borrowed from Andrews and tossed them on the table. "And I raise you another hundred grand."

The saloon was thrown into stunned silence at the huge raise.

Lucas studied the new stack of bills.

Cypher sat back in his chair and tapped the points on his teeth. He mentally pleaded for McCain to step into his trap.

"Jamie." Lucas waved to Bowen. "If ya would be so kind, a sheet of clean paper and a pen."

Cypher heaved up in his chair and stuck out his finger like it was the stock of a bullwhip. He leveled it at Lucas and snapped, "McCain, remember, we agreed, no IOU's."

Then Cypher's tone softened and he leaned back into his chair and soft as silk he rubbed his hands together. "However, McCain, I might accept a goodly number of your fine Texas Longhorns."

"Keep your pants on!" Luke shot back. "I know the rules."

"Cypher must have been expecting Lucas to bet his cattle." Bowen stabbed out his third cigar. "What is that sleaze up to?"

RE-DEAL

Bat angrily gripped his cane. "That vile man needs to be stopped once and for all!"

"Now, Mr. Cypher," Lucas said. "Since all yer worth is in the pot, I'm gonna make a wager so large ya can never match it."

"Here is the stationery, Jamie." Masterson set a sheet of paper and a pen with an inkwell in front of Lucas.

"Thanks."

Lucas dipped into the ink well and began to scrawl. When he finished, he held the paper up for all to see.

"Mr. Cypher, with this here deed for my ranch and cattle, I call yer bet and raise ya 3,000,000." He returned the finger in the face. "Remember what ya said, Mr. Cypher. There will be no IOU's."

"This is good." Bowen nodded his head. "Lucas is finally going to get revenge for the stabbing death of his beautiful wife."

With the hope of finally stopping the evil man, Lucas threw the valuable paper, which represented his entire fortune, on top of the pile of cash. He followed this with one more addition. He pulled from his coat pocket a solid gold lighter with his name written in diamonds. "I'll also throw my last piece of value, my own two hands as yer hired help, and my gold lighter for good measure."

The only thing Luke didn't bet was the aces and eights belt buckle presented to him by his wife. The crowd gasped at the multimillion-dollar bet and agreed it must be the biggest bet in history.

Cypher wasn't satisfied—he wanted it all. He pointed to the gold belt buckle and asked, "How 'bout that Dead Man buckle?"

"Ya call what ya see!" Lucas snapped.

The onlookers endorsed Lucas's play with more cheers, laughter, and applause.

Sitting on her seat, the angel-in-human-form was absorbed in her knitting and didn't see the bet. As her charge bet his huge ranch, she held up her scarf and gave it a satisfied nod. "Yep, I sincerely suppose Lucas's loveable little Davy William will want this for his wonderful wardrobe."

Cypher laughed along with the crowd. Inside he smiled at his soon-to-be victory. He shook his head and said, "Yes sir, I should've known. I should've known you and all your wealth would bear down on a man and try to raise him out."

He pulled a document out from his coat pocket. "Well, all I have is just, well, just a little something." He nodded toward Governor Prince. "I discussed with the good governor before hand, and he said he'd oblige to sign this for me should this turn of events come about."

"What? Unfair!" Lucas exclaimed. "Mr. Cypher, you were the one who demanded that there would be no boundary on raisin' or any IOU's allowed."

"Governor Prince," Cypher nodded to the obese governor, "roll on over."

Prince foamed at the mouth at the prospect of increasing his land holdings with the McCain properties. In the fashion of a large ocean-faring vessel leaving the harbor, Prince's wide girth lifted from his chair and grandly sailed across the saloon and docked beside John Cypher. He put on his spectacles. He looked around and noted Devol's steel glare and his trigger finger tapping the pearl handle of his Colt 45. He looked back at Cypher and his blubbery lips started to work.

"John, you know I'm always willing to be helpful in special circumstances."

Cypher laid the official-looking paper down for Prince to sign.

Prince's eyes blinked above his metal-rimmed spectacles. The document actually turned all his family holdings over to Cypher. That was not the way John Cypher explained it would read. He craved desperately that everything would go according to plan, or he would be in court trying to recover his own property. He licked his lips and said, "Oh, John, this, this, is not exactly what I understood our agreement to be.

RE-DEAL

But, you understand, this territory is our family property, which we had hoped would one day become a bona fide state of the Union."

"His Honor has long been the kindest, most generous official of this fair land." Cypher clamped his arm around the governor's fleshy shoulders. "Don't you think, Buckskin?"

"Yep." Buckskin grinned with a sadistic anticipation. "I reckon. So far."

The governor's eyes shifted to the penetrating pupils of Doc Holliday, then he observed Devol take an intimidating step toward him.

"As I say," Prince went on, "I always try to be of service."

He signaled for a pen. Cypher released Prince, and the governor placed the document on the table. His fleshy parts twitched excitedly as he dipped the pen in the inkwell. The idea of all this new land caused sweat to form on his overblown face.

He just hoped Cypher would live up to his end of the deal.

"Simple signature, pal." Cypher placed his hand on the back of the governor's neck and squeezed. "Just your JH, nothing fancy."

The governor flinched as he picked up the pen and dipped it. He wrote quickly and deliberately, while Bowen and Masterson looked questioningly at one another. The collection of lawmen, ranchers, and gunfighters was quiet and still. Cypher eased the governor away and swooped up his bet. His lips turned up, a final smirk of triumph.

"As I was saying, I have just a little something." He held up the document high for all to see. "I call your 3,000,000, McCain, and raise you the entire territory of New Mexico!"

The appalled crowd jeered in protest.

"Quiet! Quiet down!" Bowen stepped up and fired his revolver upwards. He turned and glared. "Cypher, it appears not everything is quite in order here."

Cypher's jaw muscles twitched, his eyes bulged. Again he held up the document and snarled. "No IOU's! No limits on raising! I got a legal document signed by the governor of this here territory, who happens to be the proprietor of this land! Now, put up or shut up!"

He slammed the document down hard on the pile of cash. No sound could be heard as everyone shrunk back.

"Very resourceful!" Lucas said with disgust. "Given that my fortune is all in the pot, I can't call this bet, and I'm compelled to fold."

The crowd went crazy with speculation.

Masterson clenched his fists. "The gall of this unscrupulous maneuver!"

"Yes, very clever." Bowen nodded with understanding. "A brilliant trap. Given Lucas's resources are all in the pot, and with no Texas governor, he can't call the bet. And since Lucas isn't a welcher, he has no honorable choice but to surrender his ranch and fold the hand. And if that's what Cypher is up to, we must stop it!"

Everyone waited for Lucas to dispute the bet, but to their astonishment, Lucas accepted the deed as a legitimate raise and prepared to throw in his cards.

"Cypher, you unprincipled sneak!" Lucas muttered. "Technically this raise is justifiable, though very unethical. But I did agree ta these rules, and I did give my word."

Lucas reflected hard for a moment. He wondered what it was going to be like to work for the evil man. He'd gotten carried away and shouldn't have tried to do the Lord's work for Him. He was also foolish to have arrogantly offered his own labor as part of the stake.

He looked straight into Cypher's dark, cold eyes. "Cypher, you are a wicked, dishonorable piece of filth, but I have no choice but ta fold." He shoved a finger at Cypher and warned, "I would advise ya ta stay hidden in that coffin ya slid from. I was wrong ta have tried ta do the Almighty's job for Him. However, I believe He'll judge yer evil ways. Now ta show ya there are still men with integrity, I'm gonna let ya have this pot. If I'd have known, I might've brought my governor along. Texas could've topped ya."

RE-DEAL

Masterson and Bowen swung their guns up at Cypher in one motion and Cypher froze. Spitting with disgusted fury, Masterson said, "John Cypher, don't touch that pot." He turned to Lucas. "Don't you give up your ranch, Luke. There's something wrong with this bet. I'm just not sure what it is."

"That's right," Bowen agreed. "This bet smells to high Heaven."

The stunned-silent room all heard the deafening sound of three hammers cocked back as Holliday, Buckskin, and Devol leveled their guns at Masterson and Bowen.

"Drop the hardware!" Devol ordered. "The fool accepted the raise, legitimate or not."

Lucas contemplated the horror of that statement. He had messed up badly. He slapped his winning four aces down with finality.

Cypher quickly reached for the pot with glee.

"John Cypher!" Lucas stood up and said, "Call yer dawgs off and tell them ta put their arms away!"

"Do it!" Cypher ordered.

Slowly all the guns relaxed and lowered. Lucas turned to his friends and said, "Devol's right—I'm a fool. But I did fold. The cash and ranch are Cypher's."

The room remained in stunned silence as Pastor Marks, the local minister who had observed the game, marched over to the edge of the poker table. "John Cypher, the Bible says that the evil sown by the father will be reaped by his children and their children. In other words, Cypher, God will require payment from your offspring for your lying, stealing, cheating, and murders."

"You're right," Lucas agreed. "Vengeance is mine, saith the Lord."

He reached down, picked up his gold lighter, pulled a cigar from his pocket, and lit it. He exhaled a cloud of smoke and watched it as it rose and then gradually diminished. He looked at the lighter one last time and wondered if his life was also going up in smoke. He carefully laid the lighter back on the pile of money and shook his head. "God have mercy on yer soul, Cypher."

He turned and calmly walked through the silent, staring crowd. He pushed through the swinging doors and left without looking back.

"Don't need no mercy from God!" Cypher leaned toward Lucas's retreating back. "Not now! You remember you belong to me now, McCain. I own you and your family along with the cattle!"

Cypher swung back to the table and embraced the winnings with a sinister laugh. He and the snarling gunfighters quickly gathered the fortune together and left out the back.

As Lucas walked through the doorway, Michala calmly continued to knit. Maria slapped her on the knee. "Hurry, Michala!"

The knitting teacher looked up just in time to catch a glimpse of her charge leaving. The angel arrayed as educator nabbed her knitting and bustled toward the entrance.

"Maria, I have ta catch Lucas."

Maria Bowen followed her, saying, "I can't believe—"

"Sorry, gotta run." As she hurried out the door, the foreigner from the heavenly realms thought, *I certainly suppose Sir Gabe will not be happy with me if I don't stay in contact with my charge.*

CHAPTER NINE

That Dainty Little Brick-Buster

The Present

Miss Guided finished the abbreviated version of the events she had seen in such detail in her mind. She looked at her charges. "As I said, Lucas might have fallen for a snooker, but he was faithful. And faithfulness is the most long-term, fruitful thing ya can have. Now come on, fellows. It's a long tote back ta town. Let's get movin'."

The expression 'tote' got the boys' attention again.

Juan asked, "Did you really mean for us to actually walk?"

"Yessiree! People laze too much. Besides, it will be good for ya'll. It'll help scrub out yer heads. Now no brooding, boys; let's get on."

As they left Miss Guided's school, they watched the warm butter-colored sunlight crest over the brow of the hill. Two hours later a tired Matt and a nonchalant Juan passed through an enchanting tree-lined park that came out in a small Mayberry-like town. Mothers played with their children; kids hung on skirts with one hand and clutched ice cream cones with the other. They stared over their wet noses at Miss Guided and the two boys as they passed by.

They passed white picket fences in front of landscaped homes. Matt could smell the lilacs coming into bloom. In the back of some of the quaint homes, Juan saw the wet wash hanging on the line. There was a screaming sound from off in the distance where two teenage boys were sawing cords of wood. The sweet smell of timber blended with the fragrance of flowers. For some reason this gave Matt and Juan a little solace—they felt safe here. They trudged on into the town.

Miss Guided pointed. "If my recollection is proper, the karate school should be just over yonder."

As the boys hiked on, their excitement grew. In front of the town drugstore, sitting on two metal milk crates, dressed in overalls and painters' hats, two leather-faced men played checkers and sucked down Cokes from old-time bottles. The older one was concentrating on his next move with his thumb stuck in the strap of his overalls. The storefronts were simple and clean with signs like Dilbert's Bakery, Donuts $2 a dozen and Aunt Birdies Drug Store, sodas 25 cents on Thursdays.

Miss Guided and her boys passed a little two-pump filling station across from an old church building under renovation. But the most unusual, and the place that caught Juan's attention, was the sign that read Murphy's Butcher Shop and Karate School.

"There it is!" Juan's voice rose in excitement. "What is a karate school doing out here in Timbuktu?"

Juan's indifferent attitude had melted away like a kid's ice cream. He loved karate. Training in the fighting arts was mandatory at the orphanage he came from, and it had been the only thing he'd really enjoyed at the Cypher labor camp. He could tell he was going to like this backward little place.

The angel-in-disguise stopped in front of the karate school. She removed a packet of blush from her little purse and gazed into the window reflection to apply some to her cheeks.

Turning back to Matt and Juan, she said, "Plant yourselves here, boys. I'm gonna visit with the karate instructor. I'll use all my powers of charm and perspiration ta obtain some lessons. When the schoolmaster makes a bargain ya'll can afford, I'll come and retrieve ya."

RE-DEAL

Matt giggled to himself. Perspiration?

She winked at the boys, then she turned and walked past the door with the sign that said Butcher Shop and entered the door labeled Murphy's Karate School.

Inside, an array of workout equipment filled the school, and a large wrestling mat lay on the floor in the center of the room. Heavy weights, stretching machines, and large hanging kick bags lined the mirrored walls. The United States and Texas flags hung from the ceiling. Between the banners stood the silhouette of a man with arrows pointing to the vital areas to strike when fighting.

Something below the silhouette caught the attention of the angel-in-human-form. A big batch of bricks was piled onto a pair of concrete blocks. *That will make a pretty pile of powdered particles*, she thought.

In the middle of the floor, a man led pushups in front of two dozen men and women.

The eager angel waved her hands like a signalman on an aircraft carrier. "Hai Karate, oh, Mr. Hai Karate. May I speak with ya for a jiffy, please?"

The head instructor, Sensei Murphy, looked up, annoyed that someone had interrupted his class.

Sensei John Murphy didn't fit the stereotypical image of a karate instructor. Instead, he was a stocky, stern-faced Irishman with a short-cropped mustache and dark red hair.

Murphy turned from his class to see a pretty young lady. Her fluttering hands, loud voice, and flower-bedecked hat contrasted with her conservative, even old-fashioned, attire.

The woman continued to flutter and bellow. "May I please talk with ya, Mr. Karate?"

Sensei Murphy completed his two-hundredth pushup and rose to his feet. "All right, all right," he snapped. "Just keep that funny hat on."

He turned to his top black belt, a Texas Ranger, and said, "Mr. Douglas, I want two hundred sit-ups from the class." He nodded toward the flapping woman. "I need to see what that babe from The Big Valley wants."

John Murphy tried to catch his breath as he hustled over to meet his strange visitor.

"Howdy do, Mr. Hai Karate." The grinning woman took his hand and shook it vigorously. "I'm Miss Guided. It's a pleasure ta make yer acquaintance. I use yer Hai Karate aftershave whenever I chop wood. It's great stuff. It really works!"

John wrinkled his forehead in confusion. He asked, "Excuse me, Madam, but you use my what?"

Miss Guided reached into her pint-size purse and pulled out a large bottle of Hai Karate Aftershave. "See! I really favor it. It's great stuff!"

John wondered where this three-dimensional commercial for stink oil came from. "First of all, Madam, my name is not Hai Karate, nor is that my aftershave. I'm respectfully called Sensei Murphy."

The woman had started to irritate him. He needed to calm down and control his Irish temper. He took in a deep breath and gradually blew it out. *Okay, that's better*, he thought. *Now maybe I can deal with this cute, confusing, young dish.*

"Shame on ya for letting out yer air, Mr. Karate." The whimsical woman waved a dainty finger at Sensei Murphy. With a twinkle in her eyes, she asked, "Have ya been breathing again? I never breathe, Mr. Hai Karate. That's how I keep my mind so clear."

John answered with sarcasm. "Miss Guided, you must be a very smart lady. I like your name—it fits."

The merry angel-in-disguise thought, *Yes, the name Miss Guided—I love it too.*

"Why, thank ya, Mr. Karate. I'm smart 'cause I exercise my memory glands daily."

Murphy shook his head clear and decided it was time to return to the world of the sane. He said impatiently, "Lady, I need to get back to my class. Is there something I can do for you?"

"Oh yessiree." Her voice turned serious. "I'd like ya ta teach yer fist- and feet-fighting formulas ta a young fellow. His name is Matthew McCain. He's an emaciated, longhaired, visually impaired ex-dope fiend. An exquisite applicant for yer karate school." She nodded with a grin. "Don't ya reckon?"

"Yeah, right! That sounds like the makings of a world-champion fighter." He fixed his gaze on the imaginative woman. "Sorry, lady, but I don't train losers. We train only those who wish to better themselves."

"Please, Mr. Hai Karate, make an exception." The undercover guardian angel turned serious. "My friend Matt has had a very vexing life. When this young fellow was in his teens, he was assaulted. The poor boy was forced to stare into the blindin' sunshine through a powerful enlarging glass. This attack horribly damaged his vision. He was still a babe in the wool and was too young ta understand that all things work together for the good ta all those who keep their faith. Instead he felt pity for himself. He hid in his apartment, shuffled cards, and abused drugs. Nonetheless, I'm gratified ta say, the young man has had a transformation in his heart." The radiance from her smile lit up the room. "He also manages some pretty slick card tricks, too."

Sensei Murphy tapped his foot as he listened, then shook his head. "That's a nice story, lady. I wish I could help you, but this is a full contact karate school. Only one in twenty students even lasts a month. Maybe your friend should try something not quite so visual, like swimming."

The visitor decided Mr. Hai Karate was going to need some supernatural encouragement. She surveyed the room and her eyes lit on the staggering stack of bricks. Pointing a delicate finger toward the concrete blocks, she asked, "What are those bricks for, Mr. Karate? Are ya erectin' a skyscraper?"

Sensei eyed the stack of fifteen two-inch thick bricks, all stacked neatly on top of two concrete blocks. He laughed.

"Oh no, I'm not constructing a building. I use those bricks to demonstrate the power of karate. I break them with my bare hands and feet. I don't mean to brag, but I can break a stack of eight with my bare hands."

"Oh, like in yer Hai Karate commercials. May I obliterate them, please, like ya do in yer TV ads?" She held up an open hand ready to hack the bricks in half. "Please may I?"

Yeah, right, Sensei thought. *A little wimpy woman like you could never even break one of those bricks.*

He told her, "If you could break even one brick, I would train all your friends for nothing."

Good! the angel thought. *That's what this heavenly hostess had a hankering to hear.* She walked over to the bricks, reached into her tiny blue bag, and pulled out her big bottle of Hai Karate. She splashed some on, then raised her hand high in the air, ready to plow through the pile.

Off to the side, the Texas Ranger was watching with the students. He was beginning to fear that this crazy woman might really try to break the bricks. He hurried over to Murphy. "Sensei, she'll bust her hand, and you'll get sued."

Sensei Murphy's eyes went wide with concern. "You're right—stop her!"

But before he could do anything, he heard a loud yell. "He-yaw!!"

The supernatural being swung her little hand down hard and crashed through all fifteen bricks. Dust flew and the blocks fractured into fragments.

The students in the school all let out a big "Hoorah!" followed by loud clapping.

Sensei Murphy's mouth fell open, while Ranger Douglas went slack-jawed with shock.

The smiling woman slapped her hands clean. *I hope I didn't over-engage my jiu-jitsu hands. After all,* the angel thought, *I'm in the guise of a fragile, defenseless female.*

She circled back to Sensei and said, "I'll go retrieve your two new apprentices."

Stupefied, Murphy gaped at the pile of rubble. *I must be delirious. Look at this mess.* He watched her exit the school.

He turned back to the Texas Ranger, wide-eyed. "Who was that dainty little brick-buster, and what have I gotten myself into?"

RE-DEAL

Outside, Juan paced the sidewalk and looked up and down the street.

Matt sat on the curb with his head hung low, trying to get over a bad headache from the drugs. He felt like a de-horned goat trying to ward off a slew of ferocious snaggle-tooth wolves.

"Boys," their rescuer waved them over, "hop to yer dawgs. Ya'll begin lessons tomorrow."

"Cool." Juan jumped up and said, "I love karate! I've been taking it since I was five."

"I can't do this," Matt said as he dragged along behind. "I can't function like others with my bli—" He stopped—he couldn't say the word blindness. So he said, "Loss. When they burned me, it messed up my ability to see anything straight on, and what is left is just rotten."

"Have faith, Mr. Matthew," the guardian-in-disguise told him. "You've just had a spell of bad luck. Remember, from sweat and yer conviction comes the pudding of life. Now chin-up, yer gonna discover how ta block and tackle those fiery darts." She opened the door and motioned them inside. "Now pound dirt, boys. Let's meet with the instructors."

The woman shepherded the boys over to the karate instructor and smiled. "Sensei Murphy, I would like ya ta make the acquaintance of these two good men." She pushed the boys forward. "This is Matt McCain and his friend Juan."

Sensei Murphy shook their hands. *McCain, huh*, he thought. *There's a name with a bad reputation.*

He wondered what he could possibly do with this blind, longhaired, pogo stick. The Hispanic boy looked tough, but the McCain kid was a mess. He realized the assignment before him was ridiculous. *But*, he thought after consideration, *a deal's a deal, even if he is a McCain. Besides, somehow this bionic babe did something no karate master has ever done, and I'd like to know how she did it.*

He shook Matt's hand warmly and smacked him on the back. "Mr. McCain, Mr. Juan, welcome to my school. I hear you both want to learn karate."

Juan nodded while Matt just stood there, a little wobbly on his feet.

Sensei Murphy smiled at Matt. "Mr. McCain, I understand you can do a trick or two with a deck of cards. Please show me something, and I'll teach you both how to handle any kind of physical altercation."

"My dad taught me how to throw a card as a weapon," Matt mumbled, "and, sometimes, hit a target."

Sensei Murphy's eyes gave an imperceptible roll. *A card as a weapon? What a joke.*

He tried to hide his skepticism. "Please demonstrate for us. I'd love to see this." Sensei pointed to the silhouette on the opposite side of the room. He said, "Slice the head off that silhouette. He's a bad guy, and he's got your mother."

Matt squinted hard to get a glimpse of what the karate man was pointing toward. He removed the old deck from his pocket, pulled out a card, and sailed it toward the fuzzy shadow of a man. He felt like his stomach was going to erupt, but he gave it his all. The card flew with great speed, but it missed the cut-out and stuck right into the link on a chain that was holding the hanging kick bag, missing the target completely.

Juan laughed. "Wow, man, what a shot. You missed the bad guy and killed your mother."

"Mr. Matt," Miss Guided asked, "may I please see yer deck of cards? I want ta try yer uncommonly slick card-throwin' jugglery."

Matt was disappointed. He had one chance to try to impress the caring and funny lady—instead, he killed his mother. He reluctantly handed the strange woman the deck.

She took aim much like a pro ballplayer, then pitched the fifty-one pieces of paper toward the picture of a person. The cards fluttered in the air like a flurry of falling snowflakes. She said with a shrug, "Oh, well."

She turned them away and headed them toward the doorway. "Come on, boys; we have no snow shovel. Let's

RE-DEAL

leave this blizzard; we have another appointment." She spun back to Sensei Murphy and said, "Catch ya'll tomorrow."

Ranger Douglas watched as the snowstorm of cards settled on the floor, all except a select few that he watched soar right toward the human cut-out, then stick firmly in four vital areas. The rest of the cards slowly fluttered down to the carpet, one on top of the other into a nice neat stack. *How odd*, Douglas thought.

Juan didn't see the four cards stick into the silhouette. He only noted the majority that fluttered in the air prior to the odd dame pushing them out. He chuckled. "'Ey lady, with talent like that, they ought to call you Miss Dealt, instead of Miss Guided."

"Yer a certain joker, Mr. Juan. Ya truly know how to tickle with a tease."

Like the Ranger, Sensei Murphy spotted the cards fly across the school. He walked over and gaped at the four cards stuck in the life size figure. He shook his head in bewilderment when he saw they were the four aces.

On the other end, Ranger Douglas scooped up the block of forty-eight cards. He flipped the cards face-up and casually looked at the numbers. Thoroughly dazzled, the Texas Ranger said, "Sensei, these cards landed in perfect order. What are the odds of that ever happening again?" Then Ranger Douglas looked back over toward the pile of rubble. "Sensei, I need to take some lessons from the great master, Miss Hai Karate."

CHAPTER TEN

Leprosy, an Old Specialty of Mine

Miss Guided looked down the street to see their next stop. She asked, "Mr. Juan, what does yer timepiece say?"

Juan checked his watch and said, "10 till 10."

"March brisk, boys. The theater is crosswise over yonder."

The trio tramped across the street past the two leather-faced men jumping checkers. They stopped in front of an old deserted church building.

"This is it," Miss Guided remarked. "Stay close."

The threesome pressed through an open door into a torn-up lobby. A man with a face as round as an orange and just about the same color greeted them. His eyes were droopy, like a basset hound, and he had a crooked grin. He wore overalls and held a hammer.

"Hi, I'm Glen, and you must be the one who buzzed our phone. You're Miss Guided, cool name. Now, I bet you're here to visit with the director, Pastor Steve Terrell."

I like this mortal man; his freckled face alone is funny. I have a hearty conviction Mr. Glen would make a good straight man for a comedy routine. Miss Guided smiled at the delicious funnies forming in her head.

"Yessiree, Mr. Glen, that's right. We're here to see the director. Can ya read our minds? I venture ta say, ya have female intermission?"

"Oh yes." Glen said with a big jolly grin. "We have both. We have females and intermission, and I love them both."

The smiling lady tapped a finger toward the hammer. "Mr. Glen, I wager ya get paid a lot a change to wave that hammer about,."

RE-DEAL

"Well," Glen nodded, "I accept the meager compensation of an honest lawyer, nothing. Speaking of getting paid, did you perhaps bring me a paycheck?"

The angel looked up toward the loftiness of the old house of worship as she recalled an old joke. "Oh, Mr. Glen, I'm grieved ta declare, I had a little problem with yer check."

Glen lifted one of his drooping eyebrows. "Well, then Miss Guided, what happened to my one and only check?"

"Well, Mr. Glen, it happened this way. Ya should first know that I have a male goat and a female goat, and I believe that one of them gobbled up yer check."

Glen hefted both brows. "A goat ate my check?"

"Yes, but don't fear Mr. Glen," she told him with a twinkle. "I have examined both goats, and best as I can tell, yer check's in the male."

Glen faced the other two and said, "If I work with Miss Guided, I can tell I would be a pauper."

"No doubt, man," Juan said with a stealthy grin. "You'd be that all right."

"A popper?" the angel asked earnestly. "Well, congratulations! Is it gonna be a boy or a girl?"

Again Matt giggled. He was already feeling better. Something about this funny lady calmed him from his bones to his brain. He wondered where this strange woman had come from and why she was helping him, of all people—a Loser McCain.

Glen glanced over to Juan andgrinnd. "I love her character. She reminds me of that great old comedian, Gracie Allen."

"Oh, yessiree, I love Gracie and the cigar she was married to. They rupture my funny bone ta fragments. That lovable Gracie and I have been swappin' cute comebacks ever since she advanced through the Pearly Gates."

"According to Pastor Steve, you have to be dead before going to Heaven." Glen chuckled. "Let me signal Steve for you." Glen cupped his hands around his lips and hollered, "Hey, Pastor Steve. There's a really funny woman here to see you."

Miss Guided inclined her flowery hat toward Matt. "That's the old-fashioned way ta reach out and touch someone."

"Yeah," Glen said with a slight bow, "it sure is. Now come on in."

He led them inside. "This is an old church building we're converting to a theater. I love acting, and Pastor Steve is a fun man to work for. You just have to put up with his preaching at you." He turned to the woman. "Miss Guided, you might not believe this, but I just started singing in the choir. And last week in church, I got up to high C! And held it for thirty seconds."

The silly woman gave Glen a wave. "Oh Mr. Glen, I don't mean ta make ya feel bad, but I got up ta P! After holding it for three hours."

Juan looked at Matt and said, "Got up to P?"

The boys looked at each other and burst out laughing.

The director came crashing through a side door. He thrust forward his hand in greeting and tried to catch his breath. "Hi, I'm Pastor Steve. Welcome to the Lamb's Theater. Please come in, but do excuse our dirty clothes. We've been working like dogs."

The pastor was a retired TV and motion picture performer from back in the sixties. The handsome actor, who had a square jaw and a full head of nut-brown hair, had wanted out of the sinful world of movies. He gave up the fame and fortune of Hollywood for future treasure in Heaven. He went to seminary, became a minister, and started a small church with a theater. He blamed his most peculiar characteristic—a hand that trembled uncontrollably—on the maddening stress of movie making.

Miss Guided appreciated this Master-loving mortal's movies. They were corny and made her laugh. She extended her slim fingers. "Oh, Pastor Steve, it's a privilege ta make yer acquaintance."

Steve could sense something special in the smiling lady. He wrapped his fingers around hers, gave a slight bow with the refinement of an earlier age, and gave her warm hand a light kiss. Then with less enthusiasm, he turned and slapped the two young men on their shoulders.

RE-DEAL

"Howdy fellows, welcome to our theater!"

The guardian angel turned to her boys. "Pastor Steve starred in two of my all-time favored movin' pictures, Invasion of the Saucer Men and Drag Strip Girl."

Steve shook his head. "Oh, no-no-no, please don't remind me," he said with a moan. "I've had a gun fight in many-many Westerns, and this is what Hollywood has done for me." He raised his steady left-hand chest high.

"Why, Pastor Steve," Miss Guided said. "That hand is firm as a foundation."

"Yes, that's true, but the left hand is not the one I shoot with."

He lifted his right hand, and it jiggled like a leaf in a gust. "This is the hand I blast with. This shaking is why I no longer want to make movies. It drives me crazy, especially when I shave. I just wish my one hand was like the other."

Miss Guided murmured, "Isn't that a peculiar preference?" She beamed and said, "Well then, Pastor Steve, I can adjust yer hands for ya."

Steve watched as she reached over and took his left hand into hers. After a short pause, something peculiar happened—his stable left hand began trembling like the right.

Steve loved a good gag. The laughter began in his grass-green eyes and then rumbled across his fair shaven face. "This is the funniest thing I've ever seen." Choking with laughter, he said, "All I need now is some leprosy, and I can shake the hide right off my weary old bones."

Wow, the misguided healer thought, *I made the Heaven-hugging human happy.*

She spread her fingers toward Steve's shivering hands. "Oh, Mr. Terrell, please allow me. Leprosy is an old specialty of mine."

In a flash Steve's face went from happiness to horror. He had no deep desire for fleshless fingers that rattled when they shook. He shoved his shaking hands into his pants pockets and said, "No thank you, Miss Guided. That's okay; thank you, anyway."

Juan watched the strange woman with bewilderment. He recalled Damen calling her an alien. He was beginning to wonder if it might be true. He was going to keep his eyes on the oddball and see what happened next. McCain, with his crummy vision, didn't see all of her bizarre actions.

Juan warned the retired actor, "'Ey, pastor man, you better get down to business before yer blind, deaf, stupid, and crash from the living. She's not called Miss Guided for nothing."

"Yes, yes," Steve said, "you're right. Thanks for the heads up."

The pastor moved toward the poor boy who had been brutally blinded. His voice filled with sympathy, he said, "I understand you want to learn how to act, and you're so good with a deck of cards you can scare the gamble out of a gambler."

Matt took in the surroundings. Drama had been his favorite class in high school, and he wanted to give this a try. He let out a breath. "Yes, Pastor Steve, I'm good with the tickets, and I would like to learn how to act. I was in theater all through high school. I wasn't good at all, but I sure am willing to learn."

"Matt, all that matters is that you're willing. If you don't mind me asking, what is your full name and age?"

Matt hoped he was not rejected because of his shameful name. "My name is," he took a deep breath, "Matthew McCain, and I'm twenty-four."

"That's a fine name," Steve said as he clapped Matt on the back. "It's one of my favorites."

Matt didn't believe that for a second. He was certain the man was teasing him. He raised his eyes and said weakly, "Thanks."

Steve could see the boy didn't believe him. He knew the name McCain was despised by most people. No matter what might be in this boy's painful past, Steve's life-giving Lord loved him. "I mean it! It's a great name, Matthew! Think about it. Matthew is the first name in the Bible's New Testament."

Matt lifted his face and smiled. Relieved, he thought, *I guess this guy's never heard about Lucas the Loser.*

Pastor Steve gave Matt another firm slap on the shoulder. He turned toward the tough-looking lad. "And Juan, your age is?"

RE-DEAL

"Twenty-one til next month," Juan snapped. "And my full name is Juan. I have no last name that I know of."

"If the name Juan is written in the Lamb's Book of Life, that's all the name you'll need."

What the hell does that mean? Lamb's Book of What?

"We volunteer here," Steve told the two boys. "Miss Guided says you might take room and board for pay. What do you think? Would you like to join us and help turn this church into a theater for the purpose of reaching the lost?"

"Well, we're both lost," Juan said with a sarcastic scoff. "So we'll fit right in!"

Miss Guided reached for the reverend's rattling right hand and shook it. "Why, Pastor Steve, ya just got yourself two excellent boys. Much obliged, Pastor Steve. Much obliged!"

Steve let loose of the lively lady's hand to face the two boys—one sorrowful and filled with fear, the other tough and showing no feeling. He shook first Matt's hand, then Juan's. "Welcome, fellows!"

Steve circled his shaking hands around his lips and bellowed, "Hey, Glen, are you still here?"

"Yes, Mr. Director," Glen replied from only a dog's bark away. "Can I help you?"

"Yes, would you please show these two young gentlemen the theater? Then show them the accommodations. Bunk them in the empty room next to yours."

"Happy to." Glen removed his tool-belt and motioned with his arm. "Matt, Juan, walk this way."

"One moment, Mr. Glen," the angel in human disguise said.

She drew her charge and his companion to the side and spoke softly. "Boys, ya know rumors have a thousand tongues. So keep hushed. Train diligent and practice fervently. Remember ta keep skunks, lawyers, and Cyphers at a distance."

She pulled a pack of cards from her little purse and placed them into Matt's hand. "Take these. Practice all the tricks yer daddy taught ya so ya can always spot a cheat. Now take these encouraging words with ya. Ponder for a spell David and Goliath. When Goliath came against the

40,000 knee-knocking Israelites, the soldiers stared up and said, 'Goliath is so big we can never kill him!' The small sheepherder David swung up his single-load slingshot and declared, 'That man is so monstrous I can't miss him!'"

"Boys, in this story, King David and the soldiers had the same situation. They just had two opposin' ways of ponderin' their choices. What I'm tryin' ta express ta ya boys, it's how ya face the mountains before ya that will determine if ya dwell in an outhouse or the White House."

After a brief pause she slowly moved her gentle gaze from one boy to the other one. She told Juan, "Keep yer head pinned beneath the line of fire. Big Lew shouldn't find ya in this haven out here." She leaned close to Juan's ear and murmured, "Keep a peeper or two on Matt for me, okay?"

Juan gave her a slow nod of assurance. "Yeah, sure, lady."

The incognito angel took them by the hand. "If ya have questions or tribulations, look deep into the depths of yer heart, boys. That's where the Creator's truth was instilled in each of ya. Yer ability for good or corrupt are both there. Have faith, boys. Now ya have much toil before ya. Remember the Almighty likes hardworkin', leathered hands with a pure heart. Now get on with ya. This little teacher needs to do some sewing and thinking. So I'm goin' on a trip, way over yonder, but never too far."

Before anyone could stop her or say anything further, the boys watched as the strange lady spun around and disappeared out the entrance.

Matt yelled after her, "You're leaving us all alone?"

There was no reply.

"Follow me," Glen said. "The rooms are this way."

The two boys tagged after Glen into the dusty old theater.

Matt whispered, "Juan, did it sound to you like Miss Guided was leaving us?"

"Yeah, I wondered the same thing."

CHAPTER ELEVEN

Fiend-Fighting Foreman

Five years later

On a clear cool morning, Miss Guided had a few free minutes. She shouted out the window of her blue buggy, "Yank it on over, Seraphim!"

The horse halted along the side of the deserted dirt road just outside the quaint Mayberry-like town where the guardian angel had left Matt and Juan. She had a few seconds to sit and knit before she checked on her humans.

Far back on the same road, a hardy Hispanic man dressed in sweatpants and a light windbreaker was out jogging. Big Lew's former orphaned wetback, the now-fugitive Juan was also called Kicker because of his fast, bone-crushing karate kicks. Juan loved learning and had acquired an excellent education using online classes at a University down South near the Alamo. He now had a B.A. in Speech Communication and a Master's in Religious Studies.

As he ran, Juan remembered that life-changing day when the Big Man in the Sky had poured joy into his heart. Ever since that magnificent moment, he loved to live life to the fullest. He relished bantering with others as well as receiving and recounting a good gag.

Juan spotted a stubborn branch spread across the road up ahead. He increased his speed into a sprint, then leaped seven feet high toward the dead, overhanging limb. He launched a double front kick, snapping off the branch. While in the air, he tucked in his knees, did a backward somersault, landed firmly on his feet, and caught the limb before it hit the ground. Holding the branch firmly in his left hand, he hacked it hard with his right hand, hewing it in half.

"I finally got you!" He tossed the branch to the side and continued down the path.

What a beautiful sunrise for pounding your dogs. Juan reflected back to how that funny female with the towering triple trotter horse spoke. His favorite pastime while running was putting Bible stories into a jargon more enjoyable to his karate amigos. Like how the Creator sent from Heaven His Son to this suspended dirtball in the sky to go to the cross to die for this humble karate-kicker's crimes and bad behavior. He realized whatever he was called to do was nothing compared to being spiked onto crossed sections of scratchy timber.

Juan thrust his arms toward the ground and executed a cartwheel. Then he twisted into three handsprings, generating tremendous velocity, and vaulted high into the air in a somersault spin. He opened into a flying sidekick into a decaying old fencepost, knocking it forcefully from the ground. He stood it back up for tomorrow's run and raced on.

Juan raised his eyes toward Heaven and prayed aloud. "Dear King of all Kings, it's me, your minor, Mexican karate kicker. Please help my amigo Matt McCain and me. Indulge this lowly act of devotion and show us amazing and mighty marvels. I'm geared up for your bidding to be executed in my life. You show the route, and I will follow faithfully."

As Juan ran along the dry road, he reflected on stirring Scriptures. Suddenly off in the far distance, he caught sight of a familiar coach. He recognized that girly blue buggy from years before. A thrill blasted through his veins.

Well, knock me out. Could this be the answer to my prayers?

He and his amigo Matt had not seen Miss Guided in over five long Texas summers—not since the day she left them in the hands of Pastor Steve Terrell. Juan ran faster to grab hold of the buggy before it pulled away.

RE-DEAL

As he hustled toward the carriage, off toward the horizon he noticed a mysterious figure that looked like a flaring gold asteroid heading toward the coach. The object floated on air by whipping golden wings that fluttered in a blur and shined like the sun. The flaming gold figure descended in a circle straight through the roof of the carriage without any damage to the top.

Inside the buggy, Miss Guided said to no one in particular, "It's time ta move and mind my two admirable mighty men."

As she put away her knitting, the golden shape of a man took form.

Outside, Juan observed a curious light shine inside the coach. *What is that brilliance?* he wondered. *It's brighter than the light of day.*

The woman's solid countenance became transparent when the magnificent being appeared and sat in the opposite seat.

The gladiator's glowing wings fluttered freely, unhampered by the corporal characteristics of the coach. His radiant form looked like molten bullion. The bearded being wore a flickering robe, a decorated belt holding a sword, and a crystalline jewel-covered helmet. Juan stepped closer and peeked inside the window. What he saw stopped his breath. As he watched, the golden glow dimmed and the bright wings slowed, then stopped, then faded away. In the pink seat, a distinguished figure slowly took on a semi-solid human appearance. However, whoever or whatever it was, Juan knew the beautified being was not a mortal man. He looked across to the opposite seat, and his heart jumped with joy. Yes, it was that wonderfully amusing Miss Guided!

As Juan surveyed the scene, Miss Guided suddenly turned partially transparent, with a light golden glow encircling her. He stared in stunned silence as the two golden translucent beings spoke.

Miss Guided tilted up her head, "Howdy, my fabulous fiend-fighting foreman."

"Well, howdy back to ya," the Archangel said. "Is ya'll doin' okay today?" The leader of the heavenly legions laughed. "Well, my funny angel, how's that? I've been practicing my Southern drawl."

"Confidentially, Sir Gabe, I think ya need ta cast yer peepers on a few more John Wayne Westerns."

"I'll give it due consideration." Then he turned serious. "My favored hilarious heavenly hostess, your uncommon style loads me with laughter. However in the Kingdom, the rest of the heavenly hosts are having a happy howl referring to you as Miss Guided. Time to time, you roughly get things right, yet not quite enough to tickle the Top." The Archangel attempted to catch her attention as she knitted. "I don't suppose you want this silly selection, Miss Guided, to stick when you have a beautiful angel name like Michala."

"Oh yes, Sir Gabe, on the contrary, I certainly seek to use this name. Miss Guided is a taintless tickling name for a teacher. I love it!"

"All right, all right, if you're so compelled," the Archangel said with a slight shake of his head. "Now, if you might be so magnanimous as to inform your Mastermind of this meaningful mission and update me with the course of your charge, Matthew McCain."

"Well, well, let me contemplate yer question. My man Matthew proceeds to places of worship on Wednesdays and Sundays." She glanced up and continued. "As does Matthew's friend and my new man Juan."

"But, if I am at liberty to ask as your entirely-too-easy boss, to which new friend are you referring?"

Worried her master might not believe she could take on a team of two, Michala evaded. "Both my fine fellows are forceful karate fighters."

Gabriel had been briefed on the faithful fellow Juan Bowen—his zealous studying of the Scriptures and his fervent prayers. The Archangel had already received permission from the Top to accept Juan's request to assist in dethroning Big Lew and his evil empire. Nonetheless, the Archangel wanted to hear the plan from the angel personally.

RE-DEAL

He raised an inquisitive brow. "Both? Again, I ask you, my glorified girl, who is this additional one?"

Michala raised her curious blue eyes without hoisting her flowery hat. She finally said, "I adopted another faithful fighting fellow; name's Juan, he's also called Kicker."

Squatting outside the pink-flapped window, Juan could barely breathe. He was witnessing something wonderful, amazing, incredible. Damen Cypher was wrong—this unusual laughing lady was not an alien. The miracle-working Miss Guided was an angel from Heaven!

Juan decided it was improper for him to be hearing this conversation. He dropped to his knees and prayed.

"I was given particulars about your prayerful personage," Gabriel said. "It's praiseworthy of you. Juan will bestow backing. My query is this: can you carry out your mission without the extra mortal so overloading you that you get preoccupied from your principal project?"

"Oh, no obstacle, glorious Gabe." The guardian angel grinned. "My two are a terrific team. They visit schools. They bolster boys to be honest and honorable. You would be enthused and inspired, Sir Gabe."

"Is that so?" Gabriel asked. "I suppose that sounds satisfactory. So, it sounds like you're set to patch your petite little lapse."

"Yessiree," she answered as animation flooded her ephemeral face. "I imagine on that estimate I'm equipped."

"Well, I must survey my amusing angel. What is your strategy to stop the serpent-supported Cyphers and reinstate the homestead back to the McCain clan?"

Michala was certain her scheme would be considered a worst-case scenario. Still, she was determined to convince the Archangel of her plan. "My new mission is to take Matthew McCain back to the past to mend the mess."

The Archangel elevated a brow. "Are you proposing taking your two charges and traveling outside-of-time?"

"Um, yes, Sir Gabe," Michala murmured. "I ponder that would be my prime plan."

Gabriel stroked his beard. The Archangel recognized that this could create the possibility for more calamity. After further reflection, he decided to allow her to proceed with her plan.

He said sternly, "Retroaction to a past period is sporadically permitted. The chances for unforeseen consequences are profoundly probable."

She raised her smiling blue eyes and said, "I'm mindful of your meaning. Fear not, my fine charitable chief, no chronicled past processes will be pushed off their presupposed path."

"You're awfully amusing, my adroit little angel," the Archangel said with a circumspect smile. "But please perform prudently. As you earlier stated, the most momentous issue is returning the ranch, and there may be no other historical alterations."

The direct contact angel was ecstatic. She was back on track with a special dispensation from her boss to take a backward trip in time. "Oh boy! We're gonna get it right this time, Seraphim." Her flower-bedecked hat bobbed up and down like a schoolgirl in spring. "Of course, of course. Thank ya, Sir Gabe! Oh, thank ya! Ya'll be pleased for sure with yer little town tutor." Miss Guided leaned across and gave her boss a big sloppy smooch on his cheek.

"My, my, Michala." The Archangel swabbed the lipstick smear from his cheek. "You have truly taken up their quaint customs."

"Ya can push on now, Sir Gabe. See ya next time ya flutter by."

Gabriel's golden wings appeared and began to flap. As he ascended through the carriage ceiling, he said, "Bear in mind my mirthful Miss Guided, you may return the ranch and relieve the McCains from the clutch of the corrupt Cyphers. However, I prefer to have no fat fish as happened with Jonah on one of your previous assignments."

"Still I fixed it." She nodded in satisfaction. "Right, Sir Gabe? And I'll fix this, too."

CHAPTER TWELVE

Assist in the Slaying

Outside, down on his knees, with his eyes lifted toward Heaven, Juan beheld the carriage once more begin to glow. He couldn't help but gape as the Archangel Gabriel transfigured into a magnificent golden gladiator and then rose through the top.

The heavenly spirit hovered. Juan was awed as he saw the angel arrayed in a shimmering robe, a decorated belt, and a crystalline, jewel-covered golden helmet. Gabriel's bearded, fearsome face gazed directly down upon Juan and smiled. The golden angel lifted his massive sword from its ruby-strewn scabbard and raised it toward the sky. His other hand gave Juan a thumbs-up, with a nod of affirmation and a supportive smile.

Inspired and in reverent awe, Juan lifted his hand and respectfully returned the same salute.

The Archangel's eyes turned golden and intense as fire. With his shimmering sword pointed skyward, he burst toward the heavens and vanished in a flash.

Whoa! Juan thought, humbled and spellbound. *That golden gladiator was cool.*

He raced back and looked into the interior of the carriage. The supernatural being had once again taken on a mortal female appearance. Juan could barely believe all he had seen.

Over the past five years, he and his amigo Matt had exhausted many weary weeks traveling the area towns trying to find this witty woman or her little schoolhouse. Now here she sat, calmly knitting. He wasn't going to let the marvelous misguided woman get away again. He reached for the door, opened it, stepped in, and entered the amazing world of the elusive angel.

Juan accompanied his words with a respectful expression of reverence mixed with a mark of mirth. "'Ey man, it's the miracle-working maiden, Miss Guided. In what region of Heaven have you been hanging your hat?"

Delight spread over the angel's appearance, and she took his hands. "Oh Juan, or should I call ya Kicker? How ya makin' it, my fighting fellow? Please snatch a scrap of seat and take a load off."

"Thanks!" Juan sat in the spot just vacated by the Archangel. "I'll snatch this already-warm one."

"I'm so proud of ya. Yer lookin' so good. And a college boy, too."

Juan looked over at the angel with a new discernment in his gaze and grinned. "Please tell me, where have you been hiding? We've not seen you for years." He paused for a second. "And what sort of supernatural spirit are you?"

The angel's eyebrows reached to her hat's brim as she realized Juan knew her identity. "Oh? I reckon I'm not catchin' yer questions."

After receiving the thumbs-up from the topmost angel, Juan knew in his heart he had a mission from the Big Man and this angel-appearing-to-be-a-person was part of his path. Speaking in his own lyrical prayer language he said, "Think about it, my adorable little angel, Miss Guided. You plainly appear, pick us a prudent place to live peacefully, tell us to train, and then you turn a tail and take the trail out of town. Now while out jogging I see your glow and that other supreme golden gladiator. In factual fame, you are Michala, and you are Gabriel's most hilarious heavenly hostess."

Oh dear, dear, Michala worried. *Did I mess up once more?* She asked, "Are ya tellin' me that ya saw my boss, Sir Gabe?"

RE-DEAL

"Yeah!" Juan replied. "I did see that cool gold guy."

Michala figured it must be fine to fill him in on her mission, or else Sir Gabe would never have permitted this mortal man to behold his glorified countenance. Her blue eyes sparkled as she gazed into Juan's honest eyes, and she smiled in gratification.

"We're gonna have fun now." She said, thrilled in her own heavenly language, "My marvelous, meek mortal, if I perhaps present to you my personal purpose on this planet and impart to you what I truly am, the secret stays between us?"

Juan inquired, "May I make known this marvelous marvel to my amigo Matt?"

Michala touched Juan on the tip of his nose with her finger. "Nobody, my karate kicker. You have received a rare peek into paradise. There is a compulsion in mankind to crave a glimpse of their Creator's complete creation. My faithful fellow, you have had a limited look. So the special secret is ours to have and hold, agreed?"

"Yes, I will do as you say. I just have a perplexing piece of the puzzle for you to explain the pretext."

"What is the particular pretext of the perplexing piece of the puzzle you perhaps would like me to provide?"

"My curious question is why is an angel here in the character of a happy human?"

Michala transferred her angelic arm from around Juan's neck and angled herself to face him. She took his hands in hers. "The aim for an amusing angel to be a temporal tutor is told this way. Regularly man may require a ration of remarkable relief, mainly your mate Matthew McCain. If your friendly, flying angel is not there to intercept her hasty human, he will handily hurry off the projection of a precipice or pace plumb into a brick building."

"You bet," Juan agreed. "It's hard to harness a blind bull in a china boutique."

"You're a gut-splitting cutter, Kicker; you absolutely are," she said with a chuckle. "Now, my fine fellow, let me provide to you the last particular perplexing piece of the puzzle. This angel's foremost task is to fix a former fumble.

"I was knitting a nice handsome neckpiece when Matt's grandfather Lucas lost his limitless lands. But I can't fix it for your friend. Matt must defeat the dragon himself. However, Sir Gabe said it's settled that you can assist in the slaying. It will be an adventure unequal to any and all of your other escapades." Michala looked into the prayerful man's eyes. "Sound satisfying? Want to go with us and war with the wicked warlocks?"

This was an answer from paradise to Juan's prayers. There was no threat of pain, plan, person, or proposal that would keep him from complying. *Besides,* he thought, *it will be tantalizing to trick my trickster, Matt.* Juan shared a conspirator's smile with the angel.

"Yes, you're being an angel tailored like a teacher is our secret. However, Miss Guided, I learned from you long ago that life is worth living when it's filled with goofy gags, joyful jokes, and Miss Guided's mirth. My question is, can we joke our way through the mission?"

"You bet! Now get on with ya."

Miss Guided pulled from her dainty purse a large wind-up alarm clock. "Yer karate class commences in fifty-eight minutes. Ya better pound yer dawgs."

Juan pointed to the huge clock. "'Ey Miss Guided, that clock is larger than that strange sack."

"Just get movin', my kickin' friend." She threw open the carriage door. "I'll see ya later at Matt's black belt exam."

Juan turned back and asked excitedly, "You're gonna be there?"

Michala didn't answer; instead she reached under her hat and removed two bobby pins and handed them to Juan. "Take these pins and keep them with ya."

"What are these for?" Juan asked as he shoved them into the pocket of his windbreaker.

Michala didn't respond. She closed the door, then shouted from the window, "Let's get on, Seraphim!"

Thrilled, Juan watched the buggy head on down the road.

CHAPTER THIRTEEN

Bloody-Looking Rocks

"499 ... 500 ... stop!" Juan punched the stopwatch. "'Ey Mano, that's 500 pushups in only twelve minutes and nine seconds. You beat me! That's a new school record!"

Matt McCain, tanned and muscular with bulging nineteen-inch biceps, stood and wiped the sweat from his brow. Though his face held an expression of confidence under his short hair, blond mustache, and nicely-trimmed beard, Matt still had inner doubts, hesitations, and fears that he tried to hide from others. His damaged vision hadn't changed. He couldn't see to read or drive, but he'd developed perceptions and abilities that Kicker and Murphy couldn't explain.

Juan stared at his sweaty friend. "Let me impart to you something I've noted over the past five years."

"What's that?" Matt swabbed the sweat from his face.

"You, my brother Matt McCain, are a monomaniacal man."

"What?" Matt frowned in confusion. "Monomaniacal man? Sounds crazy."

"It is. It's someone who won't stop digging until he's in China. I've seen you exercise card techniques for ten to twenty hours a day twelve months at a time." He punched his amigo. "And now you just had to push until you passed my perfect pushup record."

"So sad, Kicker." Matt kicked at the air. "You snooze, you lose. Now I'm warmed up. Come on—let's go a few rounds."

All the younger students gathered around the fighting ring to watch the advanced belts spar. Matt was getting ready for his black belt test later in the day. He put on his boxing gloves and went three rounds with Juan, who had already received his third degree black belt two years earlier. Both men were fit and flexible, and each displayed amazing agility as well as a mastery of difficult fighting skills. Even though Matt could see very little, he seemed to sense Juan's every move.

Sensei Murphy yelled, "Yamay! Stop fighting. Gentlemen, get your weapons and show the students your stuff."

As the two fighters left the ring, Juan shook his head. "You must have sonar like a bat. I can't get how you block my superman kicks."

"That's it," Matt replied with an outward expression of confidence. "You guessed it—it's my bat-like sonar." But inwardly he thought, *Whoa, I got lucky again.*

The chief instructor, Sensei Murphy, turned toward the younger students and asked, "How about those legs on Kicker?"

At the mention of his name, Juan turned and did a standing split, with his foot slapping an imaginary target two feet over his head. The students whooped and hollered.

Matt grabbed his metal cane, the one given to him by that strange woman, Miss Guided. He missed her and wondered whatever happened to her. Sometimes he had the same odd dream—the one where she said something about going back in time and fixing the game.

He hoped he would see her again someday. Matt stepped to the front. He used his cane to move everyone back. He spun his cane, attacking multiple imaginary opponents, all to the cheers of the others.

Sensei Murphy turned to the younger students and embarrassed Matt by saying, "In my thirty years as a martial arts instructor, I've never had a student who has so acutely developed his sixth sense. For some unexplainable reason, Mr. McCain has the ability to see without seeing. Some of you may remember when that strange woman introduced us to Mr. McCain. It was over five years ago when that little lady busted all those bricks. Look at Mr. McCain now. He's able to feel what kick or punch his opponent is going to throw before he even throws it."

Murphy glanced up at the clock. "In about eight hours he's testing for his black belt. I want all of you who can to follow us to our other school down South to cheer him on."

It's not true; it's not true, Matt thought behind a blush. *I wish I had the same confidence in myself that Sensei has in me.*

Not to be outdone by his friend, Juan took down his set of nunchakus. He went through a martial arts kata, looking much like Bruce Lee, and ended with a back flip into the splits. He jumped up and took a bow, enjoying the loud applause.

"They love us, Mano," Juan said. "Got to get out of our gis, guild our gullet with grub, and get. You got a gig in one hour at the theater. Let's put it away. Time to change."

"Right, Kicker. Do you have a buck for a sandwich?"

"I don't know," Juan said with a snicker. "Let me see the sandwich."

"You crack me up." Matt pushed his goofy friend forward. "Let's hustle."

As they headed toward the dressing room, Matt asked, "Don't you think of anything but eating?"

"Nope," Juan replied. "Food, fighting, and faith—that's all for me."

"Food, fighting, and faith, huh? What about the other F, females?"

"Not for me, Mano. Like the dude from Tarsus, I'm a bachelor to the rapture."

Juan loved Matt like a big brother. But regardless of how much he tried, Juan couldn't persuade his amigo to let go of the guilt Matt carried in his soul because of Juan's Mexican brothers who blamed the McCains for their sorrow. Then there were the sinister Cyphers stalking them like wild animals.

Matt was full of fight, but he wouldn't put his trust and faith in the Father. Juan prayed, preached, and pushed, but something kept Matt from letting go of his will and trusting in the Team Up Top.

However, Juan thought with firm faith in the Father, *now that the Big Man has sent this amazing angel Miss Guided, maybe this sad situation will improve.*

As they hurried to the dressing room, Matt asked Murphy, "Sensei, do you think I know enough to survive against all those crazy people out there?"

"Yes!" Murphy answered firmly. "You're strong and fast; you hit like a bull; and that weapon you call a cane is more deadly than a knife."

Juan removed his gi top, and the myriad scars lining his back appalled Sensei anew. He knew three men named Carlos, Gustavo, and Escona inflicted them with a riding crop. He remembered seeing the Cypher goons at his school down South, and he longed for the day they again walked through his doors so he could share with them his hammer-like fists with their razor-sharp, calloused knuckles. Murphy lowered his eyes in disgust and unwrapped his black belt.

He asked, "Mr. McCain, does your question have anything to do with the Cyphers?"

"I told you about the 200,000 dollar offer from Big Lew to deal Texas Hold'em in his big anniversary game." Matt removed his gi and slid on his black dress trousers. "I told him to forget it! Now he's trying a different approach." Matt put on a white wing-tipped gambler shirt. "I was on a flight to a show when some stranger in the seat next to mine said he had a proposition for me."

He encircled his neck with a black string tie. "He said his name is Rosa, and he's a diamond broker from South Africa. To show me his good intentions, Rosa tried to offer me a five-carat diamond ring. I told him to keep it."

Juan shoved his nunchakus in his back pocket. "Don't forget the business card."

"Right, Kicker." Matt accented the white shirt with a fancy brocade vest. "This goon tried another bribe. He suggested that I might like to perform on the Tonight Show. He gave me a card with the business and private numbers of the Tonight Show host."

Ranger Douglas fumed. "I had the department run the numbers, and they were legitimate."

"Last month after a show in Vegas," Matt sat down to slip on his black ropers, "I went out to eat, and this same suspicious character was waiting for me in the lounge."

"I was with him," Juan said. "It was weird, like something in a Godfather flick."

"He asked us to join him," Matt went on. "I had some time to kill before my next lecture on catching card cheaters. I decided to find out what he was up to. This Mr. Rosa knew all about my family and our troubles with the Cyphers."

There was a loud bang as Juan executed a jump-turn crescent kick, slamming his locker closed. He said, "Rosa had the guts to talk about paying 400 big ones to buy a judge for a murder he arranged."

"I asked you to stop kicking your locker closed," Murphy snapped. "You're wearing it out."

"Sorry, Sensei. Can't help it. It's so much fun!"

Matt pulled a pack of cards from his locker, opened the box, then fanned them a few times to make sure they were still new. He placed them into his back pocket and turned back to Murphy. "The scary part was when he offered to have a family member, or anyone else I chose, bumped off."

Sensei Murphy frowned, concerned for the life of his most unusual student. He asked, "Why all the subterfuge with underlying threats?"

"As far as we can tell," Ranger Douglas cracked his knuckles, "Cypher is holding another one of his illegal high-stake poker games. Our inside sources tell us there'll be seven players, most from other countries. This big anniversary game will have two drug kingpins, two arms dealers, a rich Middle East terrorist, and Mr. McCain's Rosa, who is a diamond dealer from South Africa. They're all very rich and each will pay 10,000,000 dollars to buy a seat at the table. In other words, there will be seventy mil up for grabs.

"This diamond merchant has supposedly heard how Big Lew wants Mr. McCain to be the dealer for the big game. Now Rosa wants Matt to accept Big Lew's offer. Rosa has bought a seat at the table, and he wants Mr. McCain to deal winning cards to him instead of Big Lew. In return, he's promised Mr. McCain half of the pot. However, I believe this is a ruse set up by Big Lew to get Mr. McCain to deal the game. But, instead of Mr. McCain receiving half the pot, I think the scam is that Rosa will be splitting it with Cypher."

"How does Big Lew communicate?" Sensei Murphy asked, a fear of more trouble reflected in his eyes. "Has he found you out here?"

"Don't think so," Matt replied. "I call my dad. He tells me what's going down."

"So, Ranger Douglas," Murphy's face mirrored his disgust, "what is the department doing to help protect Mr. McCain from these goons?"

"We're keeping an eye on the theater," the Texas Ranger told them. "Kicker is also getting his firearms license."

"Yeah, man." Juan drew his finger from an imaginary holster and pointed it like a gun. "I'm getting bad! Call me Holliday."

"I want you to keep yourself in fighting trim, just in case." Murphy placed a hand on Matt's shoulder. "The Cyphers are vicious. They always get what they go after, and in this case that's you."

"Don't worry, Sensei. All winning streaks come to an end."

Matt wondered if the bad guys ever did get their just desserts. He was starting to doubt. After five years of hiding from Big Lew and his evil clan, he could feel Cypher closing in on him and his poor family. His family had been in Big Lew's clutches all this time—Matt realized Cypher had been biding his time for his own evil purposes. Matt had never really been safe. Now he could feel time running out.

RE-DEAL

"By the way," Murphy asked, "whatever happened to that pretty babe that busted you into my school? What was her name? Miss-Miss-Miss Guided!"

"Don't know," Matt said with a distant gaze. "Haven't seen her since that day. But I sure would like to thank her."

He knew it was because of Miss Guided that he and Juan were still alive. He still had deep seeds of guilt about the Lucas curse. From the research he, Juan, and the Texas Ranger had done, he felt his family was directly responsible for the poverty throughout Mexico. They had been appalled to learn how the Cyphers throughout the twentieth century had controlled the politics, which, in return created a whole country of the poor and downtrodden. This made the country ripe for Cypher to provide cheap labor across the entire United States.

As Matt and Juan traveled around the country to police departments and casinos lecturing on cheaters, they could see Cypher's dirty work everywhere. After a hundred years of political manipulation, Cypher's evil influence reached into the agricultural industry, hotels, casinos—all the many businesses and industries benefiting from cheap labor. The cruelty and suffering sickened Matt and increased the guilt he felt as an ancestor of Lucas McCain. Matt had always traveled incognito and spoken secretly, but he was just now beginning to realize how dangerous his opposition to the Cypher reign of evil was.

Murphy slapped the Texas Ranger on the back. "Mr. McCain, if you ever see that pretty brick-buster again, Ranger Douglas wants lessons."

Sensei Murphy's comment snapped Matt from his inner reproach. "If I see her, I'll tell her."

He pulled his talking clock from his pocket and pressed the talk button. The clock said, "It's ten o'clock AM"

When Matt shoved his timepiece back into his pocket, he felt a small box. "Sensei, Ranger Douglas, let me show you what I've been saving my money for. It came in the mail yesterday."

He pulled out a small jewelry box and opened it to reveal a gold cross hanging from a delicate chain. A ruby decorated each end of the cross and a larger stone adorned the center. Matt's face lit with pride and pleasure.

"It's for my mom. The cross is gold and the red stones are real Siam rubies. The last time I saw her—over five years ago now—I pushed her down and told her to shut up and other mean things. I've wanted so badly to tell her how sorry I am for being such a thankless rat."

"That's cool, Mano," Juan said. "I'm sure she'll love it."

"I can't wait to give it to her and tell her how sorry I am. I should never have waited this long. But, we've been so busy, and you know how it is, being on the lam and all. I am so glad we're finally getting them out and away from Cypher. I've felt so guilty all these years. My dad said he's earned enough money to make a new start. The only downside is that my dad feels like he's had to compromise his values for so long, and it's driven him to drink."

"We're behind you all the way, Matthew," Murphy told his student.

"Yes, that's right" the Ranger agreed. "And the new home for your family is ready, as well as a new job for your dad."

"I can't wait to be with them again. I just wish I would have done this much sooner." Matt paused and took a deep breath. "And I hope that Big Lew and his murderous bullies don't do anything to keep us from being together and starting a new life."

Kicker asked, "What's the little paper in the lid?"

Matt closed the box and shoved the case back into his pocket. "That's a message for my mom, explaining the meaning for the cross."

CHAPTER FOURTEEN

Burn Those Eyes

He nodded to his friend. "Let's go, Kicker." Matt turned back to Murphy and the Texas Ranger. "I'm off to do a benefit performance at the Theater for some young men from Boys' Town. Thanks again for everything, Sensei. You too, Mr. Douglas." Matt tightened his belt and put on his hat. "We'll see you tonight."

Matt and Juan walked toward the dressing room exit. Matt ran squarely into the doorframe, knocking off his cowboy hat. He grabbed his head. "Ouch! Doggonit! I did it again!"

"'Ey Mano, "Juan snickered. "Someone moved the door again."

Matt chided himself as he reached for his hat. *I can step into the ring with a top black belt, but I can't even walk through a doorway without cracking my thick skull.* He rubbed his head and replaced his hat. This time he made it out without making any new dents in the wall.

"Like I told Miss Guided," Juan laughed again, "you run around like a blind bull in a china shop."

"What? Told who?"

Juan suddenly recalled Miss Guided's angelic persona was a secret. "Um, Gu-Gu-Guided. Told Miss Guided."

"What?" Matt stopped cold. His excitement shot to the roof. "Oh, you saw her!"

"Yeah," Juan said with a grin. "She might be at your test."

"What!" Matt playfully slugged Juan on the shoulder. "Why didn't you tell me? That's great!"

"Told you now. Didn't you hear me? I heard myself. Sounded good."

"Kicker!" Matt raised his knee as if to throw a kick. "One of these days!" He lowered his leg. "We've covered every inch of this countryside trying to locate her schoolhouse. Now you don't tell me when you finally find her!"

"'Ey Mano," Juan said with a smile. "She asked me to zip it. I think she wants to surprise you."

Matt could only shake his head in bewilderment at his friend. "Yeah, right," Matt said with a snort.

Matt and Juan emerged from the dressing room, Juan in casual clothes and Matt in his riverboat gambler outfit. These fancy duds elicited admiration from Sensei Murphy's younger students.

"Kicker, hold up for a minute." Matt stopped at Sensei Murphy's desk to use the phone. "I need to call my dad. He wants to come see the test."

Jim McCain sat in his new condo at an 1885 faro table given to him by his boss, Big Lew.

He cried, "Oh God, help my boy wherever he is, and me too. Help me get off the booze. I know Cypher is gonna do somethin' bad, and I don't know how ta stop him."

Cypher's threats again pulsed through Jim's head. "You won't have four mouths to feed, nor will you even have three. You will only have two."

Jim didn't like Big Lew having him use his advanced card skills more and more to control Cypher's crooked games. He wished he'd stayed toiling in the ranch's hot fields and had never picked up a deck of cards. He regretted the day he and his son Matthew had showed their boss their hard-practiced card moves, especially the new slick ones he learned from Professor Vernon.

Dai Vernon, Jim's sleight-of-hand teacher and a world-famous card magician, was called The Professor. Vernon was so good that many years before he had even fooled Houdini, the great escape artist. Professor Vernon had a fascination with old gamblers. He'd heard the story about Jim's grandfather, Lucas McCain, being cheated out of his million-acre ranch. Dai Vernon looked Jim up and offered to trade magic lessons in exchange for a look at Jim's grandfather Lucas's papers and diaries.

Over the years, each time Jim found a new document or newspaper article about his grandfather and the swindle, Professor Vernon stopped by. The card lessons were hard. But as the world-renowned Professor demonstrated the different card sleights, Jim learned many difficult gambling moves, such as dealing off the bottom of the deck and even the most difficult of all, dealing the aces from the middle of the pack. Jim started teaching the moves to Matt a year before he started grade school and was impressed at how easily his son mastered these complicated techniques.

The ringing of the phone interrupted Jim's reflection. He reached over to the wall and grabbed the receiver. "This is Jim."

"Pop, it's me."

"Matthew! Son! Been hopin' you'd call. You doin' okay?"

"Yes, good, Dad. And you?"

"Ain't doin' so good," Jim allowed. "Miss ya! Told Big Lew no more dealin'."

"That's why I called. I'm now ready for my black belt test. I want you to come watch. We can firm up our plans to get you all out during the drive."

"I'm afraid. Big Lew's been makin' bad threats against you and our family. He's told me several times, 'You will not have four mouths to feed, nor will you even have three. You will only have two.' It's the hundred and twenty-fifth anniversary of the big game—the one where the Cyphers won Grandpa Lucas's ranch. He brags that his games are the biggest in the world. Son, I hear this Texas Hold'em game will have 70 million on the table. That's why he wants you to deal this particular game. I'm losin' my touch with the cards. So to make sure the game is in his control, he wants you. Son, we got ta run, now."

Matt knew the time had come to get his family out, but first he needed to get this black belt test out of the way. He had trained so hard, and he was sure a few more hours wouldn't matter. He wanted his father to see the test, but he knew his ma and sis would freak out at all the violence.

He asked, "Are Mom and Debra okay?"

"Yes, for now—they're at Gram's. But I'm worried bad!"

"Okay, Dad," Matt said. "Meet me at the normal spot, and we'll decide what to do."

"What time?"

Matt turned back to Juan and asked, "Kicker, what time do you think we'll finish the Boys' Town show?"

"Shows at noon. Say one-thirty."

Matt spoke into the phone. "Dad, it'll take us an hour to get to you, so we'll meet you at three."

"I'll be there. I'll make sure yer ma and Deb stay at Gram's."

"Good, Dad, I'm gonna get you all out fast. Sit tight. Love ya."

The line clicked dead.

In the condo next to Jim's, Damen's drug dealer Tom watched the caller ID from a telephone line coming through a hole in the wall.

Tom grinned with satisfaction. "Got it, Damen. Small town, about an hour or so from here."

Damen punched his cell phone and dialed. When Carlos answered, Damen said "We found them." He read the address. "Take Gustavo and go!"

Damen's eyes went black with anticipation. "I'm finally going to get Magoo, the little punk Juan, and hopefully, that crazy blonde dame who snatched them! I curse them all, and I curse my old man for beating me until I zapped Magoo's eyes!"

He remembered the day his old man's guards dragged him in to see his father after he lost the school debate to Matt McCain.

Big Lew sat in his library slapping a riding crop across his palm and seething over his moronic son's failure. He

RE-DEAL

resolved not to take Damen's embarrassing loss or any more of the boy's disobedience. Big Lew had a plan for the genius McCain kid, and he wanted it carried out. When he pushed the button under his desk, two of his guards shoved Damen into the room, and the boy fell to the floor right in front of his father's massive antique desk.

Big Lew stood and bent over his splendid piece of furniture and holding a riding crop screamed at his son. "I gave you an assignment to show your worthiness of the name Cypher!" He slapped the desk hard with the whip and glared down at his cringing milksop son. "My question is, boy, have you carried out this little task?"

"I'm so sorry, father." Damen pinned his eyes to the floor and tried to decide what to say. "But, but, my kind father ..." No acceptable excuse came to him so he blurted out, "I just can't find a big enough magnifying glass to do the job the way I know you want it done."

"Don't give me that crap!" Big Lew snapped. He grabbed the whimpering coward, ripped the shirt from the boy's body, and grabbed the riding crop from his desk. He screamed a curse as he swung the whip. "You disobedient piece of squalor! I told you I want that boy's eyes fixed! And losing to a McCain—I should kill you for that!"

Damen screamed as the riding crop smacked across his naked back. "Ow! Ow! Ouch! Please stop!" Damen begged. "I'm sorry! I'll do it now!"

"This time I want you to take care of it once and for all!" Spit flew from Big Lew's mouth as he cursed. "This idea is brilliant!" Once more he swung the riding crop, again scorching the skin like a red-hot branding iron. "From now on, you useless piece of dog feces, if you ever want to be lord of this manor, next time I give you an order, you will carry it out immediately, or you'll lick spit!"

Damen hated his father so much he could taste it. He dreamed of thrashing him in the same way the evil man whipped him. But Damen knew all he could do now was plead for the tyrant to halt.

He choked out, "Okay, my wonderful father. Now please, please, stop!"

But Big Lew didn't stop. He raised the whip and split Damen's flesh a fourth time before he tramped back to his desk, threw down the whip, and pulled out a large magnifying glass.

He thrust it forward and snapped, "Take this! You have no more excuses! Now wash the blood off, you filthy piece of crap! Put your shirt back on and get the hell out!"

Damen choked back his tears as he got dressed. He shoved the magnifying glass into his back pocket and left. He whimpered from the burning pain from his bleeding back.

Someday, he thought, *I'll be boss and I'm gonna fix him good.*

Damen entered the family's main house and crossed a marble hallway into the formal dining room. He climbed on top of the eighteenth-century Chippendale dinner table and kicked the fine china off to shatter as it hit the marble tile. He jumped off and exited out the back door. He walked over a bridge spanning one of the ranch's three Olympic pools, jumped on his Honda, and rode for a good mile to a football-field-size fountain. After circling around the pool, he parked in front of a two-story mansion with a spiral staircase out front. Cypher used the building to give the appearance that his so-called adopted boys were living well. The boys actually lived in the second-floor bunkhouse with the rest of the workers. The first floor was a sixty-corral horse stable housing Cypher's million-dollar horse collection.

Damen hopped off his motorcycle and ran up the spiral staircase into the boys' living area. Because he was the son of the powerful Big Lew, he expected these wetbacks to do anything he ordered them to do, and he couldn't get himself to do what his father commanded.

Carlos, the most aggressive Mexican, said, "Hey man, it's my good bro Damen." Carlos's saw Damen's red eyes and the blood seeping through the back of his clothes. "Hey man, you look like you've been hurt. What's the matter?"

"Yeah man, can we do something for you?" two other workers, Escona and Gustavo, asked.

Determined to show he could scare and wield power like his evil father, Damen tightened his mouth; his voice cracked sourly. "Yes, you can, and you're all going to do exactly what I say! We need to fix something for my father."

"We'll do anything for you, man," Carlos said. "You're our bro. You just tell us what the problem is, and we'll take care of it for you."

"That's right," the other two agreed, arrogance in their voices. "We'll help you do anything you need done."

"It's my father's idea; he thinks it will make Matt McCain a better dealer." Damen pulled out the magnifying glass and explained what they needed to do. "Can you all take care of this for my father?"

"No problem, man," Gustavo said with a sadistic smile. He was only twelve years old when he cut a hole in the back of an old lady after stealing her purse. That had been one of Big Lew's many tests, trials to see how far Gustavo would go to prove his obedience.

"Hey, man, no problem." Their leader Carlos came right to the point. "As you know, we were taught many special things at your father's orphanage. That's why he chose us, my bro."

"Don't worry, bro," Escona agreed. "We'll take care of this problem for you. We'll make your father proud."

"Listen," Damen ordered. "Tell McCain if he mentions any names his little sister will be next."

As Damen left he thought with disgust, *I hate when those low-life Mexican wetbacks call me bro.*

Damen shook his head to clear the memories, pulled an envelope from his pocket, and handed it to Tom.

"Here's the ten grand. Take care of the McCain dames. You get the other half when the job is complete. You have the driver ready?"

"No problem." Tom took the money and shoved it into his coat pocket. "He has a big truck and is ready to go."

"As soon as that ol' geezer leaves, take care of business! But, remember," Damen warned in a cold voice, "it must look like an accident."

CHAPTER FIFTEEN

That Name Mr. Cheat

At Pastor Steve's theater, Matt fanned his deck of cards for the excited orphans from Boys' Town. He told them in his cowboy character's voice, "I'm going to show you some of the sneaky sleight-of-hand techniques used by the old riverboat gamblers. They used these cheating moves to skin coin, clothes, and sometimes even the hide off your bones."

Matt and Juan had helped Pastor Steve build this small theater/church, which seated up to 154 of the little town's inhabitants. The seats were raked steeply on three sides, making it easy for everyone to see Matt's poker table and the card show.

After the card show Pastor Steve always liked Matt to share with the boys some of the choices he'd had to make when he was younger, and Matt was always happy to do so. Pastor Steve had done so much for him and his best friend Juan that he and Kicker helped the minister whenever they could.

"Boys, when I was your age, I was attacked. From that assault, I lost most of my vision. Over the next few years, I felt sorry for myself, so I sat in my room and played with my cards. You see, after the attack, I was enraged, yet the loss of sight turned out to be a blessing from above. We've all heard how after losing one of your senses, your others become more pronounced. What I thought was a bad situation led to my independence. Now I'm capable of

RE-DEAL

performing the dishonest moves with cards like the old riverboat gamblers. That's given me the opportunity to bring to light cheaters and their dishonorable ways." He stood away from his card table. "Before we hit the road, are there any questions?"

Juan sauntered on stage to help. He pointed to the back of the room to a boy who looked to be about twelve years old.

The young man yelled out, "Mr. Cheat! How do you think you would have done playing against some of those Old West card sharks?"

"I like that name, Mr. Cheat," Juan told the lad with a laugh. "It fits! I believe I'll use it." He faced Matt. "Well, Mr. Cheat, could you have whipped 'um good?"

Matt also found the name Mr. Cheat amusing. He'd wondered about cheating the cheaters for years. Ever since the day he had met the woman with the triple-trotter horse, he'd fantasized about journeying to the past and winning back their family's ranch.

"That's a very interesting question. By today's standards most of those old gamblers were clumsy. The klutzy con men used elaborate devices worn under their clothing to conceal the aces. The grotesque part was that if those gamblers couldn't swindle you out of your coin, they'd slay you instead, then take your money anyway. Then there was a gambler named Andrews. That skilled man published a book back in 1902 on how to cheat at cards. The book was called *Expert at the Card Table.*

"Andrews was reputed to have been the foremost charlatan of all. In contrast, to answer your question about beating them, I wouldn't cheat. Cheating is robbery, and that's dishonest. I'd rather expose their tricks, and then see if they could prevail in a fair game."

Juan thrust out a head-high sidekick. "Mr. Cheat is taking his black belt test tonight, and he needs his rest. He'll be fighting ten black belts. One of his fights will be yours truly. We must give him time for a beauty nap, so we will turn things back over to Pastor Steve."

"Thank you Kicker." Steve stepped to the front of the stage. "Before we let you go, let me share with you a quick story that will illustrate God's love for each of us. I grew up in Duluth, Minnesota. In this town there was an old drawbridge that would rise to let large boats go through. My father and my uncle were the draw bridge attendants. My uncle had only one child, my cousin Tracy. On Saturdays either my cousin or I would get to go to work with our fathers—we traded off every other week. On the occasion I'm telling you about, it was Tracy's turn to go with his dad. The inner workings of the bridge were complex and looked much like the inside of a watch, except much larger. On this weekend, Tracy was watching the massive gears as the bridge was lifted to let a boat pass.

"My uncle received a call that a passenger train was coming and he should quickly lower the bridge. My uncle had set into motion the lowering of the bridge when he heard a loud scream. My cousin Tracy's clothes had got caught in the gigantic gears, and he was going to be crushed if my uncle didn't stop and reverse the lowering of the bridge. At this same moment the passenger train was only seconds from the bridge. My uncle was in a terrible situation. He had the choice of letting his much-loved son be crushed in the gears or allowing the train to fall into the icy river below, killing hundreds of men, women, and children." The minister paused. "The passenger train passed over the bridge safely without incident or loss of life."

The kids saw that the pastor had tears in the corners of his eyes.

Pastor Steve went on. "No one inside that train ever knew my uncle gave his only son for their lives." Steve removed a hanky and wiped his eyes and blew his nose. "The Bible says that all have sinned, in other words, done things we know to be wrong, and come short of the glory of God. Like my uncle, who didn't want for a second to give up his son, our father God freely gave His only Son in exchange for our sinful lives. Man chose to separate himself from God

RE-DEAL

by his bad actions. From these wrong choices, a price had to be paid. If we don't just pass by in the train of life, but stop and accept God's Son and His payment for our sins, the grief in our lives can be replaced with joy and with our names written in the Lamb's Book of Life. If you have any questions or would like to come back to hear more, we have services in this theater every Sunday at ten and seven. And we'll even come pick you up. Now would you all please give Matt and his friend Kicker a big hand?"

CHAPTER SIXTEEN

Staring into the Blazing Hot Sun

After the applause and bows, Matt left the stage. "I'll be right back. I need to run to the dressing room and get my gi and karate bag."

"Okay, Mr. Cheat, go get your things." Juan snickered aloud. "Mr. Cheat, that label really fits. It's not as cool as Kicker, but 'ey Mano, it's not bad. I'll get the truck and meet you out front. We need to get your pa and some sleep. I want to be refreshed for your test. Don't want to make it too easy for you."

"Kicker, sometimes I fret more about battling you than I do Ranger Douglas."

"No doubt." Juan grinned. "Meet ya out front."

Matt went back to the dressing room and changed. He snatched his cane and workout equipment. He was placing the gift for his mom in his karate bag when the dressing room door flew open. Damen Cypher's goon, Carlos, shouldered his way in and slammed Matt against the wall.

Carlos peered hard into Matt's damaged eyes and lashed out. "Hey Magoo! We finally meet again."

Matt cringed. He'd known this day would come, though he hadn't been expecting it so soon. Miss Guided had said he'd be safe and wouldn't be located here.

Matt demanded with icy venom, "How did you find us?"

Carlos scowled as he glowered deep into Matt's eyes. "Gave your old man a new phone. Had caller ID, very useful. Now I have a message for you from Big Lew. He said he's

RE-DEAL

tired of hunting you down. He told me to tell you that you better take the 200,000 bucks he's offered you to deal in his big Hold'em game. This is your last chance. If you don't take this final offer, your family will endure," he smiled sadistically as he said, "permanent consequences."

"Not interested." Matt used his cane to force his attacker back. "I won't use my skills to cheat for any amount of money."

"Oh, well, looky here." Carlos noticed the walking stick. "I see the fried-eyed Magoo needs a cane now. That's too bad for the poor, helpless, blind boy."

Matt felt an icy place deep in his gut erupt into fury and heat at the hated expression *blind boy*. He tried to stifle the sensation, but a fuse had started to sizzle. When the flame reached his emotional limit, he exploded.

"If you even touch my family, I'll hunt you down! And so help me God, I'll rip your arms off and shove them down that sharp mouth of yours! I also suspect you were behind one of those bags with that magnifying glass."

Matt remembered the terror that had filled his body and mind on that horrible day. He had struggled and tried to scream, but he was held tight. The most terrifying part was that no one made a sound. At one point, he had seen one of his attackers; however, the paper sack covering the assailant's face prevented him from identifying his foe.

His blood chilled as he remembered the cold stare from eyes filled with pleasure for the evil they were about to inflict. He had felt his head being twisted to stare into the blazing sun intensified by the magnifying glass. Matt had cried from the intense pain and reflexively bit the hand that covered his mouth.

His attacker had cursed. "Ah! The Loser McCain bit me!"

Another voice ordered, "Shut your fat mouth!"

The last thing Matt remembered about the attack on his eyes were the words whispered into his ear just before his attackers left him helpless in the field. "Listen to me, Loser McCain. If you mention any names, your little sister will be next."

Matt had never mentioned any names. He'd never known for sure who had attacked him, but he was sure Carlos had something to do with it.

"Yeah, right! Ancient history," Carlos scoffed. "And untrue besides. You ingrate! You owe your extraordinary touch with cards to me. It wasn't an attack—it was for your own benefit. Big Lew wanted to improve your touch with the tickets."

"I'll make you a deal." Matt gripped his cane with fiery anger. "Tell that big rat to fork over the ranch his family robbed from us, and I'll come teach you how to play Old Maid."

"No deal! Here's something else for you to consider. Suppose a meat axe were to fall from the sky, then stab across your old man's hands, chopping his thumbs off. It could happen. It's a nasty world out there, Magoo."

Carlos grinned as he advanced.

Matt always suspected Carlos had been the beast that actually held the blinding magnifying glass as it seared his eyes. Now he'd as much as admitted it.

"I'm going to make you hurt, Magoo, and I'm gonna enjoy every minute of it."

Matt stood in a relaxed fighting stance, gripping his cane. He stared impatiently through the corner of one eye, waiting for his opponent to make his play. After years of dealing with the evil scum, Matt knew exactly what he was going to do.

Carlos struck hard. He threw a thrusting front kick toward Matt's stomach.

Matt stepped back, easily avoiding the kick. At the same instant, he twisted his wrist counterclockwise, causing the solid metal weapon to swing around with potent force, crashing hard into Carlos's shinbone. Matt was shocked that the technique actually worked. The cane stopped the kick cold and Carlos shrieked in pain.

Matt yanked up with the cane, hooking his attacker's ankle. He slid in and lifted the snared foot and swept the floor with his left foot, making contact with Carlos's supporting

RE-DEAL

leg. Matt shoved with his foot so hard Carlos fell hard on his back. Again he surprised himself.

Carlos grunted. "What the hell?" He didn't hesitate, but quickly lifted his legs to free himself from the cane. He did a backward somersault and landed back on his feet. "You son of a drunk! Where did you learn to fight? I'm gonna make you hurt for that!" He reached behind his coat and pulled out a large knife. "I'm gonna slash your blind head off. I don't care if Damen offs me for it."

"I'm giving you fair warning." Matt circled the floor, gripping his cane like a Samurai sword. "You better back off or you'll be swimming in stars."

Although Matt felt scared and hesitant, he knew his range with his rod was two feet greater than the thug's reach with his knife. Then Matt noticed the blade flicker from the light overhead. He decided to make the fight a little more fulfilling. As the two longtime foes circled around facing each other, Matt thrust his solid aluminum walking stick straight up into the light bulb, plunging the room into blackness.

"What the hell's that for, Magoo?"

"Hell," Matt said with a tiny flicker of sorrow. "Hell is the place all right. It's gonna be your hot new home if you don't change." He goaded, "I had a notion you might like a less permanent taste of your own wicked medicine."

"Ya little blind creep! I'm gonna rip your head off and shove it down your neck!"

Carlos swung the knife wildly and hit Matt's cane.

At that instant Matt knew precisely where his opponent's head was. He pivoted to the left and, with all his weight behind the metal cane, he hit his assailant on the side of his head so hard that Carlos collapsed to the floor like a sack of dead, rotten fish. Matt grabbed him by his long, greasy ponytail. He heaved the metal bar over his head, preparing to crash it into the skull of his enemy. Then Matt restrained himself.

He twisted his head toward Heaven and pleaded, "Forgive me, God. I'll let you take care of him in your own way."

Matt cautiously let go of the oily mane and stood to his feet. He spun his cane like Kicker spun his nunchakus, then grabbed his karate equipment and ran out front to find his sidekick. Matt thought about his problems with Damen Cypher and Damen's depraved father, Big Lew. Despite his defiance, Matt knew that the Cyphers were holding the winning hand. Just as they had for over a century. If he could have only been there, maybe things would have come out differently.

He raised his eyes in the direction of Heaven and pleaded, "I need a miracle, dear God. What can I do? It seems like the evil Cyphers always win."

There was a loud screech as Juan fishtailed alongside Matt in his dented, four-colored pickup truck. Juan had used that old gold coin given to him by Miss Guided to buy it. It now made sense to him that she had told him it was round so trade it in for some wheels. Even though the truck was ugly, it ran and got him and his amigo around. He stretched over and opened the patched passenger door.

"'Ey, it's my excellent amigo, the card-shuffling bat. I'm finally here. Hop in, Mr. Cheat."

Matt hurled his bag and cane into the back of the ugly truck and clambered in, shaking.

"Let's hustle, Kicker. Carlos has stumbled on to us. Though to his shock, I left him deflated back in the dressing room."

Juan pressed the pedal to the floor and peeled out as disgust spread over his fearsome face. For years this foe had used a biting riding crop across his blistered back.

"Carlos? The pimp has found us? And you left him flat on his back!" He looked over to Matt. "Next time save a shot for your amigo."

CHAPTER SEVENTEEN

Hacking off Thumbs

After the crowds cleared from the show, Gustavo, who had watched the show from a concealed seat in the theater, ran out and hopped into the driver's seat of a new Ford pickup. His irate foreman Carlos waited in the truck with a goose-egg-sized knot protruding from his skull. He removed the rubber band from his ponytail and shook his throbbing head, then attempted to hide the lump with his long, black hair.

Gustavo slammed the door. "I know where they're going. They're off to that karate school across the border. You know the one—it's behind that rat-meat taco stand. Down the alley from Cypher's slave-pit, the one we were dug out of. Remember, we fought in a couple of their black belt tests."

"Oh, that dump! I curse that part of the ghetto."

"Maybe I can fight in Magoo's test." Gustavo glanced in the back and spotted his karate gi. "Remember, Murphy makes the fighter take on the first ten black belts that show up. I'm gonna stomp it hard. I want to be his tenth fight."

Carlos punched the redial on his cell phone.

Damen answered on the first ring. "Did you find where Magoo and that bizarre blonde are hiding?"

"We didn't find the alien." Carlos rubbed his throbbing head. "But we did find that little turncoat Juan; he was with Magoo. They're gonna pick up the geezer and then head down south to Murphy's hard-style karate school, the one close to your father's flesh farm."

On the other end of the phone Damen faced his old man. "We found Juan and Matt McCain, my dear kind father. Gustavo and Carlos are gonna catch up with them at a karate school—the one by your labor farm down south—snatch them, then bring them back."

"If you fail again," Big Lew glared at his son, "it will be your thumbs I have Gustavo hack off! Not Jimmy's! Now tell them to be mindful of my property. Tell them to be especially careful with Matthew's priceless fingers!"

"Yes, my caring father," Damen said with scarcely-concealed mockery. He spoke into the phone. "Carlos, get them and deliver them back to the ranch. My father said to be careful with Magoo."

Big Lew raised a fist ready to belt his son for calling his prize dealer Magoo again.

Damen cowered away from his old man. "I mean Matthew. Oh, and be very careful of his delicate, dainty, precious little fingers."

"Got ya!" Carlos said. "You're telling us we can hurt him a little first?"

"That is correct. You understand me then?" Damen said as he smiled at his father.

"Yes, I do!" Carlos snapped his cell phone closed and ordered Gustavo, "Let's get to the border fast!"

Gustavo grabbed a bottle of wine from under his seat and took a long swig. He passed the bottle across to Carlos, then pounded down hard on the gas. He asked, "Why does Big Lew make such a fuss over this runt Magoo?"

Carlos's head throbbed. He took a long gulp before he answered. "I've seen the best mechanics on this miserable planet. Big Lew welcomes them all. Everyone accepts the conditions—if you're caught cheating in one of Cypher's big games, you're dog rations. That's why Big Lew wants Magoo to be the house dealer—he's the smoothest cheat any of us has ever tried to catch. Besides, no one ever suspects that Magoo could possibly be able to control the cards. Big Lew uses him for cover; he tells the other players that to make

RE-DEAL

sure everyone is satisfied the game is honest, he's using a blind dealer."

"Isn't Cypher scared one of these characters will identify Magoo? After all, we've seen him on dozens of those goofy TV programs, bragging how he can cheat and no one can spot him."

"This is a cheater's game," Carlos explained. "However, most of these suckers come from other countries. They're all very rich and want the bragging rights to say they played in the longest running, highest-stake poker game in the world. Did you know it now costs ten mil to buy a seat at the table?" Again he rubbed the knot on his head. "I would strangle my mother for that kind of cash."

"You did," Gustavo reminded him. "But you did it for nothing!"

They came to the border and crossed. After they were clear of customs, Gustavo pushed even harder on the gas. He wanted to get to the karate school first. Their F-350 roared down the roadway, and they managed to get there ahead of McCain. Gustavo parked off to the side, where they sat and watched.

After a short while, Matt, Juan, and Matt's father Jim pulled up in front of Murphy's Mexican karate school.

"I see them!" Gustavo pointed at the arriving vehicle.

The two Cypher toughs watched with satisfaction as Matt, Jim, and Juan stepped down from the banged-up piece of junk they called a truck.

Jim had a slight frame with hunched shoulders and a kind face. He wore a cheap suit with a decorative Western belt buckle made of gold.

Carlos pointed to Jim. "That Dead Man's Hand buckle supposedly came down from Loser Lucas McCain. It's the only thing McCain didn't lose in the poker game that made the Cyphers so rich." He groaned. "I'll stay here. You go inside and lash Magoo good for me, okay?"

"Yeah," Gustavo answered with disdain. "It will be my gift to my bro!"

Gustavo was glad that Damen gave them the okay to inflict a little painful torment on Magoo before they hauled him back. They knew Damen scorned his vicious old man. He also hated Magoo, and any time he could lash out and hurt either one, he did so with relish. And because they knew Damen would take over some day, they were exhilarated at the opportunity to give Magoo a good thrashing to help Damen out. Besides, they both enjoyed administering a little pain now and then. It gave them pleasure.

Jim looked around at the karate school, a graffiti-covered, concrete-block building about fifty feet long. The windows in the dilapidated old structure were protected with iron bars and didn't open. The trashcans were spilling over with garbage, and the luminous radiance of the eyes of a large rat stared out from a can, then hastily slithered off.

"Yeek! Rodent paradise," Jim said with disgust.

Juan forced himself to face the impoverished filth. This deplorable dwelling-place awakened a deep depression in him, reminding him of damp, dark weather that chilled to the marrow. His bright, brown eyes went dim as he recalled when he was a young boy, rummaging with his sad sister for something to eat.

He enlightened Jim. "On those days we couldn't steal our meals, we dined with those rats in those enjoyable buckets of plenty."

Jim looked at Juan with a questioning glance, then continued to examine the privation and squalor.

Juan's sad face lightened. Thanks to Pastor Steve and knowing what it meant to have his lowly name listed in the Lamb's Book of Life, torment no longer trailed Juan like a pit bull. Juan's once-angry nature had mellowed. Pardon-granting from the Master Man in the Sky had healed him from his childhood memories of bobbing for garbage. He learned that joy is a judgment that comes from choosing to shove away self-pity. Juan had decided he wouldn't cling to memories that no one would want anyway.

RE-DEAL

Jim asked, "Why does yer karate man insist upon testin' across the border in this foreign country?"

"Why do we test down here in this Disneyland of pleasure, you ask? Well, Mr. McCain, it's easy to explain. It's because of all the corrupted law firms called Dewey, Cheatum, and Howe! If you get bruised, banged, or busted down here, you can't sue. Besides, what's your objection with this uptown place? This is the affluent side of town. Maybe some day I'll show you the side I grew up in; it's where Big Lew's human breeding farm is located. Now follow me. I'll show you a real upscale Mexicano karate school."

They tramped over the blowing garbage into the dilapidated building. Jim gaped at the graffiti-covered, faded-yellow-block walls. There was no air circulation in the packed, scorching-hot chamber. He wondered how the fighters would be able to breathe. As Jim continued to scan the room, he saw the fighting ring was a rough, scratched-up, wood floor. In the corner he spotted a changing room with a filthy toilet. Jim was shocked to see about 75 people crammed around the room and others squeezed on three long, makeshift benches.

He elbowed Juan. "Why is all them there sardines crammed into this dump?"

Juan laughed heartily. "They're all anxiously waiting for the bloodbath to begin."

Matt socked Juan in the shoulder and grinned. "Thanks for the vote of confidence, Kicker." Matt wanted his dad to see the gift he got for his ma. "Dad, let me show you something."

He removed the item from his bag and showed it to his father. "It's for Mom. It's to let her know how sorry I am for all those years of trouble I was and to let her know how much I love her. Do you think she'll like it?"

"Oh, son." Jim admired the jewels in the gold cross. "Yer ma will love it!"

"I can't wait to see her again." Matt returned the gift to his bag. "We're all finally going to be free of that evil family."

CHAPTER EIGHTEEN

The Tenth Round

Ranger Douglas walked over to Matt's group. He gripped Matt's hand and smacked him on the back. He asked Jim, "May I speak to Mr. McCain for a moment, please?"

"Yes, sir," Jim said. "We'll go find us a seat."

Matt and the Texas Ranger stepped to the side away from the gathering. "I have some good news and some bad news."

Matt's face went grim. "First, tell me the good news."

"We drew numbers to determine the order you'll fight everyone." The Ranger grinned. "The good news is, I drew number 1 and will be your first fight."

"If that's the good news," Matt asked, "how much worse can the bad news be?"

"The bad news is," Ranger Douglas's smile vanished, "that sadistic Gustavo showed up. He drew number ten and will be your last fight."

Matt staggered slightly, filled with a sudden stab of doubt. He wondered why his enemy was able to participate. He didn't want to fight the man.

Matt looked up and put on a self-assured face. In the most confident voice he could muster, he asked, "Why is that Cypher henchman here?"

"I'm sorry." Douglas shook his head. "Sensei Murphy sent out a notice to the other schools. He asked them to send over a black belt to help with the test, and Gustavo showed up. I informed Sensei Murphy I didn't like the idea

RE-DEAL

of Gustavo fighting in your test. Nevertheless, our honcho Sensei Murphy has confidence in your fighting ability. So, Sensei is going to let Gustavo participate."

Matt considered the situation. Uneasy and scared, he knew his only choice now was to pray for strength. He clapped the Texas Ranger on the back. "Thanks for the heads up. Now, please excuse me. I need to put on my sparring gear."

Matt was working his way to the dressing room when his blood froze as an arm clamped around his shoulders. As Matt dreaded, it was Gustavo. Like Matt, Gustavo stood five-foot eleven. But Gustavo was thirty pounds heavier, weighing in at 210 pounds. He possessed a flattened face like a skillet and a smashed-in, sideways nose. Kicker had many times described to Matt how Gustavo looked like a bulldog that caught a semi. For years Matt suspected that Gustavo had been one of the three attackers with the magnifying glass. Matt didn't want to fight the sadistic brute.

Gustavo clutched Matt's neck. "Hey, loser Magoo! I have you in the tenth. I'll make this a humane battle. I'll knock you out fast!"

Matt ripped the arm from around his neck. "Get your putrid paws off of me!"

But before he could react to Gustavo's intimidation, Sensei Murphy stepped over. "Pardon me, Mr. McCain. I have some folks from the media I want you to meet."

Before he moved on, Gustavo hissed into Magoo's ear, arrogance in his warning, "Magoo, make sure you don't wear yourself out fighting those other nine black belts. You'll need your strength in the tenth round for me." Gustavo cracked the knuckles on his fists as he swaggered away.

Sensei Murphy scowled. He wondered if he was making a mistake by letting Gustavo fight in McCain's black belt test. He knew the Cyphers and McCains had been in a battle of good versus evil for over a hundred years. Nevertheless, he believed Mr. McCain was going to kick the brainless Cypher goon's fanny. So he would let him participate.

Murphy turned back to a short, fat, female. "Mr. McCain, I'd like you to meet Ima Slime. She's from the Dallas Times Herald."

"That's Ima Slim!" the reporter said in a huff.

"Oh, sorry, Slim." Murphy turned to a man standing next to Ima. "And over here I'm privileged to introduce you to Jack Crack, ace reporter. He is from a north Texas ABC affiliate. They are the same reporters who dogged Ranger Douglas during the Bad Bob case."

"Yeah," Ranger Douglas said as he joined the group. "I reckon you're now gonna hound our fighter Matt."

The Texas Ranger was a good ol' country boy from the small Texas town Matt and Juan were hiding in. During the previous year, using his karate skills, Ranger Douglas had unarmed and single-handedly taken down Bad Bob, The Necktie Murderer.

Bad Bob had killed seven women, all found strangled with one of their husband's neckties around their throats. The Ranger had exchanged himself for a hostage, who happened to be the daughter of a prominent politician. The girl had been freed. Then with a 44 pressed between his eyes, the Ranger disarmed the larger man.

It had taken two only strikes—one to knock away the gun, the other to lay Bad Bob flat. Since the Texas Ranger had lived up to the Ranger reputation as a fearless defender of the law and daringly saved the life of the daughter of the politician, Douglas had received national exposure as a hero.

But to Douglas and Murphy's growing irritation, the media liked to keep tabs on Murphy's school and the Ranger's life. The two reporters caught wind of a partially-sighted man fighting ten black belts. To Murphy's aggravation, they insisted on covering the test.

"Mr. McCain," Sensei Murphy continued with an undertone of ridicule. "These two very highly-worshiped news-slingers thought a visually impaired, ace card mechanic battling ten black belts would make for an absorbing story."

Jack Crack, ace reporter, looked toward Murphy. "Did you say the fighter we drove all the way out here to see is named McCain? As in Lucas the Loser?"

Matt's heart sank. He wondered if there was any place on the planet where he could be free from that accursed name.

RE-DEAL

"Crack," Murphy shoved the reporter to the side and whispered loudly into his ear, "if you continue to want Ranger Douglas's cooperation and mine, you will be respectful of all my students. Then you will go back and write a decent story about an amazing man."

"Of course, Mr. Murphy." Jack straightened his tie and swallowed hard. "I didn't mean—"

"Never mind. I don't need your excuses. Just get over there and do your job."

The reporter moved back over to Matt. He spread his made-up lips, showing his perfectly-aligned, bleached-white teeth. "Mr. McCain, we are honored to be here to see your test. Do you mind if we ask a few questions?"

"Sure, whatever," Matt said. "Ask what you like. But please don't mention the name of Sensei Murphy's Texas school."

Matt recognized it was likely too late and Big Lew probably already knew where he and Kicker had been hiding out. Matt hoped, but doubted, the reporters would give their account only of the fighting and the test. Matt didn't want their location known, nor did he want to read all the sickening *blind man overcomes tremendous obstacles* crap.

The Texas Ranger and Kicker wrapped Matt's hands, then slid on his boxing gloves for him while the reporters beseeched Matt with ridiculous questions like, "How does it make you feel to get punched in the face when you can't see?"

Matt excused himself after the interview to do a quick warmup before the test started.

After the warmup, Sensei Murphy shouted, "Fighters, put your gloves on. We're going to start the test." He pointed across the room. "Would everyone else please stand against the walls or take a seat."

Jim squeezed between two excited spectators. They told him they came to all the tests to see the blood splatter. Jim didn't like to hear that. He pointed to Matt. "The fighter testin' is my boy."

Then Jim's attention was drawn to the fighting ring where his son was ready to start. Jim watched as his boy began with a series of strange moves he called katas. This was followed with a form establishing his son's mastery with his cane. Then came the part Jim dreaded, the ten fights his son said would be the hardest part. In the first round, his boy fought his friend, the famous Texas Ranger. The Ranger pushed Matt hard, but Douglas didn't try to knock Matt out. The second round was Matt's good amigo Juan. Kicker likewise fought his boy hard, yet clean. Nevertheless, the next seven fighters Matt fought were not so charitable.

Only one more, Matt thought, exhausted. His heart rate was racing at 185 beats per minute and piercing chest pains came with each breath. He was bloody, bruised, and beat, and he felt like he was fighting for his life when he at last had to face Gustavo in the tenth.

During the one-minute break between the ninth and tenth rounds, Juan massaged his amigo's tense shoulders. "'Ey Mano, you only have one more round. You can do it!"

"That's right," the Ranger agreed, as he turned to his physician who had come down with them to be available in case of any injuries. "Hey, Doc, wave some smelling salts under Mr. McCain's nose."

Seated tensely in the front, Matt's father wondered why he had come to see this frightful test. He could hardly watch as his son took such an awful beating. Yet to Jim's surprise, his son was holding his own. In fact he'd whipped that last fighter good.

Jim motioned for Juan to come over. "Why does Matt persist in puttin' himself in all these daft situations? I think he's done forgotten that he can't see so good."

"He didn't forget; however, those other fighters did. That last fighter barely endured the three minutes. Matt knocked him into next week, and that was after Matt had already taken on eight other fighters. Your headstrong son trusts that real potential comes from taking action. Not from having others do for you. That skill and strength are items of the mind and spirit, not of a crippled body."

"It scares me to see him fighting so many mean-looking fellows." Jim took a shot from a bottle of liquor hidden in a paper sack. "That's why I brought this Southern Comfort." He held up the bag. "Want ta catch you a little snort?"

Juan twisted his face with distaste. "No, thanks, Mr. McCain."

Jim slugged back another drink, and his face went white with fear. The bottle almost slipped from his hand as he watched Gustavo step into the fighting ring.

"I know that man." Jim's voice shook. "He works for Big Lew, and he's mean, real mean! Calls himself Gustavo. He's roughed me up before."

Juan nodded as he remembered all the scars striped across his bare back. Juan knew the wretched Gustavo well.

"Don't worry, Mano," Juan said as he stepped back over to Matt. "The Big Man is with you, and the Texas Ranger and I are right behind you." He rubbed a little Vaseline around Matt's eyes. "Hurt him good for me, Mr. Cheat."

Matt was so drained he doubted he could even stay on his feet. He was terrified of Gustavo and wondered why he did such crazy things. But he tried to swallow his fears as he gave his friend a nod with a half smile.

Jim clenched his hands hard around the bottle. He was trying to control his urge to attack Gustavo before the monster hurt his boy. But he was a weak, broken man and knew he could do nothing.

As Matt stood up from his break stool and stepped into the ring, Gustavo's eyes glazed over with anticipation. He hissed at Magoo, "Hey blind boy, you're dead flesh!"

Juan searched the small room. The marvelous Miss Guided angel told him she would be here. He wondered where she was or if she was even going to make Matt's test. He turned back to his friend's final fight. Juan watched with worry as the two archenemies squared off.

Gustavo watched for Murphy to give the command to begin. When Murphy raised his hand, Gustavo lunged forward and coldcocked Matt with a dizzying roundhouse kick to the side of his head. Then he charged Matt hard and ran him out of the ring into a partition wall. On the wall was a shelf lined with karate trophies. The shelf collapsed down hard onto Matt's head, then crashed noisily to the hollow wood floor.

The kick ruptured Matt's eardrum, and the trophies left a few lumps on his head. Juan and a half dozen other black belts rushed in to jerk Gustavo off Matt. The cameras zoomed in like a buzzard on a dead carcass, while Gustavo received a warning from Sensei Murphy. "Back off, boy!"

Matt realized he had to forget controlling his punches. He had to stop the twisted creep attacking him so viciously. Gustavo was not here to give him a good fight—he was here to kill him. And because of Matt's weak vision, he had to make every kick and punch count. He had no room for blundered strikes.

Sensei Murphy turned back to Matt. "Are you okay, Mr. McCain? Can you go on?"

Matt felt a trickle of blood dripping from his ear. But he wasn't going to stop for anything. He didn't want to expend any energy by talking so he just nodded his head yes.

Sensei Murphy bellowed, "Fight!"

Gustavo was ready. He employed his thirty-pound advantage and charged in like a freight train. He threw a front kick followed by a right punch that knocked Matt flat on his rear. Gustavo spotted another opportunity for a torturous cheap shot. While Matt lay gasping on the floor, Gustavo drove his knee, with all his 210 pounds behind it, into his opponent's gut. A grunt of expelled wind shot from Matt.

Sensei Murphy yelled, "Part them, now!"

A swarm of fighters rushed in and pulled Gustavo off of Matt.

Matt lay there trying hard to catch his breath. His lungs felt like they were on fire. But he wasn't going to get up; he needed the few seconds of rest.

"Get up, Mano!" Juan yelled. "You have less than two minutes to go. You can do it! Come on, dig deep!"

Matt rolled back to his feet. As soon as he was back up, he heard Sensei Murphy shout, "Fight!"

RE-DEAL

Matt determined he wasn't going to let this weasel get the best of him. He told himself to dig deep, then looked up and said, "Give me the strength, God." He rubbed the blood from his nose and right ear. He took a deep breath, lowered his hands, and dropped into a deep back stance. He was going to leave himself open, hoping to lead Gustavo into a trap. He muttered, "Come on, you sleazy sucker!"

Gustavo spotted another opening and smiled. He charged in hard and fast, and this time he realized he had fallen into a trap.

Yes, I got him! Matt was thrilled that Gustavo ran right into his devastating jump turn kick, knocking him flat on his fat rump.

The roar of approval from the crowd at this tenth round show appeared to enrage Gustavo. He sprang to his feet. Without bothering to wait for Sensei Murphy's command to continue, he threw a slamming roundhouse kick toward Matt's ribs.

Matt knew from Juan that the Cyphers were raised to fight dirty. So even when separated, he always tried to keep his hands up and elbows in tight. But even with these precautions, Matt didn't see the kick coming. He caught the force of a roundhouse kick on his right forearm. Matt heard a snap and felt a horrible surge of pain.

When the two fighters were separated, Matt told the Texas Ranger, "I believe that punk has cracked a bone in my arm."

"I think you're right," Ranger Douglas agreed after he felt the bones on Matt's arm. "I'm sorry, but I have to stop the test."

"No!" Matt slurred from his mouthpiece. "No, Mr. Douglas! Please don't stop the fight!" He removed his mouthpiece and pleaded, "To go this far and not be able to finish would be far more agonizing than any pain from a lousy broken arm."

Ranger Douglas had been in situations like this before and knew how his comrade felt. In spite of his concern for Matt, he agreed to let the test continue. "Okay, but favor that elbow."

#

Back up north, Matt's mom Mary and sister Debra were walking back from the Bible bookstore to Gram's house. They had gone out to stretch their legs and to do a little shopping. Mary handed her daughter Debra the new Bible she had just bought.

"Debra, The Inspired Words inside this Book have made a wonderful difference in my life. It has put music in my mind and happiness in my heart."

"Thank you, Mama." Debra took the Bible and held it close to her heart. "I'll treasure it forever."

Without any warning, Debra saw a large 4 x 4 truck with a full-frontal steel grill roar down the street, headed right at them.

Debra and her mom had no chance to move. The truck plowed into them with full force, and both were killed on impact.

#

Matt and Gustavo again squared off. In this exchange, the two fighters tied each other up.

Gustavo whispered into Matt's bloody ear, "Hey, fried-eyes, how did you like our little prank with the magnifying glass?"

"Stop fighting!" Sensei Murphy yelled. "Separate! Go to your corners. Now!"

Gustavo didn't separate like Sensei Murphy commanded. Instead he rammed his knee hard into Matt's groin. Matt staggered and grabbed himself as he began to black out.

"Oh," Matt wailed feebly as pain surged forth from his loins like water bursting from a fire hose. "You ... coward."

Ranger Douglas spotted Gustavo inflict the excruciating cheap shot on his friend. He bolted in and hoisted Gustavo off the ground by his gi collars and hauled him away to his corner. Douglas's face twisted with disgust at the smell of cheap wine on the punk's breath. "Hey you slithering boozer, if I see one more cheap shot, you'll be an extinct piece of meat! Now listen carefully! I'll rip you in pieces right here in front of everyone, and I'll have Sensei Murphy's blessing."

Gustavo was a big coward when faced with someone his own size. "All right! I'll play by your dumb rules."

RE-DEAL

Sensei Murphy turned to Juan. "Kicker, how much time is left on the clock?"

"Thirty seconds."

Sensei Murphy turned back to his soon-to-be black belt and said, "Mr. McCain, you're doing great. You're as good as done. Just keep your mind clear like water but cool like ice. Now let's finish the test off strong."

Juan continued to look around for the elusive angel Michala, but he didn't see the angel anywhere. He was beginning to wonder if he understood what she said about coming to Matt's test or if the entire incident in the buggy was just his insane imagination. One thing he knew for certain, she wasn't here.

He watched as his amigo frantically gasped for air. He knew Matt had to face his enemy for another thirty seconds. In the ring thirty seconds could seem like a lingering lifetime.

Matt was bent on drawing Gustavo in. He stood there holding his throbbing groin. He intentionally left his head wide open, waiting for another attack. Gustavo took the bait and charged in.

Matt shifted into a strong front stance. With all his weight behind the punch, Matt nailed the other fighter in his crooked beak. There was a big crunch as blood splattered everywhere and covered both fighters. Even through the gloves, Matt's hammer-hard fist stopped Gustavo cold. Matt couldn't see that his punch caused Gustavo's eyes to bulge and become lifeless like those in a gutted shark.

Matt wasn't done yet. He paid back the low blow with his knee to Gustavo's groin. Then Matt whirled around and nailed his opponent's right ear with a spinning elbow.

Gustavo was dazed. He teetered for a moment, then collapsed onto the hard floor.

Matt was still filled with rage and charged again.

Kicker screamed, "Tiempo! Time!"

"Stop!" Sensei Murphy yelled. "The test is over! Mr. McCain, Matt. You're done. Finished! You can stop now!"

But Matt was in a delirious state. He was running on adrenaline and didn't grasp what Sensei Murphy was trying to tell him. He was struggling with pains that assaulted his body from everywhere. He again charged after his enemy whom Matt could not see was passed out on the floor. Matt ran and tumbled over the body. He rolled back and wrapped his broken arm around the man's neck. He started to squeeze. Juan and Ranger Douglas jumped in and jerked Matt off Gustavo's unconscious body.

Kicker again yelled, "Stop, Mano! The test is over! You've earned your black belt!"

"What?" Matt finally came to his senses. He stood to his feet. He spit out his mouthpiece and ripped off his boxing gloves.

The ecstatic throng climbed over the senseless body of Gustavo. They all wanted to praise Mr. McCain for a good test.

But Matt was so delirious, exhausted, and thirsty, that he ignored everyone. Their words and screaming were all fuzzy to him. He stumbled through the throng to the washroom for a desperately needed drink. Inside the bathroom he fell to the floor gasping for air. He unknowingly cupped his hands and reached into the toilet bowl and sucked down a big gulp of the dirty water. As he slowly came to his senses he realized he was drinking from a dirty flush toilet.

Juan slipped in and discovered his friend down on his knees talking to the toilet bowl. He said with a chuckle, "Too many blows to the brain. That's not punch you're drinking. You're punch drunk." He chortled. "Come on, Mr. Cheat. No need praying now. The test is over! Now get up! Sensei Murphy is eager to present you your black belt."

Juan threw open the bathroom door and pushed his amigo out to a thunderous ovation. Leaning against the block wall was a semiconscious Gustavo.

As Matt passed, Gustavo spit out, "I'll get you for this, Magoo!"

But because of all the applause and whistles, Matt didn't see or hear his old enemy's threats. Gustavo crawled outside to his truck where Carlos was cleaning his pistol.

Sensei Murphy wrapped the black belt around Matt's waist and said, "We expected a great deal from Mr. McCain,

RE-DEAL

and he gave it." Murphy placed his hands on the shoulders of his most unusual student. He looked him in the eye and grinned. "How would you like to do this again next week?"

After food, drink, and much celebration, everyone funneled out.

Outside by Juan's truck, Matt said, "My body feels like it's been through a meat tenderizer." He touched his swollen arm with two fingers. "My arm is killing me. However, the Ranger's doctor said it was a clean break and I might not need a cast. He said it should heal fast. The best thing is, I kicked the fat fanny of that pig Gustavo."

Jim pushed his way through and caught up with his son. "Wow, son, I never knew ya could fight like that. I'm so proud of ya."

"He's not too bad." Juan grinned. "Now, if you wanted to see a real test, you should have come to mine. My feet were like lightning. They flew from beer belly to kisser. I whipped all ten black belts. Just like Superman."

"Yeah, right!" Matt said with a laugh. "More like little Miss Muffet. I had to nurse you for —"

Matt stopped abruptly as he felt something hard and cold jam up against his neck.

"Don't move!" Carlos slid the pistol higher up Matt's head. "Don't even think about it!"

Carlos seized Matt's father and herded the three men forward. He shoved the old man into Juan's dirty truck where his partner Gustavo waited. He slammed the door and said, "Take him back to Big Lew!"

Carlos turned back to Matt. He grabbed his karate bag and told him firmly, "Don't say a word or the ol' geezer is dead!" He shoved Matt and Juan into his own truck and snarled, "You drive, little punk deserter!"

For one final time Juan fleetingly gazed around for the guardian angel Michala. She was nowhere to be seen.

CHAPTER NINETEEN

Only Two Mouths to Feed

Juan drove while Carlos rode in the passenger seat holding the gun ready. Matt sat squeezed in the middle. Carlos punched redial on the phone and, to his shock, the boss Big Lew answered.

"Do you have my merchandise? Is he okay?"

"Y-y-yes, sir," Carlos stammered. "Yes, sir, Mr. Cypher, sir, I have him. But I heard him say something about a broken arm."

"From what?" Big Lew questioned. "You haven't damaged my property, have you?"

"Sir, McCain took his black belt test. He received some hard blows."

Matt yelled toward the phone. "Not as hard as I gave your pig, Gustavo!"

"That's right!" Juan yelled across the cab. "And Cypher, you're next!"

Carlos shoved his pistol across Matt straight into Juan's face. "Shut up, punk, and drive!" Carlos kept the gun leveled at his victim as he moved the phone back to his ear. "Where do you want me to take them, sir?"

"Broken arm, you say?" There was a pause as Big Lew decided what to do. "Take them to Cypher Medical."

The hospital was one of many institutions that used Cypher's money and his name and showed him in a good light to the gullible masses. Big Lew knew it also helped keep heat off his less altruistic money-making activities.

RE-DEAL

"Take them to my brother, Doctor Archfiend Cypher. I'll phone him and tell him to expect you. That arm must not affect his dealing. I can't believe you fools let him do such a thing!"

"Sorry, sir. Now what do you want me to do with this fugitive punk, Juan?"

"Bring him back to the ranch and put him on ice. I'll deal with him later. Maybe I'll barbecue him and feed him to Chopper and Butcher."

"Got it," Carlos said. "Be there fast!"

Carlos snapped the phone closed. He stared with pleasure into Juan's defiant eyes. "Punk, Big Lew has a surprise for you."

Carlos picked up Matt's bag and started rummaging through it. He found the little jewelry box and opened it. "What's this?" he taunted. "A gift for me?"

"None of your business!" Matt grabbed for the box. "Now give it back!"

"Shut up, or I'll shoot the renegade beside you in the leg!" He opened the box and looked inside. "Well, isn't this pretty?"

Carlos removed a small piece of paper from the lid. "Well, well, what do we have here?"

"That's none of your business!" Matt repeated. "Put it back!"

Carlos unwrapped the little piece of paper and read the message aloud. "Mom, I'm so sorry for all the times I didn't listen to you and was so ungrateful for your constant kindness, love, and concern. This small cross is to ask you to forgive me like you talk about God's Son forgiving us for all our bad deeds. I'll tell you the meaning behind the red rubies after you read this. I love you, Mom! Your loving son, Matt."

"Well," Carlos looked up, "isn't that nice. But I don't think your wonderful mother should have to wait." Carlos quickly rolled down his window and laughed. "I'm going to send it to her by airmail."

"No," Matt screamed. "Give it back!"

Carlos secretly palmed the valuable cross and gold chain. He heaved the empty box out onto the street where it was immediately smashed by the tire of a car in the next lane.

"Oops, it looks like your sweet little gift might not make it. That car flattened your little present."

In the other truck, Gustavo was filled with rage over the humiliation. He also hurt badly from his aches and pains from the whipping he took in the ring. He decided to break away from following Carlos and stop and buy some wine to drown his fury and kill the throbbing pains.

By the time he got back to Cypher City he could scarcely see the numbers on his cell phone. After three aggravating tries, he threw the phone over to Jim McCain in a huff and ordered, "Ol' Geezer, get Damen on the line and shut up!"

"Y-y-yes, sir," Jim stuttered. "B-b-but, wh-what is ya gonna do with my boy? Pl-please don't hurt him."

Gustavo backhanded Jim across the mouth. "Shut your face and dial!"

Jim wiped a trickle of blood from his lip. He punched in the number and got through to Damen.

"Yes?" Damen snapped on the other end of the line. "Is that you, Gustavo?"

"Yeah." Gustavo snatched the phone back and slurred, "It's me."

"Oh, so it's you, wimp! We might need to send you back to that orphanage for some retraining. Carlos said you got your butt kicked by that blind Magoo!"

"That's BS!" Gustavo shot back. "It was just a lucky shot! Now what do you want me to do with the ol' geezer?"

Always one maddening problem after another, Damen thought. He wanted some assurance his old man would give him credit for how efficiently he got rid of the McCain broads for him. Yet he knew he wouldn't. *I hate that old man!*

"Dump McCain off at the morgue. There was some kind of an accident. You know what I mean. The cops are

RE-DEAL

searching for him. My father thinks the shock will bring both McCains back onto the reservation. When you dump the geezer off, tell him my old man wants to see him when he's finished looking at Escona's handy work. Then get your whipped butt back here—fast!"

"Yes, sir." Gustavo's voice barely concealed his anger.

He pulled up in front of the morgue. Gustavo shoved McCain from the dirty truck out in front of the public entrance. He then drove in a rage back to the Cypher ranch.

Jim rushed inside to see what had happened. He identified the massacred bodies of his sweet wife and beautiful daughter. Grief-stricken, he began to sob. Tears poured down his cheeks as he felt the pain of the loss of his angelic daughter and heavenly wife to the core of his being.

He remembered Cypher's wicked threats that had kept him in line and dealing for his evil master's card games. "You will not have four mouths to feed, nor will you even have three. You will only have two." Jim feared his darling wife and precious daughter's deaths were not accidental. Again the words came back, "You will only have two."

The thought that the wicked man might also kill his wonderful son pulsed in his head like a second heart-beat. *I still have my boy Matthew. I got ta help him.* He moaned in agony. *But what do I do? That venomous Cypher is so merciless I believe he would kill another. I love my children more than anything else. Oh my dear Mary and baby girl, I love ya.* Jim decided he couldn't take the chance and cried bitterly. *Oh God, help me! It would kill me if I lost my last child. I can't believe it. Like Big Lew always boasts, "Cyphers always win!"*

Jim got a ride from the morgue back to the Cypher ranch, and he was taken to Big Lew's library. Even though Cypher was in his fifties, the malevolent man still stood tall and powerfully built. His pale gray complexion looked like he never went outdoors. Cypher was well dressed in his expensive Western black suit and black hat.

Jim looked into Cypher's dark eyes and his stomach knotted with fear. He could see deep into the vacant soul and saw nothing but a dark evil chasm. Cypher was filled with blind hate that couldn't see murder or hear the screams of the children he beat. He reminded Jim of a medieval sadist who poured gas on a dog and lit it on fire. Jim wished, *If only I could leap over the table and crush the skull of this slithering seed of the serpent.*

But to protect his last child, he lowered his eyes in shame and stammered, "Mr-Mr-Mr. Cypher, sir, if you let my boy go free, I'll keep workin' for ya."

Cypher didn't say a word. He just puffed on his Cuban cigar.

Jim sat with his head bent low. Tears rolled off his cheeks and rained on the shiny, dark wood floor. He mourned the loss of Mary and Debra. His chest began to heave. His brittle heart felt like it was being cruelly, brutally, ripped in pieces. After what seemed an eternity, Jim watched as Big Lew drew back his lips into a demonic smile, exposing the family trait, jagged teeth.

For a moment Big Lew contemplated the ash on his long, rare cigar. Finally he looked up and spoke slowly and coldly. "McCain, you will deal, and so will your son. You both are my property. Now, get the hell out!"

Jim went home, took a drink, buried his head in his hands, and wept bitterly.

CHAPTER TWENTY

Seventy Mil up for Grabs

Eight Days Later

"Okay, Governor," Big Lew said as he clapped Blight Willis on the shoulder. "My team and well-washed fluid assets are in position for your presidential run. Your little Arkansas is our neighbor and we Southerners must stick together. Just remember our little agreement."

"Yes, yes," Blight said. "I won't forget. That VP spot is yours."

Governor Willis was Big Lew's bought-and-paid-for boy for the White House. *You're a weasel like no other*, Lew thought, satisfied. *And a first-class weasel at that. I have never seen anybody BS better than you. You can really feel their pain.*

Big Lew opened the door. "Escona, take the fine Governor back to the airport."

He turned back to Willis. "Mr. President, our country's best days are ahead." *And after a little accident when I become top dog, this country will have days like never before.*

Big Lew closed the door, moved back to his desk, and sat down. It was time for him to convene the players who were to help in his scam during the big 125th anniversary game. This would be the biggest swindle since his grandfather cheated Lucas the Loser out of his ranch. He needed untraceable cash to grease the campaign. But things weren't falling into place in quite the way he needed them to. Right now his great plans were in a very delicate state. And if he didn't get Matthew and Rosa to cooperate sufficiently, hell forbid, he might be forced to play an honest game.

The first thing he needed to do was somehow convince Antonio Rosa that his prize mechanic Matthew McCain would deal. And secondly that his obstinate prodigy would deal Rosa the precious winning aces. He pulled from his desk an expensive bottle of single malt scotch, poured a two-finger shot, and slugged it down. He then hit the button on his speakerphone and snapped, "Send in my kid and Rosa."

Cypher's guards escorted the diamond dealer Rosa into the lavish library. Big Lew stood and moved across the polished mahogany floor to greet him. A cocky Damen followed Rosa in and moved over to his old man's priceless desk, flopped down in the seat of power, and thrust his feet up onto the desk. The guards moved back against the wall and stood with their arms folded.

Big Lew stepped over to receive Rosa, a thin, dark-skinned man with a huge nose. Dressed in an Armani suit with a seven-carat diamond ring on his left pinky, he had little, brown, pellet eyes that never stood still. Big Lew raised his hand and approached the merchant, who met Cypher's meaty hand with his own petite one. Big Lew's eyes pierced deep into Rosa's suspicious eyes.

Big Lew thought, *I know you're rich, Mr. Rosa, but standing before you is obscene wealth and power like you've never seen nor comprehended prior to me. So you better listen carefully to my words.*

"Mr. Rosa, thank you for coming on such short notice. Please, it's necessary to our plans that you lay aside your concerns for putting up ten mil to assure yourself a seat at my table. This is a freeze out, a winner-take-all game. And the winner, which will be us, will split seventy big ones. In other words, you will take home 35,000,000 dollars. But more meaningful than the money, you'll have the self-satisfaction of saying you were the victor in the richest and most coveted annual Texas Hold'em game anywhere on the planet." Lew softened his tone as he went on, "Now again I'm asking you not to fret. For 125 years we Cyphers have prided ourselves on the canny ways we determine the winners."

RE-DEAL

"Indeed?" Rosa answered. "Suppose I should lose? After all, I couldn't get this Matt McCain to covertly side with me in the game."

Big Lew smiled and gave Rosa a pat on the back as he walked him back to the door. "Don't worry— my top mechanic Mr. McCain will positively deal the game. When he identifies you at the table, to get back at me, I know for certain he'll make sure that you're the winner. Trust me, I have it all worked out. When the game is over," he pledged with a self-assured grin, "we'll divide the riches. You'll secure a place in history, as well as world-renowned fame."

He thrust out his large hand toward Rosa. The South African took it reluctantly, as if he were being offered the business end of a diamond-back rattler. After they shook, Big Lew opened the elegantly carved door. "My chauffeur will take you back to your penthouse at the Cypher Hotel. Just sit tight, and when everything is in order, we'll call."

Big Lew closed the lavish library door and walked back to his fancy desk. He scowled at his son sitting in his overstuffed leather chair. "Off! Now!"

Damen quickly moved to a chair on the opposite side of the desk.

Big Lew sat down in the monarch's rightful place and stared coldly at his son. "Like our shrewd, cunning patriarch, John Lew Cypher, always said, 'To all suckers, may we feast on your corpses.'" Big Lew cackled. "What a gullible chump Rosa is. Trusting that I would actually split any profits with him. My grandfather prescribed the pattern of shrewdness Cyphers are to live by, and we do it flawlessly!" He glanced over at his descendant and frowned. "Well, at least some of us Cyphers do."

Yeah. If you only knew the truth, Damen thought, tickled with himself. He knew he was foxy even by his father's standards. His father didn't see what Damen was doing behind the scenes and how he was the one really in command. He chuckled at that sardonic twist. But to get his inheritance, he knew he still must play the part of the docile son.

He said with feigned concern, "We're still in a predicament, my illustrious father. Like Rosa, I couldn't get Magoo to deal for you either."

Big Lew's unblinking eyes peered through his kid as he slowly absorbed what Damen had uttered. His lips split apart and he snapped, "Boy, do you want to know what I think?"

No, I don't, Damen thought but didn't dare say aloud. *I don't care what the hell you think about anything. You'll soon no longer matter. Before long I'm going to cut your throat and take over this empire.*

But to play the game, he gave a Machiavellian smile and answered. "Yes, my scholarly father, I want to know the pearls of wisdom that are going to flow from your lips."

Big Lew stubbed out the remainder of his cigar and jumped to his feet. He leaned across his desk and backhanded Damen in the face, knocking him out of his chair.. "You're still a good-for-nothing piece of crap."

He settled back into his throne and pulled from his humidor a fresh cigar and lit it with the late Lucas McCain's antique gold lighter. "Don't fidget, you piece of monkey mess. I did your simple task for you." Big Lew puffed on his cigar until it was lit. "My boy Matthew will deal. Those relations do what I command them to do. It's been that way for 125 years. We have held the whip hand over that fool Lucas McCain and his descendants, and it's not going to change now! Stick around, and I'll enlighten you on how to control peasants."

CHAPTER TWENTY-ONE

Vowing to Never Cheat

Big Lew pressed a button under the antique secretary and the massive doors flew open. In marched ranch security with Matt and Juan, followed by Carlos and Gustavo armed with shotguns.

Matt had his arm wrapped with a splint, and there was black and blue bruising around his left eye. Big Lew had his brother Doctor Cypher dress him in some supposed fine apparel—nauseating stuff—for the game. Matt felt like an effeminate sissy. He wore a short-sleeved turquoise-blue silk shirt and expensive charcoal-gray dress slacks and black Italian patent leather shoes.

Juan had been kept locked up since Matt's black belt test and hadn't been allowed to change. He was still dressed in his karate gi bottoms and a light windbreaker with his fighting footwear.

Gustavo's nose was still swollen and more crooked than ever. Carlos wore his long hair down around his shoulders. He was trying to hide the black and blue knot he had received from Matt's cane.

"Oh, my prize dealer, here you are." Big Lew strolled over to Matt and shook his head. "But look at you."

He clicked his tongue as he studied his card mechanic. He was surprised to see how strong and hardy Matt looked. The boy's chest and biceps bulged from beneath the silk shirt.

He said, "Wow, how you've filled out over the years. But participating in such violent activities like this black belt test—I'm appalled you would do such a violent thing."

"Yeah, right." Juan spoke up with a sneer. "You being appalled at violent activities is like a skunk being offended at your stinking son's body odor."

"Shut your face, little punk!" Damen hissed. "Bear in mind to what fine omnipotent man you are speaking. Look around at this splendor! We are Cyphers! Another designation for Cypher would be God!"

Yeah, dim Damen, Little Lew, Juan thought. *Your pomposity will be your waterloo. Just like Nebuchadnezzar, you will eat grass. Like you, Cypher, nasty Neb created a self-admiring monument. His princely palace had a wide wall so immense five full chariots could spurt side by side around the rim of his fancy fortress. However, after old Neb beat his chest bragging about his God-like attainments, the Big Man brought Nebuchadnezzar down to his gnarled knees. For seven years the potentate crawled around on all fours. His fingernails were like the claws on a big buzzard and he gobbled green grass like a heifer. Cypher, one day you will be down like a milk cow gorging on meadow grass as everyone guffaws.*

Big Lew looked over and seared holes through Juan. "Barbecued or raw? I suppose my dogs will be happy to feast on you either way." Lew looked back at Matthew. He shook his head and then clicked his tongue again. "My boy, you have been such a pain in the butt to find. Well, I'm glad to have you finally back home with me where you belong."

Matt paled.

"But your hands, my brilliant experiment." Big Lew looked at Matt's fingers. "I read about your black belt test and saw a clip on the news. You took a very foolish risk. My brother Doctor Cypher took care of your priceless fingers for you, I trust?" When Big Lew noted the mutinous, defiant look on Matt's face, he exploded. "Now why do you continually take advantage of my benevolence?" He pointed to Damen. "I've made sure my son treats you like one of the family."

This garbage can is full of crud, Juan thought. He wanted to speak up again, but as he'd learned from Michala, he knew to wait for just the correct comic moment.

RE-DEAL

Big Lew nodded toward his son. "I also gave Damen and my special boys—Carlos, Gustavo, and Escona—explicit instructions to take care of all your needs."

Lew turned back to Matt with a fatherly smile. "Matthew, are you ready to put aside these little differences between us; next, show me some appreciation for my special attention I have showered on you; then kindly come to work for me?"

Matt scowled and crossed his arms in defiance. However, he'd forgotten about the splint Doctor Cypher had placed around his forearm, and making this insulting gesture proved cumbersome. He unfolded his arms, stood up straight, and thrust out a defiant fist. Even though Matt could not see anything straight on, he did what his director, Pastor Steve, taught him—that was to give the impression that he was looking straight into their eyes.

He shoved a bold forefinger at Cypher. "The only reason I let your goons drag us here is to tell you to your face that I want my father released from the sick dishonorable duties you have given him. As well as to let you know nothing on earth will ever cause me to cheat for you again. I will in no way compromise my values for anything. Especially for something as stupid and transitory as your filthy money."

Big Lew blinked. "Everybody wants money. Wealth means power, and power means domination. Domination approaches omnipotence, and everyone wants to be God. Only we Cyphers approach that, but you could get much closer."

"I won't do it."

"We'll see, Mr. Matthew McCain. We'll see." Big Lew turned to Carlos. "Bring in Matthew's father."

A door in the back opened, and Carlos pushed Jim through it. Jim raised his sorrowful eyes. "Son, son, yer ma and Deb are gone. Both ... dead. Hit by a truck." Tears welled up as he pleaded, "Pl-please Matthew! Don't go getting' mixed up with Cypher. He's evil!"

Carlos took the butt of his shotgun and struck Jim in the belly. "Shut up, geezer!"

Matt watched his good father gasp for air as he dropped hard to his knees. Matt cried out, "Dad, Dad! Are you okay?"

"Leave the poor man alone!" Juan screamed. "Let's see you come face me! I want to see if you wet your pants like your goon Gustavo!"

"You wicked butcher!" Matt advanced toward Cypher. "So help me—"

Before Matt could continue, he was struck in the stomach like his father.

"How did that feel?" Carlos snarled as he wrapped the barrel of the shotgun across Matt's neck and stood behind with the side of the gun pressed hard against his throat, pinning him tightly. "Now, Loser Magoo, let's hear you gripe."

"I'm so proud of ya son." Jim may have been crouched on trembling legs, but he was not going to shut up. "I hope that ya understand that I dealt for that bad man ta be protectin' ya."

"Yeah, another Loser McCain!" Carlos taunted.

"That's right," Jim said. "I'm a loser." He pleaded, "My dear son. I have wrecked my life. Please don't go ruinin' yours too. I beg ya, please get away from this evil family."

Big Lew turned to his son. "Make yourself useful, you no-account louse! Now have the ol' wino shoved in the meat-locker until after my boy, Matthew, deals the game."

Damen ordered two guards to grab Jim McCain. As Jim was dragged away, he continued to urge his last child to stay away from that monarch from hell.

He cried, "Don't do it, my son. Don't deal for that evil man. I know somehow he's responsible for Mama and Debra's death. His exact words were, 'You will not have four mouths to feed, nor will you even have three. You will only have two.' Listen ta me, son, he told me if I tell ya, you would be next. Be careful, please!"

"That's it!" Gustavo released Magoo with a shove and ran over and slapped the old man down. "Shut your puking mouth, ol' geezer!" He faced the guards and growled, "Get him out!"

RE-DEAL

The two watchmen seized Jim under the arms and hauled him away.

As Jim was dragged out, he yelled back, "Always remember I love ya, son!"

Matt's father's words that his mother and sister were dead had hit him like hammer blows. His mom and sister were dead? Most likely murdered! "You will not have four mouths to feed, nor will you even have three. You will only have two."

The terrifying words sent Matt's mind into a tailspin. He could no longer think clearly. Tears streamed down his cheeks. Pain seared through him, and guilt overwhelmed him. Matt knew he should have gotten them out instead of going down south for his test. He was so selfish. It was all his fault.

All he could do now was moan. "No, No, please, not my family too! No, no, my mom! Not my sister, too! Both dead? No, no, it can't be true!"

"Shut up!" Big Lew thrust his hand palm out and barked, "I don't have time to be civilized anymore. You've exhausted my pleasant and civil period."

He gazed deep into Matt's burnt eyes, and Lew's eyes began to glow with the fires of hell. He spoke clearly and deliberately. "Mr. Matthew McCain, you will deal! Or your father will die. Slowly! Unlike your dead preachy mother and your little dog-faced sister. Trust me, with them, I was merciful. They never knew what four-wheeler pounded them into the dirt."

Big Lew and the conspirators smiled in satisfaction.

Matt's brain was close to bursting. There was only rage left inside him, a constant maddening stab of fury. He was trapped, nowhere to go and no one to turn to. What could he do now?

"Matthew, it is six o'clock." Big Lew glanced at his gold timepiece. "You have forty-eight hours remaining. By 6:00 PM two days from now, if you're not in this place ready to deal, your father will depart this world. For now, I'm going to give you forty-seven hours on the house to contemplate your options. Carlos, take these two and carefully shepherd them to the wine-cellar and secure them. But before you go ..."

Big Lew circled Juan like a shark ready to strike a wounded fish. He stopped and stood in front of him, grinding his teeth. A malignant grin spread across his face. "Juan, my runaway chattel, I wonder if I should barbecue you first and peel the flesh off your carcass, then feed you to my tykes? Or, should I leave you raw?"

Juan struggled to harness his pent-up fury, simmer it, check it. He vowed, *No more*! He said, "Is that so! Take this!" With his entire might Juan leaped up and threw a jabbing jump front kick, striking Cypher square in the throat.

"You can't hurt me!" Lew did not flinch or move.

Juan saw Cypher's eyes were frighteningly lifeless, like a demonic ventriloquist dummy.

"So," Big Lew asked, "you think your pathetic martial arts skills can best mine?"

Swift as a stroke of lightning Big Lew struck with inhuman cunning and speed. With one hand he grabbed Juan by the collar and with a malevolent shriek hoisted him off the floor.

"Wow," Juan said. "Been working out on the weekends, huh?" He spit right in Cypher's face and said, "You stink and need a bath!"

Damen stifled a smirk and quickly snatched the fancy gold lighter off his father's desk and shoved it into his pocket.

Big Lew roared like a animal as he swung his right palm across Juan's face, cuffing him twenty feet across the room. Juan landed with a thud at the feet of one of Lew's stuffed grizzly bears.

Gustavo moved over and used the butt of his shotgun to prod him back to his feet.

Matt tried to help, but Carlos released him with a shove and pointed his shotgun right between his eyes, holding him at bay.

Gustavo threw open the two library doors and gestured with his weapon. "Magoo, get that bratty fugitive up and get going."

CHAPTER TWENTY-TWO

Two Bobby Pins

Carlos was in front and Gustavo at the rear as they bullied Matt and Juan across the ranch and down into the shadowy wine cellar. As they descended the steps, the stillness was eerie and appalling, like a cold depressing dungeon or a torture chamber in a European castle. At the bottom, Carlos snapped on the light. He led them between rows and rows of costly bottles of aging wine.

He halted in front of a two-inch thick oak door and removed from his pocket a ring of keys. He inserted one and opened the door to a room about twelve by twenty with walls that smelled like cedar. Stretched across the back wall were Big Lew's investment bottles of liquor, many over a hundred years old. Carlos shoved Matt and Juan inside.

Gustavo grinned. "Magoo, I hear your ugly old lady and stinking sister look better now. Just feeling' a little rundown is all."

"Yeah." Carlos laughed. "It's too bad you didn't have a chance to give your homely ma that little cross. It might have helped with her depression."

The two thugs guffawed with satisfaction at the sick goads.

"One of these days, we'll get you both!" Juan cried out.

Carlos only laughed harder as he closed and locked the door.

Matt was in shock, his thoughts shattered, and his mind blurred. His fractured arm ached and his ruptured ear throbbed. However, the ache in his soul drowned out the physical pain. The emptiness he felt was unbearable. He was numb, with no room inside for any new emotions. His eyes welled up again. Matt was beyond pain as he had ever known it before. If he tried to talk he would only cry, but the agony was too much. He began to bawl convulsively, like he did back when his eyes were burned.

Juan saw the devastation in his friend's face. Matt's grief looked so deep Juan thought it could never be erased. He didn't know what to say. So for the silent second, he decided it seemed better to say nothing and let the guy have time to grieve. Juan opened and closed his hands into fighting fists. He wanted to hit something hard, anything.

Inflamed, he thought, *If I could only get alone with that butcher Big Lew. I'd tear the tyrant to pieces with my two bare hands. But, I kicked him hard right in his gullet and it didn't bother the brute. There's something wrong with this picture, something spooky about that man. Cypher must be a servant of Satan.*

Juan heard Matt sobbing even harder—crying uncontrollably. He saw the damp drops of rain streaking down Matt's cheeks. He placed a hand on his friend's shoulder and said in shared sorrow, "I'm so sorry about your ma and sister and your father. In spite of his failings, your dad is a kindhearted man—he's the dad I never had. My friend, I don't know what to say."

Matt inhaled sharply, trying to restrain himself. His mom's kind, caring face kept flashing into his mind. She'd never get his gift nor hear his apology. He sobbed, choked, then said slowly, "Don't say anything. Just give me a minute."

He fell to his knees and prayed aloud, "Oh God, give me the faith of a mustard seed, before I finally give up completely."

"Me too, Man in the Sky," Juan said as he lifted his eyes toward paradise and prayed with his buddy. "Just the faith of a little seed."

Juan felt his freezing arms, and for the first time he noticed the temperature was frigid. This vault was like an icebox, cold and clammy. "Mano, it's cold in here."

RE-DEAL

As Juan paced the perimeter of the room, he identified with the various Bible dudes like Peter, Paul, James, Silas, and every other believer in the Big Man's Son who had spent time in a dreary dungeon while innocent. He paced around trying to stay warm. He pounded his fist on the walls to see how strong they were. Behind the cedar siding was cement, and the walls were solid as a stone. There were no windows and the door had no knob, only a double-cylinder deadbolt. He could see there was no way to get free.

Juan thought prayerfully, *If I only had some picks I could open that lock.*

He searched topside and spotted one small vent. The hollow reminded him of a blowhole on the top of a mammoth sea mammal. It was the source for the frosty air. Still he could see it was far too small to scramble through.

As he searched, the walls seemed to pulsate, like they were breathing about him. This must be something like the Old Testament dude Jonah felt when he was turned into fleeing fish bait. It must have been bad when the baiter became the bait and got imbibed and burst forth in the belly of a denizen of the deep. The excitement started with the swallow, then swelled as Jonah slid like a lad on a water ride down into the stinking stomach full of the next day's waste. *One day,* Juan thought trustingly, *if this poor fellow's prayers are answered, the Cyphers will become fertilizer that will grow fields of flowers.* However, in contrast to the story's swallowed celebrity, Juan knew they needed not to flee, but to face their foes.

Unlike the Bible lad Jonah, they didn't have three days to stew in the smelly juices. He and his amigo Matt needed to move out of this stinking cellar before Cypher created more mischief or terrified Jim any more. Frustrated and at a loss, Juan forced his fingers into the pockets of his windbreaker. He felt something poke his forefinger.

He tugged the two thin items from his pocket. He could hardly believe what he was holding in his hand. They were the two bobby pins the pretty angel had handed him as he left her carriage. He was upset for forgetting to thank her for showing him the joy of humor. However, he was starting to wonder if he'd actually met an angel or if the episode in that girly buggy had really happened. *But the pins are here. Which means she was real.* He smiled. *Thank you, Lord!*

He faced his friend and said, "Mano, we're back in business." He placed the pair of pins close to Matt's face and said, "Let's blow this joint."

"What?" Matt wiped his eyes. "How do you propose to blow this joint? We're locked behind this big oak door. I felt the door when we were shoved inside. It's over two inches thick."

"The day of your test Miss Guided gave these bobby pins to me." Juan showed Matt the instruments for their escape, "I guess somehow, in some strange way, she knew we would need them."

"That's all the help she gave? Two lousy pins?" He scoffed. "And where is she anyway? I thought you said she was coming to my test." Matt lowered his head in defeat. "It doesn't matter anyway. She's nothing but a bad dream." He thought about his ma's cross crushed under a vehicle. "And my poor mother. She'll never know how much I loved her."

"I know it's tough, Mr. Cheat. Come on now. For your father, you must buck up! Now consider what the greatest author in the annals of mankind said about demoralizing circumstances."

"There you go again." Matt lifted his head and muttered, "Talking like a college boy. So, a writer, huh? I'm sure you mean Tom Clancy."

"No," Juan said with a laugh, happy to finally be engaging his friend. "I'm referring to Paul, the guy who wrote most of the books in the New Testament. My question to you, Mano, is, do you think this dude whose letters blanket the planet, put pen to parchment as he leisurely drifted down the Jordan River while drinking the real thing? No, the apostle scrawled the books of the Bible while crammed in a dark, dank dungeon.

RE-DEAL

"That, of course, was after he was beat with rods, shipwrecked, cursed, and stoned and left for dead. By the way, that was not stoned with drugs, but the old-fashioned way, with real rocks—big ones, hard ones. For all that battery and abuse, the fellow's direct response was to say, 'Rejoice in the Man in the Sky, and again I say rejoice!'

"The Apostle dude went on to say, 'My amigo and I are conquerors through the Creator Man who pumps us up and makes us capable for battle.'"

Juan watched in disappointment as Matt just stood there and said nothing. He lightly shook his friend on the shoulder. "Come on, Mano. I know the devil has hurled everything, including a filthy toilet at us—which, by the way you drank out of—yet I know you can do it!"

Matt sniffed and wiped away the tears with the back of his hand.

"Look at what you've accomplished so far." Juan nodded. "Your cards, your black belt, your pathetic acting. Come on, Mr. Cheat, buck up. If not for yourself, then for your father." Juan again nudged Matt, hoping the warring words and clever kidding about the novel name Mr. Cheat would cheer him up.

"Nothing more vexing than an educated wetback," Matt said as he snickered at the silly name. He kind of liked it. "I should have never let you attend college. However, I think you're a little off in your recounting those Bible verses."

His amigo's reaction was paltry, but Juan was still pleased. "Mr. Cheat, at Cypher's slave camp we were taught how to pick locks, and now it's gonna pay off big time."

Juan watched as his melancholy amigo looked up with an encouraged expression. Good, he was coming around.

He slapped Matt on the shoulder. "Come on, Mano! We're gonna get out of here and fix this horrendous predicament, as well as set your father free. Just relax and trust that our lives are in the hands of the Big Man."

Juan straightened the two pins. He took one and stuck it between the distended door and doorjamb. He bent one end into a ninety-degree angle, then pulled the pin free from within the frame.

"Let me explain what I'm gonna do. This pin I just bent," Juan handed it over for his friend to feel, "will act as my tension wrench. The other pin I'll use to pick the lock."

Juan stuck the short end into the cylinder, and with the second hairpin he delicately maneuvered the metal pin within the crack as adroitly as a surgeon performing surgery and manipulated the tiny tumblers. A moment later, Juan heard the customary click. "It worked. We're free!"

He turned the temporary tension wrench and pushed the oak door open a crack. He searched outside and saw that the cellar was clear.

"The coast is clear. If you want a tour of this nightmare leviathan, follow me."

CHAPTER TWENTY-THREE

Claiming the Goon

"A tour of what? Leviathan? There you go again, talking like a college boy."

Juan removed his picks and put them in his pocket, then blazed a path out of the prison.

"This way," Juan said as they tiptoed through the wine cellar. "Around this corner are the stairs, which will lead us out of this pit."

Big Lew had left Gustavo behind to stand guard duty. However, rather than doing his job, Gustavo was hiding around the corner chugging down a bottle of Big Lew's expensive wine. When he heard voices coming his way, he tried to stand up, but after downing the wine, all he could do was stagger to his feet and lean against the wall. He waited for them to round the corner.

As they traveled through the medieval-like dungeon, Juan called to mind the writings of his best-liked monarch, the giant soldier-slayer, King Dave, the Psalm writer. "During those days I travel through Cypher's haunted hollows filled with dark dragging forms of frightening fatal fiends, I will fear no servants of Satan."

"I know this putrid place inside and out," he told Matt. "I'll have no problem getting us off this modern-day slave camp."

As Juan and Matt approached, Gustavo smashed the bottle against the wall. He held in his hand a long jagged piece of glass, ready to carve his foe like a Thanksgiving turkey.

Matt's stomach turned when he recognized the sound of glass breaking. As he and Juan turned to look, their nerves tingled like live wires.

Without any warning, Gustavo slammed a roundhouse kick straight into Matt's midsection.

"Ah!" Matt cried as the blow knocked the butterflies right out of his stomach. He groaned, but he took the blow. He staggered, then he steadied himself.

Juan turned just in time to see Gustavo coming at Matt with the glass razor. He yelled, "Look out, Mano! The drunk has a razor-sharp piece of glass!"

Gustavo swung and caught Matt on the arm with the splint, and Matt felt his skin tear. A deep searing pain shot through him, but he struggled to ignore it. The rage and frustration inside him seemed to rip and clutch at his gut, tearing his flesh from within. The inner hurts were so great they overpowered the physical pains. Matt knew one thing—he was not going to die here in this dungeon. He also knew the attack came from the flat-nose wino, Gustavo. Matt could smell his alcoholic breath across the room. He was so choked up with anger and hurt for the slaying of his mom he could hardly contain the turbulence he felt rumbling around inside.

But something was wrong. He remembered Gustavo came down here with a shotgun. But for some reason the drunk was coming after them with a crude, jagged piece of glass. He realized the lush must be planning on doing something really sick.

He yelled, "Kicker, quick! Turn out the lights, now!"

Juan ran over and flipped the switch at the bottom of the steps, and the room was encased in total blackness.

"Kicker, stay back. This goon is mine."

"You got it, Mr. Cheat. But I'm here if you need me, Mano."

"Now we're even, you smelly lummox," Matt cried. "Let's see how well you fight in the dark. What's the matter, Gustavo? Cat got your tongue?" Matt's coarse whispers were intense and frightening as a roar. "Or are you afraid of a poor little blind man?"

RE-DEAL

Matt knew he should turn the other cheek. But as his shattered heart pumped his own blood onto his new clothes, he realized that after the slaughter of his dear mama and sweet sister, he had no cheeks left to turn.

Gustavo yelled, "Fried-eyes, how did you know it was me down here?"

"Your evil silence smells just like it did years ago when you attacked me with that magnifying glass. I have no doubt you also had something to do with the vile massacre of my mother and sister!"

"Why you piece of Lucas trash!" Gustavo slurred like a street drunk and screamed a curse of pure hatred. "Magoo, I'm going to slowly cut your ugly blind head off and feed it to my bitches."

"Yeah? You think so? No one else would have you but a sick dog."

"I'll get you for that!" Gustavo slashed across the darkness with the makeshift razor, but he couldn't find his victim in the dark. He slurred, "Where are you, Loser Magoo?"

In the blackness, Matt moved around like a whisper. He knew his lurking attacker would never know where to strike. Matt was used to fighting in the dark. Even though his body was sore and not yet healed from his test, his reflexes were still sharp and well honed. He swept his left foot across the floor and made contact with the heavy drinker's shoe. With his foot Matt hooked Gustavo's foot and lifted it high up into the air, throwing his foe off balance. Matt folded his leg back and sprang forward with a crashing sidekick, driving the heel of his boot into the drunken assailant's previously broken nose. The forceful strike splattered blood everywhere.

Gustavo screamed, his nose gushing with blood. He tried wiping it off on his sleeve.

"Turn on the light, you coward!" Gustavo cried out as he swung wildly. "It's not fair fighting in the dark!"

Matt cocked his leg again and threw a low shattering sidekick, landing it on the drunk's left knee. Matt shifted his weight forward, driving Gustavo's knee backward into the concrete floor. The force of the blow folded the knee opposite to its natural direction. In the silent darkness, the noise of the bones folding backward and cracking like dried twigs sounded ear piercing. Matt followed the kick with a right punch that drilled into the bully's eye socket.

Gustavo screamed as he fell toward the floor. He thrust out his hands to break the fall. He forgot he was holding a piece of broken glass and as he hit the ground, the glass knife he was holding sliced his palm wide open. He rolled around, crying from the pain.

"That was for my mom and baby sister." Matt was so choked up with exasperation he could only murmur, "Now, get up and fight like a man!"

Gustavo still held on to the blood-drenched glass dagger. He swung out desperately, but like a snowflake in a flame, somehow the blind man vanished.

Gustavo yelled, "Grilled-eyes! You're a stinking coward! Now be fair! Turn the lights back on!"

Matt moved close to the tough guy's ear and whispered in cold hard tones, "Gustavo, my sister and ma are in Heaven. However, you're not. I should kill you, right here, right now, and send you straight to hell! Still I'm not gonna butcher you, like you were gonna do me. I'm gonna let you lay here and contemplate what a poor little blind man did to you."

Gustavo gave a primal scream as he lunged for Matt's throat, "Aaaaaaaaahhhhhhhhhh!"

Because of his broken leg, Gustavo fell back to the hard cold floor and lay there, his body contorted, unable to get up.

Drained of all feeling and emotion, Matt hurried away, back toward his friend. "Kicker, where are you? Let's leave this dungeon."

"I'm right here by the light," Juan said.

He flicked on the light and examined Gustavo. He gaped at the thug's face and ripped right hand. Both were

RE-DEAL

blanketed with oozing cherry-red blood. But Juan grimaced at the goriest sight of all, his long-time tormenter's leg. It was bent backward in a forty-five-degree angle, inverted at the knee with his shoe far from the floor.

Juan said with a touch of pity, "That's right where evil belongs, defeated, flat on the back."

Gustavo rolled around, shrieking like a baby. He stifled his sobs as his eyes met Juan's. "Help—me—you—ungrateful—little—traitor!"

Juan thought about the scars across his back he'd received from the sick, sadistic Cypher slaves. A deep-seated rage inside Juan increased, and he battled the urge to bury the broken bottle in the boozer's body. But Juan figured his Father upstairs would take care of the tippler in His own time.

"Take this," he said as he pulled a bar rag from a hook. "Use it to stop the bleeding, and when you feel up to it, there's a phone here on the wall. You have my permission to reach out and touch someone. However, we need a head start, so you'll need to find the light switch in the dark."

Gustavo groaned as Juan turned away and snapped the light off. The lonely, impenetrable blackness again consumed him.

CHAPTER TWENTY-FOUR

Two Bloody Thumbs

Kicker spun and forced his friend up the steep stairs. "Let's get. The work trucks aren't far from here. They always leave the keys under the seat."

In ten minutes of stealthy movements, Juan had them safely at the ranch's motor pool. They slipped into one of the vehicles and drove off the one-time McCain homestead. As they left, one of Cypher's security guards spotted the truck with Matt in the passenger seat. The guard called in the sighting to his boss.

The guard reported, "Carlos, sir, I just received a call from Gustavo. He said the two jumped him and escaped. At the same time I spotted an unauthorized truck leave the ranch; inside was McCain and that renegade Juan."

"I'll take care of it from this end."

As the two sped away, Matt considered his dire situation. He was fighting the searing pain from the wound on his arm, but that pain was overshadowed by the agony of the loss of his mom and sister Debra.

Matt ripped off the splint and tossed it to the floor. That spooky Doctor Cypher had said it was a clean break and he didn't really need the splint if he didn't do any heavy lifting. Now it was covered with his fresh red blood from the cut with the glass dagger. Matt was glad the arm brace seemed to have retarded the depth of the stab wound. However, he knew he needed more than a splint to help him now.

RE-DEAL

He finally understood why his dad had continued to deal for Cypher all those years. His loving father had lived under the appalling threat of Cypher killing his whole family. Now Cypher had actually done it—he'd killed Matt's saintly mother and his radiant younger sister.

Knowing his mother would never receive his gift of repentance and love caused Matt's heart to sink further. Then there was his dad. Matt didn't know what to do. He couldn't compromise his values, yet there was no way he could let his father be murdered like the rest of his family. And he had only two days to fix this situation.

Juan said in a near-whisper, "I'm gonna work our way back to Murphy's school. We're lucky it's getting dark. To keep out of sight, I'll take all side streets. It'll take about two hours to get back, but it'll be safer. I think we should try to find Sensei and the Texas Ranger. Maybe they can tell us what to do."

"Sounds okay," Matt said without emotion. "Do what you think is best."

Poor guy. What could Juan possibly do to help? As he drove, Juan wondered what had happened with the amusing angel in human disguise. He now understood more clearly why that senior angel called her misguided. He wondered if the angelic woman was a washout after all.

After two hours of cautious driving through dark neighborhoods, Juan finally pulled up in front of the karate school. They jumped from the truck and ran to the building, only to find the windows broken and the school trashed.

"Bad news, Mano." Juan looked around with caution. "It looks like Cypher's goons beat us here. The place is a mess. Come on, quick! Let's head back to Steve's theater."

As they hurried across the street toward the theater, a deliveryman met them. "Package for Matthew McCain? Is that either of you?"

"Sure, that's us." The surprised Juan stopped in the street.

The deliveryman handed over the small square box.

Juan took it and said, "It's for you, Mr. Cheat. A peculiar package."

"Thanks, Kicker," Matt said listlessly. "You're a good friend."

He took the package, wondering how anyone knew he was here. "Who's it from?" He held it out to Juan.

"This is curious." Juan said as he examined the package. "No return."

"Well, let's see what's inside."

He took back the package, opened the box, and pulled out a piece of rolled-up white butcher paper. He unrolled the paper and discovered two bloody thumbs—wrapped around the body pieces was the cross he'd intended to give to his mother. Matt dropped the package as his senses were suddenly overwhelmed with horrifying, twisted, impressions of depravity.

"No! No! No!"

Kicker couldn't accept what his eyes told him was true. They were real bloody thumbs, cut from a human body, wrapped with his amigo's gift. It was a hideous trick to get Matt to deal. Juan realized there were no limits to which Big Lew would not go to get his way.

He prayed, "My loving Lord, I lay my life before you. My feet are ready to fly in the faces of our formidable fiendish foes."

"Here's a note." Even though Matt feared the worst, he had to know. "What's it say?"

"Oh no! Listen, Mano, it's bad. 'Now less than forty-seven hours to decide or the rest of your ol' geezer will be mailed. Oh, and Magoo the cross is a gift from Carlos to remember your mother by. Merry Christmas!'"

In the shadows, the sadistic deliveryman, Escona, smirked at Matt's pain.

"Damen did this!" Matt dropped to his knees and cried toward Heaven, "Do anything to me, God. I don't care anymore. Just please, please, help my daddy!"

But things just got worse. The headlights and screech of tires of Big Lew's limo followed by two other cars caught the boys' attention.

RE-DEAL

Damen, Carlos, and his guards jumped out and dashed over to surround Matt and Juan. The guards grabbed Matt, Carlos grabbed Juan, and they all pulled stilettos. Damen put on a show to show his old man that he could lead, that he was the macho stud horse his father claimed to be. That he was ready to take over the family business.

He snapped like a drill sergeant. "As my extraordinary godlike father would say, move and your ol' man will die!"

Juan watched as Big Lew lumbered from the limo. A sickening smile played at the corners of his mouth—the most arrogant look Juan had ever seen on the always-arrogant face.

"Don't move, Matthew my boy," Big Lew said with menace beneath the tone. "Or your thumb-less father will cash in his chips!"

Big Lew stopped to light up a cigar and patted his pockets for the gold lighter, but it wasn't there.

Carlos reached into his pocket, pulled out a box of matches, and tossed them to the boss. "Sir, catch!"

Big Lew snatched the box from the air and lit up. He puffed a few times, then blew out the smoke toward Matt. "So, you received our thoughtful little care package." He puffed again then leaned into Matt's face and blew out another cloud of rank smoke. "Hope you've been practicing. Saturday you'll turn the fortunes of many a wealthy guest."

He stared at the slobbered end of his cigar. After a long moment he asked, "Now, are you ready to stop playing these foolish games and take the substantial rewards I have offered you? Think about it—you'll be rich!"

Juan, held hard in a bear hug by a nervous amateur guard, watched Lew's moves. Carlos stood stone-still holding a stiletto and taunting him. Juan figured any dummy who used a back-gripped bear hug to hold a captive was more of a ruffian than a fighter. He could break free from his captor with his martial arts skills.

However, he still had to get past Carlos and his knife. Like Paul of Tarsus, Juan was ready to fight the noble fight and to take a stand on the evil day.

He looked up and prayed silently. *My flying feet are in your hands, my only Father.*

Matt felt ready to explode. He couldn't believe Cypher would think that money could make up for the loss of his ma and sister. His heart pounded so hard he feared it would jump right out of his chest. He felt everything closing in around him, like he was being swallowed up in a pool of quicksand.

He gasped out in fury, "I'm never controlling your games again. Now, my dad, tell me now, where is he?"

"Oh, my, my." Big Lew clicked his tongue. "After you ran off, the drunk has again declined in similar fashion. No, no, can't afford that."

"Good!" Matt fired back. "That makes two of us. Your thugs can kill me right here and now, but I won't deal."

"And what would that accomplish?" Big Lew asked in a milder tone.

He needed the kid's skills for this particular game. All the players were card-savvy and could spot a good card mechanic, but no one could spot his prodigy. However, he wasn't used to having anyone defy him— especially when he'd offered so much money.

And imagine making such a fuss over a couple of useless women. Lew had never heard of such laughable behavior. Why would anyone care about ugly dames anyway? You could buy them anywhere, and they were cheaper by the dozen.

Lew again clicked his tongue and shook his head. "I hate to hear the youth speak of death so. No, no, child, death is so anticlimactic. What can an old frump like me say to the next generation?" He turned toward the limo and signaled to Escona. "But, perhaps a son may yet listen to his father."

CHAPTER TWENTY-FIVE

No Thumbs

Inside the limo, Jim watched as the scowling bodyguard opened the door. He couldn't even push the man away because his hands were so bulky with bandages. Jim bent low as he tried to hide the pain from his terrible ordeal.

Cypher had warned Jim that this was his last chance. He had to get his son to deal, or there would be even worse than what he received for his boy. Jim wasn't going to let his last beautiful child die.

As soon as the limo door opened, Juan could see Cypher had carried out his threat. He cried, "Matt! It looks like this wicked butcher has hurt your father! His hands are wrapped, and I see blood." Juan's eyes were drawn to the dead thumbs wrapped with the chain holding the bloody cross. "Mano, my brother, I'm so sorry. As we suspected, the thumbs are your father's."

Jim looked up at his son and lifted his impotent hands into the air. "Oh, no, please don't ..." Jim started to cry and couldn't go on.

Big Lew sauntered over to his retired dealer and held up his hands. Lew wore a pained expression across his face and said with feigned sorrow, "Matthew, both of your father's thumbs have been removed." He shook his head. "I don't know how this happened, something to do with a meat axe falling from the sky."

Lew was glad he never had the burden of any feeling or compassion for anyone, including his now thumb-less dealer. However, he was exhilarated by how pain and the threat of pain generated such fine loyalty, the kind of allegiance and cooperation he needed to keep his businesses running like his expensive watch.

He said with a regretful shake of his head, "It's really a shame, Matthew; it really is. However, sadly, this means your old man has officially retired from the card table. Now if your father retires from life, that will be your choice."

Big Lew snubbed the flame end of his cigar out on the thumb-less old man.

"Yoweee!" Jim screamed, in pain from the fiery ash. "Stop!"

"Mano, he's burning your father!" Juan struggled to get loose. "Fight me!"

Carlos backhanded Juan across the face and shoved the knife close to his throat. "Shut your trap, you little traitor!"

"Dad, Dad!" Matt cried out as he looked out of the corners of his eyes to try to see his father. "Talk to me! Dad!"

"This is for me, son, but not for you." Jim held up his wrapped hands. "They can't do this ta you, my wonderful son."

"There, now," Big Lew said. "Sound advice from a venerable father."

Deep from within Matt's soul came a scream, a battle cry, a groan of grief and anguish, followed by fury.

"Butcher! First my mama. Now you take my daddy's thumbs! Wicked! You wicked piece of scum! Oh God, help me!"

Big Lew removed Jim's Western belt and fancy buckle from around his waist, then had the bodyguard shove Jim back into the limo. He raised the antique gold buckle up to the boy's view. "Can you see this?" Lew asked.

"That's Lucas the Loser's old buckle." Matt struggled desperately, trying to wear down his guard's grip. "You can keep the losing piece of crap!"

"This buckle," Lew cinched the belt around Matt's waist, "was passed down from generation to generation. Wild Bill

RE-DEAL

Hickok was shot dead while holding these cards, aces and eights, the Dead Man's Hand!"

Matt continued to struggle against the grip of the two guards.

"Your cooperation for the game is now non-negotiable," Lew said. "It's a done deal! The question is whether you care for your father and want him to remain whole. Well? I'll let you figure that one out for yourself.

He checked his watch. "Now, you have forty-six hours and twelve minutes remaining. Should you do well in the gaming Saturday, your father perhaps will yet live to see another day. As well as a bonus for you too. But if not ..." He left the threat hanging in the thin air.

Matt summoned every ounce of energy together as he screamed at the top of his voice, "Help me, God!"

He slammed the bodyguard's faces into each other and broke free. He then shoved Damen aside and ran toward the limo.

The bodyguards jumped back up and grabbed the younger McCain as he writhed and screamed, "Let—my—dad—go!"

From off in the dark distance came a strange clattering along with the call of a stallion. The buggy careened around the corner, spraying a fog of sparks from the massive wheels.

Big Lew's eyes went wide and bulged out. He growled, "What's this? No driver?"

The air was pierced with the sounds of pandemonium. Miss Guided called from within the coach, "Haaaa! Seraphim!"

Big Lew watched in terror as the weird vehicle ran full bore toward him and his men. The knot of struggling guards dove in all directions, trying to avoid being trampled as the thing halted with a spray of sparks.

"Kicker," Michala opened the door and yelled out. "Snatch Matt and heave him aboard!"

"It's that wacko!" Carlos yelled to Damen. "She's back!"

Juan jumped for joy at the sight of the misguided angel. The arrival of her coach gave Kicker his opportunity. As the thug Carlos turned to look, Juan kicked the knife clear. When Carlos turned back, Juan kicked him squarely in the chin, knocking him backward to the ground. Then Juan slammed the same forceful foot on the foot of the incompetent guard who was hugging him hard.

Kicker crashed the back of his head into the hoodlum's face, breaking his nose. Blood splattered far and wide, and the captor loosened his bear hug. Juan swung an elbow backward, smashing the guard in the solar plexus and knocking the wind out of him. Kicker dropped down and grabbed one of the goon's legs and lifted it up between his knees, causing the man to fall solidly to the street and crack his head hard on the sidewalk. This whole series of martial-art moves took five seconds.

I'm slowing down a speck, Juan thought. *Still there's time for more fighting fun.*

He jumped high into the air and drove a flying sidekick into Big Lew's back, smacking him to the street.

"You're mine!" Carlos recovered and dove after Matt. But he missed and cursed, "Damn you!"

"I won't damn you," Juan snickered. "But someone else might."

"Quick! Kicker," Michala screamed. "Snatch Matt up, heave him over, and shove him into my buggy. You get in too!"

Juan helped his amigo inside the carriage, and then hopped in after him.

He grinned and shouted, "We're in. Go, Miss Guided, go!"

"Giddy up, Seraphim, dump this town. Quick!" Michala yelled to her horse. "Back ta my little red schoolhouse, now!"

Seraphim reared majestically as he screamed his call.

"Whoa!" Carlos shrieked as he rolled out of the way of the buggy as it took off like a shot.

RE-DEAL

"What's all this?" Big Lew screamed. "Get up, you stupid bullies! Catch that buggy!"

All of his henchmen jumped into their cars and screeched out in the direction of the mysterious coach.

The buggy turned down a side street and ran full speed down a dead end alley straight toward the side of Pastor Steve's converted church.

Juan shouted, "Miss Guided, stop! We're gonna crash!" But Seraphim did not stop; he only sprinted faster. Juan tried a second time. "Lady, stop!" He turned back to his friend. "Hold on, Mano. We're gonna splatter!"

The coach ran right into the wall and then through it.

Big Lew's limo turned down the same alley. They drove up to an old brick church building where the cars came to a noisy stop. The men jumped out and looked around the dead end alley in bewilderment.

"What is this?" Big Lew cried. "You fools! Where did they go?" He knocked Damen to the ground and barked, "You louse!"

CHAPTER TWENTY-SIX

Forty-Six hours to Death

Carlos's superstitious nature was trying to take over, but he wasn't going to let it keep him from making a good impression on his boss. "The eerie woman said something about a little red schoolhouse. I know where it is. "Follow me."

They quickly turned around and the limo followed after Carlos with a screech.

Inside the carriage, the boys watched as the horse and buggy seemed to melt right through the theater's wall. In the instant before hitting the wall, the buggy leaped forward and in less than a nanosecond pulled up in front of Miss Guided's schoolhouse. Juan and Matt experienced the impossible, but exhilarating, sensation of simultaneously accelerating and retarding at lightning speeds. Seraphim picked up an easy gait on the gravel-covered drive to his mistress's red schoolhouse.

Although Matt's heart ached from the appalling memory of his disfigured father, he was thrilled to see this inexplicable woman again.

Michala reached across and touched his hand. "How ya makin' it, Matt?"

"Lady," Matt mumbled. "I mean, Miss Guided ... missed you. Where have you been? I've dreamt about seeing you for years."

Juan simply stared at the angel with a reassuring smile.

RE-DEAL

"But my poor dad," Matt mumbled to himself. "What to do? Can't compromise my values, and I have only forty-six hours. Dear God, help!"

"Come on, Mr. Cheat," Kicker said. "You're staring a gift horse in the face. Come on, Mano, blind faith is your papa's only chance. You got the blind part. Just need the faith."

"Ya bust me up." Michala unleashed a wholehearted laugh. "Ya sure are a card, Kicker; ya really are."

"Yeah," Matt said with a small grin. "You're funny, Kicker."

"In my fancy," Michala said with relish, "that name Mr. Cheat is especially entertaining." She turned to Juan. "Who came up with that there funny label?"

"Someone at Matt's last show. I think the name should stick. I'm a kicker and he's a card cheat, right?"

The carriage bounced over a bump in the road and halted in front of the schoolhouse.

Michala pushed the hair from Matt's sorrowful eyes and lifted his chin. "Come on, Mr. Cheat. I know things have been a little fitful. However, I have a new strategy. This revelation came ta me like the powerful force of the Big Top's sheet of lightning during that foretold crucifixion."

"Big Top?" Juan questioned. "You mean like the circus?"

"Wow, Kicker. Ya really bust my sides. Ya really do." She explained with a giggle. "Big Top is the Most High, the Almighty, the Master of the Universe." The pretty gal handed Juan an old paper and pointed. "Please recite this ta Mr. Cheat."

"It's an old-time newspaper." Juan took the paper and read it to his pal. "It's dated January 28, 1882." He looked up and grinned. "Whoa, that's as old as Matt."

"Funny, Kicker." Matt rolled his eyes. "Just show Miss Guided you can now read the words as well as you can read the pictures."

"Okay, be cool, be cool." Juan looked down at the old paper and started reading at the top. "'John Cypher Lays out Monumental Poker Challenge. The notorious gambler,

John L. Cypher, yesterday made a public proclamation that he could beat Texas land mogul, Lucas McCain, in a gentlemen's game of poker.'"

"What?" The words got Matt's attention. "What's that? Lucas the Loser?"

"Keep reading," the incognito guardian angel said. "Now listen, Matt."

"'John L. Cypher,'" Juan read on, "'laid down the rules of the game so as to invite only those players who can bring 100,000 dollars to the table' —"

"Stop. That's fine readin'." Miss Guided took one of Matt's hands into hers and said, "A vision without a plan is nothin' but a hallucination. So while ya have been gettin' strong I have been workin' on a stratagem ta get yer family's homestead back. Seraphim is gonna take us back ta the past and then tote us from town ta town. Yer gonna earn 100,000 dollars ta play in that there big game and then try ta whip John L. Cypher."

"How's he gonna win that kind of money?" Kicker asked.

"Well," the angel-in-teacher-form told him, "that answer comes from another dispensation, which I am sorry to say, I haven't quite found yet."

"I know how!" Matt said as excitement filled him. "Miss Guided, if what you say is true and we can return to the past, I might be able to use my bang-up math talents to earn enough money honestly to enter the poker championship, then sit down and beat that wicked butcher's grandfather!"

"Oh, Matt." Michala noticed the blood on his clothes. "I mean, Mr. Cheat! Look at that ugly cut."

"What are you talking about?" Kicker cackled. "That's just a petite, wee, little scratch. I never felt a thing when that dog-face Gustavo cut him."

"Yer so silly, Juan." Michala snickered. "Now let me see what I have in here."

Juan smiled as he watched her reach into her pea-size purse and pull out a first-aid kit.

RE-DEAL

"Roll up yer sleeve, Mr. Cheat," Michala told Matt. "I'm gonna attend ta that nasty wound."

As she doctored his cut, Matt wondered if they really could go back. Contradictions attacked his mind from every angle. Yet in the history of the world, he knew stranger things had happened.

After thoughtful consideration he said, "Miss Guided, I believe that miracles didn't go by the wayside 2,000 years ago. Funny lady, I believe your faith is strong and powerful, like the miraculous Mother Theresa. For some reason I can certainly not define, I believe you can take us back in time."

"Oh good. I'm glad ya do Mr. Cheat. I think it's the only way ta halt that iniquitous man."

At least I hope it will, she thought to herself. *Or I might be suspended and end up sitting on a cloud sewing.*

Matt took charge. "Please let me tell you my ideas. I've dreamt about doing this for years. If we can go back, I'll need to establish myself as a champion poker player. During this time, like you said, I'll need to earn at least 100 grand to qualify and then buy a seat at the poker championship of the West. This way, I'll be able to play in the same game as my great grandfather, or better, I might be able to stop him from gambling his ranch. I'll establish my reputation by exposing the dishonest gamblers and their cheating methods. This should encourage them to play honestly, or they'll be forced from the game."

"Yeah," Juan pointed his forefinger like a gun and grinned. "That's unless another player blasts them first."

This could work. Matt was finally feeling a bit hopeful. He pulled a pack of Bicycle cards from his pocket.

He fanned them out. "To get a feel for the times, I think we should start in Deadwood, South Dakota. In this town the Marshal, Wild Bill Hickok, didn't allow firearms within the city boundaries. That should hopefully cut down the risk of any unwanted gunplay. My thought is to work our way forward through time and establish a champion poker reputation as we earn the money for the big game."

"Wow," Michala said. "Ya really got this thought out."

"Kicker," Matt reached into his pocket and pulled out a small roll of bills and handed them across. "This money will have to be our grubstake. How much do we have?"

"Wow, Mano, you have 320 dollars here." He remarked with mock motivation, "All you need is a scant 99,680 dollars more, and you're ready for the big game."

"I think that doctoring should do it." The slice in the skin melted together as the broken bone inside fused. Miss Guided gave Matt a good-humored slap on the hand. "There ya go, Mr. Cheat—all better."

Matt had to admit that since the first day he met her, this extraordinary woman had captivated him. Something about her he couldn't understand or explain sent his heart pounding and his blood rushing. Ever since that horrible drug overdose, when for a moment, an all-too-short moment, he could actually clearly see her bright blue eyes and beautiful, kind face, ever since that day he had fantasized about being with her again.

He wanted to give her a little expression of thanks for her kindness. He clumsily reached across to give her a little thank-you hug. But at the moment he did, she slipped away from his attempted embrace by bending down to pick up her bag.

Darn! What a klutz I am, Matt thought in embarrassment. He hoped Kicker hadn't seen his failed amateurish attempt. Matt knew his friend would rib him big-time if he did.

Michala placed the first-aid assortment back into her sack. She pretended not to notice Matt's effort to embrace her. She particularly favored her handsome new human. However, any sort of romantic contact between guardian angels and their humans was prohibited.

She said, "I think I better run inside and pack a few provisions. It sounds like this jaunt will be a lengthy one. Conceivably, a full twinkling in time."

A full twinkling in time? Juan wondered what that meant. *Must be angel talk.*

RE-DEAL

"Wait here, boys." Michala opened the door and stepped down from the buggy. "I'll be back in a jiffy."

Juan watched as she stepped out and shut the door. He reached across, mischievously slugged Matt in the arm, and said with a snicker, "'Ey Mano, you can't gull yer brother. I saw you try to kiss her." He laughed heartily. "Trust me, Mano. You're not in her class."

"Yeah? You think so?" Matt tried to hide his embarrassment. "I wasn't trying to kiss her. I simply wanted to show Miss Guided my gratitude for her generous help." He chuckled. "Besides, do you think she'd go for a smart mouth like you?"

"Very likely," Juan said with a self-assured smile. "I'm the handsomer."

Handsomer, Matt thought, depressed again. *Not my family, not any more. Other than my dad, they're all gone.* His true dilemma was his loving father. He had to stop thinking about how much this mysterious lady charmed him.

The coach door was thrown open and the lady in question stuck her flower-covered head inside. "Hi, boys. I hope ya didn't think that I had forgotten about ya. However, I'm finally back."

She hiked up her long blue skirt, daintily scaled the step, and sat down beside Matt, facing her snow-white horse.

Matt's temperature rose a couple of notches. He scooted over, delighted to have her so close to him.

"Mr. Cheat." Michala clutched a cane. "I got yer weapon." She handed the cane to Matt and held up her blue bag. "In case of a dilemma I packed a few things."

Juan was mystified with her puny little purse. He didn't see how that tiny tote could hold even two packs. However, he knew somehow it could.

Michala opened her purse and pulled out two long sticks connected by a short brass chain. "Kicker, here are yer nunchakus." She passed them to Juan with a wink.

"Thanks." Kicker stuck them in the small of his back hidden under his windbreaker. "What else did you pack?"

"Oh, well, let me see. Just the usual things one takes on an expedition like this. Ya know, Kicker, pen and paper, cards, knitting, oh, and a cannonball. Just the customary particulars."

A cannonball? Like the pins, Juan knew to note that odd item for future reference.

She turned serious, "Oh yes, there is one more thing I forgot ta mention. Once we depart from one time period, we can't turn around and go back."

"Okay." Matt wondered why that made any difference. "Whatever you say, Miss Guided. It's your horse and buggy, and you're the driver."

He was starting to wonder if this delightful woman had a screw loose or something. But he really didn't think so. When he contemplated the miracles throughout history against the absurdity of this idea, the supernatural occurrences won out. Matt believed it could happen.

The time-traveling guardian asked, "Mr. Cheat, what time does yer slick-talking watch say?"

Matt pulled out his clock and pushed the talk button. A synthesized female voice spoke. "It's 8 o'clock PM."

"Mr. Cheat, can ya set yer watch ta do a 46-hour countdown?"

"Sure, Miss Guided." Matt programmed the clock. "But what's the countdown for?"

"It's like this. Mr. Cypher said ya have forty-six hours left ta make yer decision. Here in the twenty-first century time will continue ta proceed forward. As we travel through the past, ya will need ta be attentive ta the hours ya deplete at each stopover. If yer chronometer gets down ta zero, yer father will be out of time. Now, are ya'll set ta go, boys?"

"Even though this suggestion is right out of a dream," Matt said as he took the cane from her, "my dad needs help. I'm ready. Let's go."

But before the coach had a chance to move, Big Lew's limousine followed by the car full of bodyguards roared up the driveway. They all jumped out and started to surround the coach. Juan peeked out the window flap and spotted Damen coming.

RE-DEAL

"'Ey Mano, we have party-goers. King Rat is back with his rodents."

"Don't mess with them, Miss Guided," Matt cried. "Take off. Let's get out of here quick!"

"Hang on, boys," the incognito angel told them. "We're facing the wrong way. We need ta go up and circle around my schoolhouse, and then we'll blast by them like a tornado." She yelled out the window, "Hyaaa, Seraphim! Leave this eon. Go rearward ta 1876!"

Seraphim reared and screamed his call. The coach roared by Big Lew, Damen, and the bodyguards, spraying pea-gravel across their startled faces.

"I've had my fill of this crap!" Big Lew started foaming at the mouth. He bashed his son on the back of his head and screamed, "Damen! You worthless piece of rubbish! Quick! This time you stop that sissified rig. Now go! Or I'll use your fruitless hide for my dogs' meals tonight!"

The sleek white horse Seraphim towed the coach at breakneck speeds without apparent effort. The horse circled around the schoolhouse, blasted back down the driveway, and ripped past Cypher's goons again.

"Stop them now!" Big Lew cried out.

Damen didn't want to become dog food. So he instinctively caught on to the back of the coach as it bolted down the driveway. He climbed up the back, flung himself onto the roof, clutched onto the gear racks, and held on for dear life.

As Matt again fell to the carriage floor, he registered a loud thud overhead. He thought it sounded like something hit the vehicle.

"No! Not again!" Big Lew raved as a frenzied demon. "Get up! Get up, you stupid fools! Catch that—that—that—thing!"

As before, all his henchmen scrambled into the cars and tore out in the direction of the coach. Once more the cars came to a noisy stop. But this time it was at the bank of a mountain where the coach had again disappeared. Cypher screamed, "I'm surrounded by incompetents! Stupid fools!"

He pulled out a stub nosed revolver and shot his driver Escona twice in the leg.

BOOK TWO

CHAPTER TWENTY-SEVEN

Traveling Outside-of-Time

On the other side of the existing, the extant, the here-and-now, they watched the night in a flash become as clear as a bright sunny day in San Antone. The abrupt lurch forward once again knocked Matt to the buggy's floorboards. He blinked a few times as he tried to get his weak eyes adjusted to the unexpected daylight.

"We're unmolested, Mr. Cheat." Miss Guided patted the seat beside her. "Why don't ya come hunker down with me on this nice cozy settee?"

Matt took a deep breath. "Thanks for the invite. But I have to say that was close. I thought Big Lew was going to stop us for sure."

"Yeah," Juan agreed. "I thought we were gonna buy the farm." He snickered. "Or at least rent it."

The angel laughed as she pulled two knitting needles and a skein of emerald green yarn from her little bag.

As soon as Matt was seated, the lightning-white horse came to an abrupt halt and Matt was again pitched back down to the floor.

"Wow!" Juan laughed. "What coordination for a black belt."

RE-DEAL

"Ya must really favor the floor." Michala giggled as she glanced down. "For myself, I find the bottom surface ta be hard and bumpy."

"Oh yes, Miss Guided, I love it down here. It's as relaxing as taking a siesta in the rear of Kicker's dirty old pickup while crossing a rock quarry."

Once again Matt hauled himself up off the carriage floor. As he sat down, he didn't see Miss Guided place an already half-knitted green shawl back into her tiny purse.

Juan hid a smile as he saw the bag swallow up the needles and scarf.

Outside, on the crown of the vehicle, Damen gaped in stupefaction at the Old West surroundings. *What's all this crap?* he wondered.

Seraphim trotted the buggy down an unpaved street past fruit groves, grazing land, and old-time storefronts. A recent rain had left the air fresh and clear. The black Dakota hills framed a landscape of tall weeds and lush trees. At the foot of the rise, Damen saw a barn and a stable where two fly-covered nags swatted their tails as they dipped their muzzles in an old watering trough.

What the hell is all this? Damen asked himself. *I was right—the witch is not from this planet. She must be some kind of unearthly space cadet with evil intentions for humans.*

"Look over yonder, boys." The angel-in-guise-of-teacher pointed out of the window toward the two sway-back horses drinking at the trough. "Remember, ya might lead a horse ta drink, but ya can't make him water."

The boys laughed and gawked at the classical Old West surroundings as Seraphim drove them through town. The wooden buildings, mostly unpainted, weren't built to last long. Pedestrians were dressed in nineteenth-century garments, and empty gun holsters hung around the men's waists.

"Yank it on over, Seraphim," the heavenly spirit called. "This'll do."

The horse pulled over at the edge of town.

"Let's go, boys. We're here."

"Wow, this is like the real frontier land." Juan opened the door and took a big whiff of the unpolluted air mixed with dirty horses and hogs. "I can tell I'm gonna miss all the thick juicy smog and contaminants." He looked back at Matt. "No chewing your air before breathing it back here, Mano."

"I've had enough from you." Matt gave his friend a shove in the butt. "Get out before I send you to your room!"

As Matt stepped out, he took a whiff. If he didn't know better, he'd swear he smelled Damen's overpowering cologne. He shook his head to clear it. He knew he must be imagining that smell back here.

"Now no fighting, boys," Miss Guided said with a giggle. "I want ya'll on yer best behavior."

As the time travelers stepped down from the brightly-colored buggy, Damen flattened himself against the roof to avoid being seen.

"I can hardly believe this. This coach thing took us back to ..." Matt looked around. "When? How?"

"Remember yer prayers, Mr. Cheat. Faith of a mustard seed transforms into a wonderful giant tree, but don't forget back home, time keeps movin' along. Ya'll have only forty-six hours ta work with. Come on now, boys; can't waste time."

Damen remained flat, clinging to the coach roof. Something was horrendously wrong—he was in a bewildering predicament. He spied Matt, Juan, and the alien woman as they left the old relic buggy and strolled toward the town. As soon as they were out of view, he scrambled down and hid behind the rig. He looked around and gawked with open-mouthed incredulity.

Just then, a large, black rat with a ten-inch tail dashed between his feet. He jumped in terror. He hated rats, especially big, ugly, fanged ones. He looked around and saw no more of the vile rodents. He'd better keep an eye on Matt and pals from a distance. So when the coast was clear and the rat was gone, he cautiously took off after them.

RE-DEAL

As the threesome moved along, they passed by an orchard of apple and peach trees. The peach trees were out of season, but the apples were in full supply. In a clearing in the midst of the fruit orchard stood a partial structure. In front of the incomplete building was a makeshift stand with a bushel of large red apples and a sign that read, 'Support our church building fund—apples $1 a basket.'

Nearby, a solitary man shaped a large log with a sledgehammer and a chisel. As the group approached, he looked up with a smile and wiped the sweat from his face with a bandanna.

"Afternoon, folks." He stepped forward with an outstretched arm. "I'm Pastor Johnny Haggai. Might I interest ya in some fine apples? All contributions go for our new church building fund."

Juan was in front and graciously took the offered hand. As they shook, Juan could see this man knew the Savior.

"'Ey man, nice to meet you. Your apples look good, Pastor, and I'm as starved as an Ethiopian missionary after a four-week fast." Juan let go of the pastor's hand, then pulled his windbreaker pockets inside out. "I'd love to help, but, as you can plainly see," he grabbed the one coin in his pocket, "I only have a nickel. It's yours if you want it."

"No bother, young fellow," the Pastor said, "keep your nickel. He nodded toward Matt. "Who's yer odd-rigged friend?"

Johnny stepped toward the man with the strange staff. He pointed to Matt's belt, which was strapped around his waist and not through the pant loops. He asked, "Does that buckle do ya any good tethered on the outside of those snazzy britches like that?"

"Give him time, Pastor Haggai." Kicker cackled. "This week he learned to put on his pants. Next week we'll teach him how to use a belt."

"Funny, Kicker," Matt said. "You're a card all right."

Pastor Haggai laughed heartily. "Yeah, I'll need ta make a message from that one day."

"Pastor, sir," Matt asked. "How much have you raised so far?"

"It's only been a year since I started raisin' funds. And the church has raised eleven dollars and twenty-two cents."

"I'm the nosy sort," Kicker declared. "If you don't mind me asking, how many baskets of apples do you need to sell to build a church?"

"Don't mind the asking at all. With labor and materials, I need ta sell 400 more baskets. It's just gonna take a mite bit a time. I work from can-see to can't-see, but like Moses in the wilderness, it's gonna be about forty years. My only burden is my banker told me if I don't make a 25 dollar payment by tomorrow morning, they're gonna foreclose on my two orchards."

Matt wondered if he should offer the man something or not. He had so little money to get started with, he needed so much more, and his father's life was on the line. He decided he'd better not take the chance.

"Come on, Kicker." Matt nudged Juan. "We need to hurry."

He faced the Pastor and looked down at the ground. "Good luck on your church. Maybe we can give later."

"We'll give later." The Pastor looked over to Michala and nodded thoughtfully. "That appears ta be everybody's favored line. But it's no matter. I trust the good Lord will provide."

"That's right," Miss Guided said. "Render and it will be rendered to ya."

The Pastor said, "Yep, the Lord will return, thirty, sixty, a hundred fold. There's just nobody in this here little town that believes the sort. So I work by myself, cut my own trees, and hew my own boards. Now, Ma'am, we have no roof or walls yet, nevertheless, next month I'm startin' ta hold services on Sundays. I'd be mighty obliged if ya'll come join us sometime."

"Pastor Haggai," the angel assured him, "I'm obliged for the invite, but next month when yer house of worship is

RE-DEAL

finished, I just hope there's room for us. Now hang on ta yer faith; we got ta run."

The pastor raised his head and said, "Oh dear Lord, give me her kind of faith." He lowered his eyes back toward the lovely lady and the two lads. "Ya'll pick you a free apple, courtesy of the church."

"Thanks, Pastor Haggai." Juan turned and yelled back, "We will. Now here's a little suggestion. You might consider shortening your name to Hagee—it's easier to say and remember."

Kicker eyeballed the fruit hanging from the trees lining the lane.

"Man, I'm hungry." Juan leaped up and plucked off a luscious-looking apple. "This'll do."

He took a big bite and was surprised to see half of a big juicy worm inside. He twisted his face in disgust at the thought of what just slid down his throat.

"Ooh yummy! Look, Mano, there's only half a worm left in this apple." He held it out. "Want the other half?"

"Eat heartily, Kicker." Michala grinned. "Ya'll get some mighty fine protein from them there delectable, luscious worms."

Juan threw the rest of the apple across the field.

"Hey, you worm-gorging pig, where's my half?"

"About 120 feet to your left." Juan wiped his mouth on his sleeve. "It's all yours."

"Thanks," Matt said with a laugh. "But next time remember you're not the only one who missed lunch." He peered around at the fuzzy images. "Now if this is literally 1876, maybe we can help someone out."

He removed his father's belt and fancy antique gold buckle from around his waist where Cypher had put it. He wanted no more comments from his goofy friend, so he laced it through the belt loops and secured it. They turned the corner and headed down the hard, red-clay mud of Main Street.

The town was chock-full of gambling establishments, and they were all open for business for the sporting men and a few women.

"'Ey Mano," Juan said with a grin. "If you don't mind your Q's and P's, I found your lodging for the night. It's the Marshal's slammer." He looked in the window. "Yep, good strong bars."

Then everyone's attention was drawn to a large crowd congregated in front of a gambling house with a large painting overhead of an enormous fully-developed male bull. Juan thought the painting was a little too explicit, except, of course, for folks from San Francisco. He read the words on the sign over the two-story wooden structure.

"'Ey Mr. Cheat, that sign across the street says, 'The Bull's Head Saloon and Gambling House.'"

"Wow!" Matt shouted. "You did it, Miss Guided. It's a miracle. Lady, you have some very unusual gifts."

"You can say that again." Juan winked at the angel.

"Why thank ya, Mr. Cheat. I told ya Seraphim would know the path."

Matt suddenly realized back here in the Old West a name like Mr. Cheat would invite a large hunk of lead right between his worthless blue eyes.

"Do me a favor, Miss Guided. When you address me in public, please call me Matt, McCain, anything but Mr. Cheat." He turned to Juan. "You too, Kicker. I don't want to catch a fatal case of lead poisoning. Especially when back here the only Doc is a psychopathic tooth fairy named John Holliday." He reached over and lightly touched Michala's soft golden hair. "Do you have a first name? Something besides Miss?"

The guardian angel pondered for a period. The name Miss Guided particularly pierced her funny bone. After a moment of meditation, she said, "I particularly cherish the proper name Miss Guided. However, if yer so compelled, ya can also call me Michala."

Matt knew he had heard that pretty name Michala somewhere before. However, for the life of him, he couldn't remember where. He casually slid his hand down her slender arm and took her warm hand into his. Matt knew he was a shy flub with a pretty woman, mainly because he'd had very few opportunities to be with anyone of the feminine persuasion. Growing up the Cyphers would never let him have a girlfriend or even go out.

And over the past five years with Sensei Murphy and Pastor Steve, he'd been so busy training with his karate and practicing with his cards he'd never gone out with anyone. Unless of course you considered Kicker, and that had been merely to fight at some other karate school or do a card exhibition at the theater. Kicker was the greatest of friends and like a brother, but totally flunked the female physical.

Matt knew he was strong and fast, and thanks to Steve, he could bluff his way through. However, he still felt anxious, defective, inadequate—and always embarrassed over his blindness. That was why he did more pushups, practiced harder, and ran further. He couldn't believe he'd actually thought the word *blindness*. He absolutely despised, cursed, and detested that word and never uttered it aloud.

In some supernatural way, Matt knew his essence, his principles, his very faith were all being tested. It went all the way back to the day when he and Juan were rescued by the mysterious, funny, and unbelievably beautiful woman. From that day, he hadn't been able to bring himself to think about any other lass.

Now he stood beside Miss Guided, right now, so close he could actually feel her warm, soft hand. He felt his heart begin to race and his face to flush. He hoped his sidekick wasn't watching him take her hand. As Matt held her soft hand in his, so stiffly and carefully, like something fragile that might break, he wondered what she was feeling.

He was so close he could look into her glowing face. He said softly, "Michala, that is a beautiful name. Michala, it sounds angelic."

Yeah, it's angelic all right, Kicker thought with a snicker. *If only you knew how angelic!*

"Still," Matt told her, "if you prefer to be called Miss Guided, Miss Guided it shall be. I like it."

A loud commotion alarmed them. Matt reluctantly let go of Michala's hand and turned to face his sidekick.

"Kicker, would you look around and tell me if the men have guns? Wild Bill didn't allow firearms to be carried in town."

Juan scanned the crowd and said, "That's a negative, Mano. I see no guns in the open. The holsters are all empty."

"Good." Matt sighed with relief. "If there's any trouble, we'll at least have a fighting chance with our karate training."

"Si, si, Mano," Kicker agreed. "I think you're right. But we're gonna need to be foxy in how we cover for your super-sonar vision. I don't want any banditos getting scared of you and chickening out without first a good, fun fight."

"Thanks, Kicker. Only you would see it like that."

"Now, boys, we're here for business—not to frolic." The angel looked down the street. "Something's happenin' over there."

The altercation arose over the vulgar painting that hung over the entry to The Bull's Head Saloon. The town Marshal, James Butler Hickok, also called Wild Bill, stepped up and planted both of his calf-hide boots firmly on the ground below the sign. His six-foot frame was perfectly proportioned, wide-shouldered with a lean waist. His long, straw-colored hair fell past his broad shoulders, and his steely gray-blue eyes held the expression of a raging bull.

Most threatening were the twin Colt 45s hanging high around his midsection. They hung backward with the handles facing forward. He wore them high up without a holster, held in place with a sash, because he could draw them much faster. And just in case, for close-in fighting, he kept a large sheathed knife strapped across his belly.

The saloon's owner, Texan Phil Cole, again refused to remove the bull painting. A swarm of incensed Texas cowboys and mean cattlemen united to support Phil Cole. A separate bunch assembled to back the Marshal.

Hickok scowled at Cole as his leathery hands opened and closed just below his handcrafted, ivory-handled revolvers. "Cole, you mad dawg, you've interrupted mi poker game. This is yer last warnin'. Take down that raw slop ya call a painting so I can get back to mi game."

Cole's olive green eyes narrowed. "Hickok, it ain't a picture of a bull. It's a portrayal of you. And I don't care what you say, it's gonna stay right where I hanged it!"

Hickok shook his head slowly as he peered down at Cole. "Don't git on yer high horse and git all stubborn now."

Matt listened to the exchange between Hickok and Cole. He tilted toward Juan's ear and whispered, "Cole shouldn't be tempting fate. Hickok knows how to use a gun, and he knows how to fight."

"Cool!" Kicker's face glowed with excitement. "That's what I wanted to hear!"

Cole pretended to turn away, but instead he reached behind his back and quickly pulled out a pistol hidden in the small of his back.

Bill noted the second-rate over-used chicanery. As swift as a stroke of lightning, Hickok's hawk-eyes bore down hard on Cole. He grabbed both 45s, and fired, blowing two mammoth holes in Cole's gut.

Cole's face contorted, then conflicted between pain and the fear of hell. He fell to his knees, then the rest of the way to the dirt, face-down, stone dead.

Wild Bill blew the wisps of smoke curling from the barrels of his irons. He strolled over to Cole's saloon and ripped down the painting, sneering at Cole's backers and daring them to try and stop him.

Matt drew closer and bumped into a hangman's platform.

"'Ey Mano," Juan snickered from behind. "You don't want to get caught hanging around here."

"Hush, Kicker," Matt whispered. "We aren't secure here."

They hid behind the scaffold and caught sight of Wild Bill as he, saloon owner Carl Mann, and some others turned and walked down the street, then disappeared around the corner. The gathering quickly shifted, thinned, and dissolved away as they all went back into their favorite gambling joints.

CHAPTER TWENTY-EIGHT

Two Twos and a Pretty Queen

The threesome from the future ran down the clay road of Main Street through the brawling town of Deadwood. As they ran, Matt realized they needed more suitable attire.

"What Kicker and I need," Matt said, "is a change of clothes or maybe a long coat. These sissy duds obviously will not do. We need to try and blend in better with the times."

"Yeah," Juan agreed. "Miss Guided looks good. I'm very dashing and debonair. But, with that jellyfish-colored wardrobe you're dressed in, you need lots of help."

"Thanks, Kicker. I don't know what this world would be like without you. But, I'm optimistic someday I'll have the good fortune to find out."

"Mano," Juan rejoined with a mocking shake of the head. "Without your amigo, you'd be as lost as a bat with 20-20 vision."

The earthly angel giggled at Juan's flippancy. She spotted an eccentric-looking man with a small chicken cage stationed alongside of Deadwood's store.

"Here's a market, Mr. Cheat. Turn to the right."

They pushed through a door with a dinging little bell hanging on it and went inside.

Coming from the bright outside to the dark inside, Matt could see nothing again. He stood for a minute trying to give the impression that everything was fine.

RE-DEAL

"Wow, Mano, we've hit the jackpot." Juan was surprised to see so many things stuffed into one small shop. "This puny store is crammed to the brim with everything from pink pantyhose for you to macho pants for me." Kicker continued to search the shop. In the corner he noted a big bed with an umbrella looking thing. "If you need your beauty rest, Mr. Cheat, there's a large four-poster bed with a top."

The wrinkled face of the proprietor looked like a weathered saddle. Standing behind his counter piled high with totes, tools, and toys, his foul-smelling two-cent cigar dangling from his lips, he peered at the three browsers.

Matt detested shopping for provisions or anything else. Besides, in places like this he was always getting yelled at for running into things. "Miss Guided, Kicker and I hate to shop. Would you please go and try to find some more fitting clothes for us?"

"Sure," Michala nodded. "Happy to."

The angel advanced through the stuffed small shop, scanning here and there. In no time, she returned with her arms piled with personals and laid the clothes on the counter.

"Here we go, boys. For you, Juan, I found a dark blue denim shirt and dungarees. And Matt, for you I located a slick pair of black pants, a white studded shirt with a black ribbon to tie around yer collar, and a nice long black frock coat. And for both of my fellows, I retrieved a pair of boots and black felt cowboy hats."

"You're amazing, Miss Guided." Matt held the boots up and squinted. "These look like they'll fit me perfectly."

"Yep," Michala said with a slight tilt of her head. "I reckon they should." She held up the boots she found for Juan and asked, "Mr. Storekeeper, is it true if I buy one boot for the price of both, I get the second one for free?"

Matt thought this over for a second. When he realized what she'd said, he chuckled. This happy queen of cheerfulness really made him laugh. She brought joy into his life even when things were so bleak.

The shopkeeper leaned across his counter close to Miss Guided. "Hey, Filly, how'd ya like a soft, horse-hair bed with a canopy?"

"'Ey, store man," Juan spoke up with a sly snort. "What kind of fools do you take us for? We'll take the bed, but you can keep the can-a-pee. We have no need for that. Besides, we make our own."

Matt laughed. He turned to the storekeeper and said, "Excuse us, Mister. We need no bed or pee. But we'd like to pay for this stuff."

The shopkeeper bit down hard on his stogy and glared at his customers.

Matt pulled out his roll of bills and removed a twenty-dollar note and slapped it down on the rickety counter. The storekeeper's eyes narrowed with skepticism. He snatched the currency and studied it.

"It ain't no good!" he snarled. "Can't accept toy money." He ripped the paper money in half and barked, "This blunt is bogus."

He jerked his sawed-off double-barreled shotgun from beneath the counter and pointed it at Matt. "Ya'll pay with gold, or ya'll put those fine garments back right fast!"

Juan realized their twentieth-century currency was no good back here.

"We'll be back for the clothes later." He turned to Matt. "Come on, Mano. Follow me." He shoved his amigo outside, then pulled a nickel from his pocket and started flipping and catching it. "Guess what? Our money is no good in this century. The suspicious weasel thinks it's counterfeit."

"Oh," said Miss Guided, "what a silly oversight."

"I can't believe it." Like Juan, Matt thumped his forehead with his palm. "How stupid of me! I never thought about that."

As the three decided what to do, Juan leaned against a little structure flipping his coin. He smelled something stinky. "What's that rank smell?"

RE-DEAL

He turned around and saw he was standing next to a small structure with a cut-out of a quarter moon over the door. Juan opened the door and searched inside and saw a brown basket full of corncobs and a seat with two holes side by side.

"'Ey Mano," Juan nodded, "it's a double-seater outhouse. This is really an up-town plumbing fixture. Where I grew up, we never had more than one hole. Mano, if you ever want to visit this fancy place, mention my name, and you'll get a good seat."

"I'm gonna give you a kick in the seat," Matt said, amazed at his friend's continued silliness. "Now let's get back to the problem at hand."

"Si, si, Mr. Cheat." Kicker stretched to snatch his nickel but missed. He watched as the coin bounced from his hand and into one of the odorous holes.

"Mano." Juan looked back toward Matt and said, "Let me have some of that worthless cash, a couple hundred dollars will do."

"Do we have time for this? Are you trying to set me up again?"

"'Ey Mano, you know your bro." Juan grinned. "Of course I'm trying to set you up."

Miss Guided could feel a joke coming their way. She cocked her hat-covered head and asked, "What's all the money for, Kicker?"

"Yeah," Matt agreed with feigned exasperation. "What's the cash for?"

"Well, Mano," Kicker explained with a barely-controlled snicker. "I'm gonna toss the pieces of money down the smelly pit, of course."

"What?" Matt's burnt eyes popped with surprise at that revelation. "Now why would you throw good cash down there?"

"Mano," Juan said with a got-ya grin. "You don't think I'm crazy enough to splash around in the smelly antique toilet just for a pitiful nickel, do you?"

The amused angel's eyes sparkled with amazement. "He has become such a humorous human. He cracks me up."

"He's cracked all right," Matt agreed. "Now, let's all look around town and try to see how we can earn some money fast. Our big problem is we have no acceptable greenbacks to even enter a small game with."

"Yeah." The undercover angel looked around. "I don't even see an oinker's ear ta construct a silk satchel out of."

Over the hill the orange-yellow sun cast long shadows as it started to set.

"We must get movin'." The lady from paradise pointed toward the setting, golden sun. "It's getting late."

The bright evening light that mirrored off Matt's brilliant gold buckle temporarily blinded Juan.

"I've got it." Juan held up his hand, blocking the bright reflection. "Mano, maybe you could hock your great grandfather's gold belt buckle or use it as security for your initial bet."

"I hate the darn thing anyhow. I don't care if I lose it." Matt shook his head. "But it's the only thing my family ever had that's worth anything." He took a deep breath. "And my dad always wore it. However, I can't think of anything better. So, does anyone have any suggestions where we should start?"

Michala and Juan looked around the now-quiet streets of Deadwood. Juan spotted the same odd-looking man he had seen before they rushed into the store. Except now the scrappy chap had three playing cards on top of the small chicken coop with a bird inside. A dirty cowboy with a crooked nose stared at the three cards. Juan aimed a finger toward the man across the street.

"Miss Guided, look over there. Do you see what I see?"

"Oh yeah, Mr. Cheat." Her hat bobbed up and down as she spoke. "There's a funny-lookin' squirt of a fellow with a skinny little chicken head and a mouth that seems to stretch from ear ta ear."

RE-DEAL

"That's right. Mano, he's doing your three card trick. Since you know how it's done, you should be able to whip him good."

"Look, Kicker." Miss Guided pointed. "It appears that the cowboy has just earned a Rhode Island Red from that there senseless chicken-head. Oh, and I should warn you, Mr. Cheat, in contrast to the others, this cowboy has a holster with a firearm strapped around him."

"Unbelievable!" Matt's eyes widened with excitement. "Just the way my dad read it to me. That's Canada Bill Jones, the snazziest three-card monte pitcher back here in the Old West."

He faced Michala. "As Kicker well knows from watching my card-cheating exhibition, three-card monte is like the shell game. Except in this confidence game, instead of trying to keep track of a pea, the gullible dupe tries to pursue a specific card. My dad read many books to me about Bill and the way he worked this scam. Look around, Miss Guided; do you see Canada Bill's menacing capper, George Devol? He's bulky and hard-featured with scars like intersecting railroad tracks all over his bald head."

"I'm puzzlin' about somethin', Matt." She cocked her head and asked, "Why would someone be hawkin' baseball caps back here in Deadwood?"

"Oh no, Miss Guided. A capper is a secret partner who's in collusion with the confidence man. They work together in an attempt to try and entice the gullible pigeons into slapping down their cash."

"It's very peaceable out here now," the guardian said as she looked about the now-quiet town. "And I see no one like you described."

As Miss Guided and Juan scanned the street ahead, one person dipped back down behind a watering trough. Damen Cypher listened carefully to what Matt and the alien woman were up to.

"Are you sure?

"There is only that there same armed cowboy with that sorry-lookin' crooked nose I mentioned previous."

"'Ey Mano," Juan asked. "Are you ready for some action? It appears that busted-nose cowboy just won some money and Canada Bill's timepiece. The cowboy is whooping it up; he's smiling and holding up the cash and watch for us to see. There's one other thing. It looks as though his right coat pocket is weighted down with another gun or something else heavy."

"That's obviously not Devol," Matt said. "The description sounds more like Broken-Nose Jack Macaw. He was the coward who put a bullet in the back of Wild Bill Hickok's head. Whoever it is, I'm cocksure certain he's working with Canada Bill. They're hoping we're chumps and will step over and engage them. Let's go, Kicker. Take me over there. But please cover for me. I don't want them to notice that I use my head to bash open new doorways where there once was a wall."

"No problem. I won't tip them off and let them know you can stop trees, trains, and walls with only your whiskered face."

Matt wanted to give the notion he was just another pigeon ready to be plucked. He sauntered over and removed his buckle from around his waist. He told the chicken-headed man, "I have no coin. But I do have this rare, priceless buckle I will stake." He handed over his buckle for examination.

Bill grabbed the gold card buckle. He bobbed it in his hand, testing its weight and feel. "Now that's an impressive buckle," Canada said. "If it's not colored lead, but real plum beaten gold, I'll accept it." He observed the card figures on the buckle. "Aces and eights? You better do better than that in this town."

Matt nodded his head. "I hope to." He placed the buckle on the rooster's box. "This game looks pretty simple and honest. I believe I might be able to follow the card."

He pushed his family treasure closer to Canada Bill. "I'll offer to wager this precious gold buckle. It's very old and is worth 4,000 dollars."

Canada Bill guffawed at the idea this sucker would believe he would be so stupid as to put up four big ones

RE-DEAL

against this small scab of gold. He grabbed the buckle from off his chicken pen and handed it to his partner and asked, "Broken-Nose, how much do ya think this weighs?"

"Stranger," Jack hefted the buckle and said with an insulting scoff, "you's dumb. You gots snookered." He cackled harder. "Ain't no more than five ounces a gold here."

As soon as Matt heard Canada Bill call the cowboy Broken-Nose, one of his father's Old West stories was corroborated for him. He realized he was living a piece of history. He was standing next to the man who would be the assassin of Wild Bill Hickok. Matt could hardly believe he was coming across all these outlaws from the past.

Canada Bill's smile evaporated, and he turned serious. "My only bet is a hundred against the jewelry."

"Deflation, Mr. Matt," the woman observed with a nod. "Bear in mind that yer precious metal isn't gonna go as far here back in the days of yer past."

Canada Bill wondered what the heck this sweet little lass meant by that statement. He shook the confusion from his brain and began the swindle.

"Two twos and a pretty queen." In his squeaky, boyish voice, Canada bellowed out, "Keep your eye on the fair ruler; she will win for you!"

"Oh, Mr. Bill—"

"Please be quiet, Miss Guided," Matt whispered as he placed his finger in front of his lips. "I need to focus."

Canada Bill started to sound like a high-dollar auctioneer.

"Here you are, Slick." Again Canada displayed for the stranger two twos and a queen. "This queen of hearts is the winning card."

Canada glanced up into the newcomer's eyes and was surprised to see the outsider was looking off to the side. He wondered why this stranger was looking away from him and not at his hands. The man's weird, crooked eyes bothered him, but he wasn't sure why. Again he flourished his cards.

"Here we go, Slick. Now here, now there. Keep your eye on the pretty queen! It's my regular trade to move my hands quicker than the eye. Now you pick, Slick!"

Canada watched as the stranger slammed his hand over the queen. His eyes flashed a tinge of panic.

"Oh, now, you've got to let the professional handle the cards, my fine young man. Please let me turn that card over for you."

"If you don't mind, I'll turn it, Canada Bill Jones."

Bill Jones' eyes flew open at hearing his full name used. He stuttered, "Wh-wh-why, I have a notion you must call everyone that."

There was no way Matt was going to permit this expert monte-thrower to turn the card over and switch it for a loser.

"I'll turn it over for you, Canada Bill."

Matt flipped the card over to reveal the winning queen. Canada couldn't believe this city-dressed stranger with the crooked eyes indeed won from him—the best monte pitcher this side of the Mississippi.

But he was even more startled that the stranger knew the full name he never used. Canada reluctantly paid the hundred dollar bet. He wondered if this crooked-eyed stranger was some kind of wizard who could see right through the cards or read his brain. Canada Bill managed to chuckle at the conjurer's incredible luck as the hen in his box squawked as it had just laid an egg.

Kicker pointed at the chicken and said with a chuckle, "It looks like Canada Bill's gonna be a papa."

Matt grinned at Kicker as he left his winnings on the box next to the buckle. "I'll play again, this time for two hundred dollars."

Bill decided it was time to draw the sucker in for the sting. He covertly winked at his partner, and Jack Macaw subtly nodded back. Canada turned around and beckoned to all. He yelled, "Fortune seekers gather round. In a moment Canada Bill offers a fine, rare, gold belt buckle to the quick-eyed that can find the baby."

RE-DEAL

As his partner barked, Jack grabbed the winning queen and bent one corner right in front of the winning, sissified stranger and gave him a knowing smile.

Just as I believed, Matt thought. *These two scoundrels are working together.*

Jack Macaw quickly returned the marked card back on top of the chicken box. Canada Bill turned around and went through the same spiel as before. But this time his chagrin turned to fear when Slick didn't fall for the bent card and again won. He wondered how this stranger kept winning. The weird-eyed man never once even looked at his hands—he just blankly stared off to the side. Canada reluctantly pulled two hundred dollars from his boot and paid the foreigner.

Canada looked up at the stranger. "Congratulations, and here's back yer fine buckle." He stood up to leave and announced to the crowd, "That's all for today folks. Canada Bill's not feeling too good."

He decided he needed to warn his partner George Devol about this wizard with the weird eyes. He grabbed his chicken box and prepared to leave.

Matt thought about Devol's description of Canada as having a chicken head.

"Canada Bill Jones." Matt grinned. "I'll just take the winnings and let you retire with your radiant hen. She's a beauty."

"Yeah," Juan said with a laugh, "you and your nagging hen will make a nice wedded pair."

Michala had to join in on the merriment. The whimsical lady lifted her blooming bonnet three inches above her blonde head. "Oh Mr. Bill, before ya go, if ya can guess how many eggs I have under my hat, I'll give ya both of them."

Canada stopped and paused in rapt attention. He was always a sucker for another man's game, and when it came to a beautiful lass, Canada knew he was a sucker's sucker.

"Miss, I'll make you a speculation. I'll give you a hundred dollars for every egg under that colorful hat."

The guardian angel gradually lowered her hat and then languidly raised it.

Canada was stupefied when he saw two eggs at rest on her lovely head. He stared as the lass removed the eggs and handed him the pair. He took them with a tip of the hat and said, "Thanks, Ma'am."

He wasn't gonna stiff this pretty lassie. Canada reached into his pocket and removed two fresh new hundred-dollar bills and handed them over.

"Why thank ya, Mr. Bill. Please enjoy yer breakfast." She gave him a sincere nod. "I pray that yer not an egg-gnostic."

The boys laughed.

Canada Bill grabbed his crate and left. He had enough of this craziness. As he split he told the small crowd, "All goes to prove Canada Bill runs an honest game."

The assembly nosily watched the defeated Canada Bill's hasty retreat.

Matt put his valuable family heirloom back on his belt. He turned to the miracle-working lady and stared in wonder. *There's something about this funny lady I truly love.*

Thrilled at their first success, Matt took her hand and said, "Like I said, there aren't many like you anymore."

"So true." Kicker said with a twinkle in his eye. "So true."

Matt, Juan, and Michala dashed back to the dry-goods store and paid for their clothes. The boys moved to the back corner of the cramped store and slipped them on. Matt was glad to get rid of the sissy clothes that the spooky Doctor Cypher had given him. He imagined with this new garb he looked like the traditional gambler with his hat, white shirt, ribbon tie, black frock coat, and his handlebar mustache. He was ready to play the part of a gambler—at least he hoped he was.

CHAPTER TWENTY-NINE

Dead Man's Hand

After they changed, Matt and Juan rejoined Michala out front.

"My–my–my, ain't ya both a fine lookin' pair all gussied up."

"Thanks, Miss Guided." Matt smoothed his shirt. "Everything fits perfectly. Now, how much do we have to gamble with?"

"Well, let's see." She counted the cash. "After payin' for the clothes, ya have a little less than five hundred bucks as yer grub-worm."

"That's grubstake, Miss Guided," Kicker corrected. "I ate the grub-worm." He turned to Matt. "How are you seeing all this?"

"Fortunately I don't have to see. My dad taught me all these old hustles. He also read to me about Wild Bill Hickok and the notorious Carl Mann's Saloon here in Deadwood. Do you see where it is?"

Juan looked around the active town. Now that the time was getting close to dusk, he noticed the rowdies were squirming out of the woodwork. Then he spotted the famous saloon across from the Marshal's jailhouse.

"I see it. This way."

Matt and Michala hurried down the noisy clanking boardwalk after him.

"I've heard rumblings about that dirty little place. And this ain't the best day ta visit." The angel wavered in front of the entrance. "Here we are, Mr. Cheat—Carl Mann's Saloon. Here's yer pathfinder, Matt."

"Thanks, Funny Lady." Matt accepted the solid metal cane and hooked it around his wrist.

"Now, Mr. Cheat." The incognito angel took Matt's hands in hers and squeezed. "Matthew, please do be mindful of the ticklish calamities or grief that can happen in these uncivil neighborhoods."

With her delicate hands wrapped around his large ones—something he'd dreamed about—he felt like he could leap over Kicker's outhouse with a single bound. He tried to appear nonchalant as he squeezed back.

With a combination of shyness and excitement, he promised, "I'll be careful, Funny Lady."

"We'll watch your back, Mano," Juan said. "Remember, no fighting fun without your friend."

"Thanks, Kicker. You're a good man."

Matt hesitated in front of the doorway. He sucked air deeply into his lungs, then slowly let it out. He wanted to prove that he could take care of himself. If maybe one day, just possibly, he could date Miss Guided, he wanted her to go out with him because he was a man she could respect—not because she pitied him.

Matt felt a drop of sweat trickle down the back of his neck. The butterflies were working overtime in his stomach, and fear shot through him. Just as quickly, he repressed it. He remembered his theater training with Pastor Steve and assumed the character of a confident man, something he hadn't been sure he could do. Then he pushed his way through the swinging doors with his friends close behind.

Across the way, Damen watched the group disappear into Carl Mann's Saloon. Dressed in scratchy, stiff nineteenth-century clothes he'd filched from a clothesline, he felt less conspicuous but more agitated. When that monte pitcher had used the name Broken-Nose, Damen knew he'd found a confederate. And now he was between two buildings standing in a small box to guard his feet from rats, conspiring with Jack Macaw.

RE-DEAL

Damen had a strategy, though first he needed to thin down the odds.

"That's the one." He shoved a finger in the direction Matt had gone. "Take care of him!"

Macaw nodded his understanding and accepted a shiny gold object as payment. "I understand."

Once inside, Matt blinked hard as he tried to get his poor vision adjusted to the dark saloon. The light from a wall sconce cast an ominous shadow across the grubby floorboards. The bar was foggy with smoke and smelled of unwashed bodies and cheap whisky. On the floor, trails of sawdust served to sop up the spit, tar, and chaw. The eyes of a large rat reflected the glare from the wall sconce as it rushed across the stuffy room.

At a long bar stood Texas cattle barons, foul-smelling buffalo hunters, blood-stained trappers, and gun-fighting gamblers, all with empty holsters —chewing tobacco, gulping whisky, and spitting. Wild Bill Hickok, the only armed person in this dark, dirty tavern sat at a table relaxing from his recent business with Phil Cole.

Hickok called out in a Southern drawl mixed with an odd accent, "You, stranger!"

Matt looked over.

"Yes, you with the crooked eyes. If ya done come in peace, ya kin check yer guns with mi deputy."

The thick smoke burned Matt's eyes and irritated his throat. He blinked hard, and then turned his head and squinted out of the sides of his eyes to try and catch another glimpse of the legendary Marshal.

"No gun, Mr. Hickok." Matt held his cane up for the Marshal to see. "I only carry this here little walking stick."

"Looks harmless enough." Hickok gave an approving nod.

Matt turned to Kicker. "Why don't you go do something useful, like pray I don't get my head blown off or something worse?"

"Si, si, jefe, I'll do it. They might make me clean up the gory mess."

"Just get over there." Matt shook his head. "And keep an eye on Miss Guided for me."

Matt turned away and casually worked his way over toward the poker table, patting his pocket with the nearly five hundred dollars he had to gamble with.

Matt understood now why Miss Guided had taken them to that old theater. It was time to put Steve's acting lessons into play.

He idly approached Wild Bill's table. "Good afternoon, gentlemen." Matt tipped his black hat. "Does anyone have any qualms with playing cards with a chap who carries a painless, unavailing, walking stick rather than a firearm? Can't see worth a darn, but I sure enjoy a friendly game of poker."

"No," Hickok said, "not at all. As long as yer blunt is green or gold, we don't stress if ya haul a cane or wear bloomers."

Matt had two burdens—first to win, second to get the Marshal away from that deadly table. He kept looking at the doorway behind Hickok trying to make him nervous. He had to get Wild Bill out of that fatal chair before Broken-Nose Jack Macaw walked through and blasted a hole in the back of his head.

Matt removed a small bill from his roll of cash and decided to try on one of those Southern accents he'd learned from Steve. He nodded toward the bar and said, "Mr. Hickok, let's step over yonder and set a spell. I'll dicker ya a shot."

"What are ya talkin' like that fir?" Hickok asked with a snort. "Ya sound really stupid! And no thanks, keep yer drink. I'm not gonna stop mi game again."

Whoa, Matt thought. *So much for acting lessons*. Again he tried to make Hickok nervous by looking over his shoulder to the door.

Hickok looked behind him and puzzled about the doorway the new guy kept gawking at. After a brief hesitation he turned back. "Besides, I don't never leave in

RE-DEAL

the midst of a game." He nodded toward the man's gold buckle. "Now that rich harness ya got there makes me think ya might be worth a gainful game of draw. Why is aces and eights worth flappin' over?"

"Aces and eights is called the Dead Man's Hand," Matt told him ominously. "And I guarantee you don't want to know how it received that name."

"I like it," Hickok said with a nod. "The Dead Man's Hand. Sounds prophetic. I'll give ya a twenty dollar gold piece for it."

It's prophetic all right, Matt thought. He wondered if he might be able to scare Hickok into shifting to another chair.

"No, I'll keep it. I trust you would find this buckle to be very doomful. Aces and eights was named after the shooting death of a famous, longhaired lawman in Deadwood born with the name James Butler."

James Butler? How does this outsider know my given name? He must have picked it up from somewhere, James Butler Hickok thought to himself. He shrugged the stranger off as just another lucky nut.

One of the players, the rich Captain Masse stood up. "Stranger, take my chair. I'm cashing in."

"What longhaired lawman?" Carl Mann reclaimed his seat at the table. "Marshal Hickok's the only longhaired lawman we know, and he's still not dead."

"What does ya mean, still not dead?" Hickok snapped.

"Just a for instance, Marshal."

"Marshal Hickok," Matt tried again. "I'd be glad to take that seat with the door to my back."

"I'll keep it, as it's brought me some luck today."

A trapper dressed in duds stiff with the dried blood and guts of his quarry strode up to the table. The stench was so overwhelming that Hickok covered his nose, pulled his gun, and pointed it at the new arrival.

"Not you, Dirty-Face Jones. Rules of the table, ya had ta bathed within a year before yer allowed ta squat at mi table."

"Now, tha's not very neighbor-like a ya. I'll go's back and drink."

Dirty-Face pouted and turned back toward the bar. Everyone there moved away as he planted himself with a sulk.

Matt pulled up a chair and squeezed in beside Hickok. Juan and Michala stood back in the shadows and watched the play.

"Let mi acquaint ya," Hickok said. He pointed with his gun toward the scroungy players, all with mustaches and dark suspicious eyes. His Adam's apple jerked.

"Right here are some good reasons I make 'em check their guns. Ya met the owner of saloon number ten, Carl Mann." He moved clockwise around the table. "That's Charlie Rich. Right there is Dark-Alley Jim, and there you got Six-Toed Pete. As mean with the cards as with the guns, these. Watch out for yer skin, Mister ...?" Hickok stared hard at the stranger. "What do you answer to, stranger?"

What a bunch of stupid names, Matt thought. He wanted a cool name, though he knew he'd be a fool to use the name Mr. Cheat. He searched his mind for something really clever. Then an old martial arts movie came to mind.

"Um-uh-um, you can call me The Karate Kid."

In the back, Juan rolled his eyes at Michala while the others looked blankly at the newcomer.

Hickok dealt the cards and said with a chuckle, "Cruddy Kid? Ya look too clean ta be kin ta Dirty-Face."

"No relation," Matt said with an inaudible laugh.

He received his five cards and his sensitive fingertips lightly touched the faces. He then raised the cards close to his eyes to try and get a glimpse. Between the two sensations, he could usually get an idea of what the cards were. Matt had started to wonder if he could do this without using his cheating skills. However, he knew he had to try.

Standing to the side, Juan soon grew bored watching the surly gamblers as they played. He was trying to understand how it was possible that he was here in the former, the past, the previous. And now he was presently watching the past pass by again.

RE-DEAL

"Michala, how is it possible within a second or two that we can be in two different centuries? Does it have something to do with what that other angel called traveling outside-of-time?"

"Yep, that's it."

Kicker was not satisfied with the short answer. He prodded. "Please explain that."

Michala focused her blue eyes on Juan's brown eyes. "Outside-of-time is where a instant is as a thousand years and a thousand years is but a twinkling. That is why the Creator can know what everyone is doin' at all times." The angel pointed back over her shoulder. "That, my little friend, is why this century and that one we came from back yonder are no longer disconnected; they can both simultaneously and at the same time be right here and now. Got it?"

Kicker stood there by himself, stunned. He tried to comprehend what he had just heard. The response had sailed like a shot right over his mystified mind. He wanted to ask Michala more, however he could tell the angel was not eager and this was not the time.

He simply said, "You bet. I got all of it."

After hours of play, Matt had accumulated a collection of odd bank notes and actual gold and silver coins. He noticed the other big winner was a dude called Six-Toed Pete.

Matt was thunderstruck at how rapidly this last pot had leaped into the thousands. He'd bet his four twos to the hilt, yet every time he raised, the Six-Toed character would raise him back even stronger. Matt wondered if he should call Pete's last raise, but he suspected something was wrong here—Pete seemed to have a trick up his sleeve.

Matt's suspicions were confirmed when his sharp ears heard a short, tiny squeaking sound, an ill-defined little mechanical noise. Because of his poor vision, Matt's hearing had become so keen he could hear a flea burp from within a dog's ear. He could tell this squeak didn't belong in this backward place—the sound came from a mechanism used to bring cards in and out of a sleeve.

He asked, "What is that tiny sound, Mr. Hickok?"

"Beg pardon? What sound?"

"A holdout device is in play." Matt twitched his head in the direction of Six-Toed Pete's coat sleeve, and then pointed his finger.

Pete's face went slack.

Hickok followed the pointing finger. In one ferocious move he stretched across the table. He grabbed Pete's arm, pulled a blade from within the sheath around his waist, and held the gleaming Bowie knife to the cheater's throat.

"Pete," Hickok ordered. "Roll up yer sleeve or die!"

"Please don't use that blade on me, Mr. Hickok." Pete yanked up his sleeve, revealing the cheating device. "Take my gain, and I'll give ya this holdout, too."

Hickok stood up and looked Pete up and down, judging his worth. He decided the scoundrel didn't merit a place in his mellow town. He shoved him away from the table, drew his revolver, and fired at his feet. Pete hopped and danced toward the door.

"Now," Hickok bellowed, "get outta mi town before yer name's No-Toes Pete!"

After Pete flew through the flaps, Hickok blew the smoke from the barrel of his gun and returned it to the sash around his middle, then sat back down in his chair. He sighed.

"Let us resume our peaceful attitude, boys." He nodded over at the sharp-eared fellow. "Much obliged, Cruddy Kid."

Hickok pushed half of Pete's money over to the Kid and said, "Rules of the table—catch a cheater, half the pot is yours."

Nearly an hour following the banishment of the fool Six-Toed Pete, Dark-Alley Jim once more picked up the cards and began shuffling them. He passed the cards to Carl for the cut. He placed the halves back together and started to deal around the table.

Matt cocked his head slightly to observe Dark-Alley's deal through the sides of his eyes. He'd been following Dark-Alley's dealing action, and he was certain this surly cowboy was using

RE-DEAL

some kind of reflector to catch sight of the cards as he dealt them. And since there was nothing on the table to hide a mirror in, the shiner was most likely hidden in Jim's hand or, more likely, connected to a ring. Matt decided, since Hickok was the only one with a gun, to risk exposing another fraud.

"Dark Alley, I prefer a smooth, quick pass from a dealer," he said.

Dark-Alley stopped the deal and stared at Cruddy. "A young newcomer who tries to mark the cards with his snotty nose ought not to be so picky, Kid."

"Hey, you're crazy. I don't mark with snot." He nodded his head, tipping his hat toward the shiner man. "Dark-Alley Jim has a shiner in his hand or on a ring."

Hickok's eyes narrowed, and he moaned in aggravation. "Another?"

Dark-Alley's eyes widened in fear. He tensed as Hickok launched his large, firm mass across the table with his gleaming Bowie knife.

Hickok barked, "It's gettin' so as a man can't have any peace a mind with his poker associates! Now show me that ring, Jim!"

"It's nothing! I received it from my lady!"

Hickok pressed the knife to Dark Alley's throat, and then he slammed Jim's hand down hard on the table, palm up. He found a pea-sized looking glass attached on the underside of the ring.

"Now, Jim, I bet that takes a hell of a lot of practice ta operate."

"N-n-no. I didn't know that was there!"

Hickok whipped out his weapon and snarled, "I ought ta let ya have it right between yer eyeballs just for insultin' mi intelligence."

He fired at Dark-Alley's feet and made him prance toward the door. "Jim, ya employed all yer luckiness and all that lingers is stinkin' manure. Now unless ya want death ta be next, ya better get off where Six-Toed ran to, before I quit bein' so understandin'!"

Dark-Alley dashed through the doorway like a frightened baby otter sliding down the gorge of a great white.

"Now," Hickok reloaded his revolvers then turned back to the table, "kin we please get down to a good ol' game based on an honest man's skills of concentration?"

"Yes, sir. I trust we can; these others seem to be clean." Matt nodded in the direction of the remaining gamblers.

The players all stared, puzzled at this spooky intruder, as Hickok slowly eased himself back into his chair. Once again he split the cash with the alert, dull-eyed, stranger. Matt again tried to get Hickok away from that chair.

"You're not very observant, Mr. Hickok," Matt said with a disapproving shake of his head. "It's pretty bad of you as the Marshal to let us get drawn into playing poker with these cheats."

Hickok pulled on his goatee with his mouth agape.

"But I really think, Mr. Hickok, we ought to have a drink. I'll buy. Or maybe we should rest a spell." Matt hoped he could convince Hickok to move out of the chair that would otherwise be the place he died.

"Are you batty? Rest? From a poker game! Stop before winning all mi money back?"

"Yes, sir. Just step over across the room."

"Will ya rest yer flappin' mouth and give us a chance to catch up with ya," Hickok snapped. "I never seen yer kind o' luck and with two cheaters too!"

He handed Matt the deck. "Now deal the cards and from now on, no nose contact!"

Matt hoped Hickok was not so dumb as to believe he was actually marking cards with his snot. He passed the deck over to Carl Mann.

"Sorry, it's Carl's deal."

Everyone made a contribution to the pot, then Carl Mann reshuffled the cards and dealt five-card draw. They all studied their cards, and Charlie Rich made the opening bet. After the first round of betting, Hickok drew two cards and settled back into his chair.

RE-DEAL

Jack Macaw sauntered in through the swinging doors and calmly meandered toward the game. Without warning he pulled a pistol from inside his shabby coat and trained it toward the weird-eyed stranger.

Juan spotted Macaw pull a gun.

"Mano, duck!" Juan yelled in alarm. "It's Broken-Nose! He's got a gun; duck!"

A deafening explosion erupted at the same moment Matt was blown out of his chair and bit the dust. Everyone in the saloon jumped.

Broken-Nose moved and leveled his firearm on Hickok. "Welcome to hell, Wild Bill!" Again he squeezed the trigger, and his pistol fired with a second thunderous blast.

Hickock's head banged on the table, and his body slowly slid to the floor.

CHAPTER THIRTY

Phantom of the Card Table

Mass confusion reigned as everyone rushed to see the spectacle of fresh dead bodies.

Through the group of gamblers, Juan saw his amigo fall to the floor. He felt the familiar hollow of fear in his gut every fighter has suffered with some serious loss. Then he saw the formidable Hickok fall forward dead, still gripping his cards.

"Hurry, Michala!" Juan cried. "Matt's been hit!"

Juan hurried through the mob. As he shoved his way between the stinking, sweaty bodies, he asked the angel in alarm, "Michala, the first bullet was intended for Matt! Why was that?"

Carl Mann bolted up and grabbed one of Hickok's revolvers. Carl aimed the gun at Macaw and ordered, "Drop the hardware, Broken-Nose!"

Jack dropped the gun and fell to his knees groveling. He wept hard and begged, "Don't shoot! I didn't mean—I mean—it was self-defense! Hickok kilt my brother and always threatened me too!"

Matt slowly opened his terrified eyes. As he lay still on the floor he wondered why there were two shots. His body tensed—every muscle, every fiber inside him involuntarily frozen. The assassination hadn't happened the way history was written. Why did one of those bullets have his name on it?

RE-DEAL

"That's a lie, Broken-Nose!" Matt grabbed his hat and quickly stood up from below the table. "You were paid to assassinate the town Marshal."

"What?" Jack Macaw almost passed out at the sight of the dead man rising like Lazarus. "I gots ya!"

"Tomorrow's newspaper," Matt faced the gunfighters and explained, "will spell out clearly how Jack Macaw was hired to murder Hickok for 200 ounces in gold dust." Matt remembered Kicker saying something about Macaw's coat looking like it was loaded down with something heavy. He pointed and told them, "If you search the killer, you'll find the gold in that sagging coat pocket."

"Wh-wh-what are ya sayin', Mister?" Charlie Rich stuttered. "Tomorrow's daily won't come out for another two months." He raised his hand and pointed a shaking finger at Cruddy. "I saw ya get blowed away, then get back up. And now ya knows the future. You's not human, you's is really a-a-a phantom."

"Don't be ridiculous," Matt said with a roll of the eye. "The bullet just missed me." He pointed to Carl Mann. "Check Macaw's pockets, and you'll see I know what I'm talking about."

Juan was relieved to see his friend was okay. He stepped up beside Matt and whispered, "I'm glad you're still not dead. But it's not the proper history. I'm confused Mano; the first bullet was meant for you."

"I know, Kicker. I don't get it either."

"Search the weasel!" Carl Mann ordered. "Check his pockets good!"

The bartender and two others pushed their way through the crowd and heaved Broken-Nose to his feet. They searched his pockets and found a bag of gold dust and a fancy lighter. The barkeeper tossed the goatskin bag to Charlie Rich, who snatched it from the air.

"The Cruddy Kid is right," Charlie tested the bag's weight. "It's close ta 200 ounces of dust."

"Look," Carl Mann held up a gold object. "This lighter was also in Macaw's pocket."

He examined the lighter, then looked back at Macaw. "You must have stole this here gold lighter from that rich Texas rancher. His name is here scrolled in diamonds."

"I don't like this, Mano. That's the same lighter as Damen used when Tom gave you that hotshot way back when."

"Carl," Matt asked, paralyzed with fright. "What name is on that lighter?"

"The name is Lucas McCain. He's a millionaire cattle rancher way down south."

Matt's mind filled with questions. *If this lighter is my great grandfather's down in Texas, how did this killer end up with it? But if it's the one from the future, how did it end up in Macaw's pocket?*

The superstitious gamblers were stricken with horror. Everyone in the room turned their eyes upon the Cruddy Kid. Carl Mann's face plainly expressed his confusion and bafflement. He motioned toward Jack Macaw.

"Give him a fair, impartial trial," Carl ordered. "Then hang him!" He spoke as the new law in town. "My vote is guilty!" His eyes drew down hard on the sucker. "You're a hanged man, Broken-Nose. Get him over to the platform and string him up, boys."

The bartender Harry and his helpers dragged out Broken-Nose as he screamed his innocence.

Masse shuffled over to check Hickok's body as everyone studied the Cruddy Kid with suspicion. Dirty-Face joined Captain Masse, and they respectfully lifted Hickok's body back erect in the chair, making the Marshal's last hand of cards public.

Masse saw they were aces and eights arranged in the same order as on the spooky belt buckle. He stared at the ominous hand and then at the Cruddy Kid's clasp. His gaze rose to Matt's face.

"Aces and eights, same as on yer buckle. Ya just told us how that buckle was named after a longhaired lawman."

RE-DEAL

Dirty-Face's normally companionable gray-blue eyes went wide with fright. "The feller is a phantom." His voice shook with fright.

"That's right," Captain Masse agreed. "The Cruddy Kid is the Phantom of the Card Table."

Outside the entrance, Damen had stood quietly and heard everything. Jack Macaw had failed him, and he had no mercy when he watched the fool Macaw dragged by him screaming like a baby.

During the chaos, Matt decided it was time to make their getaway.

"Kicker," Matt whispered as he sidled up next to his partner. "Can you help me pull my winnings together? I think it's time we move on."

Darn! No flipping fun? Juan wanted at least one sparring sport before they left.

Kicker quickly collected his amigo's accumulation of cash and secured it inside his coat. Then he reached behind into the small of his back and extracted his nunchakus.

Michala moved forward to join her charges. She'd stayed off to the side to give them the chance to handle the situation on their own. So far she figured they were doing fine.

"There are some weird things going on in this place," Matt whispered as he took her hands in his. "My great grandfather Lucas's gold lighter was discovered on Jack Macaw."

"Yeah." Juan was still disappointed there was no fighting. "It's the one Damen was always swiping from his father, Big Lew."

"Oh, is that so?" Michala squinted at Kicker's downcast face. "Juan, where is that delightful smile of yours?"

Juan's lips turned up on the ends as Miss Guided handed Matt his cane, and the trio stepped toward the door.

"Gentlemen," Matt said to the suspicious gunfighters. "We're going to run down to the jailhouse and get the deputy."

As they started to head out, Carl Mann and his bunch rushed over and stood in front of the doorway, obstructing their way. Carl moved forward in front of the Cruddy Kid holding Hickok's revolver. His followers stayed with Mann, blocking the exit.

"I'm the new Marshal in this here town." Carl glared at Matt. "Now ya opened up a swirl of dust, Kid."

"Yeah, Crud," the superstitious Charlie Rich agreed. "Seems to me, you opened up more secrets than a dude ought to have a right to."

"Knows the ways of the crooked and knows what's gonna happen afore it does." Dirty-Face said, "He's a definite phantom."

"Yeah." Carl waved the firearm toward Cruddy. "He's Hickok's angel of death, no doubt."

Matt's weak eyes darted here and there, trying to focus on the action. He felt like the night was about to explode all around him. *Come on, McCain. Let your training kick in. Like Sensei Murphy says, "Keep your mind clear like water but cool like ice."*

Matt slowly relaxed, and all his senses became intensely acute as he surveyed his surroundings. He gave a subtle, unnoticeable nod to his sidekick.

Juan received his amigo's miniscule signal. After a second to consider the situation, he kicked the six-shooter from Carl Mann's hand, smacking the gun across the saloon.

"Let's roll, Mr. Cheat!" Kicker whooped. "It's party time!"

Juan smacked his foot up the side of Charlie's head and spun his nunchakus. He and Matt jumped and swung, delivering blows as fast as they could throw them.

"We're having' fun now!" Kicker roared with a sunny smile.

He gave a piercing karate yell as he cracked a jaw with a sidekick while his nunchakus smashed hard across Carl Mann's mouth. He heard cusps and cavities crumble.

"Sorry!" he said with a grin. "Nothing personal, just removing a little decay!"

Everybody joined in. Brawlers used chairs as clubs, and large men fell into tables, smashing them to pieces. But the

RE-DEAL

pair from the future with their simple weapons and karate skills displayed amazing agility as they avoided fists, chairs, and bottles. The sheer number of ruffians invigorated Kicker but began to slow Matt down. He felt like his heart rate shouted above the noise of the yelling, cursing, and bashing-in of the bar.

Carl Mann spit out a half dozen teeth, then wiped blood from his lip. "I'm gonna kill that phantom!"

"There's nothing like a good brawl to finish the day off right," Juan bellowed to his bud. "I'm sure glad they consider this relaxing sport back here!"

Carl saw the phantom was exhausted, so he quickly spit out a couple more teeth, grabbed the Crud, spun him around, and landed a heavy blow to his stomach. He followed that with an upper cut to Cruddy's cheek.

The blows sent Matt flying out the door. He was exhausted, and the jolt rattled him right to his bones. He landed on his back in the hard dirt road—groaning, dazed, and confused. He tried to shake his head clear. He squeezed his eyes closed, then opened them and looked around. He could faintly see that night had fully set in with a bright moon in the sky. He could hear the loud racket of the fight still carrying on inside.

And he could swear he smelled Damen's stink oil. He shook his head again; he must be more dazed than he thought if he was imagining a smell from a century in the future.

CHAPTER THIRTY-ONE

Gold Lighter

Damen watched as Matt sailed right by him. *Good riddance to you, Magoo,* Damen thought with a snort. He slipped into the saloon, but avoided the action by staying back against the wall. Damen looked around and spotted his old man's lighter. He grabbed it and pocketed it along with some of the cash loosely spread across the filthy floor.

An immense rat was fleeing across the counter of the bar. Harry the tapster grabbed an empty whisky bottle and slapped it hard off the edge of his just-washed bar.

"Out of here," Harry screamed, "or I'll make lunch with you!"

The rat twirled through the air across the room and landed with a squeal on Damen's back as he was bent down grabbing the money. He sprung up like he was being attacked by the devil himself. The rat clawed against the back of the shirt. In a panic, Damen smashed his back hard against the wall, crushing the rodent. The monster rat fell to the floor.

I hate rats! Damen railed. He slipped out the rear and ran back to the weird blue coach. He wasn't going to be left behind here with these vile creatures. As Damen slipped down the boardwalk, he could feel the left-over rat remains dripping down the back of his scratchy shirt.

Juan executed a backward handspring off the bar onto a table. He flew high into the air and came down, issuing twin sidekicks into the faces of two barroom brawlers. As he

RE-DEAL

flipped high in the air, he thought he spotted a familiar foe. *But it can't be Damen Cypher! We left him a century in the future.*

As he tried to get a better look at the figure slipping out of the saloon through all the hubbub, Juan landed on his feet like a feline lands on all fours. *That scurrying-away weasel is Cypher's son. Or is it?* Kicker clambered to get a better view and was caught off guard by two gunfighters who grabbed him and simultaneously slugged him in both eyes. Stunned, he soared out of the saloon into the street next to his amigo Matt. Juan was followed by the crowd who also poured outside.

Matt jumped up and ran over to help his friend.

"I think I saw ..." Juan's eyes rolled back in his head, then he fell limp.

"Saw what?" Matt tried to pull his sidekick to his feet. "Kicker, can you hear me?"

Juan fell back to the ground. He rolled his eyes again and mumbled, "We're having' fun now!" He again slumped over.

"Kicker! Are you okay, buddy?"

The last determined ruffians—the spooked Charlie and the empty-mouthed Carl—came staggering after the Cruddy Kid.

"Let's kill the Crud!" Carl staggered toward the Kid.

Matt leaned Juan against a watering trough to give him time to come to his senses. Then he grabbed his cane and finished off the last two cowboys with two desperate swings of his rod. With everyone subdued, Matt slumped to the ground next to his buddy.

"'Ey Mano," Juan said with a misshapen smile. "That was a blast. I'm ready for seconds."

"What?" Matt rubbed his aching jaw. "You're crazy!"

"Yea-ha!" Michala rushed over, whooping and cheering. "That's what I say is a real hoe-down, boys! Ya both waxed down this den like King David himself!" She grabbed their grubby hats and weapons from the ground. "Now let's get a move on boys. Play time is over."

She pulled them both to their feet. She handed them their hats and weapons, then hustled them back towards her horse and carriage.

"I must be dreaming," the dazed Kicker declared. "I thought I saw that creep Damen."

"What's that, Kicker? Who did ya see?" the disguised angel asked.

"No, Kicker," Matt told his friend. "Damen was the fight we had before we left the twenty-first century."

"You must be right." Juan shook the cobwebs from his head. "Wow, I haven't had this much fun since Mr. Cheat's black belt test."

"Huh?" Matt asked with an exasperated roll of the eye. "You call this fun?"

"Yep! Hope the party isn't over yet."

"Yer silly, Kicker. You boys ain't gonna last long if all yer gonna do is fight yer way through this jaunt. Now, let's get movin'."

They hurried toward the buggy. On the way Juan spotted Macaw on the old hangman's platform, crying like a baby. Juan stopped and Matt ran right into his back.

"Kicker, use your taillights next time you're gonna stop like that."

"Si, si, Mr. Cheat. Next time I'll put on my emergency flashers." He pointed to the platform. "Mano, look over there. It's Macaw giving his final sermon on that hangman's hangout."

"Please," Macaw begged. "I'll do good! I don't wants ta see hell yet!"

Jack was pleading for one more chance so he could change and see Heaven when the trap door dropped open and he fell toward the ground.

"Oh no!" Miss Guided held her breath. "It looks like that there flimsy platform gave way!"

They all watched in shock as the body fell towards the dirt and then abruptly stopped two feet before hitting earth.

"Macaw was just hanged," Juan told his friend. "Matt, your pop would be satisfied." He turned to Michala and asked with mock gravity, "Do you think that man got hurt when that small platform fell open?"

Macaw hung there swaying with his eyes unblinking, fixed in fear.

RE-DEAL

"No, he got lucky," the angel said with an inner sorrow she attempted to conceal. "It looks like that rope around his neck broke the lost man's fall."

She sighed and thought, *Another soul for Satan.*

"Wow, Miss Guided, that was a colossal understatement," Juan said grinning. "It did more than break his fall. It broke his scrawny, immoral, villainous neck."

"Please you two," Matt said nervously. "Stop telling morbid jokes. Now let's get back to the coach, fast!"

"Si, si, jefe; be cool," Juan said with a broad smile. "It's just another bat finding his way back into hell."

As they moved down the dirt street, Hickok's body was carried past them.

Matt paused and shook his head. "I hoped to have stopped that death."

"The best intentions, Matthew." The undercover angel took one of Matt's hands and imparted a tender squeeze. "Ya gave it."

They quickly moved on down the road.

"Matthew, how much did ya win in there?"

"Not sure." Matt turned to Juan. "Kicker, do you still have the winnings?"

"You bet." Juan nodded and patted his pocket. "Right here, safe and sound."

"Before Broken-Nose busted up the game, I remember being up to around 5,000."

"Oh?" Michala said with a nod. "Not bad for a few hours' effort."

"We still need another 95,000." Matt wondered if she would consider letting him use a trick or two. "You know, it would go faster if I controlled the cards now and then." He glanced out of the corners of his eyes at her. "What do you think, Miss Guided?"

"No!" Somewhere in the dark a night owl hooted. "That's not the way ta do it, not by a sight, Matthew. Not by a sight. Shame on you for ponderin' such. You combat evil with good. You just pushed yer body ta win; now push yer mind too."

Darn, I knew better than to consider cheating, Matt scolded himself. *What was I thinking?* It was more than just that, Matt didn't want this pretty lady to look at him like he was one of the scoundrels they'd seen in action.

"Just clowning around, Funny Lady," Matt said. "I do know better."

Kicker looked around again. He was certain he'd seen that sneaky Cypher seed slithering in the saloon—at least he thought he was sure.

He asked, "Miss Guided, you don't think there's any chance somebody else could have hitched a ride back here?"

Matt and Michala looked at him like he was a loon. The three time travelers were 125 years in the past. He realized what he'd asked had to be absurd. He decided that figure he'd taken to be Cypher had to be some other sorry-looking sap.

"I mean..." He sighed. "Oh, never mind. Like my amigo said, must be too many blows to the head." He decided to switch the subject. "Where to now, Mr. Cheat?"

Matt was just rolling that around in his head. He loved the stories his father had read to him about the riverboat gamblers. He always wondered what it would have been like paddling up the Mississippi playing stud with some of those old celebrated dandies.

"The places where we can have the longest winning streaks possible." Matt spoke with confidence. "In transit during the lengthy voyages down the Mississippi."

"Riverboats?" Juan asked, wondering if those tooting tubs might have sufficient space for more amusement. "Like big ones?"

"Yes, stern wheelers," Matt replied. "A pleasant way to see the country."

He also thought the cruise might make for some quiet romantic time with the pretty lady walking next to him, Miss Guided, Michala. *Michala?* Matt wondered. *I'm sure I've heard that name before.* He shook his head clear. *I have no time to think about girls now.* He had to stay on track and remember his first order of business was to earn money to get his father free.

CHAPTER THIRTY-TWO

Planting Seeds

The trio hurried down the dirt road they'd first come in upon. The road was peaceable and hazily lit by the moon. They passed the same apple orchard where they met the clergyman. Matt's sharp ears heard the sound of someone whimpering. As they drew closer Matt recognized the heavyhearted sound to be the voice of Pastor Haggai. The minister was praying fervently with sniffs and sobs.

"Oh, my Lord," he prayed. "I gave it my all, but, I'm sorry, Lord, it just weren't enough. The banker is gonna take back my trees in the morning."

The moonlit night was so quiet that the three couldn't help hearing every word of the man's pleadings.

"'Ey Mano," Juan whispered. "The Good Book does say contribute to the Man in the Sky, and He'll give it back in heaps and piles. What do you think? Should we support the Bible dude?"

Matt's mind was in a quandary. He believed he should help; he just feared the idea of spending even one penny. Images of his maimed father and reflections of his mother's cross wrapped around bloody thumbs tormented his mind.

Then there were Pastor Steve's words, "You can have no harvest unless you first plant your seeds."

What to do? Matt fretted. He knew what Pastor said was true and what Kicker wanted to do was the wise thing. Yet he just didn't know if he should take the risk now. But he decided, what's a few hundred when needing so much?

"Kicker, peel me off twenty-five dollars. No, no make it ten percent. That should be about five hundred bucks."

He turned and spoke in a soft undertone to Michala. "Miss Guided, do you have any kind of writing instrument with a scrap of paper?"

"Naturally, Mr. Cheat." She removed the writing items from her bountiful purse. "Those particular valuables were ones I packed before we departed."

"Good. Please write on the paper, 'This money is to build your church. May God bless you.'"

The radiant lady scrawled the words Matt spoke to her.

"Here ya go, Mr. Cheat." She handed him the paper. "Just as ya said."

"Thanks." Matt handed the note to his friend and whispered, "Kicker, roll the cash with a small rock into this paper and carefully lay it by the minister, but don't let him see you."

"Si, si, Mano. Don't get lost. I'll be right back."

Kicker bundled the money for the building fund inside the note and sneaked up in back of the praying man. The clergyman was in such fervent prayer he never noticed when Juan laid the donation beside him.

Juan stepped close to Matt's ear and murmured, "Mission accomplished, jefe."

"Good job, buddy. Now, let's get out of here, quick!"

The angel was elated with the boys' actions. She knew the multiplying power of the freely-sown seed.

"Alike ta Johnny Appleseed, ya don't know what a fine orchard was just planted here on this day."

Seraphim watched the threesome with big, bright eyes as they closed in on the coach. Hiding behind the buggy, a shaking Damen peeked around the edge.

When they arrived at the coach, Matt stepped ahead of Juan, opened the door for Miss Guided, and offered his hand.

RE-DEAL

"Yep," she seized his hand with a smile. "I think something's happening to ya, Matthew."

The angel-in-human-form hiked up her skirt and climbed in. Juan lifted his hand daintily toward Matt like the angel had.

"Sorry, not my type." Matt kicked Juan in the butt. "Now get in, sweet-boy."

Without warning, shots reverberated nearby. The two gamblers Matt had earlier exposed as cheaters, Six-Toed Pete and Dark-Alley Jim, were running down the dry-clay street. With the death of Marshal Hickok, they had retrieved their firearms, and with these weapons they had regained their strength.

"There he is!" Pete cried out as he aimed his gun. "Kill 'im!"

Both pointed their pistols and fired.

"Whoa!" Matt screamed as his hat was shot from his head. "It looks like Kicker's fun is back."

As he bent down to grab his hat, he heard the gamblers drawing closer.

"Cruddy Kid!" Dark-Alley threatened, "Give back our coin, or we'll blow your phantom head off!"

"That be's right!" Six-Toed Pete shouted. "I wants that phantom's toes to touch the daisies."

From behind the coach, Damen silently cursed the alien woman. He didn't want anything to do with this mysterious contraption. However, he had no choice. He hated rats and wasn't going to be left behind. During the commotion, he jumped into the back of the trunk.

He wasn't going to hang around a place where they dangle you from a rope before you have a fair opportunity to bribe the judge. Damen squeezed in and closed the hatch, sealing him in darkness. He felt claustrophobic and something else. Surely it wasn't another rat! He took his hand and carefully felt the fuzzy and hard thing alongside his body. He cautiously felt animal substance, but it was too big for a rodent.

But he could tell it had bone and hair. And hoof? His body stiffened as he lay in the dark tomb. He was sickened to figure out it was a piece of a horse leg⊙it must belong to that spooky white broomtail that pulled this rig. Damen needed to breathe deeply to keep from panicking. *But how can I take a deep breath lying in this dark, gloomy, alien's coffin with this piece of dead horseflesh lying next to me? What have I ever done in my good upright life to deserve the punishment of having to tour around with rats and horse rot?*

Outside Matt snatched his hat as more shots bit the dust. He straightway boarded the coach.

"Go! Michala!" Matt yelled. "Sorry, I mean Miss Guided. Please take off, fast!"

"Okay," she said with a relaxed, unruffled smile. "From this piece of earth, do ya know the time and locality ya would like ta visit next?"

"Anywhere, Miss Guided." Matt's alarm intensified. "Just get us out of here, quick!"

Michala relaxed back into her pink seat in complete calm. Without saying a word, she reached into her little purse and pulled out her knitting. She sat trim and erect as she hooked her needles in and out of her green yarn.

It seemed to Juan the angel was coming up with some new funny.

"Well," she grinned and giggled. "Mr. Cheat, I need ta acquaint Seraphim with a destination. Or we may end up in Tim Buck Two, or worse, we might land in Tim Buck Three."

Kicker wondered how Miss Guided could stay so calm and collected and speak silly jokes while everybody wanted to layer them with lead.

"I've got it!" Matt said. "Riverboats, two years in the future!"

But Matt and Juan were both stunned and horrified, as Michala did not tell Seraphim to get going. They watched in shock as she calmly put her knitting away, opened the coach door, and stepped down from the carriage.

"No, Michala!" Matt cried out. "Don't go outside! It's too dangerous!"

RE-DEAL

But it was too late. She was already out and the buggy door closed. On the outside of the fancy buggy, the disgruntled gunfighters took aim at the opening coach door. When Miss Guided stepped out, they aimed their Colts and fired.

But suddenly, with neither warning nor explanation, in the blink of an eye, darkness turned to noon, and the bright light flooded the black, blinding everyone. The shots went wild, missing Michala and the buggy.

"Two years forward, Seraphim," the heavenly spirit told her horse.

Seraphim whinnied as if he understood. Miss Guided strolled back to the buggy and climbed aboard. Just as quickly as it had appeared, the blinding light disappeared, plunging the historic town back into the black of night. She sat back down into the seat. She reached into her puny purse and pulled out her needles and yarn.

"Are ya ready, Mr. Cheat?" She looked up at the perplexed pair. "We can go now. Seraphim knows the route."

Once again the disgruntled gamblers fired on the coach. Matt thought if Michala didn't hurry he was going to need a clean pair of pants.

"Yes, Miss Guided." He pleaded, "We're ready; let's go!"

No sooner did the request leave his mouth than the coach transported the travelers toward their next stop. And as before, Matt again tasted the hard floorboards.

CHAPTER THIRTY-THREE

Excellent Powers of Constipation

"Mr. Cheat, would ya like me ta yarn ya a pouch full of soft down feathers?"

"No, thanks." Matt shook his head in frustration. "My throbbing skull molds perfectly to the floor of this hard wood carriage."

"What a talented black belt!" Juan laughed heartily. "Wait til I tell Sensei Murphy. He'll bust you back to a pink belt."

Matt climbed back into his seat. "You're a true friend, Kicker. You give real meaning to the saying, 'With company like you, who needs lawyers?'"

"Both of ya be quiet and hold still." The angel shook her head. "Look at ya both. Yer bruised faces are a mess."

As Michala nursed Matt's wounds with a damp cloth, Juan noticed his timepiece's second hand had ceased spinning around its face.

"Miss Guided, my watch stopped."

"Oh, don't worry about that. It stops only when outside-of-time."

At the mention of Kicker's broken watch, Matt wondered how much of his father's precious time had been used up. He pulled out his timepiece and pushed the button. Its soft female voice said, "38 hours 6 minutes 45 seconds remaining."

"Whoa! Miss Guided, we've already used up eight hours. It seems like we were only in Deadwood for an hour or two."

"Yeah?" Juan grinned. "Like they say, Mr. Cheat—time flies when your feet are flailing in foes' faces."

RE-DEAL

Miss Guided began to wipe the filth and blood from Juan's face. "Please don't fret, Mr. Cheat. It was only 7 hours 53 minutes and 15 seconds. You just picked up 6 minutes and 45 seconds. Yer such a clever fighter." The angel pinched Kicker on the cheek and shook her head. "But must you relish brawling so?"

"I started training at five," Kicker told her as he plopped his hat back on his head. "Big Lew breeds fighters down at his so-called orphanages."

Michala's cheerful face turned reflective. "I know all about those forced labor camps and how yer family got caught."

"I was raised in one. My poor ma was forced to give me and my sister up, then she was sent to a sweatshop."

"You were not meant ta be brought up there."

"Are you telling me I should have had a real loving family?" The thought thrilled Juan.

"Yes, my friend. Son of Bowen, great man of God."

Behind them, Damen, claustrophobic from being squeezed inside the back of the trunk, could breathe only in short panting breaths. Still he attempted to hear and make sense of everything. He knew his and his old man's survival depended on how he dealt with this predicament.

Baffled at what had just happened, Matt asked, "What was that bright light back there?"

"Well, confidentially, Mr. Cheat, between you and me, I gather we were favored ta experience a fascinating and rare reverse eclipse."

In the trunk, Damen scoffed. *Reverse eclipse. Ha! That's a big pile of bull! She has to be an extraterrestrial! No worthless dame could do all this!*

"Reverse eclipse?" Matt asked. "I've never heard of such a thing. Will you please clarify what that is for us?"

"Why sure." The angel-in-disguise smiled. "A reverse eclipse is where the bright sun in the sky temporarily moves between this populated terrestrial planet and the nighttime moon hoverin' above."

Or, she thought, *it's when an angel doesn't want to drop a stitch during gunfire. Knit one, purl a double, knit one, purl a double.*

Matt wondered why the hot sun didn't turn them into crispy pieces of bacon. However, what he really wanted to understand was how they were back here in the Old West.

"Well then, Funny Lady, can you spell out how in a second or so we can be in two different centuries?"

"Yeah," Kicker jumped in. "Please explain that to my poor, uneducated amigo Matt."

"Okay, but I ask ya, please don't be insulted as I clarify something so uncomplicated as time continuance."

"Remember," Kicker said with a snicker, "Matt is a little thick in the cabeza, so explain outside-of-time to him very slowly."

"Of course, Kicker, I'll elucidate ta my dynamic duo as clearly as I know how. Outside-of-time is from where the Lord of Lords reigns. It's where every day is existing now. Beginning with the devourin' of the fruit in the Garden of Eden ta the return of the King of Kings on His white stallion." She looked across and smiled at Juan. "The King's mount is an uncommonly refined charger. My favorite factor is he has some of Seraphim's blood in him."

She resumed her knitting. "Knit one, purl a double. As I was sayin', outside-of-time is where a second is as a thousand years and a thousand years is but a jiffy. That is why yer Creator can consider what everyone is doin' at all times. First grade arithmetic will tell ya His Majesty has a thousand years of seconds ta note yer meaningful one second prayer. And if my mental math is proper, that is 525,600,000 minutes to listen to ya. That, Mr. Cheat, is why this century and that one ahead of us are no longer separated by time. They are both the existing, the present, the now."

As Matt sat speechless while Juan grinned at the angel's perplexing explanation, the inside of the coach lightened and in a flash night became day. Matt's eyes again throbbed from the burning light, but this time he at least managed to stay in his seat.

"Wow. You did it, Mr. Cheat. You succeeded in stayin' off that hard floor. Yer genius overwhelms me."

RE-DEAL

"Why thank ya, ma'am," Matt said in his best John Wayne accent. "Yer a woman of good breedin' yerself." He pounded on his chest. "And you ain't seen nothin' yet!"

Juan checked his watch, and to his surprise, the second hand was moving again.

"Stop banging your chest, Cheetah, and tell me what that babe inside your talking timepiece has to say."

Matt punched the button. "38 hours 6 minutes 40 seconds remaining."

"Did you hear that?" Juan asked excitedly.

"Hear what?"

"Figuring it took you about five seconds to punch your clock, as we were on the road moving through time, not even one second advanced as we went from where we were to where we are now."

"Kicker, I guess that college learning did you some good. You're going places. You don't miss a trick."

"You bet." Juan looked at the angel and winked. "Outside-of-time is very interesting."

In the darkness of the trunk in the rear, Damen's contempt for the two fools' gullibility almost made him forget his predicament. *Outside-of-time! What a bunch of crap!*

Miss Guided placed her knitting back in her bag. "Mr. Cheat, yer takin' a venturesome risk gettin' on those steamboats without the coach."

"I know, Miss Guided. But if Seraphim has set us down at Natchez, Mississippi, in the late spring of 1878, we might find the legendary gambler George Devol loaded with some of his biggest winnings aboard the Robert E. Lee."

"Time is running, Miss Guided," Juan said. "Only 38 hours to collect ninety-five grand, then go and try to win the game. Oh boy, I see more merriment coming up."

"Yeah, Kicker. Devol was a vicious fighter. Using his head as a weapon was part of his winning strategy on the boats for forty years."

"Now, Matthew," the guardian angel said. "You already proved you can fight. This time just try and use yer head."

"Like I told you," Matt said, rubbing his tender cheek, "Devol was famous for using his to smash things, including people. However, I remember vividly his cheating tricks from the book he published in his old age."

"This scoundrel wrote a book also?" Kicker asked.

"That's right. And I know about all his tricks."

The trio looked at each other and said together, "Let's get him!"

When Matt opened the carriage door, a cool breeze filled the coach. They stepped down from the buggy and found themselves in 1878 in bustling Natchez on the bank of the booming Mississippi River. People and porters laden with luggage were heading toward the large white riverboat that towered four stories over the dock.

In the back, Damen slowly opened the trunk hatch and looked out, then he slipped from the trunk and blended into the crowd.

After she and her charges were out of the coach, the angelic lady said, "All right, Seraphim, now, boy, pick us up at the dock where we're gonna land. Giddy up!"

"'Ey Mano," Juan said. "Did that book tell you where this big tub is gonna end up?"

"Good thinking, Kicker." Matt turned to Michala. "Miss Guided, tell Seraphim we don't know where this boat is going."

"Oh, Seraphim," she shouted toward the horse. "We don't know where that there little canoe is gonna drop anchor. See ya there."

Seraphim looked back and reflected a clear understanding in his eyes, then he faced forward and picked up his gait.

The palatial riverboat, the Robert E. Lee, was docked at the wharf. Nearby the travelers saw a prize ring had been set up and a large crowd had gathered.

The mob howled as a man in circus-ring-master garb challenged, "Is anyone willing to step in the ring with Willie Carroll? Willie is a parentless stray from overseas and the man with the hardest head in the world. If anyone is able to last just three minutes with Willie, he will win five hundred fresh crisp dollar bills!"

A strutting gambler sauntered down the Robert E. Lee's gangplank.

"My name is Devol," the gambler said. "I'll take that bet, and I won't even remove my coat. It'll be that fast!" He removed a roll of bills from his long, black frock coat, held them over his head, and waved them around. "And I'll take any bets you cowards want to make."

Matt said, "Devol did us a favor and revealed this anecdote in his biography. If we put our cash on his book, we'll definitely clean up."

And so they did. The fight was brief; before Carroll knew what happened, Devol charged in like a crazed bull and used Carroll's own weapon, his rock-hard head, and gave Carroll's skull a bone-crushing head-butt, knocking him out cold.

"All right Mano," Kicker cried. "It really helps to study your history. You just won fifteen hundred bucks."

"Oh, Mr. Devol," the anonymous angel stepped over and said, "that's a lot of money ya just won. Would ya like ta donate ta my new research project?"

Devol eyeballed Michala lustfully. "And what is your new research project, hon?"

"Well, Mr. Devol, I'm endeavorin' ta find a cure for death."

"Did you say a curative for death? What kind of flighty professor are ya?"

"Oh, yes, Mr. Devol, I did say death. Ya understand more of Natchez's inhabitants die from death than from any other cause."

"Wow, woman, with a steel trap like yours, you could melt ice."

"Why thank ya, Mr. Devol. That's because I have excellent powers of constipation."

He groaned, shoved her aside, and with the arrogance of a conquering gladiator, swaggered back up the gangplank.

CHAPTER THIRTY-FOUR

Old-Fashioned Royal Flush

The rustic cranes finished loading the cargo and the steamboat trunks, and the riverboat blew its whistle. Michala paid for three tickets and a cabin.

"Come on, boys. Let's not miss the pretty little bobber."

"Little bobber? This tub is huge. Lots of room for good wholesome fighting fun." Juan jabbed Matt playfully on the arm. "Come on, Mano. Let's hurry—new adventures are just across that gangplank."

Hiding in the crowd, Damen dashed toward the boat as soon as the group was out of sight in an ocean of ladies' bonnets and men's cowboy hats. He bribed the deckhands with some of the cash he'd picked up off the dirty floor back in Deadwood.

Juan led his traveling companions toward the prow of the vessel. They squeezed their way through the impatient throngs. Juan gave little consideration to the parties of pompous-looking tycoons, but he and Matt did tip their hats to the women. After a few fraught minutes, they reached the front.

"'Ey Mano," Kicker said as he slipped up to the bow of the boat. "It's pretty cool up here, huh?"

"Really cool, Kicker." Matt looked over the rail and breathed in the fresh air. "This is a far cry from that smoky armpit back in Deadwood."

They leaned over the rail and watched as the elegant boat pushed its way up the current at about two knots.

RE-DEAL

Michala pulled from her tiny purse her needlework, a long, emerald-green scarf. She draped it over her shoulders and cuddled it closely around her in the brisk breeze. Her long, golden hair floated and whipped in the blustering wind.

"Mr. Cheat." She pulled a key from her pocket. "What do ya say we find our cabin? It's gettin' a mite bit nippy out here."

"Sure, Miss Guided."

"Yeah, Mano." Kicker took the key from Michala. "I want to make sure the plug is securely fastened in this tub."

Matt chuckled. "Okay. Let's go check that plug."

Damen watched from a safe distance as Matt led the woman inside the boat, Kicker close behind.

Once inside, the trio snaked their way through the twists and turns of the legendary vessel. They strolled along floral carpeted passageways illuminated by wall-mounted oil lamps.

Matt explained, "We now have more than six thousand dollars to gamble with, and we couldn't be in a better place. Since cards were one of the few diversions from the monotony of the long voyages, everybody played."

"Here we are." Kicker glanced down at the tag attached to the key and then up to the cabin door. "Yep, sanitarium number seven."

Juan used the skeleton key to open the door, and they entered their stateroom. A solitary oil-burning lamp along with light from the tiny porthole illuminated the inadequate furnishings. There was a cot fit for one; a throne-like chair with a large hole in the bottom and a porcelain bowl under it; and, on a small ledge, a hand-size washtub with a pitcher of water sitting in it.

Juan pointed to the cot. "Mano, unless you want to sleep stacked like a Gag-in-the-Bag triple-decker, it looks like you and I'll be sleeping under the stars tonight." He then noted the old-fashioned toilet and snickered. "Mr. Cheat, I want you to close your eyes and tell me what beats four of a kind. But first I'll give you a clue."

"Do we have time for this, Kicker?" Matt asked.

"Won't take but a second. Now no peeking." He took his friend by the shoulders and slid him across the small room. "Sit down, Mano, and experience an old-fashioned royal flush."

As Matt sat down and felt the hole in the throne, he realized he'd been had again.

"Miss Guided," Matt said with a roll of the eye and a shake of the head, "did we really need to bring this joker on this trip with us?"

"He's a card all right, Mr. Cheat. A real joker card."

After a good laugh, they quickly freshened up.

As Matt dried his face, he asked, "Well, Kicker, are you ready to go whip some gamblers? We'll do better with two players, rather than just me."

"Not me." Juan shook his head. "I told you many times before, I hate cards. You play—I'll whip 'um."

"Chicken!" Matt placed his thumbs under his armpits and flapped like a bird. "Cluck-cluck-cluck."

"Yeah, chicken sounds good. We haven't eaten since we, well, well, since we left home 130 years from now. That is, of course, unless you think a taste of an apple and half a juicy worm amount to much of anything."

"Yeah, I'm hungry too," Matt agreed. "And I didn't get my half of that savory worm."

"Miss Guided." Matt rubbed his hungry stomach. "What do you say after the game tonight, we leave Kicker with the worms, and you and I go out for a bite."

"Go out for a bite?" she asked. "Well, confidentially, Mr. Cheat, after the game I'm gonna be slumbering on this comfy little cot. But Matthew, if ya like, I can bite ya now!"

Matt laughed. "Let's go look for the gambling parlor. Maybe we'll also find some grub."

Juan and Michala nodded their agreement and followed Matt out the door.

However, as Matt waited for Juan to lock the room, the mention of food caused him to recall how his loving father was locked in a meat locker somewhere in the future. The sobering thought made his stomach drop like a free-falling elevator. Cypher's fierce words came flooding back to his mind, "Forty-eight hours and your father will die. Slowly."

Forty-eight hours, now less then thirty-eight. Matt's mind flashed back to the thumbs wrapped with his mother's cross. His breathing accelerated as his emotions once more plunged into a terrifying panic.

"Let's not forget about my dad! We need to hurry!"

Juan gave his pal a pat on the back. "Don't worry; you have help from above. Trust me."

"Thanks, Kicker. I need to always remember that."

But Matt questioned his own abilities. If his friends only knew how scared he was, they'd probably call him a coward or chicken, or they would chastise him for not trusting that his prayers had been heard. The question that kept rattling around in Matt's brain was why anyone, especially God, would pay any extra mind to a poor, crippled descendant of a man whose actions had caused so much pain and suffering.

However, Matt knew for certain his prayers had been responded to. Otherwise, how could they be back here in the Old West? The biggest stumbling block and the thing that kept Matt's stomach churning like a cement mixer was that he knew the success of this trip was up to him, his actions, decisions, and abilities. That thought again sent Matt's mortar-crammed stomach plunging like a skydiver with a defective parachute. How can he possibly do this?

CHAPTER THIRTY-FIVE

A T-Bone Steak Game

As Matt turned to go, he bashed his noggin on the doorframe. "Darn!"

"Don't worry, Mano," Kicker said. "Your bat sonar is fine. Some prankster just moved the door."

The three left the room and worked their way through the elegant passageways toward the main gambling saloon. They passed more well-dressed businessmen and couples. Some of them nodded; others looked Matt over with alarm.

"'Ey Mano," Juan said. "Some of these people are giving you the evil eye."

"Do I look okay? No worms stuck between my teeth or anything?"

"Boys, I've heard enough about worms today. Now ya look fine, Matthew. Just keep yer eyes straight ahead, and we'll let ya know what's comin'."

"Yeah, Mano. Just keep your mouth closed, and no one will see what's wiggling between your teeth."

Matt was troubled, worried they wouldn't allow Miss Guided—or was it Michala Guided? Or just Michala? Was Miss Guided only a stage name, like Mr. Cheat? Michala, Michala. Where had he heard that name before? Matt hoped they'd let her in the traditionally men's-only gaming areas.

"Better keep between us." Matt positioned Miss Guided between them and slipped his hand around hers. "They don't normally allow women upstairs in the main saloon."

RE-DEAL

"Ya sure know yer history, Mr. Cheat," the angel disguised as a teacher said. "All that readin' certainly paid off."

"It sure did. Thank goodness for my good ol' Dad's stories. But who would have imagined I'd ever need them to survive?"

Matt felt a horrible, frightening chill come over him as he remembered the horror of the package with his father's thumbs and the tragedy of his mother and sister's murders. He muttered to himself, "Mom, Sis, somehow I'll get the Cyphers back for their evil deeds."

Kicker said a silent prayer. *Please, Big Man, help my amigo trust in You with all his heart and not lean on his own faulty understanding. And me too.*

They arrived at an ornate staircase, and as they started to ascend, a burly bouncer stopped them.

He thrust out his strong arm. "No guns or women allowed in the gaming area. You must check all yer firearms here."

"We have no guns." Matt opened up his coat for examination. "Feel free to search us."

"You bet. I'll do just that!"

Matt held his solid metal cane openly in his hand while the guard first frisked him, then moved over to his friend, where the checker found Juan's chucks. He pulled them out and asked suspiciously, "What are these?"

Kicker grinned. "Why, they're nut crackers, for very big nuts, of course."

"Where have you ever seen a nut that big," the guard asked. "I say there's no such a nut."

"Oh yes," Juan answered. "We've all seen one. I guess you've never been to Hawaii and seen a coconut." He reached for his chucks. "I'll show you how they work." Kicker took the nunchakus from the perplexed guard and placed one stick in each hand. He made an open and closing motion and said, "See, very handy. Every little lady should have one. In fact, I'll sell you this set to give to your wife for only a thousand dollars. No, no for you, only five hundred dollars."

"What?" the guard scoffed. "Five hundred dollars for two sticks and a piece of chain! You must be cracked! You keep them. I'll make my own."

"So we can go?" Matt asked politely.

"Yeah," the guard replied with a sneer. "You can go. They'll appreciate a couple of dupes like you up there." He turned back to his post with a scoff. "What kind of fool do you take me for? Five hundred bucks just for two sticks!"

The group moved on up the stairs, and once out of earshot, they all let out a big laugh.

"Good job, Kicker," Matt said with a shake of his head. "We have our weapons, and he was so confused he said nothing about Miss Guided going up to the gambling hall with us."

They stepped into the noisy casino atmosphere of the main gambling saloon. The room was a mosaic of bright colors and dark carved-wood, felt-covered poker tables. The place was bustling and smoky with the masses dressed in expensive clothing. Most were crowded around the poker tables watching the action.

"Wow, this place is appealing. If they'd just get rid of all the smoke and booze, it would be exquisite," Miss Guided said.

"Mostly wealthy," Juan said as he looked around. "It looks like five tables playing. The center table has the most impressive gamblers with one big winner."

As they strolled into the saloon, Michala received a collection of hoots and whistles. She smiled shyly and waved, charming everyone. Matt expected some kind of protest at a woman in the saloon, but no one complained.

"Mano, look over this way." Juan pointed. "The big winner at that center table is that ugly dude with the rock head."

"I reckon yer right, Kicker," the angel agreed. "Same scars all over it. Based on the large piles of money, it's a T-bone steak game he's playin'."

T-bone steak game! Kicker gazed over toward his friend and saw a smile grow across Matt's face. He appreciated how the amusing angel could relieve Matt's anguish with jokes and joy.

"You mean high-stake game, Miss Guided," Matt said. "That's great—just what I'm looking for."

"But I don't like that stake. He's too mean. You oughtta play a different table."

"I don't think I should, Funny Lady. The clock is ticking. We need to win fast and win big."

"That's it," Juan agreed. "We've got to take the risk, Miss Guided."

"I expect yer right." She studied the players and nodded. "There are some mighty well-heeled folk at that table."

"Can you describe the other players with Devol?" Matt asked in a low voice.

"Sure," Michala murmured. "There's five other well-dressed folks seated around Mr. Devol's table. Straight across from him is a man of the cloth, all dressed in black with his stiff, bleached-white collar turned up. He's lookin' very embarrassed and is nervously shufflin' his last three silver pieces. Next is a young fellow, obviously just married. I believe this because he's still donned in a custom weddin' tuxedo."

"Yeah," Juan nodded, "but my favorite is the man next to the honeymoon kid. The dude looks slick, like an aristocratic English lord or something."

Juan noticed the nobleman's cigar went out in his hand. The man, wearing a look of exasperation, re-lighted it and exhaled the cigar smoke up into the air. The prototypical person of leisure. Juan shook his head. As he looked closer, he saw a baroque bottle of liquor next to the aristocrat.

"Mano, it looks like the outlandish-dressed foreigner is sloshed from drinking French brandy. He's intently trying to focus on his cards. I think he's trying to decide if he should quit. Nope, he's not quitting. It looks like he's so intoxicated he's peeling off his gold watch, rings, and diamond studs and tossing them into the pot."

The womanly-appearing angel waved away the smelly smoke. "Fillin' the table are two rich-lookin' men who seem to be very bored. Like the Englishman, they're both puffing on stinky, long, black cigars."

Suddenly, the room went quiet as a man entered the gambling hall, sucked in his paunch, and raised his hand, signaling silence. "Welcome, folks. I am the captain, John W. Cannon. You're traveling aboard the fastest steamboat afloat."

"Devol." Cannon pointed a finger at the big gambler then gestured to the young groom. "Be considerate of that young fellow I just wedded. His well-to-do father is a good friend of mine. If you're not fair as you play, I'll set you off this boat without obliging to stop."

Devol gave a faint nod to the Captain. He casually took a sip of his brandy while he eyed the large lady's ring the groom was fingering nervously.

As Captain Cannon turned to go, he spotted Matt, Juan, and Miss Guided. He walked over and shook the men's hands. "Welcome aboard, gentlemen." He turned to the woman, took her hand, and kissed it. "Madam, you're the loveliest lady I have ever had grace this steamer."

"Why thank ya, Mr. Cannon." She curtsied. "I'm pleasured for sure ta make yer acquaintance." She reached into her small blue bag and took out a grapefruit-size steel ball. She handed it to him and said, "Mr. Cannon, please take this gift for yer friendly hospitality."

The Captain took the heavy ball. He looked at the ball, then at the miniature purse and shook his head.

Juan's spirit leaped within. He was overwhelmed how the angel always knew what weird item was needed. He wasn't sure what the ultimate use would be, but he knew this cannonball would somehow be important.

Cannon said, "Ma'am, might I ask what this steel ball is for?"

"Why, it's a cannonball for yer cannon, Captain Cannon."

"For my cannon you say? Why, thank you, Madam." He set it on the bar between an old compass and a ship's wheel. "It will make a nice addition to my souvenirs." He turned back and suggested, "Maybe later you and your friends might like to join me for a stroll around my winning vessel."

"We'd be privileged, Captain." Matt slipped his hand into Michala's and gave it a slight squeeze. "That might make for a pleasant diversion from this long voyage."

"We'd be pleasured for sure, Captain Cannon." She disengaged her hand from Matt's and shut her purse.

"See you tonight." The Captain turned and paraded out, waving to everyone.

CHAPTER THIRTY-SIX

Used Card Lot

Devol turned back to the players and snapped his fingers. "Gentlemen, let's get back to the pursuit of wealth redistribution!" He called to the tapster. "Bartender! This deck has gone soft! Let's get another over here pronto!"

The haggard-looking bartender snatched a new deck of cards and hurried over to Devol's table. Devol gave the bartender the old deck, then made a show of taking the new, unopened pack from the tapster. He held it up high for all to see as he opened the cards.

"A fresh deck so everyone knows at Devol's table we play only a gentlemen's game."

"He certainly makes a fuss about a new deck," the angel observed. "Do ya know why?"

Matt nodded. "Yes, I do know the reason for Devol's peculiar behavior. He was known for changing the positions of figures on the backs of cards. For example, if there were little birds on the backs, where they were would tell him if the card was an ace or a two." He leaned over and whispered, "Kicker, can you see what the bartender is doing with the old cards?"

Juan whispered back, "It looks like he's shoving the cards into the trash behind his bar."

Matt's eyes lit up. "Miss Guided, would you please go over and offer to empty the garbage? Then bring me back the used cards. Kicker and I'll meet you outside in the passageway."

RE-DEAL

"Why sure, Mr. Cheat. I'll be right back with the rubbish."

Matt and Juan stepped outside, careful not to draw any unwanted attention to themselves, while the angel disguised as a lady strolled over to the boat's bar.

"Oh, Mr. Bartender," she exclaimed with a grin. "Would ya like me ta empty yer trashcan filled with those dishonest cards that characterize the aces with cute little birdies? It would be my pleasure ta do that for ya."

"Right away, ma'am." He snatched up the can and almost threw it at her.

"Thank ya. Yer very helpful."

"And it's mighty nice to have a softer person on the team," the barman responded.

Outside Matt and Juan watched as an endless army of fluffy white clouds drifted across the river, casting shadows that turned the water a deeper blue. Juan stood with his hands in his pockets, bracing himself against the rail.

"Mano, how can you outdo that rock-head?"

"I don't know, Kicker. I'm still working on that problem." Matt was worried and seriously starting to consider whether it might be okay if he cheated, but only the other cheaters. "Kicker, what do you think about fighting fire with fire?"

"'Ey Mano. Remember the Old Testament dude, Jacob's preferred son, Joseph. The teenager was used by the Big Man to sustain his people during destitute days, and he did it without fighting fire with fire. But, like we might have to do, Joseph had to first go through a ten-round, heavyweight kickboxing championship bout to demonstrate his moral muscle.

"Listen Mano, you might think your black belt test was hard. Joseph's test started when he recounted to his eleven brothers a prophetic dream where they all bowed down before him. To make his brothers even more upset, his pop presented him with a slick gold-medal-winner's cloak. Round one, Joseph received a bloody shot to the nose when his resentful siblings cursed and scorned him. Round two, he captured a kidney shot after the eleven brothers ripped the custom wrap from his back and then dipped it in beast blood. Round three, his feet were kicked out from beneath him. The brothers betrayed him and hurled him into a hellish hole. Round four, while on his back, he was stomped in the gut as the older siblings suggested they might slay him.

"Round five, the forsaken boy was forced to his feet, and more wisely than whacking him, the jealous kin auctioned Joseph off to some clan called Midianites. Round six, Joseph took an uppercut to the chin when the monstrous Midianites made a hasty harvest after retailing Joseph to some dude known as Potiphar. Round seven, the wearied warrior wasted some teeth after running from Potiphar's lustful lady, as she secretly strove to sexually assault the innocent man. Round eight, the perjuring princess delivered an after-the-bell groin-shot by falsely accusing him of rape.

"Round nine, Joseph received a standing eight-count as he spent a decade in a non-air-conditioned, dirty Egyptian dungeon. Round ten, Joseph's knees were knocked out from under him when his prison fellow forgot to inform Pharaoh about Joseph perfectly interpreting his dreams. Because of his inconsiderate comrade's absentmindedness, Joseph spent a few more years down in the depressing brig.

"At length, after long, lonesome years of pushups and shadowboxing, Joseph's forgetful cellmate finally remembered to recount to the rich ruler Joseph's God-given gift to decipher dreams. Finally after ten brutal rounds, the bell rung. The fight was over. Joseph triumphed. He was brought together with Pharaoh. After Joseph informed the Pharaoh of his future, he went from the pit to the palace in a single hour. He was positioned with all power, at the right-hand of the mightiest potentate on earth.

"Precisely as told in his long-ago dream, and Mano, all without fighting evil with evil. Then his starving, unsuspecting siblings sought out the sovereign. They were brought and bowed before their unrevealed royal brother. Joseph put

RE-DEAL

his arms around his brother's necks and said, 'I am Joseph.' Each and every brother openly wept tears of joy."

Juan looked at Matt and said, "The lesson from this story is if a boy can't bear the body blows, he can never handle the power of success. Besides, Mano, you know Michala won't like that excuse for you to be another con man. Remember Joseph endured many body blows, the pit, a lustful woman, and dirty dungeons—all without fighting fire with fire."

"I know; I know. But Kicker, I still think it's cool. Our time is running, and the other way is too slow! Don't torment yourself. I'll be fair. I'll only cheat the other cheaters."

The direct contact angel stepped outside and found Matt and Kicker talking as they casually leaned against the rail.

"Here ya go, Mr. Cheat." She handed him the trashcan. "There are enough antique cards here ta open up a used card lot."

Matt grinned at her silly play on words. He pulled a pack from the can. "Thanks, Funny Lady. Any problem with Devol's stooge?"

"Nope. But the poor young man did seem very nervous and fidgety. That is, until I offered to get rid of the marked cards for him."

Juan asked, "Did you actually tell the bartender you knew the cards were crooked?"

"Why of course, you silly boy," Michala said. "We always should be truthful."

Juan turned toward Matt, hoping his amigo was listening to the wisdom from Matt's undercover guardian angel. Juan lifted his leg and tapped his boot tip on Matt's cheek. "Did you hear what she said, Mano?"

"Yes, I did, Kicker. I did."

Hiding off to the side, Damen was hanging onto a pole, trying desperately to watch and hear this bunch. He detested boats, and he hated watching this unstable vessel churn its way up the river. However, his only way back to the future and his old man's power and fortune seemed to be the weird woman standing between his two enemies.

Matt nodded his understanding. Like his buddy Kicker, Matt was continually amazed at the lovely woman's daring. Even more astonishing—it always seemed to pay off. He realized his intention to cheat the cheaters was immoral, so he decided to be like Joseph and play honestly.

He got down to business and examined Devol's used cards. However, because of the attack with the magnifying glass, he couldn't begin to tell if they were marked or not.

"Miss Guided, I want you to watch carefully as I riffle the cards." Matt held the cards up close to her eyes. "This is an old gambler's trick to detect readers."

"Yeah, I know this one," Juan said with a nod. "I learned it from one of Big Lew's goons."

"Did ya say readers? I thought ya called these colorful pieces of paper playin' cards."

"Oh yes, sorry, Funny Lady. Let me explain. 'Readers' is the gamblers' name for marked cards." He held the cards up closer to her face. "Now watch what I'm gonna show you." He thumbed the cards like a cartoon book. "Now watch the designs on the backs very closely."

As she watched Matt riffle the cards, the little birds in the design didn't stay in the same place. So as Matt sprung the cards rapidly one card following another, like a moving picture, the birds became alive and were animated, moving around in the otherwise consistent pattern.

"My lands, that Mr. Devol is tricky! I noticed petite little birds bouncin' back and forth, like night bugs flying around a hot light bulb."

"Yes, just as I thought," Matt said. "These are readers all right. The designs all look the same until you swiftly leaf through the pack like I just did. It takes a pro like Devol to read the little changes on the backs of these tickets."

"That's the scheme all right. And every time gravel-brain requests a fresh deck, he gets the same setup. This way he always knows who has the dough-winning hand," Kicker said.

"But not this time," Matt said. "Devol spends a lot of time fixing the decks up. In his book, he admitted that using

RE-DEAL

the bartender to switch in marked cards was his preferred ruse. Now if the table gets down to only two players, I should be able to beat Devol at his own crooked game."

At least he hoped he could. He took a deep breath, brushed his hair back, and spoke with an outward show of confidence. "Come on. Let's go watch."

Michala shoved Devol's old marked deck into her purse, and the time travelers quietly went back inside.

CHAPTER THIRTY-SEVEN

Phantom Gambler Bull

Once inside, the trio watched Devol skin five gullible suckers out of over 27,000 dollars; 15,000 came from the young groom alone.

Michala shook her head. "That poor faulty suitor. That ignorant new husband not only squandered his entire wherewithal, it looks like he also forfeited his new bride's weddin' ring."

"Yeah," Kicker agreed, "but it looks like the groom is luckier than that clergyman."

They watched as the minister stared at his dwindling stack of coins. The man of the cloth lifted his gaunt face towards Heaven and prayed just above a whisper. "Oh dear Lord, please help me break even. I really need the money."

"Stop right there, preacher!" Devol thrust his heavy head forward and roared, "I'll have no praying at this table! Asking for supernatural intervention during a poker game is cheating! And at this table, all cheaters die!"

Devol's eyes cut like steel into the praying gambler. The clergyman turned so white that his face matched his bleached-white collar. Sweat began to pop out of his face and crawl down his cheeks as the swarm of onlookers shrank back against the saloon walls. Devol reached across the table, grabbed the preacher by the back of his turned-up collar, and bashed him with his mammoth skull. Unfortunately, the clergyman's head was not as resistant as Willie

RE-DEAL

Carroll's, and it imploded as easily as a melon. The man dropped to the floor like a sack of dead bullfrogs, knocked out cold, maybe dead.

"Barkeeper!" Devol hollered. "Remove this bloody mush melon from this table and feed him to the fishes!"

Devol circled the glittering heap of money, including the brilliant diamond ring lost by the foolish groom. He slid the gain over to his ample heap of spoils. He looked at the remaining players and said, "You're all safe now that the cheating preacher is meeting his Maker."

The guardian angel said, "Matthew, I don't think ya should play cards with that Mr. Devol. Ya might end up with an awful bad headache, and I didn't pack any butt-burn."

"Did you say butt-burn?" Juan asked. "What are you gonna do? Light a match and throw it in Matt's trousers just to get rid of a headache?"

Michala laughed. "Oh Kicker, I sure like the way ya can joke around when ya'll are in such dangerous surroundings." She drew closer and dropped her voice. "If I must, I'll spell it out. I said butt-burn because I don't believe it's lady-like ta use the normal word for anti-inflammatory pain pill."

"What?" Matt asked in confusion. "Miss Guided, if this isn't one of your silly jokes, then what the heck are you referring too?"

"If I must." Michala blushed as her blue eyes darted to the right then to the left. "The normal word for anti-inflammatory pain pill is," she delicately cleared her throat, "ass-burn."

Matt and Juan laughed in unison. Matt thought this funny lady had the oddest and quaintest sense of humor of anyone he'd ever heard. He continued to smile as he took one of her delicate hands and held it between his.

"That's aspirin, Miss Guided. Still, if Devol's foolish enough to fight us, he might be the one needing some butt-burn."

"That's right," Juan said. "And I'm the foot doctor. After my foot finds your face, you'll need a doctor."

"Kicker, you crack me up." Matt faced his lovely lady friend. "However, I don't have any choice but to play the rock. I'm here to accumulate a very large bankroll while at the same time trying to establish myself as a card player with a reputation. Now I think I can beat Devol, but not with those marked cards. Or Miss Guided, do you think I should just try to out-cheat him? I can, you know."

"Oh, no-no-no. Just because Mr. Devol is not playin' fair doesn't give ya the excuse ta be dishonest too. Those that cheat ta make it in life end up as captain of the chamber pot. Besides, ya would be welchin' on our agreement if ya don't win honestly."

Their eyes held for a moment. Matt knew she was right. Standing this close to her, face to face, almost lip to lip, he could almost see how beautiful she was. He loved her peaches-and-cream skin; inquisitive, clear-blue eyes; and long, blonde hair—the soft shiny hair that fell over her shoulders, so long, like a tempting shelter, so attractive he wanted to bury himself in it.

It's amazing, he thought, trying to cover his emotion. *This beautiful woman always seems to help keep me on the right path. And like the gambling groom, I wonder if there might be a wedding in our future, too?*

"Hello!" The incognito angel squeezed his hands. "Are ya still with me, Mr. Cheat? Hello. Matthew, yer not payin' much mind ta me, Matt."

Matt shook his head clear. He nodded, embarrassed that she'd caught him daydreaming about loving her. He wondered if she could see what he was thinking behind his broken eyes.

"Sorry, Miss Guided. I was thinking about that poor groom and his bride." He looked into her eyes. "You would make a beautiful bride."

"Wh-wh-why thank ya, Matt," she stuttered. "But weren't we talkin' about you not cheating against that Mr. Devol?"

"I've had enough of this mush," Kicker complained. "Stop flirting with her. I'm sorry to tell you this, Mano, but she's out of your league."

RE-DEAL

"Oh, you're right, Kicker." Matt tried to cover his embarrassment with a joke and a laugh. "I forgot we let you drag along with us." He released Michala's hands. "Kicker, how am I going to get rid of those marked cards?"

"Oh, Mr. Cheat." Michala opened her petite purse. "Do ya remember right before we left, I packed a few things?"

She reached into her purse and pulled out three new packs of cards. Kicker took a pack and compared it to the pack in play.

"Wow, Miss Guided," Kicker declared. "I can't believe it. These cards precisely match Devol's old-style marked cards."

"That's a master stroke, Miss Guided," Matt said with delight. "You're an expert prestidigitator." He nodded back towards the bar. "The problem is, how do we switch these standard cards for Devol's marked ones?"

Kicker thought it highly amusing that Matt couldn't see all the many miracles Michala performed under his nose. Matt hadn't been blessed to see her with her angel superior, but surely he should recognize that she did things no ordinary human could do.

"'Ey Mano," he said. "Let me switch those cards for you. This goes back to my training at the Cypher madhouse. I'll be able to switch them with no detection."

He held out his open hand and the angel slipped him the other packs.

"Wait here." Kicker covered the cards with his hat. "I'll be right back."

"Okay Matt," Michala said as she narrated Kicker's card caper. "Juan is movin' his way through the crowds of gamblers and spectators. He's casually slippin' up ta the side of the bar. It looks like Kicker's waitin' for the bartender ta turn away. Oh good, the spirit dispenser has turned ta help someone. Why look at that! Kicker's movin' with the practiced speed and coolness of an urban shoplifter. There he goes—he's slippin' the three new decks onto the top of Mr. Devol's marked packs. Uh-oh, the bartender's turnin' back. Oh good. Kicker resumed his stance at the bar just in the nick a time. Here he comes; he's on his way back."

"Mission accomplished, jefe, a piece of cake."

"Good job, Kicker. But it disturbs me how easily you fell back into using those sneaky talents. And you preaching to me about fighting fire with fire." Matt turned back to Michala, took one of her hands, and gave it a gentle squeeze. "Here we go, my beautiful angel. It's time for the battle."

With cane in hand, Matt turned away and casually walked back to the tavern with Juan. Michala followed behind them, sat on a couch off to the side, and resumed her knitting. Matt and Juan leaned on the bar, waiting to make their move.

Juan asked, "Why did you call Miss Guided an angel?"

"Why not? She's as close to an angel as I've ever known."

Juan was relieved. His amigo was only using the word as an expression of endearment. If he only knew.

Then a conversation at the bar between a cowboy and a gold miner from Deadwood caught the two boys' attention. The gossip caused both their stomachs to flip with apprehension. They listened as a scabby cowboy asked the gold miner, the wealthy Captain Masse, "Ya don't believe that Phantom Gambler bull, does ya?"

"Practically the whole town of Deadwood swears it," the Captain replied with a confident nod. "The Phantom knows yer thoughts, yer tricks, knows even what ya been doing before ya get to the table. And he don't need no gun, 'cause the Phantom fights faster than you can shoot at him."

The cowboy said, "Good thing for us he hasn't been spotted since Hickok was shot two years back."

Masse tapped the empty holster that had held his ivory-handled pistol before Captain Cannon had it checked during boarding. "We still keep a lookout for the Phantom with his strange eyes, his kicking friend, and that Dead Man belt buckle."

RE-DEAL

Juan's mind marveled at the overheard conversation. He hoped for more fun for the foot doctor. He felt his back pocket and patted his chucks.

"Heads up, Mano," Juan said. "The dude who bet his wedding ring is quitting. And it looks like he's pretty wasted too. If you want to play granite-head one on one, his table is empty." He tapped Matt's gold cards on his buckle. "And close your coat and hide that buckle before Captain Masse recognizes you."

Matt pulled his coat over the buckle. He was surprised to hear that he was now called the Phantom. He hated the name. It sounded like someone evil.

"Oh dear." Matt took a big breath, slowly let it out, and grabbed his cane. "Well, Kicker, here I go. It's time for me to match wits with boulder-brain."

Matt straightened, ambled over to Devol's table, and addressed the fearsome legend.

CHAPTER THIRTY-EIGHT

Matching Wits with a Rock

"Mr. Devol, this is my first time aboard a riverboat. I'd consider it an honor to play with a celebrated gambler such as yourself."

Devol studied the new arrival. "Boy," he said, "you have to have a lot of money on you to last at my table."

"Well, at least I can say I once played with the legendary gambler, George Devol."

Legendary? How old does this stranger think I am? A hundred or something?

"Then sit down, boy, and let's get the skinnin' over with." Devol placed the deck on the table. "I'll even let the youngster have the advantage of the first deal."

Matt thought he was off to a good start—he had an invitation to take a seat at the richest table on the boat. But he didn't like Devol's demeaning overtones, and he still needed to get rid of Devol's crooked cards.

"Maybe I shouldn't play after all. I'm told that I see no better than a bat. However, even I can see those cards look awfully shabby."

Devol said, "So you have a problem with this deck, huh, boy? Well, I can fix that." He turned toward the bar. "Bartender, bring me a new deck. So if there's any other cynic out there, they can also see this is a gentlemen's game."

Devol turned back and looked hard at the stranger with the cane. What troubled him about the kid was that

RE-DEAL

he couldn't see what was behind those weird, un-focusing deadeyes.

The bartender reached under the counter and grabbed the deck on the top of the stack. "Here you go, sir."

Matt hid a little sigh. This was the moment of truth. Time to play heads-up with the rock. He sat down in the seat left vacant by the unfortunate newlywed.

Devol made another big spectacle as he took the cards and broke the seal. He handed them over to Matt to shuffle.

The hours passed at a plodding pace for the fidgety Juan. He watched from the periphery, wondering if his Superman feet would be able to chisel a happy face on that scowling stoneface.

Michala opened her purse and pulled out Devol's pack of cards and handed half the deck to Juan.

"Kicker, let's go practice throwin' these cards like Matt. I think it'll help with the monotony."

"Good idea." Juan's eyes lit up. "Matt and I used to do this all the time at the karate school." He glanced around and spotted an empty Victorian chair forty feet down the hall. "A wormy apple says I can hit that chair."

As time passed, the pile of winnings beside Matt grew higher. A small group of onlookers had gathered to watch the newcomer whip the tough gambler. Devol was using great self-control to keep himself composed. He couldn't understand how this uncorrupted deck got mingled with his marked cards. He pushed the large pot of money toward the clever stranger and flung his losing poker hand down.

"Congratulations—again."

"Actually," Matt said with a nod toward Devol's pile of goods, "I'd be happy to take that wedding ring as part of the winnings. I might need that someday."

The spectators eyed each other, laughed, and shook their heads. Devol never took his eyes off Matt's eyes as he tossed the six-carat ring onto his pile of winnings. He took some cash out and pushed the rest toward the dead-eyed stranger.

He griped, "I don't think I feel comfortable with this deck. Barkeeper, new deck, now!"

The tapster's fingers nervously fidgeted on the bar. He quickly reached down and removed another new pack of cards.

Devol's eyes smoldered at his associate as he followed the nervous man's every move. As soon as the bartender arrived at the table, Devol yanked the deck out of his hand.

He turned back to the table. "Always good to get a fresh start."

He studied the box. They looked like his good cards, all right. Devol breached the seal and opened the new deck. He shuffled and set the cards before Matt for the cut. Devol picked up the deck and dealt. He watched and, as before, the stranger picked the cards up and held them up to his nose. This odd action bothered Devol. He wondered if this was some clever new denoting technique.

"Hey," Devol growled, "yer not marking those cards with snot rot, are ya?"

"What? Of course not. Tell me what the benefit would be of marking the cards on the faces? The cards are already marked on this side."

"Then hold them back away from your face. Don't want yer juices on my cards."

Darn, the rock can't see the backs, and I can't see the faces.

Devol carefully lifted his eyes and glanced across to the stranger's cards, but again saw no marks. He then glared at his supposed ally. He knew that calling for a new deck so soon would raise suspicion.

Devol glared at the bartender and saw the man tremble.

Matt was beginning to feel the heat of Devol's prolonged anger from his continuous losses. Devol had obviously become so dependent on having his cheating advantage that he'd lost his gambling guts.

Now Matt decided to confirm this belief. Considering that he couldn't hold the cards close enough to get a good look anyhow, he was going to go for broke. He was going to play every hand as if he held a royal flush. Matt counted off a stack of bills and a single gold piece.

Then he said without any emotion or change of expression, "I'll open the bet with five g's."

Again Devol squinted a little harder to search the backs of his opponent's cards. Once again his fears were corroborated. These were not his good cards—there were no marks. Devol looked back at the bartender, then back to this unknown kid. He was bothered by the stranger's deadeyes; they seemed to look right through him. Devol hated this—the kid's weird eyes were throwing his game off. He couldn't tell if deadeyes was bluffing or not.

Now he was down over 12,000 dollars. Devol caught the eye of the nervous-looking barman. He finally figured it out. The bar-bum must be a double-crosser. He must have partnered with deadeyes, and they both must be scamming him. That must be why deadeyes was holding the cards so close. They must be passing some signals or something. He hesitated, his mind working feverishly. Should he fold with triple fives? Again he scrutinized the fidgety barkeeper and decided he was going to fix this problem before they went any further. He shuffled his winning three fives back into the pack.

"Take the pot," Devol growled. "I fold!" He pushed the deck aside. "Don't move, stranger! I'll be right back!"

Everyone rushed out of the way of Devol's steamroller stride toward the bar. Devol grabbed the tapster by his pants and neck and shoved him out the back. Once outside, Devol hurled the pleading man overboard as easily as tossing a toy doll. He turned to go back inside when he was stopped by a grinning man who had observed his disposal of the bartender.

Damen Cypher lit a cigar with his old man's gold lighter. "George Devol," Damen blew out the smoke, "my father use to tell me stories about you."

Devol's cold eyes bored holes into the cocky kid. "And who might yer daddy be?"

"I'm sure you've heard about the silver quarry in Tombstone called the Cypher Lode." Damen offered his hand. "I'm Damen Cypher."

Devol knew the quarry owner, John Cypher. He studied the arrogant stranger and nodded. "Yeah, there's a resemblance."

The two shook hands.

Damen said, "I can tell you something important about your opponent in there." He tossed Devol the gold lighter with the name Lucas McCain scrolled in diamonds. "I'm sure you'll recognize that name."

Back inside the boat, the passengers were so involved with their own gambling that only a few, including Michala and Juan, had seen Devol drag the bartender away.

Juan decided to do a little leg-limbering in case there might be a little ballroom dance after the grueling game. He also tucked two cards in his pants pocket. The heavenly teacher told him that one never knows when something as small as a card might come in handy. He was learning never to doubt an angel. He glanced down at his watch and saw that time was getting short.

He slipped up next to Matt. "Mano, it's six o'clock."

"I know, Kicker. It's a slow process trying to win honestly."

CHAPTER THIRTY-NINE

Cutting the Ace

Devol entered the saloon and slammed the door closed. He stormed back toward his table and bellowed, "Matthew McCain!"

The two boys turned wide-eyed in the direction of Devol's booming voice. Devol shoved a finger directly toward Matt.

"Boy," Devol growled, "yer family's roaming way past those wide fences of your plantation. You're all so honest, good, and smart!"

What? Honest, good, and smart? You think Lucas the Loser is good and smart? He was beginning to wonder if he had the wrong impression of his great grandfather.

Devol chuckled. "We need to hurry and put you McCains out of business before you take over the world!"

"Mano," Juan whispered. "How did marble head find out who you are? Your name was never spoken."

"Don't know, Kicker. It seems like someone just clued him in to who we are. The question is, who?"

Devol glared across the table at the McCain kid. He opened his hand, revealing a gold lighter. He tossed it to the table and dared, "I have a challenge for you, McCain. That is if you rich folk have any guts."

"'Ey Mano, something's up." Juan was stunned to see the ancient artifact. "That's your great grandfather's lighter the stone-head threw on the table."

"What?" Matt's mind was reeling again. "How can that be?"

"Don't know," Juan said. "But don't worry. The foot doctor is on duty."

The card games across the saloon stopped as the people caught wind of the developing battle.

Matt speculated about which of the many tricks Devol revealed in his book he would implement now.

"Mr. Devol, what kind of challenge are you proposing?"

"It's simple, McCain. It's an uncomplicated, double or nothing, winner takes all. I'll bet you your 12,000 dollar gain that with only one try I can cut the ace of spades."

The spectators all chuckled and shook their heads with disbelief.

"They don't think I can do it." Devol stuck his finger in Matt's face. "How about you, deadeyes?"

Deadeyes? Where did that come from? Matt brushed that thought away and focused on the challenge. From Devol's biography, he knew what the tricky head-butter was up to.

"Okay, Mr. Devol, but only if we use a new deck, and I get to shuffle, and we have a third party cut."

"I see. Okay, we'll do it your way."

"Here's my 12,000 dollar bet." Matt stacked up his nice large pile of bills. "Now let's see you cover it."

Devol thumbed off 12,000 dollars and tossed it on top of Matt's money.

"Bartender!" He caught himself with a chuckle. He'd forgotten he'd fed the double-crossing bar-bum to the fishes. He looked over at a deckhand and ordered, "You boy, get us another pack of cards!"

The waiter ran back behind the bar and grabbed a new deck. He brought it over to Devol, who handed it to McCain. Matt opened the deck and removed the two jokers. As he shuffled without any fancy show, he secretly palmed out a card.

Matt sat the deck in the middle of the table. "Mr. Devol, would you like to pick someone to cut?"

Devol spotted the research nut he'd run into earlier. He nodded toward the dame. "Let's have that pretty little babe

RE-DEAL

over yonder come and cut. Professor Nut, I want you to help me with a little research project of my own."

"Why yes, Mr. Devol." Michala glided across the room to the table. "I'd be happy ta assist ya with yer project."

"Cut this deck for us," Devol said with a lustful twinkle in his black eyes. "And take yer time."

As Devol watched the dame cut the deck, he smirked in self-satisfaction. He scanned her from her feet slowly up to her face, stopping at her clear blue eyes. Devol suddenly felt exposed, naked, reprimanded, and he didn't know why.

He shook it off and said, "Very good, sweetheart." He turned back to McCain. "Now, boy, are you ready for me to cut the ace of spades?"

"Anytime, sir. I really want to see this."

Matt gave a slight nod to his sidekick. Kicker caught the communication and prepared for action. Michala watched them with a supportive smile.

Suddenly, with the speed of a doctor's bill, Devol reached behind his coat and whipped out a sleek dagger and stabbed the deck all the way through to the table with a mighty blow. The crowd guffawed and clapped with surprise. Devol stood beaming with triumph. He spun around and laughed and basked in the crowd's amazement at his inventive victory.

"There you have it, McCain!" Devol bellowed. "I cut the ace of spades just as I said I would, and it's a perfect cut, right down the middle. All yer winnings of the day, McCain, back into my hands! Yer a stupid dupe falling for such a doltish trick!"

Matt moved back from the table and spoke loud enough for everyone to hear. "I think, sir, that you will find the ace of spades is the only card in that deck that is unharmed."

Matt slowly pulled from his pocket a card and flipped it over, revealing the ace of spades. The crowd fell silent while Devol stood grinning. With a confident smile, Devol yanked the dagger from the pierced deck and spread the cut cards across the table. He looked for the ace of spades. It wasn't there. Devol's face went slack. He frantically rustled the cards around trying to find it.

He looked up and growled, "There's no one who can palm a card without me spotting him!"

"The Phantom Gambler can!" Captain Masse cried out from the back.

The crowd reacted with excitement as they stared in amazement. Devol seemed to remain in perfect control, but his eyes couldn't hide the image of a ticking bomb ready to blow. In a flash he whipped Matt's coat back to reveal the notorious buckle.

"Yer the Phantom of the Card Table!" Devol stepped back. "Canada Bill told me about you. Yer the self-righteous gambler who exposes our little innocent gambling aids." He shoved a crooked finger toward the buckle. "And I heard about that sequence of cards now christened the Dead Man's Hand! And yer about to become a dead man yourself!"

"Kicker, get the money." Matt moved back by his friend. "Guess it's time to shut down."

Juan grabbed the cash and secured it in his pocket.

"Hold it!" Devol whirled around. "Not even a phantom can go without me giving him leave!"

I'm not a phantom, Matt silently complained.

Devol sprung like a battering ram with his head aimed at McCain's chest. The crowd bunched up like sheep as they moved back against the outer walls. Devol's large, hairless head reflected the light from the bank of chandeliers like an oversized cue-ball. The glaring reflection helped Matt keep track of Devol's location.

As Devol rammed his way forward, Matt thrust his hands out to meet Devol's shoulders and used the momentum to flip his opponent over his head. Devol flew through the air and crashed to the floor. The onlookers reacted with shock at the tricky maneuver. Devol jumped to his feet and turned with fury to throw a table to the side as he advanced on Matt.

As Matt started to back his way toward the door, Captain Masse cried out, "Don't let the Phantom escape!"

Two of Devol's confederates lunged and grabbed Matt by his shoulders. Just as quickly as he was captured, he thrust both his arms to the sides and grabbed the thugs by their necks. He pulled his knees up to his chin, did a backward somersault, and flipped away.

"Cool move, Mano!"

As others charged in, Juan broke their stride with several penetrating kicks. Devol charged like a raging bull. Matt saw him coming and executed a jump kick to Devol's chin, which merely diverted him to the side.

Michala moved about gracefully, avoiding fists and feet. Matt delivered a crashing hook kick to Devol's left ear, followed by a spinning heel hook to the other ear. Devol merely shook his head from the blows and grinned at the invigorating stimulation that came from a sharp smack to the head.

Devol glared hard as he refocused his eyes on Matt. "You dead-eyed phantom! I'm gonna' get you and pop yer head like an irritating boil."

Kicker recalled the clash with Carroll. He recognized that Devol's head was hard as a hammer.

"Mano," Juan yelled out, "concentrate on boulder-brain's body. I think your heels crashing into his head turns him on."

This time as Devol ran in, Matt executed a perfectly timed jump sidekick, which penetrated deep into Devol's soft lower gut. Gas shot from all orifices like a stepped-on bullfrog. Devol grabbed his gut as he gasped for air. Matt lunged again and a step-across sidekick smashed a savage boot into Devol's kidney. The hard-headed man was propelled across the room where he demolished a door and fell outside.

A burst of cold air filled the saloon, causing the flames in the oil lamps to flicker. Devol followed the door down onto the deck where he lay motionless. The end of the fight signaled the onlookers to scramble after the money littering the floor. This precipitated a real brawl, every man for himself.

"Mano!" Kicker grabbed Matt's cane and handed it to him. "It's party time!"

With his cane spinning and making contact with heads and shins, Matt fought off several men at a time.

Juan's adrenaline pumped and his heart raced. He cried out, "We're having fun now!" Kicker's legs were doing the splits as his heels and nunchakus left swollen impressions on the chins and ears of the ruffians. But to his discontent, the skirmish was short.

"Stop fighting and listen!" Matt cried out. "I'm only interested in the money I won fairly. If anyone else wants to try and take my winnings, like Devol, you'll also wake up with a severely bad headache."

"Boys," Michala said with a shake of her head, "all this jumpin' and kickin' must give ya both a heapin' dose of prostration."

"It does that, all right." Matt draped his tired arm around Juan. "You're the college boy here. Tell me, does it give us prostration?"

Juan was laughing in between gasps of air when Captain Cannon entered the gambling hall. At the sight of the Captain, everyone settled down and went back to play. Michala and Juan counted the money—over 24,000 dollars in bank notes and one twenty-dollar gold piece.

"Mr. Cheat, put this in yer pocket for cab charge."

"'Ey Mano." Juan held up the uncut ace. "We have all this cash because that over-grown thug couldn't even cut one little ace."

Juan handed Matt the money, and he quickly stuffed it into his coat pocket.

"I've never seen anyone so easily whip Devol before." Captain Cannon stepped over with his hand outstretched. "I ordinarily will not even permit Devol on my boat."

As the Captain shared stories about George Devol, Damen wormed his way into the cabin. He pocketed the lighter and snatched the dagger for Devol. He slipped up beside Devol and slapped him until he regained consciousness.

Damen handed him the knife and said, "Kill the Phantom, and I'll tell you more winning secrets."

"Mano, watch out!" Juan's eyes widened as he spotted the revived fighter running their way. "That crazy Devol is going to try and cut your ace again!"

RE-DEAL

"Captain Mule Face, you're first!" Devol lunged with the knife toward the Captain's turned back.

Kicker spotted the cannonball the amazing angel had brought from the future. Now he knew what it was for. He grabbed it and hurled it across the room toward Devol. The iron ball hit him in the head and caused the knife to fall short of the Captain's back.

Kicker followed this by jumping and driving a flying sidekick into the still-dazed Devol's chest, knocking him back outside. The fight, armed-against-unarmed, surged out onto the outer deck.

Damen cursed when he saw Devol falling his way. He slipped around the nearest corner to keep from being spotted.

"The Phantom is gonna die!" Devol growled as he shook his head clear. "I'm going to cut yer head off and feed it to the fishes!"

Devol surged forward with his knife in hand, slashing towards the Phantom. Matt delivered a crescent kick to the knife hand and a leg sweep to the feet. This caused Devol to fall backward and hit the railing, flipping over the side. He fell, cursing, down to the icy water.

He surfaced and bellowed, "McCain! You—are—a—dead—man!"

As Matt finished with Devol, Juan disposed of one last aggressor. Those unwilling to fight went back into the saloon in fear. Michala's eyes danced with delight, and Matt breathed an inward sigh as everyone watched Devol slowly dog paddle to shore in the pale moonlight.

"Wow, Miss Guided!" Matt said. "Devol never touched us. It shows you the power of karate."

Juan looked over at the miracle worker Michala. Kicker knew there was more than the might of the martial arts taking place on this time-traveling trip.

CHAPTER FORTY

Licking the Leftovers

"Kicker, do you see my great grandfather's lighter?"

They looked everywhere, but the lighter had disappeared as quickly as it appeared.

"No, Mano. It's gone. Someone must have snatched it while we were having fun."

"So you're the Phantom." Captain Cannon moved over and slapped Matt on the back. "Wow, that was a good fight. I've never seen anyone use a cane for a weapon." He faced Juan. "And you young fellow, I never knew a fellow's legs could split apart and kick like that."

He turned back to Matt. "Mr. McCain, I've also heard of your reputation. If you don't mind, I'd like to hear exactly what happened to Wild Bill Hickok. Bill was a friend of mine, and I was saddened when I heard that he'd been killed. Why don't you and your young fighting friend and that lovely lady come be my guests at the Captain's table for supper tonight?"

"Thank you, Captain. That's very gracious of you. We're privileged, and we accept your invitation."

"We eat at eight," Cannon said as he turned and walked out. "See you then."

As soon as the Captain left, the card tables were righted and the gambling resumed as if nothing had happened. Matt felt a tinge of guilt for wanting to feast at a time when his father was imprisoned and bleeding in a meat locker. Still he was looking forward to some relaxed time with this amazing, amusing lady.

Michala, Michala. I know I've heard that name somewhere before.

RE-DEAL

Later that evening, the passengers, including the newly-married couple, that had been at the poker table gathered around the Captain's banquet table. The groom still wore his black tuxedo, and the bride joined him dressed in a lacy white gown. Next to the happy couple sat the aristocratic English nobleman, and next to him were two bored-looking, cigar-smoking businessmen. The one person missing was the poor clergyman Devol had thrown into the river. The Captain's guests feasted on fried ham, sweet potatoes, collard greens, and fresh-made custard pie.

Juan thought the meal was as fine a supper or Thanksgiving feast as he'd ever enjoyed. Aside from the five holiday meals with Pastor Steve, Kicker couldn't recall sitting and actually enjoying a genuine Thanksgiving dinner for himself. Growing up, he was the one who had the privilege of licking the leftovers from the plates while cleaning up after Cypher and his family.

"Excuse me." Juan lifted his plate. "I'll take another great big slab of that grilled hog meat smothered with some more of that cream sauce."

"Ah, yes." The Captain laughed heartily. "I like to see a young fellow eat swine like a hog."

"He has a hollow leg with a hole in the bottom, Captain Cannon," Matt said. "I should have given you fair warning."

The angel laughed along with the mortal folks. She reached under the table and took her charge's hand and whispered, "Matt, how would ya feel about givin' the bride back her symbol of their binding love. After all, her poor, naive husband was swindled out of it."

Matt hoped something would develop between him and this special lady. "I'd like to keep it," he whispered back.

"Matthew, rings and things are like yer packs of cards. Ya don't care for them unless they're in a special combination that has genuine importance."

"Yeah," Kicker said in a low voice. "You know, Mano—like Queen Victoria's toilet water."

"What?" Matt twisted his face in confusion. "What piece of foolishness are you talking now?"

"I understand what Kicker is tryin' ta say. It's what the Queen privately calls a royal flush. Ya know, a ten to ace in the same suit. Now there is a combination with value."

"That's right, Mano," Juan agreed. "So give it back."

"Just keep stuffing your fat face," Matt snapped with pretend anger. "And mind your own bee's wax."

"Yeah," Kicker continued, "do you have any bee's wax? Honey would be good on the bread."

Matt decided to ignore his friend. He felt so exhilarated at the feel of Michala's gentle hand touching his that Kicker's silliness didn't bother him. He also figured that feeling her soft hand in his was worth more than a replaceable ring.

"Okay, Funny Lady," he said. "I believe I got your point. You want me to make what I do count for something. I agree with you, and I'll give the ring back."

He released her hand and let his open palm fall onto her lap where he gave her leg a tender squeeze.

The angel in human form dropped her fork, flabbergasted at what she'd just felt. She could sense the significance in Matt's caress. As an angel in human form, she felt unfamiliar sparks through her female frame.

Matt smiled as he pulled from his coat pocket what he thought must be at least a six-carat diamond.

He handed the ring across to the groom. "Please take this wedding ring and put it back on your lovely bride's finger. And keep it there where it belongs."

The young groom took the ring with a look of both surprise and contrition.

Matt added, "And don't play cards anymore. You've got too much to lose."

"Why, thank you, sir." The young groom bowed slightly and asked, "Can I make it up to you somehow?"

"Yeah," Matt replied with a slight nod. "How about saying something nice to your lovely new bride?"

RE-DEAL

Michala was misty-eyed as she watched Matt. She leaned over to Juan and said softly, "This is wonderful, Kicker. Quite movin'." She nodded toward the beautiful weeping bride. "Look—real tears."

"Yeah, pretty cool, I suppose." Juan lifted a fork full of ham to his hungry mouth, hoping he'd never surrender to the trap of marriage. "But I have a question. Why does a bride dress in all white?"

Miss Guided wiped a tear from her eye. "Why, Kicker, she's dressed in all white because it's the happiest day of her life."

Kicker crammed his mouth with the tasty ham so he wouldn't say what he was thinking. *If that's the case, then why is the groom dressed in all black? Like the Tarsus dude Paul, I'm a bachelor to the rapture.*

The thankful husband turned to his wife and said, "Sweet darling, I'll never gamble again."

The Captain pushed his chair back from the table as he watched the happiness shared by the couple he had recently married. He gave a moan of pleasure as he pulled an ornate gold cigar case from his coat pocket. Cannon removed a cigar and went through the ritual of lighting and inhaling.

The bride smiled as her repentant husband took her hand and slid her ring back in place.

For the moment Matt forgot about his problems and felt a shiver of elation even in the midst of their current problems.

The angel blotted her eyes as she felt Matt take her hand again and give it another soft squeeze.

The clacking forks and knives suddenly stopped as Cannon sucked in the paunch at his belt. He stood and raised his glass for a toast. "Here's to the Phantom!" He turned back to the couple. "Hear! Hear! To a long and fruitful life, with lots of babies."

Matt didn't like being called the Phantom, yet he was sure the Captain meant no offense.

Everybody nodded as the group clinked glasses. After hours of food, laughter, and conversation, the time-travelers started back to their cabin.

CHAPTER FORTY-ONE

Marriage and ... Things

Juan walked with Michala just ahead of Matt. He nibbled on tidbits left over from the captain's feast as he debated with himself whether he should let the angel know how much Matt liked her. He downed the remaining morsel, then he sailed the saucer off the side of the boat into the night.

"My, my, Kicker." Miss Guided shook her head in amazement. "Yer stomach should not be rumbling from hunger for a mighty long spell."

"As an angel in human form," he lowered his voice even more, "can you marry and ... things? You see, I think Matt is starting to like you more than just as a friend."

She was temporarily set back at the suggestion. "Well, confidentially, I've never had that question asked of me before. As a direct contact angel, I suppose marriage is in my vast periphery of options. But I have never utilized it."

"I just wanted to give you a heads-up. And thanks for helping my friend." Kicker hesitated as he recalled how Cypher used to have him whipped with a riding crop. He lifted his thoughtful gaze. "I would like you to know, I'm also very thankful."

"Why thank ya, Kicker. It's my pleasure, too. Your faith and funnies are fabulous."

Matt caught up with his companions. He placed an arm on each of their shoulders and stuck his head between theirs. "What's all the whispering up here?"

RE-DEAL

"'Ey Mano." Kicker clapped Matt on the back. "Just explaining what an amateur you are with the ladies."

Matt stopped Juan and slugged him playfully in the shoulder as Michala continued to move down the hall.

"Thanks for the help," Matt said, feigning hostility. "Next time I need the backing of a neophyte, I'll call you."

"Any time, Mano. Gonna explore the boat and try to find some more grub. Then I'm gonna crash on one of those fancy chairs in the hallway outside that built-for-one cubicle."

"Where do you put it all? I've never seen a hog eat like you."

"Got to keep my Superman feet charged up." Kicker lowered his voice and said, "I got your message that you would like time alone with the miracle worker. So why don't you take her for a little stroll around this bobbing bathtub?"

Matt's heart skipped a beat. He was surprised his sidekick called her a miracle worker, though she seemed pretty amazing to Matt.

"Thanks, my zany friend, but for now I'm only interested in helping my dad get free from that butcher Cypher. But, please save me a nice warm chair. After I walk her back to those pitifully-furnished quarters, I'll join you. Remember, make sure you first bite the worms before they bite you. Happy hunting."

Matt hurried and caught up to Michala, again wondering where he'd heard that name.

"Miss Guided," Kicker hollered. "If Matt gets fresh, zap him!"

Kicker turned away and headed toward the kitchen. Michala moved back and met Matt.

"Matthew, where is Kicker off to?"

"He's exploring." Matt took her hand. "It's a beautiful night. What do you say we do the same?"

"I'd be pleasured, Matthew, but just for a brief spell."

Damen had been standing at the top of the stairway listening. He'd been shocked and infuriated at how easily the two had taken care of Devol and the others. Now he had to come up with another plan to rid himself of the men and to get hold of the woman and force her to take him back to the future. He followed behind Matt and the woman as they wandered toward the prow of the boat.

Matt walked Miss Guided up to the edge and leaned over the rail with her. The night was clear and cool, with a bright moon overhead. They watched the bulky paddle wheel slowly work its way up the current. Off in the distance, little cottages nestled among the tall, leafy magnolias and red oaks. The reflection of the moonlight glimmered in the smooth river, and lightning bugs flitted across the black-velvet sky. Far away, the crickets battled the June bugs for top billing.

Matt was relaxed and comfortable right here with the fine woman, a rare treat for him during these strange jumps through time. He wanted to savor the moment, though he continued to have stabs of guilt about losing focus over his mission. However, he thought some release of tension might help keep his skills sharp during the fights, and more importantly, the games.

"Brrr!" Michala wrapped her arms around herself against the crisp evening. "It's chilly out here."

Matt removed his long frock coat and wrapped it around her, then arranged his arms around her waist and gently pulled her close. He gazed into her eyes. She was close enough for him to see her fuzzily. She smelled and looked so nice.

Then he remembered where he'd heard that beautiful name Michala. It was the name of Lucas the Loser's son's tutor.

Michala looked directly into his eyes. "What burning conviction are ya suppressin' in yer heart, Mr. Matthew McCain?"

Matt wanted to tell her how his love for her was growing. But he didn't know how to say it, or even if he should. Given the combination of miraculous circumstances and dreadful conditions they were brought together under, he didn't know if it would be proper. He released his arms from around her waist and ran one hand up her arm to her shoulder. With his other hand he lightly touched her soft rosy cheek with his sensitive fingertips.

"Grandpa Lucas had a tutor named Michala," Matt murmured. "Love that name. It's beautiful, like you."

Michala smiled at the memory of her past charge's son, Davy William.

"Why thank ya, Matthew." She gazed back into the eyes of David's grandson. "Ya really are a sweet talker; ya really are. And I think I like it."

Matt wondered if his sentiment for her was evident on his face. As he admired the moon shining on her blonde hair, he thought it looked like spun threads of gold. She was so beautiful, inside and out. Again he mused that maybe he didn't have the right to consider romance at this crazy time in his life.

"Michala, if you don't mind, may I ask you something?"

As the beautiful lady nodded, Matt caught a glimmer of the bright moon shining in her soft blue eyes.

"Sure, anything ya like Matt."

He decided to ask something that had been rattling around in his head like seeds in a dry gourd. "Has anyone ever asked you to get married before? Uh, I'm sorry that's not what I mean. What I intended to say …"

Matt stifled a moan. He'd meant to ask if she'd ever been asked to go on a date. Not get married. But such a strange, unexplainable feeling had risen in him that he seemed to lose all control of his tongue. He was worried she was going to think he was a zealous fool.

Again the angel was set back at the inquiry. *Twice in one night,* she thought in surprise. *Funny time—always the finest way to get free from a fanciful difficulty.*

"Oh yes, I've been asked ta get married time and time again."

"Is that right?" Matt asked with a touch of jealousy. "By who?"

Her sky-blue eyes sparkled bright from the moonbeams. "By my mama and papa." She gave Matt a gentle jab in the rib and grinned. "Got ya, Matthew."

Matt released a breath of air, glad that it was only a joke. He was also relieved that she didn't think of him as an offensive idiot. Maybe there was still a possibility she'd go out with him.

"Funny Lady." Matt spoke nonchalantly to cloak his fear. "You're really wonderful. Do you ever dream of going on a real date, with me, sometime?"

"Dream of going on a date? Oh no, I never have nightmares. Just kiddin'. I love dates, just so long as they're pitted."

She did it again, he thought. *She ducked another question with a joke. How does she do it so easily? I certainly do love this funny lady. She really knows how to put joy in my pained soul.*

"Miss Guided. Michala." Matt lightly held her by the shoulders. "I'm amazed how you can take any question and turn it into a silly josh."

"Call it divine perspiration." Unsettled, she tried to turn the topic back to their task. "What time is it gettin' on to be?"

Matt pulled his clock from his pocket. When he pushed the talk button, the synthesized voice seemed loud in the quiet of the night.

"23 hours 5 minutes 10 seconds remaining."

The voice shocked Matt from romance to the reality of how little time his father had left. Big Lew's threats kept blazing around like a wild fire in his head.

"Miss Guided, I've used up half our time, and I'm only a quarter of the way there. I'm not earning money fast enough." He took her hands into his and said, "We only have time for two stops. I need big games. Next let's stop in Tombstone, and then I should have enough money to try the rich Andrews House in Carson City."

Shivering off to the side, Damen took note of the places Matt was headed to next. He had to stop McCain before he

RE-DEAL

spoiled the Cypher family's fortune. And the worst-case scenario would be the loss of Damen's birthright as the new Cypher lord. His eyes gleamed from an evil malignancy deep within his soul. Like his old man, he would and could do anything to make sure these three didn't affect his ascension to the Cypher throne.

The guardian angel in disguise told her charge, "You'll need yer quietude. Let's head back."

Matt led his treasured lady friend back to her berth. They stopped at the door where she removed his coat and handed it back to him.

"Much obliged, sir, for the use of yer nice warm coat."

Matt slid his coat back on and stood by the door vacillating. He wanted to touch his lips to hers. After an uncomfortable hesitation, he took one of her dainty hands between his strong fingers, slowly raised it to his lips, and kissed the back of it like he'd seen the Captain do earlier.

"Good night, Miss Guided. Sweet dreams."

"Thank you. Snatch yourself a few Z's too, Matthew, sweet ones."

Matt's gaze lingered on her as she closed the cabin door. As he walked down the hallway toward Juan, he bashed his head on a dark wall lamp and knocked his hat off. With a mild curse at his blindness, he replaced his hat and joined Juan on a chair in the passageway.

Kicker sluggishly slid one eye open, shut it, then snapped both eyes open. He was lounging with his head cocked in a sizing-up sort of way.

"Yer not barbecued beef. You must have been a gentleman. Too bad. I could have used a little midnight snack."

Matt flopped down into the Victorian chair next to his comrade. "I know how to handle the ladies, Bro."

"Yeah, right," Kicker said with a chuckle. "You couldn't tell the difference between the lips on a female from a frog."

Matt draped his coat over his body and covered his face with his hat. "Good night, Kicker."

Apprehension and concern again consumed Matt. He tried to turn off the brutal scene with his father, the bloody thumbs, and the cross—the moment kept playing over and over again in his mind.

After an hour of exhausted worrying, he finally dozed off into a fitful sleep.

The next day after a long dinner—with thirds for Juan, they packed and cleaned up. Then they joined the passengers waiting on the brisk sunlit deck to de-board.

Anxious and a little embarrassed after the moonlit walk with Miss Guided the night before, Matt knew he liked her, but he still didn't know how she felt about him.

Kicker said, "I'm wondering how stone-head knew your real name."

"I don't know. That also has me baffled. I still haven't figured out how my great grandfather's lighter was in Macaw's possession back in Deadwood and is now here with Devol." He turned to Michala. "You're very quiet today, Miss Guided. What do you think? How did Devol know my name?"

"Well, Mr. Cheat, there's an intricate network of forces out there for ya ta bang yer purposes against. And yer actions and conduct against this malevolent malignancy will determine if yer devoured or receive yer designed blessings."

"Whoa, Mano," Juan said. "It sounds like you're gonna have a battle with the devil himself."

"That's it, Kicker," the angel said with a nod. "And Matthew, I know ya have it in ya ta combat the pressing lion before ya."

"Don't worry, Mano," Juan told his amigo. "If that lion tries to eat you, I'm sure your stringy, bad-tasting flesh will cause him to spit you right out."

Everyone was laughing at Juan's silliness when Michala spotted her stagecoach and Seraphim.

"Boys, yer chariot awaits. I see Seraphim and my buggy waitin' for us at the boat landin'. That was a very nice trip, don't ya reckon?"

RE-DEAL

"Yes it was, Miss Guided," Kicker said. "I believe that newly married man learned a valuable lesson about the crooked ways of the world."

In his hiding place, Damen tried to figure how he was going to get aboard the outlandish vehicle without being detected. He couldn't wait to get off this boat.

When the gangplank lowered, the three travelers alighted from the steamer and walked over to the buggy and Seraphim. The majestic white stallion let out a big happy-to-see-you whinny.

CHAPTER FORTY-TWO

Too Ornery to Live In

Matt was overwhelmed at how something unseen continued to encourage him from within. He knew this remarkable lady's allegiance to, as his sidekick put it, the Big Man in the Sky, had something to do with the help he was receiving. Yet there were other disturbing, unexplainable things taking place during these fascinating trips through history.

As much as Devol's knowing his name and the mystery of the lighter bothered him, Matt knew that to fret over the unknown would only distract him from his mission. Somehow he was being tested. His father's life depended on his honestly earning 100,000 dollars against a bunch of cheaters and killers. The one good thing Matt was discovering was that his great grandfather Lucas might not be the stupid loser he'd always believed him to be.

Matt slid into his seat. He reached into his inner coat pocket and removed his fat hoard of cash.

"We have over 24,000 dollars here," he said. "The bummer is we still need about 75,000 more to buy a seat in the big game."

He punched his talking timepiece. "Time remaining 8 hours 10 minutes 40 seconds."

"I made a serious blunder. No more riverboats. We're trapped aboard, and they use up too much of our short time. We need places where we can get in and out, fast."

RE-DEAL

"Well, then it sounds like it's best we shove on down the line." Michala pulled out her knitting. "So, Mr. Cheat, where to now?"

"Let's go," Juan mumbled. A molar in his mouth hurt, whether from a cavity or from a crunching fist in his face he didn't know. "I have a toothache, and perhaps the skip through time will fix it."

"I know the place, Miss Guided. The year, 1880; the place, Tombstone, Arizona. That's our next destination. When we get there, if our human garbage disposal still has a toothache, there's a dentist there who might do a little fang-yanking for him."

Crouched outside the coach, Damen shivered in fear. *Not Tombstone! I hate snakes!* The coach started forward, leaving him squatting alone on the ground. Even at the risk of scorpions, sidewinders, and head-scalpers, Damen wasn't going to be stranded here in nineteenth-century squalor. He lunged forward and grabbed hold of the backend of the buggy and again prepared himself for the miserable experience of being hurled from one generation to the next.

"Hang on, fellows!" The angel cracked the window and cried, "Hyaaa! Giddy up, Seraphim. Let's pound a hoof and whirl a wheel. The time, 1880; the place, Tombstone, Arizona."

With a characteristic lurch, Seraphim, the coach, and the four travelers again pierced their way through time.

Damen was gasping and breathless as he scarcely made it inside his hiding place before the carriage had departed from the wharf. He fretted over the horse's leg beside him and the snakes he expected to face at the next stop.

Years later, or maybe it was only a minute—the boys really couldn't say for certain, the stagecoach set down in the town that proclaimed itself "too ornery to live in."

"Miss Guided," Juan said with a couple of nods and a broad grin. "From what I've heard from Matt, Tombstone is a pleasant place for a family outing. It's filled with Apaches and rattlesnakes, and there's always a constant fifty-mile-an-hour breeze to keep the dust from settling on the 110-degree streets."

"That's it," Matt agreed with a sweaty nod. "That's the way my father read it to me. In this crazy town, there are brutal deaths every day. The thing in our favor is the gambling houses are always open for business."

Seraphim halted the carriage in front of a place called The Grand Hotel.

"This is your stop, Mano." Kicker made a grand gesture. "Tombstone, a place named for all those who blocked bullets with their bodies."

Matt threw the door open. "Let's hustle!"

They jumped down into a dirty silver-mining settlement. The late summer sun was descending behind the barren foothills, casting long shadows and bringing down the temperature.

"Wow, Mr. Cheat. It's as hot as a goat's bottom in a pepper patch."

The setting sun tormented Matt with the realization of the brief time remaining.

A little while after the buggy had come to a halt, Damen opened the trunk and peeked out. He spotted the woman running after Matt. He looked hard down at the hot, sandy dirt for anything that might creep or crawl.

"Hold up, boys!" Michala cried as she caught up with Matt and Juan. "Let's stay together."

As the group trudged down the dirty road, the dust slapped their boots and throats. They came upon a large graveyard filled with dozens of leaning crosses and tipped-over gravestones.

"'Ey Mano." Kicker pointed with a chuckle. "That memorial says, 'Told You I Was Sick!'" He pointed to another. "And that one over there says, 'Played 5 Aces, Now Plays a Harp!'" He elbowed his amigo and chuckled. "With five aces, I would guess he's more likely playing the devil's pitchfork."

The three laughed as they moved on down the hot road. They passed by the harness shop, then the blacksmith, and

RE-DEAL

then they spotted the famous Oriental Saloon. By the time they set foot in the foyer to the gambling hall, they were a sandy shade of brown from all the wind-blasted dirt. Once inside the lobby, they brushed their clothes off and tried to wipe the dust from their irritated eyes.

"Come here under this nice whirlin' fan, boys. I want to clean yer dusty faces." Miss Guided removed a hanky from her handbag and helped the boys wipe the soil from their faces and watery eyes. She placed the wipe back into her bag.

"Matthew, ya sure know how ta pick fanciful places ta take a girl."

As Matt felt her hands touching his, he tried to steady himself. Although he didn't want to concede the powerful emotions swirling around in him for this beautiful, whimsical woman, he had to admit he loved Michala and wanted to tell her so. However, he still didn't have the nerve.

"'Ey Mano," Kicker said as he gazed around the gaming house. "This place isn't as nice as the tooting tub, but I can tell there's real money here. And the fancy bar-back across the room is filled with bullet holes. Maybe more fun, huh?"

He picked up a copy of the local paper, The Epithet. He moved under the fluttering fan with Matt and Michala.

"'Ey Mano, listen to the headline on this paper. It says, 'Dead Men Don't Lie!'" He glanced up and grinned. "If they don't lie, well then, what do they do, sit up?"

"Yer an unfailing card, Kicker. Ya positively are!"

Matt thought the lovely lady's laugh was like the delightful tinkle in a music box. "Yeah, Kicker, keep it up, and I'll put you on display with the prancing pigs at the local carnival."

After the three were out of view, Damen slipped out of the trunk. He placed his foot right beside a large sunning rattlesnake. He heard the well-known sound of the rattle and his bowels almost busted loose from fright. *No! I hate slithery crawly things.* He had to bite his tongue to keep the words in his mind.

He moved along the boardwalk, trying to keep out of sight. He watched as McCain and the others entered the Oriental Saloon. He peeked around the entrance and watched as his enemies laughed at some old newspaper. He slinked behind them straight into the gambling saloon and out of sight.

The travelers entered the primary gaming hall. Matt's focus was drawn to a thunderous hacking cough.

He whispered, "I hear the respiratory problems of a direly diseased man. I have no doubt it's that tuberculosis-infected gambler, Doc Holliday." He challenged his friend. "Kicker, if you still have that toothache, it's said that with one shot, Holliday can extract a tooth from twenty-five yards."

"Thanks for the concern." Kicker gave Matt a mischievous slug on the shoulder. "My tooth is all better."

"Miss Guided," Matt whispered. "Describe to me the other card players you see."

"That poor, ill Mr. Holliday is sittin' at a full table of miserable-lookin' poker players. At the next table is a tall, handsome United States Marshal. He's dealin' cards on a table with a picture of a pretty, orange tiger on the felt."

"Wow, Kicker, another legend. That officer is Wyatt Earp, and the game Wyatt's dealing is called faro. He was part owner of this saloon. It was supposed to be the fanciest and most profitable casino in Tombstone."

Virgil and Morgan, Wyatt Earp's brothers, were amusing themselves adding more holes in the dark wood of the bar.

Michala spoke with a worried shake of her head. "As I see it, Matt, I imagine with all the loud discharges I don't need ta tell ya that there are guns. Those two boys seem to be as crazed as two hoot owls in a single burrow."

Matt said after a long deep breath, "Well, that explains the holes Kicker mentioned. But I have to go play. Crazy or not, here I go."

CHAPTER FORTY-THREE

Doctor of Psychopathology

Matt bumped his way through the crowd, followed closely by Kicker and Miss Guided.

Inside the casino, the dentist Doc Holliday stared at the newcomers. At the sight of the girl, he made a quick attempt to straighten his wrinkled black suit and the lopsided bolo around his neck. He slammed back a shot-glass of hooch; he hacked, coughed, then choked up some of the whisky with phlegm.

"Fetch the lady a sarsaparilla." Holliday nodded toward the bartender and wheezed. "Then show her the door. No dames allowed. Would the gentlemen like to join our little poker game?"

With every word, Holliday exhaled vile, bitter-smelling fumes.

"Whoa, Kicker!" Matt said as he shook his head clear. "With that breath, Holliday could take down an army of commandos alone."

"Yeah," Kicker agreed. "You play him, and I'll get the mouthwash."

Matt propped his cane up against the bar, and pulled a one-inch thick roll of bills from his coat pocket.

"Doc Holliday." Matt fanned out his cash. "I've acquired a few dollars. When a seat becomes available, I'd like to join you."

As Holliday's eyes feasted on all the currency, he hacked up more death spew and wiped his thin mouth off on his moist coat sleeve.

Gesturing toward an occupied chair, he said, "Sit down stranger! Josh was about to get!"

"I have no such aim," Josh said. "Mr. Holliday, you got thousands of my dollars. And I ain't wantin' to leave until my luck turns."

"It just turned," Holliday growled. "Good night!"

Quick as a stepped-on sidewinder, Holliday pulled from his breast pocket a two-shot forty-five-caliber derringer and blasted Josh dead. All gambling paused as curious eyes turned to witness Josh getting blown out of his chair. Holliday sat there calmly holding his belly-buster with a wisp of smoke curling from the barrel.

The coarse men at Holliday's table were accustomed to flying lead. However, after determining faro might be a less molesting game, they quickly grabbed their chips and moved to Wyatt's table. Other gambling cowboys and rustlers gazed over and spied the dead man. However, they mellowed once they recognized it was merely Holliday behaving the gentleman by freeing a chair for some outsider. They all resumed their drinking and gambling.

One intoxicated scoundrel dubbed Buckskin stood to his feet. Buckskin received this moniker because he outfitted himself in all-male-deerskin leather. His velocity with a six-shooter had relegated to the soil mounds of worm chow. He downed his potion and staggered toward the dead soul. He squatted down and checked the lifeless corpse.

"Not too shabby for point-blank range. Right twixt the eyeballs." Buckskin's mouth wobbled into a demented grin. "Nonetheless, Doc, yer still as slow as a tipped-over tortoise."

Holliday grinned as phlegm oozed from the edges of his tight lips. He calmly turned to Wyatt. "Self defense. Right, Marshal?"

Wyatt and his two brothers, Virgil and Morgan, were all United States Marshals. The brothers were apt to overlook the keen points of the law when they became bothersome with their personal interests and benefits. This afforded the Earp brothers the covetous position of defrauding the gullible dopes, then pulling out their badges and guns and running them out of town. Holliday was a good blade to have in a gunfight, so Wyatt kept him around even though he thought he was a smelly psychopath.

"That's right, Doc." Wyatt nodded. "I saw what happened, and it was a clear case of self-defense. But, remember, when you're in town, carrying a non-concealed weapon is prohibited."

"Don't worry, Wyatt." Doc opened his coat. "Look, it was hidden."

Wyatt nodded his approval and turned back to the bar. "Ned," Wyatt said to the bartender, "fix me the usual."

Ned insisted, "Wyatt, tell yer brothers to stop shootin' at the bar, and I'll pass ya my specialty."

"Sure," Wyatt yelled. "Cut the fire, boys."

Holliday glared at the newcomer. "Stranger, show the babe the door. Now! Then sit down. It looks like it'll be just us two!"

Matt's stomach jumped with panic. Holliday's invitation sounded more like an ill-tempered order rather than an invite.

"No siree, Matt." Michala moved close to Matt and pleaded. "I don't think ya should play cards with that Holliday. I suspect he's a Doctor of Psychopathology. Please, Matthew, let's find a different game somewhere else. I want ya ta fulfill the chore the good Lord assigned ya. But ya can't do it if that Holliday gives ya a lead-filled prostrate corpse."

"Yeah," Kicker said with a chuckle. "I don't want you to have any excuses for dying around on the job when there is still work to do."

"I can't, my funny friend." Matt drew close to Michala and lightly held her by the waist. "I need to keep playing, and this is the richest place in town."

"Again yer not payin' me much mind, Matthew. Do I need ta get rough and square yer ears?"

"Oh, no. I hear you just fine, Miss Guided. But, our time is running out, and it doesn't matter where we go. All the players seem to be dangerously crazy." He faced Juan. "Kicker, I'm sorry, but someone needs to stay with Miss Guided. Considering I'm the only one who will play cards, that leaves you, my friend. Come on, Kicker, let's step outside. I need you to protect this fine woman for your amigo." Matt turned to Doc Holliday. "I'll just take the lady outside and be right back right ready to play."

As Matt pushed them forward, he didn't want his allies to realize he was afraid to remain alone, by himself, without them, his faithful backup. But he needed desperately to know he could take care of himself without anyone having to watch over him. Furthermore, he knew it was his family's fault that they were all in this mess in the first place.

As Damen watched Matt leave, he saw his chance. He hurried over to the sick Holliday. Damen handed the gunman his father's lighter and beseeched him to step aside for a minute. "I have something important to say to you about the man you're about to play against."

Outside, the time travelers walked back to Seraphim and the carriage. "Don't fret, Miss Guided," Matt said. "I'll be okay. While I play, see if you and Kicker can rustle up some chow."

"Sure, Mr. Cheat." Juan patted Seraphim on the nose. "Yeah, I'm sure Seraphim would like a burger and some fries. But Mano, at the first sign of trouble, you call on your amigo, the foot doctor, okay?"

Matt nodded and tried to chuckle. "You got it, my friend."

Michala pulled some cards from her bag. "Come on, Kicker. Let's go practice throwin' cards and find some grub."

"Yeah, good idea." Juan rubbed his starving stomach. "It's either been two hours or two years since the last time we've gobbled down anything, and I could eat a horse."

At that moment Seraphim looked over and let out a curious whinny.

RE-DEAL

"Sorry, Seraphim," Juan said. "Nothing personal. I meant to say elephant, barbecued and smothered in onions."

"Miss Guided, don't let this hollow leg pester or irritate anybody out of their food," Matt said. "He can only have worms, and if a circus comes to town, stick him in the Marshal's jail until the elephants are gone. Do that for me, okay?"

"Why, of course," she replied with a snicker.

Matt leaned over and gave Michala a soft kiss on the cheek. "Thanks!"

The direct contact angel's eyes went wide with surprise. She held the cards out for Kicker to take.

"Thanks," Kicker said as he grabbed them. "Now zap him!"

"Miss Guided, is it true that in some parts of Africa, a man doesn't know his wife until he marries her?"

"Mano," Kicker said with a sly grin. "You are really countrified when it comes to women. That's the way it is in every country on the planet. That's why the Tarsus Dude never got hitched."

Michala chuckled at Kicker's silliness. She turned back to her charge and took his hands into hers and gave his fingers a gentle squeeze to impart some encouragement and assurance.

"Matthew, contemplate any predicament like one of yer poker hands. Ya can guise a wimpy pair of deuces into a triumphant winner. In contrast, if ya swindle, indeed five aces will be defeated. Ya beheld the words on that old tombstone back yonder that said, 'Played Five Aces, Now Plays a Harp.' Hence bestow all the effort yer Maker put in ya."

"Thanks, Michala." This time Matt leaned forward and gave her a quick peck on the lips. "I'll make sure those ducks are wild."

"I saw that!" Kicker cried with an accusing shake of his firm finger. "Those ducks aren't wild, you are!"

"You just keep your feet ready. And after you gorge yourself, brush your teeth or I'll send you back to the dentist in that saloon."

CHAPTER FORTY-FOUR

No Playin' with a Spook

Matt reluctantly went back inside, leaving his friends with the horse. He was falling in love with Michala, and he didn't want her around all these menacing gunfighters. He most certainly would prefer to operate apart than to risk endangering her. He knew Kicker would watch after her with his life. He took in a deep breath and blew it out, then pushed his way through the swinging doors of the Oriental. He gripped his cane firmly as he headed back to Holliday's table.

"Gentlemen." Holliday belched. "May I have your civility? We're favored to have with us today the Phantom of the Card Table. No one has yet figured out who he really is or where he comes from. Now I am gonna acquaint you to his misdeeds and multifarious masks. He beat Canada Bill at Bill's own game. He predicted the death of Wild Bill Hickok, then whipped the undefeated fighter George Devol. His on-the-road-accomplice, that marm you all just saw leaving, calls him Mr. Cheat. A very entertaining name, yes?

"Now back in Deadwood, he called himself The Cruddy Kid. Why anyone would favor to be identified with bull hockey is beyond me. And, have you noticed his appearance is much like that rich rancher, Lucas McCain? I have crossed McCain's path on plenty of occasions. This Phantom could be Lucas's kid brother. They look alike because they are kin.

RE-DEAL

His true name is Matthew McCain. However, his comrades just call him Magoo. That designate I can't puzzle out neither. But considering I suppose the Phantom is here to challenge me to a card duel, I require that the remainder of those who don't want to play move back and give us some room!"

Everybody registered the menace beneath the polite tone. They all scrambled to comply with the dangerous Holliday's request.

Whoa! Matt wondered. *What happened while I was outside?* He felt like his heart just vaulted into his throat. He started to panic. Matt realized Michala was accurate in her reckoning, and he'd better get out fast. Something uncanny was going on, and he didn't think he should stay and find out what it was. Matt circled around and dashed back to the exit where he ran square into the leathery chest of Buckskin.

Buckskin twisted him around and shoved him back toward Holliday's table. "Get back over yonder and hunker down! Yer not gonna be leavin' until yer bankroll is scattered."

"All right!" Matt wrenched himself free. "Just keep your grubby paws off the merchandise!"

Matt realized he had to sit down and play. His father's life was in the balance. And he remembered how agitated the other players got when he clutched his poker hands close enough to his face to figure out the value of his cards about half the time.

But, the biggest blow to Matt's ego was that most of the cash he'd won so far hadn't come from any actual gambling proficiency. The money had come from unmasking cheats at Hickok's table and from keeping Devol from his marked cards and from knowing Devol's cut-the-ace con.

Matt realized Holliday would be wary of any odd behaviors. He decided that if they played only games where most of the cards were face up, things would be easier. With Holliday, he needed to see every card in play. Now if he could just exploit his abilities with the cards it would be no obstacle to trounce the cheating Holliday.

But, why can't I use them? After all, wasn't it God who gave me my talents in the first place? No, no, Matt reproached himself, *that's wrong to think.* He shook his head clear.

He was trying to rationalize wrongdoing. Matt knew he was being tested, and the wonderful Miss Guided would be upset with him for even contemplating such a dishonest impulse. He didn't want to disappoint her. He loved her. So he would play straight.

All those years he'd fantasized about beating the scoundrels, he'd envisioned doing it by playing on their own cheating level. At which, with his touch perception and expertise, he would slaughter them. He never thought he'd have to try and beat them honestly, especially since he could barely see the cards.

Matt decided the best way to cloak a problem and liberate any suspicion was to lay the predicament out for all to see. So he turned and faced Holliday straight on.

"Doctor Holiday. If I'm gonna play at your table, I have two requests. I'll play as long as you have at least 20,000 dollars to gamble with."

Holliday scooped up the numerous bills in front of him. He held them up in plain view. His bloodshot ice blue eyes glared coldly.

"Don't worry, Phantom. I've got what it takes to take what you've got! Moreover if I need more bank notes, Wyatt is part owner of this saloon and he'll back me any sum I lack." He looked over toward the Marshal. "Isn't that right, Wyatt?"

"Yeah," Wyatt nodded. "Anything you say, Doc."

"Any others want to join in?" Holliday surveyed the room. "Virgil? Morgan?"

"We're gonna sit this one out," Morgan said. "We ain't playin' cards with no spook!"

"Cowards!" Holliday slurred. He looked back to the Phantom and asked, "And what's your second petition?"

The whisky-filled breath reeked so intensely that Matt felt like he was about to succumb from the stench.

RE-DEAL

"As you may or may not know, to some extent I came by my notoriety as the Phantom of the Card Table on account of I see no better than a bat." He held up his cane. "So, if you don't mind, I'd like to play only five-card stud and have Wyatt declare the face-up cards as they're dealt."

Holliday slammed back one more shot of his foul-smelling booze. He set down the bottle as he nodded. Holliday stood up from his chair and held onto the table until he stopped swaying. He stumbled over and held a murmured conversation with Wyatt and Buckskin. Wyatt stayed but the gunman left. Holliday blundered back to his table and steadied himself by gripping the back of his chair.

"Sit a spell, Phantom," Holliday snapped. "Wyatt will turn his faro game over to his brother, Virgil. Then he's gonna come read the cards to you as well as deal the game."

Matt preferred having Wyatt deal rather than Holliday. He leaned his cane against the bar and hesitantly sat down across from the Doctor. He wished he could call on Michala and Kicker for support, but he was trapped.

Holliday glared across the table and spit. "We have all heard of yer mysterious exploits in Deadwood and elsewhere. Presently we're gonna see what you can do opposite a genuine gambler."

Wyatt Earp sat down, gathered the cards together, and shuffled. "The game is five-card stud, no rules, no limitation on betting, anything goes."

They both anted, and Matt opened the first round of betting.

Outside Michala moved the coach in front of the Oriental. She waved for Juan to halt his card flinging for the moment and come sit with her. "Kicker, let's see if we can find something to eat."

Juan climbed in and sat across from her.

The guardian recognized her adopted charge was deep in thought. "Stop agonizing, Kicker. Matt can take care of himself." She pondered for a period, then mumbled, "At least I hope he can."

"Man, I'm famished," Juan said. "I've hardly noticed how little I've eaten since, well since ..." Kicker stopped to consider how long it has been between meals. "Miss Guided, when was the last time we foraged for grub? Was it yesterday on the riverboat? Or has it been two years since we bobbed around in that tub? Yeah, yeah, I expect I'm accurate in my analysis. We went forward two years. That's a lengthy interval between foodstuffs. No wonder my stomach is grumbling."

Juan was ready for another romp. He felt for his head-knocking nutcracker. It was gone. "Darn," Kicker complained. "Left my chucks outside. I'll be right back."

"Now!" Damen ordered. "Get them!"

The carriage door flew open. Buckskin and Damen reached in and grabbed the two and dragged them out. Damen cracked Juan on the back of his head with a borrowed gun.

Stunned, Juan fell to his knees, grasping his hurting head. "You—scum—bag!" he whimpered.

Damen kneed Juan in the eye and followed that with additional kicks to the face and body.

Buckskin's dark olive-green eyes gawked carnally at Michala. "The lady never got her sarsaparilla." Buckskin clutched her tiny wrist and tipped his dingy hat with the point of a large dagger. "Cain't allow that! Ya might thinks yer in a den of thieves and cutthroats."

Michala maneuvered herself between Kicker and their two adversaries.

Even though Juan was confused from the crack on the head, he gradually forced himself back to his feet.

The angel could see Kicker was stunned. She wanted to protect him from the two villains. "Kicker," she said. "Please get back in my buggy so Seraphim can take ya somewhere safe."

"Hello, my pretty little alien." Damen pointed the pistol at the irritating woman. "My private investigators were correct. You are from outer space."

RE-DEAL

Juan thought he heard the angel tell him to flee. He was appalled to see Big Lew's evil son standing before him. He had to tell Matt Damen was back here in the gone-by. He attempted to take off but his feet failed.

Damen grabbed him by the hair. He wrapped his arm around Juan's throat, then pointed the gun at his temple.

"Kid, my old man would like to barbecue your flesh and feed it to his dogs."

CHAPTER FORTY-FIVE

A Dame Worth More Than Five Bucks

Back in the Oriental, the game was not going Matt's way. The pot stood at around 11,000 dollars, and both players were going for the jugular.

For the inaugural hour of play, the putrid fumes emanating from Holliday had so distracted Matt that he couldn't concentrate, and he'd lost over 5,000 dollars. But at last Matt had been dealt a hand that should let him take the winnings so they could move on to their next stop.

But Matt had already lost twice because he'd misidentified the cards, and he wanted to be positive. For the third time, he brought his hole card up close to his eyes and squinted hard. This time he was sure it was the nine of spades, giving him four cards aligned in the same suit. He was taking a big gamble by going for broke and betting on the come, especially with Holliday sitting pat with three-of-a-kind. But time was passing too fast, and he had to finish this game—and win it.

Holliday had discovered that swapping cards in front of the Phantom was like plucking feathers off a dead Apache Chief. With three sevens showing, he palmed his facedown card and traded it with the last seven he'd concealed up his coat sleeve. Now he held four sevens. He leaned back in his chair, confident he'd prevail.

Matt knew that cards had been dropping from Holliday's sleeves into his liver-spotted hands since they'd begun to play.

RE-DEAL

Wyatt dealt Matt's final card and to the shock of everybody, Wyatt declared it to be the eight of spades. The Marshal laid it along side Matt's ten, jack, and queen of spades.

Matt took a deep breath. He could scarcely believe his luck, without cheating or wild cards. His straight flush would thrash anything Holliday had, even if his down card was a fourth seven.

Holliday's glassy eyes ballooned. He knew he was in big trouble—Wyatt had already signaled to him MaCain's down card. To keep the winnings, he had to force his opponent to fold his superior hand. The arrogant Cypher character had told him his relation, John Cypher, had found from experience this kind of play never failed. *It's convenient I met that resourceful Cypher fellow*, he thought. *It's gonna be a fruitful day.*

Holliday reclined back in his chair and jerked the bottle from the table. He filled his mouth with more hooch, inclined his head back, gargled, then swallowed. "Phantom, it's imaginable that you might think that you have a superior hand than me, but I know you don't! So, my mysterious little spook, you may as well just fold, climb back in that sissy buggy I understand you sally abroad in, and get!"

"Is that right, Doctor Holliday?" Matt knew there was no way Holliday could quell his straight flush. "If you think you can trounce my hand, let's see you bet those sevens into this potential killer straight flush."

Holliday faltered. He looked around for his backup. If the pelt-cloaked gunman Buckskin didn't show up, Holliday knew the infamous Phantom would financially ruin him. He looked around the room, then laughed and clapped his hands together. "Be patient, be patient. I'm just considering my bet."

Holliday's fingers drummed on the table. At that moment Buckskin rushed in and gave Holliday the high sign. Just as quickly, he turned and hurried back out. Holliday reached into his wrinkled coat pocket and pulled out the gold lighter supplied to him by the Cypher kin.

"My opening stake," Holliday flipped the gold piece onto the table and snapped "is one million bucks." He settled back into his chair and smiled.

Matt didn't like the sound made by the hard object as it landed on the table. He couldn't see it, but he knew it wasn't coin. And it couldn't be valued at a million dollars. He picked up the article Holliday had tossed into the pot. His stomach dropped to his feet, and his mind reeled with emotions and thoughts. *How can this be? It's Grandpa's lighter, again.*

He couldn't keep his voice from trembling. "Where did you get this lighter?"

"I understand that gold piece is over 100 years old. For my part," Holliday said, "I find that hard to suppose, but who am I to differ? However, that's my million dollar bet."

The saloon doors flapped open, and Buckskin pushed Michala through the door and to the bar. He held a dagger firmly across her throat.

Damen shoved Juan in front of him, clutching a gun to his prisoner's head.

Kicker's face was swollen, his eyes blackened, and his clothes torn. Even though his mind was muddled, his spirit didn't waver. He still trusted the Big Man with faith and joy.

Damen knocked Juan to the dirty floor, then laid the gun on the bar close at hand.

The wide-eyed angel wondered if Sir Gabe was right. To go rearward was a really misguided idea.

After Damen checked the floor for snakes and rats, he drew closer to McCain, but not too near, skittish of Matt's cane and feet.

"Hey, Magoo, do you recognize my voice? I'm the one who arranged for your close-up view of the fiery blazes of hell!"

"Damen Cypher, it's you! I had a wretched feeling I got a whiff of you back in Deadwood! As for hell, if you don't beg pardon, hell is where you're headed!"

"Now, now, Magoo, there's no actual Heaven or hell, and I can prove it. If there was some kind of Supreme Being,

RE-DEAL

tell me this. Why did it place that tempting fruit tree with a seductive snake in that Garden?"

He looked down at the floor again, then back toward Matt with his pistol at the ready. "Was that fruit tree put there purposely to tantalize that stupid dame into screwing up? That way some evil being could gleefully hurl humanity into some kind of fiery furnace! What kind of perverted presence would order that? No god would do that on account of there is no god! I told you years ago, we evolved into gods on our own. And, we Cyphers are superior to McCains. That's why Cyphers own the McCain spread, not you. I'm rich and powerful—you're not. I have this slippery little alien under my control—you don't. Therefore, stop trying to be something you're not. A superior evolved being like yours truly."

"Oh yes," Matt goaded. "I remember. You came from a monkey with a kitchen knife. I'll spell it out fast. Why was the tree put there? Mankind has no free will if we can't choose. The tree was put there so humanity was not just a walking gadget. Man had a choice—opt to embrace the almighty Creator or your father, the Cypher snake."

At the word snake, Damen pointed the firearm toward the floor but saw no snakes.

"Very funny, but ludicrous. Now, Loser Magoo, let's ease off for a moment and reconsider the opportunities before us. Like your fantasy babe in the garden, you have two options. If you throw in your cards and stop attempting to get our ranch back, you secure your little magical alien back in one piece. If you do not fold, then you get the pretty little thing returned in two."

A dreadful jolt of fear shot through Matt's body. "Damen Cypher, you depraved piece of scum! If you dare harm my woman, I'll track you down, and may the God you don't believe in forgive me, for I'll rip you to pieces and feed your scraps to those dogs your evil old man is always babbling about!"

"Well, isn't that nice? So the intruder is now your woman?" Damen took a long icy look at Michala. "Perhaps

I shall have a little amusement with her just prior to carving her up, when I actually savor the taste of the space creature's green blood."

Kicker was attempting to regain complete consciousness by rolling around in his head some of his best-liked Bible accounts. *Now,* he thought, *Isaiah was a Bible dude who could scrawl consoling Scriptures. Mexicanos and their amigos that rendezvous with their glorious God on His ground are within reach of renewing their swift kicks to the rump of Satan's seed. The Big Man's amigos shall mount on wings as eagles and fly with infiltrating sidekicks. Godly guys shall kick and not cultivate a fatigued physique. Mexicanos may get pounded with a pistol by a sadistic Cypher but not faint.*

Kicker's head began to clear and he reached for his chucks. Then he recalled they were still outside.

However, he felt a couple of cards in his coat. He recalled the angel had said his cards could come in handy. He slipped them out and held them in his hand. The courageous shepherd David, who later became King Dave, only had a puny slingshot and a prayer, but he brought down the giant Goliath. After the daring Dave lodged a stone inside the forehead of the gladiator, the shepherd gave the Goliath a haircut right below the ears, yet above the combater's collar and triumphantly carried the head to King Saul.

Kicker looked upward and silently uttered, *Thanks, Man in the Sky. With the strength of Your spirit inside, I know I have sufficient power for all perils.*

Holliday coughed up more spew. The Cypher relation had promised that he knew how to make McCain quit and that he would only take half the winnings. Now Holliday reasoned out the scheme.

The Phantom supposes a dame is worth more than five bucks, he thought. *What a fool! Anyone who thinks a dame has actual worth deserves to lose.*

"Phantom, like the Cypher blade said, toss in your hand and get your little girlfriend back in full capacity. But if you don't give up and fold your hand, then you win her back in scraps!"

RE-DEAL

Holliday's bellowing voice made Matt's insides quiver.

Holliday again coughed, choked, and spit. He removed a handkerchief and wiped his sweaty face.

"Doctor Holliday," the lady said. "Ya don't sound good. Did ya know an untreated grippe could pester on for an entire week? Yet, with fine doctorin', a cold can pass away in a scant seven days."

Holliday cleared his throat and growled back. "That's valid thinking. Here's to ya, doctor!"

He inclined the decanter of bathtub gin and embraced another long swig.

Matt didn't know if he should scream, cry, or kill. He had already lost his mother and sister. For now his father was alive, but bleeding, inside some meat locker facing Cypher's menacing threat. Now less than eight hours remained.

Over the past few years, Matt had ardently prayed for some relief. But no ease had ever come his way. Bad things just seemed to pile on. Maybe Damen was right. What sort of God would make a man go through so much? And now he was being compelled to sacrifice the life of either his loving father or the beautiful woman he was growing to love. The thought of choosing between them made him ill.

For now, Matt recognized he plainly had only one option. He lobbed his winning cards to the table. "I fold. Take the money! But, please, please! I beg you—let my friend and the lady go!"

CHAPTER FORTY-SIX

Not a Rubber Blade

Holliday scooped up the money and stuck it in his dingy coat pocket. He lurched to his feet and kicked back his chair.

Foam oozed from the edges of his mouth as he barked, "Now that I've made the celebrated Phantom yield, I'm gonna see if he bleeds." His glazed, bloodshot eyes looked over to his cohorts. "Buckskin, let me borrow yer skinner."

The angel admitted she might need to exploit some of her divine endowments. The host of the heavenly hordes didn't declare she was prohibited from using her paradise powers. She was simply supposed to stay away from fat fish, and there were no fish around this dry, dusty desert.

"Mr. Holliday, I'm obliged ya fancy ta be safe and use Mr. Buckskin's rubber play-pretty." She lifted her hand and dislodged the knife at her neck.

Buckskin tried to stop her, but his paralyzed arms had no strength.

Juan's eyes lit up as he watched the angelic woman slip free from her captor, all the while keeping the sharp edge of the knife under her control.

Buckskin scoffed, "Lady, that butcher blade ain't made outta no rubber. It's made a cold steel."

"Rubber, you say." Damen handed Buckskin his gun and snatched the dagger. "Let's see what occurs at the moment it impacts flesh." He turned to Holliday and said, "Allow me, Doc."

RE-DEAL

Matt's apprehension swelled, and he tried to work his way back to the bar where he'd left his weapon. Just then Damen lunged for his arm, pinning it to the top of the bar. He raised the knife and plunged it down hard into the back of Matt's hand. However, when the tip of the blade made contact with Matt's flesh, the blade folded backward like a wet noodle. Then when Damen pulled the knife back away from his hand, the blade straightened back out.

"What's this?" Damen lifted his eyes and glared at Buckskin. "I can't believe this! Can't anyone get anything right back in these ancient dung heaps? What kind of gunfighter are you anyway? Carting around sissy kid toys!"

"It ain't no playthin'," Buckskin argued. "I used that sharp sticker ta cut the hide from the bucks I used fer these duds."

Damen shrieked, "Oh yeah, watch!" He laid his hand flat out on the bar, then raised the knife high over his head. Just like he'd done to Matt, he slammed the pointed blade down hard into the center of his soft palm. But, this time the razor sharp blade didn't bend. Rather it remained firm, splitting through the flesh, pinning his hand to the bar. In shock Damen screamed out in tormented agony, "Curse you!"

"Somebody needs to stop the Phantom once and for all." Holliday tipped the bottle and sucked down the last drop. "It appears it's gonna have to be your friendly neighborhood Doc."

Holliday was fast on the draw, but Juan was ready. He sailed the two cards hidden in his hand toward Holliday's head. The spinning cards soared at a tremendous speed across the saloon. Like a viper's venom, the cards separately struck each of Holliday's bloodshot eyes, temporarily blinding him and causing him to drop his gun and grab his irritated eyes.

Matt knew he could depend on his sidekick to initiate another painful brawl. And he knew his body was going to hurt, again, so he might as well get it over with. Matt flipped over the poker table and retrieved his cane. Armed with only their martial arts expertise, Matt and Juan stood side by side and faced down the Old West brawlers with their weapons. Matt dropped into a solid karate stance with his cane held like a samurai sword.

"Oh no, here we go again," Matt said. "I hope we're ready."

"Yeah," Juan replied, rejuvenated. "It's time for my favorite dance, the hoof-in-mouth jig!"

Buckskin raised the pistol toward Matt's head and aimed the gun, ready to fire. Miss Guided saw him raise his small two-shot derringer.

"Matt!" she shrieked. "Behind ya, firearm at six o'clock!"

Kicker looked and ducked, just as Matt spun around. Matt's rod crashed down on Buckskin's gun arm, fracturing his wrist, and the gun fell to the floor.

Juan kicked the weapon, and it slid into Holliday's barf.

Buckskin yelped and grabbed his wrist. "I'll kill ya!"

Marshal Wyatt Earp reached for his drink and leaned back against the bar, relishing the evening's entertainment.

Damen screamed in agony as he tugged on the knife pinning his hand to the bar. There was a sharp cry of pain as he liberated the blade from his bloody hand. He raised the red dagger and lunged after Matt. "I'm the one that's gonna kill him!"

As Damen ran past Juan, he stuck out his foot, and Damen tumbled to the filthy floor.

"Mr. Evolution Man," Kicker said. "Allow me the courtesy of returning the lashes your father ordered to be put across my back."

Kicker executed triple back handsprings followed by a somersault propelling him high in the air. He dropped down hard on top of his enemy's head. He drove his heels hard into Damen's skull and knocked him out cold.

The Earp brothers clapped. "We ain't seen a show this good since the shootout at the OK Corral," one said.

Juan's eyes sparkled with excitement. "Mano, all we need now is some dressing, and we can stuff this monkey."

RE-DEAL

"We have no time," Matt answered. "Let's abandon him for the dogs. They can always use him for a fire hydrant."

"Yeah! I like it!" Kicker grabbed their hats and handed Matt's to him.

"Phantom," Holliday bellowed out. "I'm gonna extract yer head from yer shoulders just like I dislodge a decayed incisor." He raised his weapon and sighted down the gun.

"Look out, Mano! Holliday at three o'clock. He has a nasty looking popgun!"

Matt spun with his rigid weapon and walloped Doc upside the head. Holliday staggered and dropped to his knees.

"Kicker," Matt yelled out. "We need to get out of here, now!"

"Yes, quick!" the angel agreed. "Let's get movin', boys, with no dalliance on the way."

Matt and Juan followed Michala as she led them out front to the coach. The faithful horse waited with the buggy. The stately white stallion gave a whinny that seemed to say, 'It's about time.'

Bent on retaliation, Holliday staggered out and spotted them running towards a pink and blue buggy. He took aim and fired a fusillade of bullets.

Matt ran into the coach and knocked his hat to the ground. "Ouch!"

"Ya ought ta open the door first, Matt. Then clamber inside. Ya'll find it preferably more efficient."

"Thanks, Miss Guided." Matt shook his head clear. "Next time I'll take that into consideration. Now hurry up and get in, you silly lady."

She scrambled into the carriage. Kicker grabbed Matt's hat, shoved him in, and crawled in behind him. They heard a gun's hollow click.

"Holliday's gun is empty," Matt said. "Go, Miss Guided, before he re-loads! Go now, anywhere in the future. Just get the coach going before we pick up any more uninvited passengers."

Holliday stumbled up and grabbed for the coach door. However, he missed, and the travelers evaporated from Tombstone and left 1880 behind.

CHAPTER FORTY-SEVEN

Son-of-a-Monkey

Michala straightened her hat and blouse. She adjusted her pink boa, pulled her knitting from her bag, and looked up with concern. "What location would ya like ta journey to now, Matt?"

"We need big games with big money." Matt let out a deep breath. "We have to go for broke. It's time for the Andrews House in Virginia City in the year 1881. I must take on Andrews, the foremost cheater of the day. We can recognize him because he'll be decked out with fancy clothes, gold, and jewels like you've not seen yet."

Juan was discouraged Matt had forfeited so much of his profit in Tombstone. If he'd stayed with his pal, the situation would have turned out differently. However, he still maintained his belief in the Big Man.

Now that Damen was in the mix, Juan figured he'd have more fighting fun, with a marvelous miracle or two by Michala. The supernatural adventures continually happening all around them amazed Juan. It amused him that Matt didn't notice most of the miracles that Juan was blessed to see.

Even with an angel working with them, Juan realized the Almighty wanted them to demonstrate their resolve without violating the truths He had fixed within their human hearts.

RE-DEAL

Kicker remembered good old Samson—now there was a Bible battler. If one could just keep the dude away from temptresses, the mighty man would be a good amigo to have on your team. Juan admired how the mass of muscle, Samson, solely with a jackass jawbone, defeated an army of Philistines. Juan believed Samson must be a master in the martial maneuvers.

Juan pondered how he would look if he let his hair grow out long like Samson. But, bearing in mind he had left his chucks back at their stop, Juan wondered where he could come across the jaw of a jackass to be used in future fights. Kicker snickered as he thought he could use Damen, but he was still back in the same place as Juan's chucks. Probably still in shock over the rubber knife turning to metal when Damen stabbed his own hand.

That marvel reminded Juan of Moses, the Bible dude with the snaky stick. He liked how Moses slammed shut the Red Sea and provided a complimentary bath for the Egyptians. When Moses' stick turned into a viper in front of the Pharaoh, the Pharaoh's shocked face must have looked like Damen's face when his knife folded backward like a worm.

Juan thought about borrowing the Bible dude's fighting philosophy. He'd bug the Cyphers with crawly creepy flies, fleas, stinkbugs, and spiders. He'd bug them and bug them and then bug them some more. Juan would do this until Big Lew would let the Mexicano people go free. However, Moses had an uncountable quantity of creepy-crawlies, where Juan was fresh out.

Somehow, someway, no matter what it took to succeed, Juan would shut down those Cypher forced labor camps—even if he had to forfeit his life. However, for the first phase, Juan would perform the Joshua jig. He'd do his fancy foot dance around any Cypher seven times, with, of course, a solid smack upside the Cypher ear each go-round. Like the wide walls of Jericho, that should send any servants of Satan headlong into hell. Merely meditating on these motivational Bible battles was getting Kicker extremely excited.

"'Ey Mano, how much time do we have remaining? Perhaps adequate time for a fighting jig or two, you think?"

Matt hit his timepiece. "Time remaining 5 hours 30 minutes 27 seconds."

"I don't think so, Kicker. We're in big trouble."

Matt reached into his pocket and dragged out his remaining cash. "We're nearly out of time," he told them. "And we've been set back big time. I was a fool and lost horribly at Holliday's table. This is all the dough we have left." Matt handed the money across to his sidekick. "How much do we have, Kicker?"

Kicker quickly thumbed through the thin collection of currency. "You have 15,200 dollars. The tooth fairy's bill was almost ten grand. Not a big bang for the buck."

Matt granted his friend a diminutive chuckle to hide his growing alarm from his friends.

He softly spoke to his hope-to-be-love. "I'm distressed, Funny Lady. My strategy to play honest with these old charlatans wasn't a very good one. My poor father has fewer then six hours to live, and I still need 85,000 dollars to enter the game."

"'Ey Mano." Kicker handed the bank notes back. "How do you think Big Lew's son-of-a-monkey ended up back here with us?"

Matt reflected back. "When we were leaving the twenty-first century, I remember hearing a thud overhead. It must have been Damen hitching a ride."

"Yeah, Mano. That explains the additional riddles, like how the gamblers had the lighter and knew your name. The primate must have been covertly sticking close, and when he saw an opportunity, the monkey's uncle stepped in and caused trouble for us."

"You're right," Matt agreed. "At least we know one thing. Thanks to you, the evil seed isn't with us this time."

"No," Juan said with a knowing shake of the head. "I think Miss Guided's cool prank with that rubber knife takes the cake."

She looked up from her knitting, agitated at openly using her supernatural abilities to win against the evil one.

RE-DEAL

"That may be so, Kicker. I'm fearful Mr. Damen could create a bitter portion of harm."

"Miss Guided," Matt asked, "What do you think he might know?"

"Matt, do ya recollect when we were standin' on the deck of Captain Cannon's riverboat? Ya talked about where we're gonna journey to next. I bet ya Mr. Damen was listenin'."

"'Ey Mano, if the missing link was eavesdropping, we could have lots of new thrills. He could be standing with two-ton muzzle-loaders aimed at us when we step down from the buggy. Even though they say to never take a jawbone to a cannon fight, it would still be spine-tingling fun."

"Kicker, if I knew what in blazes you were talking about, I'd say you're crazy. However, my pop's time is running out, and I have no time to interpret your nonsense. We must push on to this high-dollar casino, even if Damen has time to make trouble for us during the interim year."

The buggy struck a hard bump as it halted in the year 1881. Seraphim looked both ways down the street, turned to the right, and pranced along at a brisk pace.

Gas lamps lit the opulent facades along Cobblestone Street of Virginia City's glittering casino district with a warm, rich glow. Pedestrians, most well lubricated by alcohol, crowded the bustling boardwalks and streets.

"There must be over a hundred honky-tonks here." Juan peeked out the window. "I like the wild names. There's The Slaughterhouse. That opera house is called The Hall of the Bleeding Heart."

Kicker pointed to another building. "That's my choice. That saloon is called The Bucket of Blood. Lots of kicking fun there, no doubt. Wow, Mano, I counted 102 casinos and only four churches. Mr. Cheat, you know how to pick pure, righteous places. It looks like all that gold has filled the town with good, wholesome family fun. Whoa, Mano, wait until you feast your sonar bat eyes on this last place."

A dazzling casino was coming into view. It looked like a multi-story, European chateau with marble steps mounting up to high Corinthian columns and archways.

"Mr. Cheat, this must be your stop. Just like you told us, this place is christened The Andrews House."

"Miss Guided, just to be safe, have the coach roll to a stop before it reaches the entrance."

Michala opened a window. "Yank it on over, Seraphim."

"Sorry to disappoint you, Mano," Kicker pouted as he gazed out the window. "No fighting festivities today. No one seems to be waiting for us."

"Kicker, the way you like to fight, I think you belong back with Samson or King David."

"Yeah Mano, give me the jawbone of a Cypher, and I'll take down an army of jackasses."

Matt rolled his eyes at Juan, whose constant joking was beginning to irritate him. He put on his hat and grabbed his cane. Then he opened the door and stepped down onto Cobblestone Street.

"Maybe Damen got struck by a bullet or bit by a rattler or just gave up on us." Matt held his hand out for Michala. "After all, it's been an entire year of lingering for the troublesome plague."

Matt wanted to sound dynamic, in control, and upbeat for his friends. But he knew it was a subterfuge, and he feared they'd see right through his phony optimism.

Miss Guided stretched out her slim arm to capture the offered hand, then stepped from the carriage. "Oh, Matthew, it still might not be safe."

"I know, Miss Guided." He pulled her close and wrapped his arms around her. "We must move ahead. My father's minutes are ticking."

As Matt held her so close, he wanted to tell her his feelings, but now was not the time.

He spoke from deep in his heart. "I was terrified today when that tanned-hide creep held that blade across your throat. I thought, I thought that I might lose you." Matt spoke with a positive tone that he didn't feel. "Miss Guided, Michala, my cherished friend, we'll just go in, win eighty-five grand, and get out quick."

In all likelihood, there was no way he could honestly earn that kind of money in five days—let alone in five hours. The stress and urgency he felt were even more relentless than before. His gut had been doing a jarring dance of dread over the last forty time-traveling hours.

Once again Matt heard the pain-racked voice of his beloved father. He shuddered with the voice screaming in his head, *Yer ma and Deb are gone. Hit by a truck!* The voice was already blaring and increasing by the second. *Yer ma! Deb! Gone!* Then there were the evil Cypher's words blasting through his mind like the explosions from bombs dropped by a B52. "Your—father—will—die—slowly!" Matt felt his chest tighten and his breathing become more difficult. Once more he envisioned his father's demise at the hands of an evil monster if he faltered.

To rescue his dad, he could see no alternative but to exploit his twenty-first century techniques to defeat the old-time charlatans. Yet inwardly he felt conflicted.

Matt wasn't certain if he should tell his beautiful ally of his intention to fight fire with fire. For the moment, he decided it would be better to wait. His discerning conscience, Kicker, wouldn't sanction his intentions to engage his expertise with the cards. So he decided to keep Juan at arm's length.

Matt thrust his head back into the coach. "Kicker, would you please park the coach, then follow in after Miss Guided and me? If Damen made it here ahead of us, it would be safer to split up and enter separately. Strive to keep out of sight. I need you to guard our backs. If you detect we require backing, render what you've been doing so excellently. Bolt in with sidekicks soaring and fists flying."

"Without fail, lover-boy." Juan gave his amigo a tap across his unshaven chin. "The foot doctor will be there, jefe."

Matt grasped Michala's hand, and they started toward the entrance of the casino.

CHAPTER FORTY-EIGHT

Erdnase — Your Name Spelled Backwards

Matt glanced out of the corner of his mangled eyes at the lady who glowed with a lovely radiance. He felt guilty, as if she knew he planned to defraud the frauds.

Off to the side of the immense casino, eyes watched Matt and the lady over the top of a newspaper. Allan Pinkerton, founder of Pinkerton's Investigating Agency, smiled as he folded the paper and rose from the bench — thrilled to be the first to spot the famous Phantom. He watched the peculiar-colored buggy as it pulled away with no driver.

But his sharp eyes turned back to the man and woman a mysterious client had paid his agency so much to find. He rushed to the back entrance and shoved his way through an obstacle course of doors to a dark wood door that blended perfectly into an ornately-carved wood partition.

The invisible door opened onto a stage in the middle of the extravagant casino where a high-dollar poker game was on temporary hiatus. Pinkerton found Eric Andrews sitting alone at his poker table with a large pile of bills stacked in front of him.

Andrews was so absorbed in his introspective thought he didn't hear the secret door open. He kept thumbing through the bills he'd just accumulated from two San Francisco suckers. He'd already won close to 150,000 dollars from the affluent men.

RE-DEAL

He glanced over his shoulder and saw the bizarre new mayor closely watching him. He didn't like how this new executive lorded over him as he played. The winnings were no consolation to him either. The previous night the mayor had tricked him into betting his palace. Then to his shock, he had to surrender it after the mayor held up a fist full of deeds and raised him half the city.

When Pinkerton pushed open the door, it blocked his view of his client against the wall. He went over to the jewel-covered Andrews and spoke softly. "Lord Andrews, I need to tell Mr. Cypher the Phantom is here and coming up the steps."

After overhearing Matt on the boat deck, Damen had tracked down and hired Pinkerton. Over the past year, Damen had used his knowledge of the future along with his inherited cunning and deceit to become rich and powerful. He'd also become the mayor of Virginia City and the owner of the fabulously rich Andrews House.

"As of yesterday," Damen faced Pinkerton and hissed, "Andrews is finished as landlord. He is no longer entitled to your admiration. Identical to most of the establishments in this insipid town of fools, I am the master of this palace. Andrews is now only the house mechanic. From now on, I am the one you will address as lord. Now apprise me of your new information, quickly!"

Damen Cypher puzzled as well as awed Allan Pinkerton. Cypher first employed him to find the well-known Andrews House. They had arrived in town less than a year ago. Within six months, Cypher owned half the places in town. Then he ran for mayor and won. Now the man had become the owner of the richest place in the country.

Cypher knew what was going to happen before it happened, and he prevailed over and over again against overwhelming odds. Allan had often wondered if Cypher had actually sold his soul to the Devil. He had dealt with the Devil before and didn't like it one bit.

"Sorry, sir. The Phantom is on his way, and the teacher woman you mentioned is also with him."

Damen's eyes crossed as he faced the detective. "Was there a stocky Mexican with the Phantom?"

"No, sir." Pinkerton shook his head. "There was only the Phantom and his cute little lady."

"I'm cocksure the wetback is around somewhere, conceivably hiding in that eerie buggy." Damen turned to the jewel-covered gambler who he realized was the forefather of his drug dealer Tom. "Andrews, I charge you with the task of separating the dame from the Lucas McCain relation. Then keep the Phantom absorbed with his gambling until we're prepared for the sting. Also, clear Mustache's table and warn her to be ready for a stranger with deadeyes."

Damen turned back toward Pinkerton. "Get the girl. Fetch her back to the camouflaged chamber and restrain her there. But don't damage the woman. I have plans for her afterward."

Damen knew he needed her alien powers to return to the twenty-first century. He had the constant reminder of the cavity on his own hand from the stab wound he self-inflicted back in Tombstone with the knife that had been a toy when used on McCain. He covered his grotesque left hand with his right. He recalled how the nasty stab wound had become infected, and because there were no antibiotics in this uncivilized century, his hand had almost rotted away.

"Use a gun," Damen told Pinkerton with barely-controlled rage. "But only as a bluff to control the woman. Knives don't work."

"Yes sir, Lord Cypher," Pinkerton said with a firm nod. "I'll get the girl and be prepared."

Allan Pinkerton turned toward the engraved wall. He applied pressure on the face of an ornate carving to open the door, then hurried out.

"Andrews, The Phantom is the best card mechanic you'll ever face. He does things that aren't even in that little instructional book you're writing."

Andrews's eyes went wide. "Lord Cypher, on whose account were you made aware I have been penning a tutorial book on card manipulation? Nobody possesses this information but yours truly."

"I know it in the same way I know you're considering authoring the book using your name spelled backwards."

Andrews's eyes went even wider with fright.

"However," Damen went on, "that's not pertinent to our situation here and now. At this moment our problem is the gambler you call the Phantom and whose actual name is Matthew McCain. This man invariably professes to always play honest. However, I don't believe him for a second, so watch his hands vigilantly. He's related to Lucas McCain, the rich rancher down in Texas. For that reason you're clear to exploit the entire resources and belongings of this gaudy place. If you quickly break McCain, this tawdry monument to stupid fools will be yours again."

Without saying anything further, Damen retreated through the same secret door Pinkerton had used.

CHAPTER FORTY-NINE

Fighting Fire with Fire

Outside, Matt and Michala topped the flight of marble steps and entered the nineteenth-century gambling palace through handcrafted teak doors. They passed through a cavernous foyer decorated with Corinthian pillars and six life-size white marble sculptures of Greek gods.

When they stepped into a huge room lit by crystal chandeliers, Michala exclaimed, "Wow, Matthew! This particular place ain't no flophouse."

Vibrant tapestries and paintings decorated the walls, and fine wood and marble furniture lined the periphery. A grand staircase formed a large horseshoe that led to private rooms on the upper levels. A five-foot elevated area with a lavish poker table dominated the inner circle of the twin dark wood stairways.

The incognito angel murmured, "Matt, I think ya should be mindful of that curious stage over yonder. It appears ta be a private area with a designated poker table and a sort of throne where an overdressed man is playin' cards."

"Miss Guided, is the man arrayed with fine clothes, jewels, and such?"

"Yep," Michala affirmed. "I reckon he'd make Elizabeth Taylor covetous. He's scattered from hat ta boot with gold and large, sparklin' baubles, and circlin' around his thin neck is a very bloated long gold chain."

"Wow!" Matt stopped to catch his breath. "That's S. W. Erdnase, which," he explained, "is E. S. Andrews spelled backward. He's a master card manipulator, all right. He was the foremost card cheat of the nineteenth century."

And, Matt *thought, if Andrews won't play straight, I'll beat him at his own dishonorable game.* He raised his head and said a silent prayer. *Sorry, Lord, but my father's life will end if I don't act now. You must understand.*

Guilt knotted Matt's stomach, and he shook his head to get rid of the thought that he was justifying dishonesty.

"Miss Guided, that stage must be the place from where Andrews conveys his cheating signals to his dealers."

"Oh, is that right?" The angel lifted an inquisitive eyebrow. "That multicolored fellow likewise authored a book?"

"He did. Positively the finest book ever drafted on card-table artifice. The book was so eloquently composed that most card men figured Andrews traveled in high circles and was very educated."

Michala smiled at the only decent asset in the place—an orchestra performing classical music. She wrapped her arm around Matt's and moved toward the orchestra.

"Matthew," she murmured. "Let's just mix in with the company. The hackles on my neck are warnin' me we're being looked at."

"Just find me an open seat at a card table so I can get warmed up and hopefully catch Andrews's interest."

"Okay, but I see no place open. Right now all the gambling tables are filled with inconsolable-lookin' players."

"Darn!" Matt whined. "If I can't sit down, I can't play. If I can't play, I can't win any money. What should I do now?"

"Don't start fretting quite yet. Let's look some more."

She led him to an empty sofa. "Hold here, whilst I scan the room."

She looked around the room, then turned back to Matt. "I did spy a particular lady blackjack dealer. She had no players at her table. She's stationed right below the roost where yer twinkling man is seated. For whatever reason ya want ta get his attention, that is yer best spot."

"Good." Matt leaped to his feet. "Will you please describe the twenty-one dealer to me?"

"Well, let me see. She's exceedingly well portioned topside, with a black silk dress split up the sides. She's suckin' in fumes from a long, rank cigar and guzzling whisky. She has two enchanting Christmas-colored eyes—I imagine you'd call them bloodshot green. She has a pancake-batter complexion, with a long, carrot-shaped, beet-red nose with a very feminine wart with a long black hair thrusting forth. Grinning below are painted tomato-red lips. She's surely a stylish woman by virtue of her treated tumbleweed hair matching the scraggy black bush above her upper lip."

Matt adored how Michala could take road kill and turn it into a Christmas fruitcake, but he was puzzled how she could abide in her joy and remain unruffled through all this. The trek through time, the stress, the crazed gamblers ... Although his fear was growing, he wouldn't let her know.

"Miss Guided, I'm not sure if you're describing a Christmas doorstop or Eleanor Dumont. Nevertheless, I imagine you're depicting Dumont, in view of the whiskered growth above her upper lip. In her later years she was known as Madam Mustache. She was one of the most memorable female connivers of that century. I certainly hope I can outdo her by employing my card-counting skills."

"I'm puzzled, Matt. Why would ya need ta count the cards? Even I know when fully vested there's only fifty-two."

"Card counting is just a way of keeping track of the pasteboards as they are dealt. This way I know when the probabilities have increased in my favor. Matt lowered his voice. "Would you please search your mysterious little purse and see if you have an ace and a face card that matches Madam Mustache's deck?"

The angel hesitantly opened her handbag and pulled out a pair of playing cards. "So, Matt, you want two cards? Like this ace and this king?"

"Oh yes! Thanks, Funny Lady!"

RE-DEAL

Guilt-ridden, Matt slid the two instruments of wrongdoing up his right coat sleeve. He straightened his coat, hiding the now-notable buckle, dusted off his hat, and picked up his cane.

"Miss Guided, would you please look around and see if anyone is outfitted with guns?"

After scanning the gambling hall, she whispered, "No one in here has an implement of hostility, not even your sparkling landlord. However, standin' beside that heaved-high spread, vigilantly watchin' the gambling tables are five treacherous-lookin' armed defenders."

"Come on, Miss Guided." He took her hand. "Let's go play some blackjack."

As they advanced toward the faro banks and roulette wheels, Eric Andrews watched them from his perch far above the casino floor.

There were no players at the blackjack table. As they sat down, Matt smelled the aroma of cheap perfume combined with foul-smelling sweat coursing from the dealer's body.

The guardian angel was burdened with Matt's intentions. Her heavenly boss had given her a task to accomplish for the kingdom. She had been given a privileged dispensation—to travel outside-of-time—to fix her earlier failure. However, she knew she was teetering in her task.

Matt had begun to weaken towards the worldly way to resolve his difficulties rather than keeping his confidence in the Creator. He had to change direction, or there would be eternal consequences. Michala decided it was essential to lighten his heavy heart so he might move back and embrace a moral mission. As before, her primary weapon was humor.

"Excuse me, Miss Dumont," she asked. "Where is yer mama, and does she know what yer doing in this playground for the undone?"

"You ask at which place my mama is?" Madam Mustache grinned, showing off her last three yellow teeth. "Why she's sitting over yonder by her spinning wheel."

"Well, isn't that proper? Yer mama is sittin' by her spinning wheel. I suppose she's makin' a wonderful new sweater for ya."

"What are you, woman?" Eleanor pointed toward a gray-haired old woman operating a roulette wheel. "My mama is right over yonder seated behind that high-dollar spinning wheel. I see that she just won five hundred dollars on twenty-one red off four dupes."

Matt chuckled at the silly interplay as he sat down and angled his cane against a stool where Michala placed her bag. "Miss Dumont," Matt said as he took a bunch of bank notes from his pocket. "I have traveled a lengthy stretch for the pleasure of a thrilling game of blackjack with you."

"Well, big boy. I can see by your irregular eyes it's not my gorgeousness that calls."

Matt wondered how she had so quickly picked up on his bad vision. As before, it was like somebody had blabbed to her he was coming.

"In spite of my meager vision, I nonetheless am partial to a stirring bout with a legendary card-player of recognized expertise. If I may ask, what's your betting limit?"

She raised the wooly bush above her upper lip in a smile, and said, "For you doll-face, I'll go up to five thousand bucks a hand."

With so little time left, Matt had to go for the big play and quick. "Madam, raise your limit up to ten thou a hand, and I'll play."

"To cover that amount, I must get permission from Mr. Andrews."

She waved to Andrews and displayed ten fingers. Andrews nodded and gave her back a secret gesture that said to double-deal him. Eleanor fluttered her bloodshot eyes as she shuffled the cards.

"Get your wage out, honey." She sat the deck down for the cut. "Let's play some blackjack."

Matt placed fifty dollars on the green felt table, and Madam Mustache started the action. Matt paid attention to

RE-DEAL

the whoosh of each card as if he were riding it to the tabletop. Miss Guided murmured the dealer's face-up card and the cards dealt to him after he picked them up. Matt monitored every card and played the percentages competently, yet his money seemed to be sucked into a cash-devouring void.

Matt would win one sequence, then turn around and suffer defeat two or three hands in a row. He watched in agony as his cash reserves dwindled down to barely two thousand dollars. At long last, after three times through the deck, and about forty unbearable minutes, the probabilities turned in Matt's favor. It was still early in the deck, with only twenty cards played. Matt had a plus count of eight, which meant there were eight more face-cards and aces remaining in the deck in relation to the low cards, the twos through sixes. The snag was that he had only two thousand dollars remaining.

He took half his cash and made a thousand dollar wager, and this time he was victorious. He made a two thousand dollar bet and won again. He allowed the bets to ride and kept doubling his winnings. He finally tossed a ten thousand dollar bet on the table.

Eleanor paused for a split second as she felt Andrews's eyes bear down hard on her. When the player won again, she had to struggle to keep her hands from shaking. Andrews was watching her like a hawk and would take it out of her hide if she lost another ten grand stake. She peeked at the top card and saw it was a six.

"That's the table limit, hon. You've been playing the percentages pretty well. Are you prepared to hazard another ten big ones?"

"Our time is short. Miss Guided, I've got to take the chance and go for it all." He turned back and nodded at Madam Mustache. "Yes, deal the cards."

She dealt the next round, and Matt's keen ears heard the whoosh of the first card as usual. However, the next card came from beneath the top card and went swish!

There it is, a second deal. She has now unfastened the door of dishonest play. To save his father, regrettably, he would battle cheating with corresponding actions of his own. He tilted his pair of cards up so Michala could see them. If his two cards were a bust combination, Madam Mustache was going to cheat him, and he should have the right to fight back. *I mean, it's only fair,* he told his withering conscience.

The guardian angel was worried her charge was no longer willing to trust in his almighty Maker, but was now ready to try to solve his problem with dishonest means. She couldn't coerce him to do what was right. The Sovereign set it up so His race would be free to choose to sin or not.

"Ya have a ten and a six, Matthew." She paused, then said, "How ya play it is up ta you." All Matt seemed to care about was winning at any cost.

Matt knew he was at a moral crossroads. If he went further and yielded to the temptation to switch the bust cards for the blackjack up his sleeve, he would be crossing an ethical boundary he knew to be wrong. A voice deep inside of him cried out for him not to go any further, not to succumb to the temptation to cheat. *Don't do it*! Matt heard the internal influence cry. *Remember King David. You might believe it to be a small wrong, but it could cost you amply!*

However, Matt chose to ignore his conscience and all the faith-building miracles that had taken place on this amazing trip. As he chose to smother the voice of his moral sense, the inner utterance slowly faded. Matt shook his head clear of the guilt. He casually dropped his right arm to his side, causing the ace and the king to fall into his palm. He raised his card-stuffed hand back to the table and slid it with his left hand, cupping them together over the losing ten and six.

As he pretended to look at the cards, he palmed the two bust cards and substituted the ace and king he'd dropped up his sleeve. He flipped the two cards over and said, "I have twenty-one. I win my ten thousand dollar bet plus an additional five thousand for having a two-card blackjack."

RE-DEAL

Eleanor's eyes widened in shock. How did that happen? She knew she'd dealt a ten and a six. She looked up at her boss, whose attention was unfortunately absorbed on the winner's skillful actions.

Eric Andrews watched as the gambler called the Phantom slipped the swapped cards into his left coat pocket. Andrews marveled at the efficient move. Only an especially educated eye like his would have caught the switch.

CHAPTER FIFTY

James Garner

A tall, middle-aged man in a tailored suit stepped up to the table. "Very entertaining play, young man."

Matt turned to face the new arrival. He could never judge what surprise would unfold next, so he fixed his hand on his cane to be prepared for a potential calamity.

Asa Turner, the Governor of Texas, stepped toward Michala and smiled.

"Madam, you're the prettiest little lady this side of the Mississippi." He took her hand in his huge one and kissed it. "Seems to me we've been introduced before. Don't you tutor Lucas McCain's boy, Davy William?"

Michala was astonished to see Lucas's refined, God-fearing friend in the gambling house of their foes.

"Why, thank ya Governor. I'm pleasured for sure ta again make yer acquaintance. Oh, and I've tutored many fine boys. And Governor, how's yer Texas campaign comin' along?"

"Thanks, Ma'am, for asking. It's going well. I hope to be re-elected."

The fellow carrying the mysterious walking stick was a dead ringer for the governor's friend, Lucas McCain.

"I'm Turner, Asa Turner." He grasped the young man's hand. "I'm here drumming up some business for my grand state of Texas."

As Matt shook the man's hand, he thought this man could crush it like an egg shell.

RE-DEAL

"Please, don't take me for a namedropper, but I must ask. You've got to be akin to an old friend of mine, a fine rancher by the name of Lucas McCain. Might you be his kin?"

Matt's heart leaped with joy, thrilled to encounter somebody who was acquainted with his ancestor. Matt knew of the well-respected Governor of Texas during his great grandfather's era. And this man, Governor Asa Turner, called Lucas his friend, not Lucas the Loser. Over the course of this trip back through history, Matt had discovered how respected his great grandfather had been. Now he was proud to be a McCain.

Without thinking, he blurted out, "You know Lucas McCain? He's my great grandfather!"

The governor turned back to Michala, cupped his ear, and gave the tutor a friendly nudge. "My hearing ain't what it used to be. What did he say, Ma'am? Lucas is his great what?"

Matt's heart skipped a beat as he remembered he hadn't been born yet. What a stupid slip of the tongue.

"What I intended to say was, I yearn for a grandfather like Lucas McCain. I've always dreamed of having a ranch comparable to his."

"Oh yes," Asa responded. "Don't we all wish for a ranch like Lucas's? Don't we all?"

Andrews wondered why this man had just fibbed to Governor Turner. Eric had met Lucas McCain once and recognized the startling resemblance between the two. Damen Cypher was right—the card Phantom could be McCain's son or younger brother. Eric stepped down from his observation perch and joined the group. As he shifted close, two of his attending guards drew in behind him.

"Asa," Eric said. "You have saved my house by interrupting a very expensive game." He faced Matt and held out his hand. "Eric Andrews, sir. And you are ...?"

Matt knew he had to mask his blooper fast. He crossed his cane to his left hand, then accepted the extended grip and persisted with more lies. "Uh-uh, Garner. My name is James Garner. I've been told I could be McCain's long-lost brother. I eventually hope to meet him."

As an accomplished poker player, once again Eric spotted the deception. He said, "You will meet the wealthy rancher if you continue playing like you did with my fine lady sharper."

Matt was startled with Andrews's admission that his dealer was a card mechanic. He wondered what that might mean for him.

Eric twisted around and eyed the woman with McCain. He bowed, embraced her hand, and kissed it. "It is my pleasure to meet you, Madam."

Worried that her charge had used trickery to win at the blackjack table, Michala wanted to keep Matt from any more infamy. It was time for another gag.

"I'm pleasured ta make yer acquaintance. Haven't we met previous? Perhaps I tutored you in a night-school class?"

"Madam," the baffled Eric asked. "What class are you alluding to?"

"I'm sure ya would recollect, Mr. Andrews." She chuckled. "The class was titled The Twelve Steps to a More Dysfunctional You. And, Mr. Andrews, you were at the head of the class."

Eric resolved to make a momentary allowance for the foolish woman's failure to realize just how prosperous and scholarly he was. But then the truth flooded back. All his assets and wealth now belonged to Damen Cypher.

"Madam." Eric gazed hard at the woman. "I believe you have erroneously confused me for another. I wasted twelve years at the university and possess three advanced degrees. I was so far above my humdrum professors that I exhausted more of the class time practicing with my cards than I spent listening to the bores. I make more money in one hour with these fifty-two pieces of paper than the tiresome pedagogues make in an entire year." He turned

RE-DEAL

back to McCain. "Considering you embrace the hazards of gaming, won't you join Governor Turner and myself for a sociable game of poker?"

This was the invitation Matt had hoped for. His time for this stop was brief, so he had to win fast and win big. If he didn't make it and his father was killed like his mother and sister, he would be all alone. Even though he had two great friends in Kicker and the funny lady, Michala, he would have another vast hole ripped in his already-sinking heart.

He answered, "Only if there are no limits on betting."

"I don't imagine Asa would appreciate that sort of hazard toward his campaign fund," Andrews said.

"You're right, Eric," Asa agreed. "Thank you anyway. I need to increase my fluid assets, not purchase you additional historic masterpieces." He tipped his Stetson. "So I'll just keep the lady company and watch."

"Well, then." Andrews gestured toward his private stage. "Shall we venture a little friendly play?"

Andrews escorted the small group toward his personal high-dollar gambling area. They approached the platform steps and ascended.

Juan had been watching the action from his hiding place at the top of the staircases. He'd noted the interaction between Matt and Andrews.

Kicker figured if Andrews was ever arrested for rustling, the town authorities wouldn't need a rope to hang the thief; they'd simply tug the gold chain around his neck. Eric Andrews reminded Juan of Tom Andrews, the guy who'd shot his amigo up with dope back in the twenty-first century, in the incident that first introduced them to Miss Guided. Not only did they have the same last name, but also they even looked a lot alike.

Something else worried Juan. Matt was wavering toward the temptation to fight fire with fire. Matt's father's life was on the line, but for Matt to win the war at the expense of his soul was not an equitable exchange.

CHAPTER FIFTY-ONE

Caught Red-Handed

As Eric walked beside Matt, he said in a low voice, "Sir, given your notable relation and esteem, you delayed too long before making your appearance at my celebrated gaming house."

Matt's insides froze in alarm. "I beg your pardon, Mr. Andrews?"

"I trust you understand what I'm alleging. I imagine you have other designates as famous as McCain. I know it's not Garner." Andrews paused, then said, "Phantom of the Card Table, perhaps? That's what everybody is calling the anomalous gamester with the aces and eights belt buckle."

At a nod from Andrews, two of his guards grabbed Matt by the coat and spread apart his lapels, revealing the infamous buckle. Matt's whole body trembled with fear, and the blood drained from his face.

"As I theorized," Andrews declared with a gratified nod, "you are the Phantom. I appreciate how you worked your card expertise in Deadwood, Tombstone, and aboard riverboats. Subsequent to winning a sack burdened with an accumulation of large bank notes, you and that enigmatic woman hop a multi-hued coach drawn by a triple member stallion and somehow mysteriously vanish."

Matt couldn't imagine how Andrews knew who he was, unless Damen Cypher had already made it here. He choked down his anxiety enough to speak. "Mr. Andrews, what clue tipped you off that I was this mysterious Phantom?"

Eric could see that McCain was enchanted with his card talents. The Phantom believed he was so clever that not even the great E. S. Andrews could snare him. It would be easy to further corrupt the Phantom by inflating his already oversized ego.

"Please, please. First, all my good friends call me Eric."

Matt thought, *Wow, this celebrated man isn't after me. Eric likes me.*

He returned the neighborly gesture. "And Eric, please call me Matt."

"Why, thank you, Matt. I must say, that was the most dexterous and smoothly executed display of palming and substituting a blackjack hand I've ever witnessed. You thoroughly stunned the educated eye of Madam Mustache, and that I am compelled to admire. In fact, you can keep the winnings. However, if you don't mind, I would like to retain the two cards concealed in your left coat pocket, solely as a memento to the most peerless card switch I have ever beheld."

Stunned at first, Matt grew ecstatic at what he just heard. He could scarcely maintain his composure. He couldn't believe what the great card man Andrews had just said about him. Yet Matt realized he'd been caught trying to cheat—no, not just trying, actually cheating. So just how good was his switch really? After all, he was caught red-handed.

Then he relaxed and realized he should have expected this. After all, it was E. S. Andrews who spotted him—Andrews, the greatest card mechanic of the day. He hesitantly reached into his pocket and removed the two pieces of evidence, hoping that no one else knew the dishonest thing he'd done. As he walked up the steps, he passed them back to Andrews.

"Thanks! This is just a little memento."

Andrews placed the cards in his vest pocket.

Slow down, Matt told himself. *You're playing with fire.* He was walking alongside a card legend his father and card teacher Dai Vernon both revered.

On the upper story, Juan saw Matt pass back the cards. Based on Matt's expression of dismay and guilt, Kicker figured his friend had been caught cheating. Kicker knew he couldn't make Matt's moral decisions for him, but he could still pray for faith and feet equipped for battle with the enemy. He petitioned the Almighty.

Eric and Matt reached the private gambling area, a thirty-by-fifty-foot stage carpeted in greens and maroons. In the center stood a poker table encircled with carved high-back chairs.

The Governor and the angel seated themselves on one of the couches that backed up to the dark rail bordering the stage. Two guards stuck by Andrews like gum to a shoe. They were dressed in suits, boots, and hats, with guns strapped around their waists.

One of the guards said to Matt, "Permit me to move this walking stick out of your way." The guard hooked the cane on the banister. "It will be right here. You can pick it up on your way out."

Matt didn't like being separated from his weapon, but it wasn't far, and he wasn't in any position to make a fuss.

The two guards moved back and took up their posts in the back corners on either side of the hidden door.

Andrews stacked his large notes in a nice neat pile. He grinned, flaunting every jewel-studded gold tooth in his mouth. "I have over 150,000 dollars in pretty money, and it's up for grabs."

Matt knew pretty money was cash won from a casino or from another player, and it was usually frittered away as freely as water. This might be a good thing. Maybe Andrews was interested in a simple, relaxing game of cards. But on further reflection, Matt knew that was probably not the case.

The direct contact angel's uneasiness increased minute by minute. She should have thought twice about supplying her charge with the playing pair.

She was a mite bit bothered that Sir Gabe would not have authorized her actions. She walked over and laid her hands on Matt's tense shoulders. "Matthew," she said in hushed tones. "I can read your mind!"

At the feel of her touch, Matt's eyes went wide with guilt. His chest tightened as he wondered if she knew that he was plotting to utilize his fancy handwork to hammer Andrews, who wasn't really such a bad fellow. After all, Eric did call Matt a friend, and said to call him by his first name. Even more exciting, Eric appreciated his card genius.

"I'm sorry, Miss Guided." Matt stood and faced Michala. "Did you say you can read my mind?"

"Yes I can, Matthew. You see, I'm telepathetic."

Matt chuckled, then sighed in relief. It was only one of her amusing teases. Then for an all-too-brief moment, he wondered if she was trying to communicate something to him. But he had no time to squander on deciphering subtle messages.

"Thank you, Funny Lady, for the entertainment." He smiled toward Andrews. "But I really must focus on my privileged opportunity to play at this distinguished man's table."

Michala shook her head. "Once again, Matthew, yer not payin' much mind ta me."

"Sorry, Miss Guided, but my mind is in a whirl and my time is short." He nodded toward Asa. "Why don't you visit with the Governor and give him some ideas for his campaign." He reached over and gave her a little peck on the cheek. "Don't trouble yourself; I'll be okay."

She shook her head again and slid back to her seat.

CHAPTER FIFTY-TWO

Not so Dumb

Eric closed his mouth in a thin tight line as he watched the weird woman retreat. He passed the deck to Matt. "Please shuffle the cards. They're an excellent new product, soon to come out, called Bicycle."

As Matt sat back down he giggled to himself at the idea that the most recognized pack of cards in the country in the twenty-first century was just now a new product. He accepted the deck and started to shuffle.

Andrews focused his attention on the Phantom's hands. He watched carefully as the supposed card wizard grasped the deck and broke it precisely in half, shuffling one card after another, in perfect, every other card, faros.

"By your elegant mastery of the paper pasteboards, I perceive that you appreciate that manipulation is more profitable than speculation." Eric gestured around the palace that was once his. "That is how I have appropriated so much wealth."

But that was no longer the case. He had yet to figure out how he was manipulated into staking his gaming empire as a bet. However, Cypher had promised it would all be given back if he could crush the Phantom.

"Permit me to state further, Matt, first I have identified you as the legendary Phantom of the Card Table. Secondly, I reason that your visual acuity is pathetic, and because of this you have an incomparable touch with the tickets. Thirdly,

RE-DEAL

if truth were told, your full name is Matthew McCain, and you are related to the millionaire down south, Lucas McCain. As a final point, I believe that you are, as well, a master of hypnosis and legerdemain. You exploit these outstanding abilities to win everybody's stake, then with these same means, you avail yourself of them by cleverly disappearing."

Matt's body tensed in shock and bewilderment. He became dreadfully thirsty, and his throat felt like sandpaper.

"May I have something to drink?" he asked with a slight cough. "My throat is extremely dry, and I'd like to have a shot of scotch and water—hold the scotch, please."

Eric was elated to see he was beginning to weaken the Phantom. He snapped his fingers and a steward in white tie and tails appeared from behind the invisible door. Andrews gave the drink orders to the butler, who nodded his understanding and retreated without delay.

"Matt, the refreshments are on the way." He leaned forward in his chair and said, "My friend, I would be interested in seeing some of your moves. Can you demonstrate a second deal or maybe a bottom deal? Or are these advanced methods out of your realm of expertise?"

Matt felt a wave of relief. Andrews was sucking up to him. But he was still surprised at the request for him to openly demonstrate a crooked deal with all these people hanging about. However, none of the gamblers below could actually see what they were doing up here on the stage. And showing his skills might be a good idea. After all, seconds, middles, and bottoms were his best moves. Eric would be astonished. Back here a middle deal hadn't even been thought of yet.

Matt picked up the Bicycles. "Have you ever heard of a middle deal?"

"No!" Andrews stifled a gasp. "No one can deal from the middle!"

"Watch!" Matt fanned the cards out perfectly and performed an array of fancy flourishes, including the yet-to-be-invented one-hand shuffle.

Aloft, Juan wondered what was going on. His friend was flagrantly performing his card show. For the next fifteen minutes, Juan watched as Matt demonstrated many of his well-mastered moves.

Eric inclined his head toward the Phantom. "Matt, my master card friend, I would be interested in learning some of your brilliant techniques. In particular, that middle deal. I have never heard of such a move."

For the second time, the heavenly guardian stood and stepped up behind her charge. "Mr. Andrews, to master, one first ought to be humble, honest, and willing. Are you willing?"

Eric could no longer contain his aggravation with the outlandish woman. He lost his composure as he snapped back, "Madam, I now recall where I spied you previously. You're with P. T. Barnum's circus. You were acclaimed as the world's most brilliant simpleton! Now lady, you may converse when spoken to." He shoved a finger toward the door. "Or, Madam, you are at liberty to lecture outside—alone!"

Matt cringed at the harsh tone between his new friend and his love-to-be. "Thank you, Miss Guided. But do you mind if Eric and I get back to the matter at hand?"

"Sorry, Matthew." She glanced at Andrews's effeminate frame. "Confidentially, Mr. Andrews, I think yer very manly, though not as masculine as yer Creator designed you ta be."

"Creator?" Andrews stood and snarled, "Woman, did you say Creator? Haven't you heard of that profound new researcher of natural science, Darwin? He has confirmed that the species originated by natural means. That there is no God, and the world didn't come into existence by an event as idiotic as the notion of creation."

This is going to be good, Juan thought as he watched from above. *Arguing with an angel about evolution. Only an atheist would be so asinine as to attack the Almighty's angel after asserting He's not authentic.*

"Now listen, lady," Andrews maintained. "All things came into existence through natural selection, what Darwin calls evolution! I can easily demonstrate he's correct, and there's no God." He aimed a long thin finger toward a painting suspended high on the wall. "Asa, do you see that priceless masterpiece?"

"Um, let me see." Asa stood and looked up. "Yes, Eric, I do."

Andrews directed Asa toward a high, enormous window. "Do you see the shining moon in the sky?"

Again Asa nodded. "Yes."

"Look closer," Andrews prodded with a smirk. "Do you see God?"

Asa shook his head. "No, no, I don't see God."

"That's right!" Andrews said smugly. "You can't see God, because there is no blasted God!"

This was right up the angel's alley. She appreciated a war of whimsical wits. "Governor Turner." She pointed up. "Ya can see the warm pleasant moon out the window, yes?"

Again Asa agreed. "Yes, ma'am, I can!"

The angel aimed a finger at Professor Andrews. "And ya can see Doctor Andrews's gold-encircled head?"

"Yes, Madam," Asa affirmed. "I see his head surrounded by the fat gold chain."

"And Governor, do ya see Professor Andrews's created brain?"

"No, Ma'am." Asa shook his head. "I don't see his brain."

"Well, there ya have it. According ta the clever professor, he doesn't have one!"

Up topside, the angel's war of wits with the gambler amused Juan. From her behavior, Michala must be troubled with Andrews. She was attempting to trick him until Matt caught a clue about the wickedness going down. Juan resolved to add to the fun.

He softly broke off a four-inch piece of cornice and said silently, *Yeah, pretty man, there's no invisible gravity, and this didn't actually fall.* Juan watched as the chunk of wood thumped Andrews on top of his head. Kicker snickered silently, then crouched low so he wouldn't be seen.

Down below, the chunk hit Andrews on the head with a thud. He grabbed his head and cursed loudly. He searched the level above and saw where the fragment of cornice had broken free. "Curse those overpriced architects," he mumbled under his breath.

Michala nodded to herself at Kicker's subtle support. "Aren't ya gratified there's no unseen force called gravity that pulls things ta the earth? That means you didn't really feel that painful crashing bop."

She smiled and slowly sat back down. Asa elbowed her and nodded his approval.

For a moment, Eric stared at the weird woman and considered there was something about her that wasn't so dumb.

At that moment his contemplation was interrupted as the hidden door opened and the steward returned and set the tray of drinks on a side table. A crystal pitcher filled with water, a bottle of choice scotch, and three shot-glasses sat on the silver tray. Andrews dismissed the attendant with a nod.

He stood and turned to Asa. "Governor, please join us as I pay homage to the illustrious Phantom. I think you will relish the sensation. This is some of my most superlative imported scotch."

Matt panicked. He didn't want any real liquor. "Eric, I, in fact, just want water."

The fright in his opponent's eyes intoxicated Eric. "Nonsense," he said as he filled the glasses with three fingers of scotch and a splash of water. "No genuine gamester tosses water." He leaned over and passed a glass across to Asa and one to Matt. He thrust forward his arm and clinked glasses together. "To the celebrated Phantom and his genuine gifts of genius!"

RE-DEAL

Matt faltered. Should he or shouldn't he? He wavered with his glass of doom. He really didn't want this drink.

"Come on, master card man," Andrews prodded. "Do me the honors and drink up!"

"All right," Matt said, his voice strained. "Here's to ya."

Then contrary to his better instincts, Matt choked down the alcoholic beverage in one gulp. He slapped back down the glass as his eyes went wide and started to well up. He hadn't had any booze in years. Once he regained his composure from the shock, he felt better, a little less nervous, a little more at ease.

"Yep." Asa sat his shot-glass back on the silver shelf. "That's mighty fine scotch all right."

"Thanks, Governor. Like another?" Andrews asked, holding up the decanter.

"No thanks. One is my limit."

Eric's gaze shifted back over to McCain. He could tell the Phantom wasn't a drinker. Much of Eric's personal high-stake profits came from rich drunks.

Without asking, he replenished Matt's glass. "Just one more before we commence play." He handed the full glass back and continued with lies and half-truths. "You are extremely proficient with the tickets for larceny. The code of the day is, if you can't spy the cheating, you can't claim it as cheating. That's why I have developed complex, cunning, entirely imperceptible techniques to create the payoff. That's why I see those secret card moves and applaud a master when I see one. I am willing to pay for the privilege of watching your approach toward robbery." He smiled. "It will make for a more entertaining game if we utilize our card table artifice. After all, poker is a game of skill. Defrauding likewise demands tremendous talent. Otherwise why is cheating cheating?"

"Here's to you." Eric picked up Matt's glass and held it out to him. "My friend, the card master."

Matt felt like evil was stalking him. But the scotch was starting to make him feel a little warm inside, dulling his inherent sense of warning. He saluted again, clinked glasses, and downed the second drink. This time his eyes didn't well up. He handed the glass back, and Andrews once again poured another.

Michala was shaking her head ever so slightly from side to side. She drew in her lower lip and clipped it with her teeth.

"I never heard of such," Asa murmured. "Why, they're talking openly about having a cheating match. If what Andrews just said is true and that's how he acquired all this wealth and treasure," he motioned around the opulent room, "then I'm not interested in any of his dirty money for my campaign fund."

The angel nodded in agreement as her hands turned tensely in her lap.

CHAPTER FIFTY-THREE

Swindling Competition

There was little time left, and Matt was ready to go for broke. He looked around and discovered that his eyesight was even more shadowy than usual. Before the drinks he could hardly see the cards. Now he'd really fuzzed up the works.

Yet if they were going to have a swindling competition, then it really shouldn't matter. His delicate touch would do all the seeing and mastery of the cards for him. He tried to shake his head clear. "I suppose we could play a game of stud poker or draw."

Eric hid his elation. Poker was precisely what he wanted to play. But then he recalled what Damen Cypher said. "You are clear to exploit the entire resources and belongings of this gaudy place. If you quickly break McCain, this tawdry monument to stupid fools will be yours again." Eric fumed inside at Cypher's insulting words.

However, his fortune depended on appeasing Cypher, who, for some reason, was in a big rush. A poker game would be far too time-consuming. He drummed his well-manicured fingernails on the green-felted poker table.

After consideration, he said, "With a master, I prefer fast, high-risk ventures. You shuffle, and then we'll cut for high card."

That would be perfect. Matt knew he would beat Eric every cut. He just needed to make the conditions so interesting and seemingly impossible that Andrews would be inclined to bet big. He pulled his large roll of bills from his coat pocket.

"That sounds fine, Eric." Matt spread the paper money across the felt. "Thirty thousand dollars says I can cut all four aces. I'll also make it more interesting. I'll let you do all the shuffling, and I'll only be able to defeat your cut card with an ace. You can even tell me from what part of the deck you want the bullets to come from, either off the top, bottom, or straight from the center of the deck. You mix and make the call."

Only thirty K? That was merely an hour's take in this casino. A relation of the affluent Lucas McCain should have more than a paltry thirty thousand. But Eric knew the true riches lay in the Phantom's knowledge and skill with the fifty-two tickets. If the Phantom could deliver what he just declared, the dividends would be far greater than the pocket change. Eric chuckled as he stripped open a new deck.

"I'll take that gamble." Andrews quickly put up the money. He shuffled and cut a queen. "Pretty lady. Bear in mind, you said you could only beat her with an ace!" He again shuffled and sat the deck in front of the Phantom. "Right now, cut the first ace to the bottom."

Matt took the deck. He was a little shaky at first, and his fingers were a bit numb from the scotch. It was foolish to have let himself get spurred into drinking hard liquor. He wanted to say a little prayer, but he felt that the Lord wouldn't forgive him nor look on his actions favorably. He had to make a go of it on his own. He'd gotten himself in this jam, and he had to get himself out.

Matt felt like the room was spinning. He inhaled deeply, repeatedly, to regain his focus from the fog in his head.

He grabbed the deck by the sides between his fingers. He let his well-practiced subconscious take over. He applied specific secret pressures to the deck, causing a weightless ace to split from the cards below. His fingertips felt dulled. Under lucid conditions he never missed the mark when it came to finding an ace, but now he wasn't convinced he had an ace. Yet all his money was on the line, and if the card wasn't an ace, his jailed father would be killed and the blame would be entirely his. He cut the deck, placing what he hoped was a life-giving ace to the bottom.

When he flipped over the deck and saw the bottom card, Eric couldn't believe what he saw.

When Andrews laid bare the lowest card, Matt could only see a white blur. He could tell it wasn't a multicolored face card, but it could be a losing two or a three. "Well," he bellowed. "What is the card?"

Andrews shook his head. "It's an ace, my card friend. That's amazing and very fortunate for you."

Matt sighed in relief. He'd done it! But this was just the first round. He must do it again.

Andrews moved the ace off to the side and again thoroughly mixed the deck. He cut a ten of hearts and said, "Ten, only three aces left. Cut this next ace to the top."

Matt took in a deep breath, a little less worried. "Watch carefully," Matt said as he cut the deck. "Here comes an ace."

Andrews laughed as he turned over the top card and saw a second ace. "My, my, another miracle. You are truly amazing, a real master." He shuffled, cut a king, then set the deck before McCain. "Big cowboy, hard to beat, and only two aces remaining."

Matt wished his teacher Vernon could see him blowing away this card legend. "To make it more challenging, I'll cut the last two aces simultaneously from the middle."

High overhead Kicker could see pride had infected his pal. Andrews would tickle his friend with flattery, and Matt would become thrilled with his triumph.

Sitting on the sofa, the undercover angel and the governor of Texas held their breath.

Eric's eyes burned into the Phantom's magnificent hands. He was trying desperately to catch these unheard-of methods. He stifled his desire to gasp in awe. As Matt effortlessly cut the two aces from within the deck, Andrews, his watchmen, and the Governor could only shake their heads in disbelief. Andrews counted out 30,000 dollars and tossed it over to the Phantom.

Matt could hardly believe his sudden fortune. Employing his deftness with the cards, in five minutes his bankroll had mushroomed to over 60,000 dollars.

"That's astounding," Eric looked up and said. "I haven't a clue how you're locating those power cards."

Matt was only 40,000 dollars from his 100,000 dollar goal. He decided to take the risk and offer to bet it all, putting him well over the 100,000 dollars he needed.

"How close can you get if I asked you to cut an exact number of cards?"

Andrews considered the question. "Always within three, sometimes two, maybe one."

"Tell you what. I'll bet this sixty grand if you cut the exact number of cards I request."

"Don't be ridiculous," Andrews snapped. "I'm no man's dolt. Nobody can be that precise."

"Well, then let's flip the challenge," Matt returned. "Eric, I have a dare for you. I'll wager this 60,000 dollars that I can cut off the precise number of cards you decide on." He elected to use a Miss Guided joke to lighten the moment. "But Eric, don't say fifty-two; that would certainly be dull-witted."

The angel saw an opening. "Oh, Mr. Andrews." Michala moved in and locked her eyes onto Andrews. "I can pick off fifty-two, and I get it correct every time."

Eric's eyes made sharp, angry contact with the woman's unwavering blue eyes. He pressed his mouth closed in a firm tight line. His voice was flat, cold as he spoke. "Madam, you can't do fifty-two. You're not playing with a full deck. Madam, let me ask you something. When you were a newborn, did your maid drop you on your little vacuous head?"

"Oh, don't be silly, Mr. Andrews." She gave a dismissive wave. "We couldn't afford a maid. My mama had ta do it."

CHAPTER FIFTY-FOUR

Never from a Guardian Angel

In his hiding place, Juan silently stretched his legs. As worried as he was about Matt, he had to smile at the angel. Even in the middle of a mess, she could take an uncivil slap and turn it into a jest.

As Juan limbered up his legs, he saw the bodyguards squeeze in close to the gaming table. He squatted low to keep from being seen. He knew drinking would lower Matt's resistance to the temptation to sin, the inclination of all humans to stray from the Savior and His Testament truths. Man hugs his own way, usually to his own harm, like the prodigal son.

The prodigal boy submitted to the wiles of the serpent to take his inheritance and run. He squandered his cash, drinking spirits and bedding strumpets. Finally, he was pitched into the pig pen and ended up sleeping with swine.

Since he had firsthand knowledge of the heavenly host, like Gabriel and the misguided angel, Kicker knew there had to be other beings—evil ones expelled from Heaven for their mutiny against the Big Man. History is filled with the servants of Satan, like Stalin, Hitler, and Big Lew Cypher.

But Paul exhorted everyone against letting the evil entities anywhere near. He proclaimed, "We are not sparring against mortal martial-art masters, but against principalities, against the rulers of this planet, against the army of immoral angels who were flung from the paradise places to rule this massive mud pie."

Juan knew the demons would use any willing man or woman as instruments for their evil. Juan could see that, as the serpent tempted Eve, Andrews was appealing to Matt's pride. The card legend was telling Matt exactly what he wanted to hear, enticing him into Andrews's control.

Big Man, Juan prayed silently, *in your Son's name, I bind the fallen fiends that are attempting to dominate the mind of my amigo, Matt McCain.*

Following his plea, Kicker slipped down the stairs. He shuffled past the blackjack table and ran right into Pinkerton and a pair of his guards. The two guards smiled as they pointed their pistols at the Mexican's temples.

"Welcome, little punk!" Damen said as he and a third guard stepped from the shadows. He scowled bitterly as he raised his deformed left hand, displaying its decayed cavity. He leaned toward Juan, his eyes cold and cunning as he gestured around the casino. "How do you like my little place? All I need now is that alien, and I'll get my revenge and ticket back home."

"Really? You think so, huh?"

Kicker thought, *The Bible Book states, "Go and play, you prosperous son of Satan. But someday you will squeal like a stuck swine because your wretchedness has spread throughout your sorry soul. Your ill-gotten gold and silver are infected, and the love of it shall feast on your flesh like maggots."*

Up on the elevated stage, Eric could scarcely believe what he just witnessed. The Phantom had picked off the exact number of cards he had requested.

Eric decided to remove the maddening woman and bleed McCain of his priceless knowledge before Damen killed him. Eric glared at the strange female, wondering how to get rid of her. His eyes locked onto her eyes; the scrutiny of his gaze rattled everyone, but for some reason, not this woman.

She gave him a wide smile, and Eric felt like he was gazing into an enchanted mirror that reflected his deceitfulness right back at him. The woman was not intimidated, nor did she avert her gaze. Eric stared at her, and his mind filled with a peculiar dread. He sensed she was the phantom behind the Phantom. Eric lowered his eyes and shook his head clear from the strange impact and turned back to his opponent.

"I don't believe it is necessary to have the teacher tending over us men, do you?"

Matt didn't want her to leave, but he realized Andrews was having a problem with her. The clock was running, and he had no time to deal with the predicament.

"Miss Guided, would you please go see if your horse has been watered? I'll join you back at the coach shortly. If you don't mind, I'd like to take a minute and swap a few card techniques with Eric."

Michala didn't like this at all. Matt was employing his duping proficiency to prevail, and he had promised he wouldn't.

"Do be prudent, Matthew. And please remember the time and yer true purpose."

She turned and went down the steps; on the casino floor she wended her way through the throngs of irritated gamblers.

"Lord Cypher." Pinkerton aimed a finger. "Here comes that lassie."

Damen glared into Juan's defiant eyes. "Your time is up!" He turned back to Pinkerton and ordered, "Get her!"

Pinkerton's jaw dropped open and his eyes bugged as he frantically looked back and forth. He blinked and rubbed his eyes, but the woman was nowhere to be seen. Where did she go?

Michala stepped outside and down the marble steps. She turned right down the footpath and gave a resounding whistle. She followed Seraphim's answering whinny to a serene side street. As she moved closer to her coach, she noticed Gabriel's glorified glow.

She stepped into the interior of her buggy and positioned herself humbly before the cowboy-garbed Gabriel. For the moment she simply stared out the window toward the celestial bodies hovering in Heaven.

"I positively have a passion to play again in Paradise." She sighed and looked at the Archangel Gabriel. "There is so much sorrow and distress down here on this pitiful planet. I am so fervently looking toward the Almighty's momentous moment when His crowned Prince of Paradise returns to claim His proper place."

"Well, howdy Ma'am." Sir Gabe tapped his toe and in flashed a bright beam of light. "Is ya'll havin' a little discommode on this here frolic? Well, my whimsical woman, how is that? I've been drilling diligently on my Texas two-step and Southern speak. Am I improving?"

The downcast angel's face brightened and a little smile appeared. "I suppose, Sir Gabe. Ya sound convincing ta me. Just keep watchin' them late night Westerns."

The leader of the heavenly hosts squirmed, then cleared his throat. He stroked his beard, tipped back his hat, and finally spoke. "My mirth-provoking Miss Guided, I'm mainly here about a further affair. Michala, you've performed satisfactorily as an on-earth angel. However, your human's heart is still hard, and your guy hasn't given himself solely over to the Savior to be grafted in as a saved son of Abraham. Your man Matthew has the Scripture inside his head but not in his heart. However, I'm compelled to repeat, your prevailing Kicker is performing to my predicted expectations."

"What? Your predicted expectations, Sir?"

"Yes, there were histories missed and histories yet to attain. I have recommended this man to the Almighty. Therefore the Father has favored your orphan as His modern Moses. Kicker is your key to the replaced present. His applied prayers and steadfast faith are rallying the hosts of Heaven behind him. But our chief concern is your charge, Matthew McCain. The Begotten Word is once again regarding you as his one and only misguided angel. The Lord of Lords loves your levity, as do we all, and He is observing this specific expedition."

He took hold of her hands. "Michala, my amusing angel, you are aware that taking man outside-of-time is seldom sanctioned. The history that isn't should be existent. My merry marm, you are the reason and the mend. But again, I'm to apprise my paradise princess, outside of the restitution of your prior human's homestead, no other chronicled history may you modify."

"Yes, my Satan-slaying sovereign, I hear ya."

Gabriel dropped her hand, leaned back, and smiled. "In the event there are any unsanctioned changes, or if your charge is engorged by an obese dweller of the deep, my funny angel may be flying in the Beyond with one wing tied behind her back."

Michala answered, "I hear ya, Sir Gabe."

"Yes, Michala, in the heavens there are a handful of hosts who are still calling you Miss Guided. As I earlier expressed, I have an inclination for the funny name. It's amusing, and it makes me giggle. But, by all means I'd rather my legendary lady not live up to the nonsensical name. Michala, I'm sure as a guardian of the Almighty-made mortals, you're mindful that an angel is at no time allowed to advance incentive toward sin. Temptation is approved to proceed from one temporal to another, and inducement for wickedness ceaselessly comes from Satan and his bootlicking lackeys. But, Michala, temptation should never spread from a man's guardian angel."

"Ta what do ya refer? Was it the foldin' knife or perhaps the two cards?"

The Archangel shook his head. "No it's not the knife. However, I must admonish you—the maneuver with the knife was risky. I pray you will never again overtly use your heavenly power in front of people. Though as you surmised, I'm certainly here with respect to the playing pair."

He hesitated. "When you provided the pair, you approved corrupt conduct. Your charge procured the means for his currency-exploiting procedures that he concedes in his soul to be sinful. We all respect the risk of arrogance from watching the dethroning of our once-divine delegate. It seems like it was a mere million millennia ago when the once-radiant Lucifer was the lord of the angelic legions and sat beside the Savior's sacred throne. Gaze at old gooseberry now. The hideous serpent slithers in the shadows, trying to seduce society, hungering to haul a myriad with him into the flaming lake of fire."

"Yes, I understand, Sir Gabe. Hell, a horrible choice to intentionally make."

"My promising angel, as I'm sure you discern, once a single step has been seized toward a direction one knows to be bad, pride pushes in and the second step is never far after. When your charge cheated that tally-to-twenty-one trial, he shamed his virtuous values. Matthew McCain has mastered a swindler by swindling. Through the whole of history, the holy have gathered that one can't conquer evil with evil. In this way, both are beat. If your man Matthew doesn't hurry and halt his dishonest deeds, it will be easier for your fellow to suppress his conviction and concede a second step toward sin."

"I fathom the peril. I made a momentous mistake. I'm remorseful, and I hope ta mend it quick. Just please don't take me off the McCain case," Michala pleaded.

"All right," Gabriel agreed. "You are authorized to advance with your assignment. But, I'll assert again, you are allowed to aid in the accruement of Lucas's assets back to his ancestry. Aside from that, no alterations of the past may occur."

Gabriel transformed back to his ethereal status. He whipped his golden wings, and they fluttered and shimmered like sunbeams.

As he gradually disappeared, his words floated back through the air. "Remember, my merry Michala, all of this particular planet's span proceeds toward one important purpose, and that is the manifestation of the Almighty's Sacrificed Son."

"For sure," the angel announced to a barren buggy. "I'm looking foremost for that momentous moment."

The carriage door flew open, and Damen thrust his smirking face inside. "You definitely are a little green-blooded alien!"

CHAPTER FIFTY-FIVE

Beguiled like His Great Grandfather

The inventive card moves he'd just witnessed stupefied Eric. He gradually raised his eyes and said, "You are a sort of Phantom, aren't you! Almost dangerous." He tossed another 60,000 dollars onto the table. "You must be the incomparable master of card table history. Capable of anything, no doubt."

Matt was thrilled—he'd thrashed the legend out of over 120,000 dollars, and the man he'd vanquished was now praising him.

Matt tipped his hat. "Thank you, Eric. Coming from a legend like you, that means something. I thank you much; however, I've got to get on my way."

"No, no, no, not quite yet. We must have one more duel."

Matt felt a chill of alarm run up his spine. He wasn't interested in any more play.

Andrews rose and stepped out to the edge of his private gambling area. His eyes scanned slowly across the gambling crowd. He removed Matt's cane from the rail and pointed with it.

"What would be the ultimate bet? The preeminent wager?" He paused and looked around the room. "I have it! My Phantom master, I bet you all of this," he waved the cane across the hall, "Mr. Cypher's entire array of treasures and his casino, that you, Phantom, can't save your Mexican and your lady."

The gambling palace grew silent. Matt's stomach dropped, and he felt cold terror grip him deep within his gut. He jumped from his chair as dread and nausea consumed him.

"Cypher?" Matt shivered and stuttered, "wh-wh-which Cypher?"

Two of Andrews's guards shoved Juan up the steps and onto the stage next to Matt. The goons pointed pistols at each of their temples.

"'Ey Mano," Kicker quipped. "Brought some friends to the party."

Two other watchmen moved forward and also drew their weapons. Matt peered out of the corners of his unfocussed eyes and found himself face to face with a vision of horror.

"Kicker, I'm glad to see you're okay. But, where's Miss Guided?"

Governor Turner rose from his seat. "Eric, don't be ridiculous!" He pointed at the four armed men. "Call off those guards, and tell them to holster their weapons."

Matt felt numb, in shock, like a thousand snickering eyes were watching him. He was beginning to understand that he had been beguiled like his great grandfather.

His voice quivered as he attempted to mask his panic. "Eric, sir, it's below you to play with lives."

"May I have everyone's attention please?" Andrews spread his arms, the cane in his right hand, and spoke like a sanctimonious preacher. "The notable Phantom Gambler, ladies and gentlemen, Wild Bill Hickok's angel of death, elusive to all, finally meets his match in this establishment. He was caught cheating by yours truly." Andrews reached into his vest and held up two cards for all to behold. "My trusting patrons, the Phantom was caught switching these cards at Miss Dumont's blackjack table. The man who exposed others for their tricks has been unveiled himself as a hypocrite and a fraud."

The swarm of offended gamblers began to gasp and murmur at Andrews's news. Then they turned their attention to Matt and began to boo and hiss.

RE-DEAL

Matt's shame and humiliation for his crooked deeds were clear on his face. Andrews's words hit him hard, almost like a death sentence. Each word felt like a bullet ripping into his guilt-ridden conscience, tearing him apart piece by piece. All he could do was tremble—he could think of nothing to say. He couldn't believe his own stupidity. Like his great grandfather, he had fallen into their trap.

He silently said a quick, desperate prayer. *Oh dear God, I'm sorry! Please help!*

But things only got worse. Matt heard a squeal come from behind him, from the opposite side of Andrews's elaborate partition.

Damen shoved the obscure door open and hauled the woman forcefully into the gambling area. He held her firmly as he shoved her forward and grinned at Matt.

"Hey, Magoo, why not see Andrews's bet with your girlfriend's pretty little thumbs?"

Kicker was sickened by the stare in Damen's eyes—a glassy grimace, worse than Juan had ever witnessed before.

The image of his father's bloody thumbs once again wavered before Matt's mind. He froze, then tried to focus his shadowy vision on Damen's gun pointed at Michala's head. Seeing her trapped in the wicked man's arms deepened Matt's stark terror and panic. He tried to stifle his heart's violent pounding by placing his hand over his chest. He felt the sweat turning cold against his skin.

"Michala." Matt pleaded in frantic harsh whispers, "You don't have to let the rat hold us. Can't you use one of your marvels to stop the Cypher brat?"

Michala remembered her commander's recent admonishment concerning miracles. "Matthew, yer holdin' the cards."

What? It was all up to him? Oh no, what could he do now? He was the one that got them into this mess! He swallowed hard, feeling as ensnared and frightened as a mouse clamped in a starved tomcat's mouth. He choked out a shame-packed plea, "Help us, God!"

"Big Man," Juan imperceptibly prayed along with his pal. "Bring down Cypher's contemptible Tower of Babel. If you require a life as recompense, I offer mine. Just rally round my amigo Matt, and help him at long last to be released from the despicable grip of Big Lew, then help him free his father." Kicker looked out the window toward the bliss in the beyond. "Please Lord, let my feet fly like a sheepherder's stone, but only if it will further Your Father's perfect purpose."

Matt's razor-sharp hearing took in every word of Juan's pleadings. The unselfish words his friend spoke caused Matt to suffer even more pain and guilt.

"Yes, God," the Governor agreed. "Just give me the grit."

Asa heaved his massive frame against the guard nearest him. This caused Juan, his captors, Damen, and Michala all to crash to the floor. Juan executed a somersault, jumped up, and landed a back-kick in a guard's belly. Andrews's watchman curled like a stuck worm and retched.

"Don't dirty the good-looking carpet." Kicker snickered. "Heave outside if you must."

He spun and spotted Damen reaching for a six-shooter. Juan sprung and flew after Damen with the hard heel of his boot. Kicker cried, "Give me the might, Big Man!"

Damen dropped Michala and lost the gun after Juan rolled them down like a bunch of bowling pins. He stood and charged after Juan with a scream.

Kicker forced a foot right into the belly of his attacker. "Heel's to ya!" he said with a chuckle.

"Curse you!" Damen cried as his belly folded around a boot heel. The blow caused him to suck air and curl down slightly, but he recovered quickly.

Andrews stepped away and signaled for more guards.

Oh no, Matt thought, *here we go again.* He tipped the table against several of the oncoming guards, and the flying money filled the air. Down below, the gamblers scrambled up the stairs and after the floating cash. The guards fired, and the crowd yelled and ran for cover.

RE-DEAL

Eric leaped from the elevated stage and flew out the door.

Juan and Matt fought faster than ever before while the guards were striving to get a clear aim.

Michala scrambled toward the steps. A sentry grabbed her from behind by the neck. She gracefully flipped him over her head and thought, *Wow, it works!*

She turned back and yelled, "Boys! Quick! Let's get movin' with no dalliance, now!"

Matt and Juan leaped toward the edge of the stage. They punched and kicked the endless supply of assailants pouring up the steps.

"Stop," Damen bellowed out. "Don't let the Phantom escape!" He signaled for Pinkerton and his guards to follow the escaping trio. "Get them!" Damen pressed an ornate carving, and the invisible door opened. He ran through, closed the door, and raced toward the front entrance.

Matt's crooked eyes darted back and forth, trying to spot a way out.

Juan wrapped his hands around the rail and yelled, "Mano, let's jump!"

Holding the handrail, Juan went over headfirst, performing a flip, and landing on his feet like a confident feline.

Matt followed behind. He grabbed the rail and slung his legs over together. He fell toward the ground, but he landed on the back of a faro dealer. The dealer cursed him as Matt scrambled to his feet.

"Matt! Kicker! This way, boys!"

Matt and Juan shoved over a large wheel of fortune, then a craps table, followed by two faro banks. As the knot of guards and gamblers tried to unsnarl their bodies, the two karate fighters made a break and trailed after Michala toward the casino's foyer. As they dashed by the Greek marble gods, Matt could hear bootsteps echoing on the polished floors as the enraged bettors and backers pursued them. Matt could also hear the Governor trying to get the guards to halt fire.

"Hold on everybody," Asa appealed. "McCains are honorable folk."

As Matt, Juan, and Michala passed through the front hall, Damen stepped from behind one of the pillars with a gun. He took aim with the pistol and fired.

The bullet whizzed by Matt's ear. "Whoa!" he cried.

"Run, Mano!" Juan screamed as he saw the gun again pointed at his pal. "Save your father! I'll stop Damen!"

Juan thrust out his arms and dove headfirst toward the floor, diverting Damen's attention. He executed a cartwheel, followed with three back handsprings, generating tremendous velocity. Juan hurdled high into the air into a triple somersault. He unfolded out of the spinning with a striking sidekick straight for Damen's face.

Kicker called out, "This is for the soldiers of the Big Man and for his Son."

Damen squealed, "Hold still, you flipping fugitive!"

Juan gave an earsplitting scream as he flew right for Damen's face.

Damen tried to take aim but finally just randomly fired. The shot caught Juan in the head, and he collapsed to the floor like a sack of potatoes, blood gushing out the side of his face.

"Bingo!" Damen bellowed.

As Matt ran to tackle Damen Cypher, he tripped over Juan's body. He screamed, "You sick butcher!"

Matt fell, and he grabbed and knocked Damen down, causing the shooter to drop the gun.

"Matt," Miss Guided screamed. "Grab Kicker!"

Matt scuffled around on the marble floor with his long-time enemy. Matt clutched the weaker man by the collar and cuffed him hard across the chin, knocking him out cold. Matt scrambled up on his hands and knees. He struggled back to get Juan.

"Kicker!" Matt cried in a panic. There was no reply. Matt checked Juan's face; there was no sign of life, and Juan was covered with fresh crimson blood. "Please God, no!" Matt cried. "Don't let him die!"

RE-DEAL

Matt shoved his arms under Kicker's neck and legs and picked him up. "Hang on, my brother," Matt pleaded. "We'll make it!" He took off running, but slipped in Juan's blood on the slick marble floor.

The gamblers charged after the Phantom like a voracious swarm of killer bees. One guard grabbed Juan's leg and ripped the body from Matt's arms. Juan's body thumped to the floor.

Matt heard a thunderous blast, and a gunshot whizzed passed his ear. He scrambled back to his feet and took off running. Another shot was fired at him and another and another. He dodged bullets as the gang of gunmen kept advancing toward him.

"Matt," Michala cried. "Let's get!"

Damen shook his head clear. "Only kill the devious Phantom," he ordered. "Not the woman. I want her alive!"

Michala seized Matt's hand and pulled him out the door.

Pinkerton signaled for more guards. "Stop them!"

"I can't go!" Matt lamented. "No! Kicker is still inside! Oh God, no!"

Matt had another flashback. A fleeting memory of his father's severed thumbs. He choked back a sob, a desperate prayer. "My poor father! I need that money!"

Michala hustled him down the stone steps as the angry gunmen poured out of the casino in pursuit. She hollered, "Move, Matthew!"

She placed two fingers between her lips and gave a piercing whistle, which was answered by Seraphim. Her horse rushed the buggy to the side of the steps. Bullets whizzed by them as Michala threw the buggy door open and shoved Matt in.

"No!" Matt cried desperately. "I can save him!"

"Sorry, it's too late!"

"No! I could've whipped that crowd!"

"Oh? Are ya gonna go back and shoot them all? Is that yer plan? Maybe ya got a trick up yer sleeve ta cheat Kicker back into this coach right here! Ya reneged on our agreement, and there's nothing ya can do about it now."

An array of nightmare voices screamed in Matt's head—his mother and sister, his pop, and now Juan. He was frantic and stuck his head out the window. Bullets thumped like hammer blows around his head into the oak panel sides of the coach then ricocheted away.

"What are ya doing?" Michala pulled Matt back in. "Get yer silly head back here!" She shouted to the horse, "Giddy up, Seraphim!"

Bullets rebounded off the buggy as they spun away and gained speed to a gallop, then disappeared back outside-of-time.

CHAPTER FIFTY-SIX

Stupid Pride

Matt collapsed on the seat of the coach, paralyzed at the nightmare that had just unfolded before him. He let his head fall forward, then shook it hard, hoping it would clear away the undeniable fact that Kicker was gone, dead, left in the past, with no funeral and no good-byes.

Matt blew out a sigh. He attempted to face Michala, but quickly lowered his head in shame. His own dishonest actions had thoroughly humiliated him. He wanted to say something, but nothing would come out. Several minutes passed in awkward, tormenting silence. They were in the buggy, traveling outside-of-time—Matt knew the time wasn't actually passing, but those few minutes of silence seemed to last forever.

He felt like he'd been shot through the gut. His strong "I-can-do-it-myself" mask was shown to be just that—a mask, a facade, a fraud, a phony. He felt anguish beyond words that because of his stupid pride, not only had he lost the cash essential to rescuing his father, but also he'd caused the death of his best friend Kicker, who'd been like a brother.

I'm a fool, Matt chided himself. He sniffed and the tears flowed. *A real sucker. I'm no better than the rest. McCain, you say you're principled. You trust in God and no way will fall. Well, you fell big-time. You had several warnings, but you didn't listen.* Matt dabbed his eyes with his coat sleeve. *Oh, what have I done? If I could only have one more chance, oh God, please just one. Kicker, Kicker, you shouldn't have taken that bullet for me. You goof! You silly, brave, worm-eating goof. I love you. Kicker, next time I'll use my body to stop that bullet.*

Matt again wiped his eyes and nose, cleared his throat, and broke the silence. "Miss Guided, can't you take the coach back before …"

His voice trailed off. It sounded lifeless and hollow as he recalled Michala informing them that once they depart one time they can't go back.

"What's that, Matthew? Go back before you cheated? So ya want an excuse ta try again? I heeded what yer Mr. Andrews declared, how he caught ya red-handed swappin' cards."

The accusation in Miss Guided's words stung deep into Matt's soul. "Oh no, that's not it at all! I don't want another opportunity to outdo that crafty Andrews." With a hopeless throb in his heart, Matt yielded his disgrace in a voice no louder than a sigh. "No, Miss Guided, that's not what I'm proposing. You should be disappointed with me. I mean go back before the bullet hit Kicker. I will prevent it from hitting my brother."

The memory of Kicker's bloody head shattered Matt's composure again. He dropped to the coach floor in a pleading position on his knees beside Michala. Tears poured from his blurry eyes. "Oh, dear Lord, what have I done? First my mom and Debra are killed, now Kicker, and because of my stupid, stupid, selfish behavior, my loving dad will be next."

Matt approached Michala as if she were the last bastion of hope for his father. "Miss Guided," Matt pleaded. "Is there anything left that can be done?"

The angel watched as the tears streaked down her charge's cheeks and fell onto the seat.

She hauled him up next to her. "Ya don't propose ta say that ya would have positioned yourself in front of that deadly projectile?"

RE-DEAL

The question seemed to dangle in the air. Matt could not answer. He had no doubt he would have done just that. But what did it matter now? Kicker was gone, and he was so, so sorry.

The guardian in human form concentrated on the trickles of contrition on her human's face. "Now hush yer tears."

She caressed his face and stroked the back of his head as he sobbed. She pulled away, took her hankie from her minuscule purse, and patted his face.

"I'm sorry, Matthew. It's partially my doin'. I should never have contributed the two cards."

Matt shook his head. "No, oh no! Absolutely not. This horror is my fault—I'm the one who broke the agreement to earn money honestly. As expected, you were correct. You can't defeat evil with evil."

His body was trembling, and he was glassy-eyed from weeping. He wiped away the tears, sighed, and used his coat sleeve to wipe the wetness from his nose and cheeks.

"I can't believe it. I really blew it badly, and all because of my foolish pride. I believed I was so clever not even Andrews could spot me." He again lowered his head in regret. "Pride, the most harmful of all sins. It was on account of his pride that Lucifer became the devil and was hurled from Heaven."

As the tears again started to run, Matt lowered himself back on the floorboards to his knees. He rested his elbows on the seat, clasped his hands together, lifted his eyes toward Heaven and prayed aloud. "Oh dear God, please, please forgive me. I was so rotten, and I'm so regretful for my cheating. But even worse, I never truly put my trust in You. Throughout my life, I only focused on all the offenses done to me. Never on all the worthy attention to detail You have continually shown my life. Like this exceptional lady, Pastor Steve, Kicker, and the extraordinary opportunity to travel outside-of-time with the hope of helping my family. My dad's hours are numbered, Kicker is dead, and it's entirely my doing.

"Over the years I have given you lip service, but unlike Kicker, I never surrendered my undivided self over to you. Again I ask You to forgive me, and like Pastor Steve would invite the kids to do, please send your Holy Spirit into my heart." He choked and sniffed. "Juan's with You, I'm certain. Please let him know I finally took the step to trust You. That I'm also very sorry and that I loved him like a brother."

Matt slowly slid back into his seat across from Michala. "We may as well return to the twenty-first century. Considering that my rotten actions have caused the death of Kicker, our time is spent, and I lost all the money, there's no reason to continue on back here."

Michala was moved. She could see her charge was remorseful for his dishonest deeds. She moved over in front of him, laid her handkerchief in her lap, reached over, and took his hands.

"It's okay." She lifted his chin. "Please look at me, Matthew. Perhaps somethin' can still be puzzled out. I'm sure ya know it does no good ta brood on the past. The Almighty doesn't languish on what's gone, so ya need not either. The Creator is acquainted with history's outcome even before that age has gone by. Hence if ya have reliance and faith on, as Kicker would say, the Big Man in the Sky, everything will be right with ya."

The woman's words and soft voice soothed like down feathers floating across his face. Her heartening words and tender touch sent surges of adrenaline through his system. His eternal eyes were opened with a song in his spirit. Matt again prayed, "My loving Lord, I thank You. I heard and heeded your hallowed words, but I never held Your healing Holy Spirit in my heart. Again, I give thanks."

The freedom and forgiveness slowly streamed a second time into Matt's soul. He wiped the wetness from his face. "What are you trying to tell me, Miss Guided? I know we can't go back. Prior to leaving on this voyage, I recall you cautioning us that as soon as we departed a time or place, Seraphim would not be able to return to that same place.

RE-DEAL

Besides, even if we could, we have no time left." He lowered his head. "And Kicker, who was closer than a brother is now gone—thanks to me."

"Take comfort, Matt. Kicker is in the hands of the Big Man, as you also are. In spite of everything, I trust ya might be able ta still rally round yer Papa."

"But Miss Guided, how could we possibly do anything now?"

"Well, Mr. Cheat." The lovely lady's eyes lit up. "We could stop in 1882, and ya could advise yer great grandpapa Lucas not ta participate in that underhanded game. What do ya say, Matthew? Let's seize the bull by the tail and go for it. We'll do it for Kicker!"

"Miss Guided, Michala, whoever you actually are, I believe there is more under that flowery little hat than you permit people to see."

"Why thank ya, Matthew. As I previously said, I'm so smart that I haven't even brought into play half my brains."

Like her previous charge Lucas McCain, Matthew had impressed her in a manner that she could scarcely describe. He'd overcome a remarkable amount. Even after falling for the evil enemy's lies, he'd gone to his knees for forgiveness and finally trusted the Savior to pull him back up by the bootstraps. Now if she could simply complete her mission and mend her prior mess, things would be all well in the hallowed heavens.

The angel asked, "What does yer timepiece say?"

Matt pulled his timepiece from his pocket and punched the speak symbol. "Time remaining 1 hour 42 minutes 13 seconds."

"Miss Guided," Matt said with a new exuberance. "Our time is swiftly passing away; however, I'm with you. Let not my selfish desires, but the Lord's divine wisdom be done. Let's go! We'll stop off in 1882, and we'll do it for Juan!"

The angel smiled. Sir Gabe would certainly be satisfied. Matthew McCain was maturing into a heartfelt man of faith.

"Hang on, Matt, here we go. Next landing, host of the poker championship, Bowen's Dining Hotel, Santa Fe, New Mexico; the year 1882."

As the pair voyaged outside-of-time, Matt wanted to express his appreciation. Deep in his spirit, he knew this woman had not been sent his way for romance. However he wondered if it would be within reason to give her one more kiss of gratitude.

He took her hands into his, shifted close to her hazy face, and placed his hands on her rosy cheeks. He moved his fingers through her golden hair to the back of her head and leaned under her hat to give her a quick kiss. Just as his lips were ready to touch hers, the coach stopped short and Matt was forced from her nearby lips to his familiar spot on the floor.

CHAPTER FIFTY-SEVEN

In Two Places at the Same Time

"Oh, Matthew, we're back in this world. Let's go warn yer grandpapa Lucas."

Embarrassed, Matt once more hauled himself up off the floorboards with a sigh. As he scrambled to his feet, he considered that Kicker's killer might be waiting.

"Miss Guided, in the event we have uninvited visitors with guns, knives, or rock-heads waiting, I think we should park on the outside of town and find another way in. I'm afraid this rich-colored coach sticks out like a two-headed hog."

"Good idea, Matt," she agreed. "We'll pull over here and walk." She shouted out the side window, "Yank it on over, Seraphim. Be careful when ya step out Matt. There's a steep holler to yer left."

"Thanks, Miss Guided."

But Matt wasn't worrying about a high hill. He was worrying about the wickedness they could face. However, he had to trust that the Big Man was in complete control.

Michala pushed opened the door, and the pair stepped out. They were puzzled to find the streets deserted. The angel looked about and spotted a single soul sitting on a buckboard.

"Hang on, Matthew, there's somebody."

As they dashed toward the buckboard, Matt reflected on the affection he had for this miracle worker. He could hardly wait for this fight to save his family to end. He was eager for his father to meet Michala—he didn't doubt his dad would adore her as much as he did. He hoped someday things would slow down long enough to tell her just how much he treasured her. But his first priority was to keep his eyes on the Big Man and not his personal pleasures.

He peeked up and prayed, "Give me your might, Big Man!"

They caught up to the driver. The angel asked, "Mr. Taxi Driver, where's all the folks?"

He lifted a gnarled finger and pointed. "Why, they're naturally down at that rich man Bowen's overpriced grub shack. That's where the big game is, ya know."

Matt asked, "What? You mean the big game has already started?"

"Reckon so. And the overrated drinkin' hole is full of bunch a killers. I personally droves Holliday and Devol me-self. Cain't find two better men fir flourishin' me business." Digger flicked a bony thumb over his shoulders toward a funerary box. "As ya see, I'm fixed fir dead dealings."

Matt's wasted eyes went wide at the mention of those murderous maniacs. He knew this meant more mayhem. However, like his late pal Kicker, he was a reinvigorated grunt in the army of the Big Man.

"Folks, if you gots twenty bucks, ya kin hop in, and I'll take ya yonder."

"So you're a corpse-carrying cabby," said Michala.

Matt patted his pockets, though he knew he had no money. Then his fingers felt a single solid circle. It was the twenty-dollar gold coin Michala had given him for cab fare back aboard the boat. This was one more marvel that was so mind-boggling he couldn't discount the coincidence. Matt's faith increased.

He peered up at the driver and said, "Take us to Bowen's place—fast!" He tossed the gold coin to the driver. "Your rates are as bad as a New York taxi." He helped Michala up and snapped, "Let's go—quick!"

As the hearse headed down the street, Matt whispered, "Miss Guided, we need some kind of disguise or those gunmen will recognize us. Moreover, if Damen is here—"

RE-DEAL

Before Matt could complete his thought, the cab stopped. "Here ya'll is. We's here."

"Well, gee," Matt exclaimed. "What a rip-off! For twenty bucks, you tugged us twenty feet." Matt figured it would be best to gain entry unobserved. "We want our money's worth. Drive us around to the back."

"Ain't no good complaining now," the driver said. "Hangs on; got ta go twixt the erections."

The cabby drove them around to the back, and Matt and Michala jumped down from the wagon. In the alley, Michala saw many people working to unload the catered food and drink. The duo maneuvered their way to the back entrance. Matt lifted his head to catch a glimpse of the workers who scurried in and out, unloading crates of bottles and vittles from a large wagon.

A supervisor abruptly shoved the latecomers toward the cart. "No taking a siesta on the job!" He thrust a forefinger at the late pair. "The two of you, snatch ya a basket and keep movin'!"

"Yes, sir," Matt answered. "We'll get right on it."

Matt and Michala merged into the crew, and each grabbed a box of bottles.

The guardian angel murmured, "Keep alert, Matt. I spied a few watchmen patrollin' the particulars."

Matt trailed behind Michala carrying the crate of booze. As she led them toward the kitchen door, Matt told himself, *In no way will I ever toss down this type of toxin again.*

As Matt moved, he used the bottles to cloak his recognizable face. However, he could scarcely see where he was going. As he tried to enter, he missed the opening and crashed into the doorjamb, causing the crate of bottles to noisily smash into his face.

Whoa, he thought, *as my good friend Kicker would have said, someone moved the door.* He breathed a sigh, shook his head clear, then cautiously tried a second time. This attempt was crowned with success. *Things are looking up*, Matt told himself. *I'm in the midst of trouble in only two tries.*

He blinked as he tried to adjust his injured eyes to the darkened back room.

"Not so clamorous, Matt. If yer compelled ta create additional doorways, please render yer refurbishing quietly."

"Miss Guided, you crack me up. Nothing rattles you."

"Hush. Lots of folks ahead; now linger close."

Matt gripped his case near to his face as he followed behind his benefactor.

Chaotic commotion greeted them in the kitchen as the waiters and cooks struggled to hold up under the demands of the major event underway. Matt tried his best to keep up with the graceful Michala. But as he bumbled behind her, saloon and restaurant attendants needed to sidestep him. Matt felt as though any moment, something would cause him to bump into somebody.

Michala ushered Matt down a corridor filled with packing crates imported from San Francisco. The crates contained bottles of fine brandy and wine. He bumped into an open box that smelled like moldy fermented grapes, reminding him of his blunder at Andrews's place and of Kicker's demise.

The angel eased them over to the back of the bar. "We can set these baskets of abominable booze down here."

They laid their load on the bar. They lingered out of the way as they attempted to learn the layout. A headwaiter came near and snatched an apron off a hook hanging on a board.

He snapped, "You two loafers, you're late. Get dressed. When the game is done, that pushy crowd is gonna demand their brew."

Matt questioned, "The big showdown game has started?"

The headwaiter didn't reply. He just rushed toward the rear.

"Matt, remove yer coat. I have a notion for a costume."

The angel pulled down two aprons. She cinched one around Matt's waist and the other around her own waist.

RE-DEAL

She placed a bottle and two tumblers on a tray and passed it to Matt.

"Here, take this tray and keep it elevated to conceal yer face." She fixed another for herself. "Follow me, Matt. And please strive ta be quiet as ya make new doorways."

In the guise of servers, they made their way into the main saloon hall. Inside, a lavish party was in progress under the sparkling chandeliers of the richly-appointed room.

They passed waiters carrying silver trays filled with draft and vittles. Most of the men held drinks and puffed on long cigars. As they moved forward, Michala found the front door parted in pieces. As she scanned the bustling room of gamblers, cattle barons, and gunfighters, she recognized some of their past foes.

In hushed tones, she said, "Keep yer famous face hidden behind yer tray, the Rollin' Stones are here. I see that hairless man with a rock for a head. He's already used his numb, gnarled noggin ta demolish the front door."

"Thanks for the heads-up. Can you please move us somewhere inconspicuous?"

"Sure," she said. "Stay close."

She led them over to the opposite end of the massive bar. "Matt, we can set these servers down here."

Matt collided with the counter, then found a place to set the tray. He kept his head low and simulated the actions of a waiter by arranging things on the bar as he attempted to get acclimated. He was eager to search out his great grandfather, Lucas McCain. But everything was so far out of focus, he could make out nothing, zip, zilch. His heart was heavy with apprehension, but his faith was in the Father.

He said a silent prayer. *I know You can see, Lord, and I trust You. Please guide us in your perfect direction.*

"Please accompany me, Matt," Michala said. "Let's stir us a stone's throw closer so ya can see."

Michala eased them over to a towering ornate pillar behind which they could study the contest.

Matt asked, "Who else do you see?"

"Well," Miss Guided looked about the huge gaming hall, "it's so chock full of bystanders that I can't glimpse a clear view." She grabbed Matt's hand and pulled him forward. "Hoof it quietly and follow me." She stopped by some steps and said, "Plant yourself here, Matt. I'm gonna look round and check out the situation."

"You got it, Miss Guided."

She went up six steps and looked around the saloon. She heard the memorable, sick sound of Doc Holliday. The ailing killer was standing in the back bearing a bottle in one hand and a brimming boot of barf in the other. She caught sight of Buckskin with his finger up his nose. Andrews was standing next to a grinning Wyatt Earp.

The very plump Governor Prince sat in an office chair. She thought, *There is Matt's grandpappy's traitor, his Judas Iscariot.*

In the center of the room, two gamblers sat at a circular poker table that was covered with cash. The crowd was quiet. There in the center of attention was her last charge, Lucas McCain. She smiled and wondered how his little son Davy William was doing. Sitting across from Lucas McCain was Satan's servant, John Cypher. Each had cards in their hands.

She worked her way back to Matt, took his hand, and led him closer to the action. "I spied two fellows playin' cards. Everyone is watchin' them. One looks jest like ya—he's yer great grandpappy, Lucas McCain."

"Matt, I can sure tell that Governor over yonder knows the four food groups."

"What do you mean, Miss Guided?"

"Why he's a little too big for his britches. You'll also need ta be very careful, as I spotted that there mad tooth fairy. He's got the drunken staggers. I don't favor drinkin', Matt. People act like they swallowed their brain, and it got stuck in their shoe and then squished. I also noticed many of his mean friends lurkin' about."

"You're right. We don't want another fight. But I do need to get close enough to stop my great grandfather from betting his ranch."

RE-DEAL

Out front, Damen Cypher paced. He knew Matt would show up sometime, and he wasn't going to let him anywhere near the big game. He looked back inside, searched the crowd, and caught Devol.

Devol slid back to the door and asked, "Seen 'um?"

"No sign of the Phantom yet," Damen replied with a shake of the head.

They went back to scanning the crowd.

"One minute," Lucas said as he finished lettering a deed to his limitless lands. He held the legal paper up for all to look at. "With this here deed for my ranch and cattle, I call yer bet and raise ya three mil." Lucas laid the document down on the mountain of money and forced his finger close to Cypher's face. "And no IOU's!"

The crowd burst into applause. On the other side of the room, Buckskin moved slowly through the crowd and paused at Doc Holliday's shoulder. Holliday nodded toward Matt and whispered something, then they moved in opposite directions.

"Oh, no! We're too late! Grandpa Lucas has just bet his ranch."

Even if he was shot on the spot, Matt had to stop this particular play. He quickly cupped his hands around his mouth and called from behind the column. "Lucas McCain! Stop! Don't fall for it! It's a trick!"

The crowd reacted with stunned cries and mutters at the interruption. The gamblers and gunmen tried to see who had interfered.

Buckskin's powerful arms grabbed Michala, and he clamped his hand down hard over her mouth. He stuck his dirty face next to hers and said coldly, "Keep quiet, babe!"

At the same moment, Damen's knifepoint met Matt's back. He hissed, "Shut your hole, Magoo!" He glared at Michala, "Any tricks from you, and I'll stick your little boyfriend!" Damen yelled out to the crowd, "Oh, excuse us, ladies and gentlemen. It's just my crazy brother. He had a few too many. Please continue."

"I've had my fill," John Cypher cried back. "Any more interruptions and I'll have you shot! Get on with it, McCain!"

"As I was gonna say, along with my ranch, I'll also throw in my last piece of value, my own two hands as yer hired help." He pulled from his pocket a gold lighter and tossed it to the table. "I'll even include my personal torch for good measure."

The crowd approved with more laughter and applause.

Damen watched McCain bet the same lighter he'd stolen from his father back in the future. He wondered if it might still be in his pocket. For an impetuous moment, he released his hold on Matt's mouth and hastily felt in his coat for the identical gold lighter. It was still there. He pondered how the same lighter could be in two places at the same time.

"Let us go, you son of a butcher!" Matt cried when Cypher uncovered his mouth.

Damen's eyes burrowed into Matt's, and his sinister smile cut like a razor. "Just about three more minutes till we're back home to Daddy." He pushed the knife, drawing a trickle of blood. "Here's a little scar I've been saving for you, loser Magoo."

Matt recoiled from the cut, then quickly recovered. "Yeah, what makes you think I won't keep yelling and let you kill me right here?"

Damen's eyes glistened. "We'll just make sure you don't!"

He clamped his hand across Matt's mouth and held the knife tight across Matt's throat, drawing more blood. He eased Matt back toward the wall away from attention. He smeared a spot of blood onto Matt's shirt and said, "I knew you'd show up in some form. We'll just wait this one out and keep things right in their intended order."

Damen turned back to the game. He watched his great grandfather manipulate Lucas McCain. He now understood how his father became so clever in treachery. Damen watched his ancestor as if he were viewing an entertaining stage show. He wanted to pick up any tips so when he took over his father's empire he would be even cleverer.

As a matter of fact, Damen thought, *I'm ready now. When I get back, I'm going to shove my father out a fifty-story window and take over.*

Damen remembered he was going to need the woman to return to the twenty-first century. "Buckskin," he whispered, "whatever you do, don't hurt that babe."

Damen thought he might have a little intimate fun with her on their way home. He'd been wondering what was under the hat and skirt of this alien.

Buckskin could see a sadistic glee in Damen's eye.

"Don't soil her," Damen warned him, "She's mine for later."

CHAPTER FIFTY-EIGHT

Card Table Phantom

John Cypher leaned back in his chair. He tapped the points on his teeth and said, "McCain, I always believed you were as low as dung on the bottom of a shoe, and this honor you always talk about is just a facade. I was prepared for this trick. I thought you might stoop so low as to try and use your wealth to unfairly raise me out." He called to Prince, "Governor, roll on over."

John Cypher pulled from his pocket a formal-looking paper and laid it out for Prince to sign. He stood and clamped his arm around the governor's shoulders, "His Honor has long been the kindest, most generous official of this fair land."

"As I say," Prince explained, "I always try to be of service."

Prince twitched excitedly as he dipped the pen in the inkwell.

Matt's eyes bulged with anger, but Damen's hand held like a vice over his mouth.

After Prince placed the signature, Cypher eased the fool away. "As I was saying, I have just a little something. I call your 3,000,000 dollar bet, McCain, and raise you the entire territory of New Mexico!"

Bowen cried out, "You can't do that!"

Masterson stepped up and fired his gun toward the heavens. "Quiet! Quiet down!" He faced Cypher. "John Cypher, it appears not everything is quite in order here."

RE-DEAL

Cypher turned aggressive, like a prosecutor coming in for the kill. He held up the document. "No IOU's! No limits on raising! I got a legal document signed by the governor of this here territory, who happens to be the proprietor of this here land!" He whipped a forefinger at Lucas. "Now, put up or shut up!"

He slammed the document down hard on the pile of cash.

"This ain't right, Cypher," Bowen cried out. "This bet smells to high Heaven."

"So this was your scam, John Cypher." Luke considered the raise and nodded with understanding. "Very clever. Given my resources are all in the pot, I have no way to call this bet."

The angel remembered what her superior had said about bending blades and making use of fat fish in front of mortals. However, she figured there were no rules against a simple hug. She forced Buckskin's hands away and stepped between Damen and Buckskin. She slid her arms around their arms and squeezed them close.

She whispered, "Gentlemen, might I interest ya'll in some refreshments?"

Damen's eyes went wide in shock at how easily she got free and grabbed hold of him. He was in such a fright he couldn't speak, and as hard as he tried to pull his arms away, he couldn't free himself from her grip.

"Quick, Matt. Go help your grandfather."

"Thanks, Miss Guided!" Without any hesitation, Matt hollered out, "No, Grandpa Lucas, stop! Don't fold the hand! The document raise is all just a big scam between Cypher, Prince, and some of these killers."

This second interruption threw the saloon into more confusion.

"Hold everything." Masterson again pulled his pistol and fired. "Quiet!" He pointed his pistol at Matt. "Who are you, mister?" He turned back to Lucas. "And Luke, why is this man calling you grandpa?"

"Listen to me," Andrews shouted. "That's the Phantom, people!"

Devol cried out, "Hell, that's the Phantom, all right! I got a grudge to settle with him."

"Yeah." Holliday coughed up more spew, then agreed with the others. "That's the card table Phantom. I whipped 'im good back in Tombstone."

The crowd was in an uproar over the mention of the famous Phantom. Everyone scrambled to get a glimpse of the mysterious gambler.

"That's right." Matt removed the apron and emphasized his buckle. "I'm known as the Phantom. Cypher is running a bluff. He's trying to force Lucas to fold with a bogus raise."

Cypher pounded on the table in rage. "There's nothing phony about it! I own New Mexico, and here's the deed to prove it!"

Bat Masterson wondered how he could possibly arbitrate this situation. Cypher had to be running some kind of a scam, and Bat knew they needed to put him out of business once and for all.

He announced, "We'll leave the decision to our most distinguished judge, the Honorable Henry Watson."

Bat knew Judge Watson was weak. He drank and gambled too much, but most of the time he was fair. "Judge Watson, sir," Bat motioned, "please come here. We need your professional opinion."

Devol left his posted position. He stepped behind the judge and whispered his threats. "Watson, listen carefully. Yer gonna verify the legitimacy of that document, or you'll sleep with the worms tonight. If ya cooperate, a thousand is yours."

Devol clamped his meat-cleaver hand on the back of Judge Watson's neck and escorted the judge through the crowd.

"All of ya lookers," Devol screamed as he pushed his way through the crowd, "out of my way, so I can let the honorable Judge pass."

Henry feared for his life. He remembered how Devol had used his head to split the door in half, and he had no desire

RE-DEAL

to sleep with worms. Besides, the grand might be lucky on twenty-one black. So Henry decided to lie. He approached the table with an air of command. He took the deed from Cypher and studied it. He wanted to give the impression that his decision would be sound.

"Confidentially," Henry explained, "this is a very unusual situation. A Governor does have the authority, and with this signature by Prince, the principal proprietor of the majority of the New Mexico territories, I believe this is legal. And because my brothers sit on the region's high court, I know they will agree with me." He turned to Lucas. "Sorry, Mr. McCain, but I must side with Mr. Cypher."

Lucas realized he was wrong for not putting his reliance in his Lord. He shouldn't have tried to slay Cypher himself. Lucas turned back to his look-alike. "Phantom, I'd like ta thank ya for yer kind effort. But, poker etiquette gives me no honorable option but ta fold. However, if my good friend Asa Turner, the fine Governor of Texas, had been here, things might have turned out different."

The saloon fell so quiet Holliday's wheezing was the only thing that could be heard.

Lucas again lifted his hand, ready to throw in his cards.

At that moment, Jamie Bowen spotted a familiar face, the face of the Texas Governor, Asa Turner, coming through the door.

Michala kept a tight grip on her two foes as she looked toward the front.

"Stop, Lucas McCain!" Governor Turner's companion called.

Ready to toss his cards to the table, Lucas stopped at the sound of the loud voice.

"Ladies and gentlemen," the voice continued, "the right honorable Governor of the state of Texas, Asa Spades Turner!"

"Lucas!" Asa cried as he hurried through the damaged door. "Hold yer cards, partner!"

The crowd parted for the governor and his companion.

CHAPTER FIFTY-NINE

Forgetting Wings and Having to Walk

Matt glimpsed the fuzzy image of the man with Governor Turner, and his mind went wild with hope. Was it Juan? Was his amigo still alive? He struggled through the throng to see.

Maria Bowen rose from the sofa when she thought she saw her son. She waved, "Raul!"

Kicker watched the confusion playing across his great grandmother's face. She had mistaken him for her son, Raul, who could be Juan's twin. Kicker threw a compassionate kiss to her.

Governor Turner shook hands with Jamie Bowen. He waved at Bat, but stared with disgust at Governor Prince. He turned toward his fellow Texan.

"Lucas, I was planning to introduce ya to my fellow Governor, Mr. Prince. He has many times talked about taking his New Mexico territories and applying for U.S. statehood. However, I fear he has thrown everything away by siding up with Cypher."

"Hey! Dignitary!" Cypher glared hard at Governor Turner. "Not even you're gonna stop my winnings."

The animated angel's heart jumped with joy to see Juan accompanying the Governor. She swung Buckskin and Damen face to face into each other, and they fell to the floor. She shrugged apologetically toward Heaven.

"Kicker!" She ran over and wrapped her arms around him. "I'm so glad ta see ya again!" She stretched back and

RE-DEAL

held him by the shoulders. "Ya look very handsome." She removed his hat. "Wow, I see over the past year, like Samson, you've let yer hair grow. Looks like 4.1 inches."

"Yeah," Kicker agreed. "And I feel stronger too."

Michala replaced the hat. "Did ya enjoy spendin' time with yer 23-year-old great grandfather, Raul Bowen?"

"Yes." Juan smiled, and his appearance reflected a new maturity. "Everyone thought we were twins. I now know who my real family would have been if Cypher had not cheated Matt's great grandfather out of his ranch."

"Well then, Kicker, can ya tell me why it took ya so long ta get here? After all, you did have an entire year to get Governor Turner and work yer way back. Five more seconds, and it would have been too late."

"Sorry, Michala." Kicker grinned. "I forgot my wings, so I had to walk."

The angel chuckled as they circled back to watch history be rewritten.

CHAPTER SIXTY

Time Remaining Zero Hours Zero Minutes Zero Seconds

Asa Turner, the Texas Governor, bore down on John L. Cypher. "Mr. Cypher, I understand you and Prince are using his land holdings to swindle Texas' finest citizen out of his ranch." Asa's eyes sparkled as he pulled a sheet of paper from his pocket. "Well, Cypher, I have a similar document." He turned to Lucas. "Luke, call his bet with the state of Texas."

"Mr. Cypher." Lucas beamed with relief. "In what I'm sure is my last high-stake game, I see yer bet of New Mexico, and I call ya with the state of Texas!"

The crowd burst into cheers as Governor Turner guffawed.

Cypher jumped from his chair, turned to Masterson, and protested. "That's not fair! McCain folded!"

Bat turned to the Judge. "Your honor, sir, I didn't see Lucas fold. Did you?"

Michala stepped up beside the Judge and gazed into his eyes. "Yer fine Judge will be truthful. His new campaign motto is, 'Honesty is the best policy.'"

Judge Watson felt as though the pretty lass could see through him, and he felt ashamed of his involvement with Cypher. Even at the risk of becoming worm food, he decided to tell the truth.

"No," he said, "Cypher is lying. Lucas didn't fold. Devol affirmed he would feed me to the worms if I didn't side with Cypher. I was watching carefully, and I can declare Lucas never threw his cards in."

RE-DEAL

"John Lew Cypher." Masterson pulled out his six-shooter and ordered, "Show your cards or fold."

"Don't worry, Holliday," Devol said confidently in the back. "We'll still win. Cypher used my stacked deck."

Cypher was tense but still confident of victory. As a backup, he knew Devol had stacked the decks before running this scam. "I have four kings, which beats that full house I know you're holding." John laid down his cards and grabbed for the money. "It's all mine!" He laughed as he circled both arms around the pile of greenbacks and the precious deed to the McCain ranch.

"Hold it, ya scoundrel!" Lucas allowed. "I knew ya stacked the deck, ya double dealin' cheater! That's why I didn't stay with that pat full-house."

Lucas wanted to work up some suspense and make Cypher sweat a spell. He spotted his son's teacher standing beside Bowen's son. "Michala, would ya please step on over." His attention was drawn to the apron wrapped around her waist. "Look at you—ya always want ta help. That's why my boy loves ya so." He handed her his poker hand. "Please tell Mr. Cypher what I'm holdin'."

She took the pile of playing cards, looked at them, and said, "Well, it looks like Mr. McCain has a pair of pairs."

"Two pairs, is that all?" Cypher screamed out. "My four kings slaughter your lousy two pairs. So that means I still win! The ranch is mine!"

"But Mr. Cypher, I hear this is a very powerful two pairs." She leaned over and laid the cards in front of Cypher. "Mr. McCain has a pair of red aces." She laid down the diamond and heart. "He also has a twin pair of black cards." She laid alongside the red cards the ace of clubs and ace of spades.

At the sight of four aces, Cypher's eyes dilated with terror, and his frame began to shake.

"My four aces whip yer lousy four kings," Lucas pronounced. "So instead of you, I'll take the winnings."

"And now, Cypher," Masterson said, "you are under arrest for the murder of three people, with more charges to follow. This time, Cypher, you won't be able to bribe your way free." He nodded at the bartender. "Send for the sheriff."

"Thanks, Asa," Lucas said as he collected his profit and handed back the powerful sheet of paper. "Here, I don't need yer State."

"I guess not," Asa allowed with a laugh. "You already have Prince's ample property. Lucas, you ought to teach him a lesson and keep the estate."

"Yer right, Asa." Lucas peered over at Prince and pronounced, "Governor, I'm gonna keep yer New Mexico lands. Prince, ya used yer massive land holdings in an attempt to cheat me out of mine. You used yer land unfairly but lost it fairly. Yer fired and are no longer Governor. You can take yer leave." He pointed toward the door. "Adios!"

The throng taunted Prince as they stripped his custom clothes off and rolled his blob of blubber out into the street.

Lucas felt an inner glow of satisfaction. They had finally crushed the killer, John Lew Cypher. He folded the forfeited deed to Prince's tremendous territories and placed it into his pocket.

"Matt!" Juan ran over to Matt. "You did it, Mano!"

"Kicker!" Matt wrapped his arms around Juan and they embraced.

Asa moved over to Maria. He took her hand and gave it a kiss. "So, this is the beautiful mother of our twins."

"Twins?" Maria replied, perplexed. "Raul is one of a kind!"

Governor Turner grinned, thinking Maria was teasing him about her twins. "Confidentially, that's precisely why I left him to run the Governor's mansion. But your other boy has some real face-kicking feet on him."

Lucas was preoccupied at the appearance of the person who called him Grandpa. "Thank ya Phantom, or whoever you are." He offered his hand. "I hope you'll stick around. I would like ta show ya my appreciation for helpin' us expose that murderin' Cypher."

Juan looked at his watch. "Matt, only three minutes left!"

RE-DEAL

"I hear you, Kicker. Time to get!"

"Matt! Kicker! Hurry!" their guardian shouted from outside the entrance. "This way, boys!"

"Raul!" Maria spotted her son running after the tutor. "Dear, please don't leave without a nice visit!"

The Rock-Head Devol along with the staggering Holliday stepped in front of the split saloon doors blocking Matt and Juan. Gripping his barf filled boot in one hand and revolver in the other Holliday said confidently, "Phantom, Yer not moving without paying the Doc!"

Again Maria cried, "Raul! Get back here!"

Oh boy, thought Juan, *more fun for the Foot Doctor.*

Juan leaped high, jabbing a savage boot heel into the growling teeth of Devol, providing a calcium snack for the rockhead and new business for the Doc. Devol's head slammed cruelly into the mahogany door he earlier cracked. The split finally gave way, and the hard piece came crashing down firmly onto Holliday's hand, knocking the gun to the floor. Juan's feet separated, driving his right foot into the smelly boot and splashing the vulgar excretions across the Doc's face. A second roundhouse to the ear put Holliday out of his gagging misery.

Devol came roaring back. Juan spun fast, driving a turnkick painfully into Devol's soft gut. "Heel, you mad dog, heel!" Devol again crashed into the doorframe and slid to the floor, finally heeling to the gentle persuasion.

"Wow! Did you see that?" Jamie Bowen wrapped his arm around his wife. "Darling, I didn't know our boy could kick like that!"

"This way, boys!" Michala urged.

The angel and Juan dashed toward the buggy with Matt close behind.

Damen shoved his way between Maria and Bowen and ran after the buggy. He wasn't going to be left behind with the rats, rattlesnakes, and scorpions.

"Get movin', Seraphim," Miss Guided shouted.

Kicker seized the coach door and swung out on it. He stuck his hand out; Michala grabbed it, and he swung her inside.

"Mano." Juan reached for Matt. "Grab my hand, buddy!"

"I can't see it!" Matt cried as he somehow managed to bound onto the moving back. "Whoa, thank you, Lord," Matt murmured. "That was close."

"Matt, heave yourself over, and we'll grab ya!"

Matt carefully climbed around to the door, and Juan grabbed him and pulled him inside.

"Seraphim, now, back to the present!"

Damen sprinted forward and threw himself at the carriage. He managed to grab onto the back and climb onto the top. He crawled to the front and pulled a lever separating the horse from the coach. He moved back to the middle of the roof, right over the open door. He swung himself down into the coach and dropped behind everyone, landing with his back up against the opposite wall. He was in the perfect position to kick everyone back out the door.

"We don't need you, Magoo!" With both boots, Damen shoved Matt off the coach.

Matt grabbed onto the door as he was shoved out and held on for dear life.

Damen adjusted and shoved again. "I don't need you anymore either, alien!" He thrust his feet straight and Michala flew out the door.

"No!" Matt wailed as Michala's body bounced by him.

Juan dove down onto Damen, grabbed him around the neck, and held him hard. "Hang on, buddy!" Kicker cried.

As Matt dangled, the out-of-control carriage hit an embankment and lurched onto the opposite two side wheels, slamming the door shut. Matt was thrown backwards into the buggy as it tumbled over and over off the side of the cliff. The only thing the three could hear as they tumbled through the air was the muffled tone of Matt's talking timepiece.

"Time remaining zero hours zero minutes zero seconds."

EPILOGUE

Back in Heaps and Piles

The sound of his talking timepiece caused Matt to again remember Cypher's sick words, "Forty-eight hours and your father will die—slowly." Oh no! They were too late!

The three travelers were thrown from the coach, and they continued to plunge. They landed on a grassy hill and rolled over the edge of a precipice. They all screamed in terror as their bodies tumbled through the air, then burst into a big body of water, totally submerged. Each struggled to swim up toward the top. As one after the other broke the surface, they gasped hard for air.

They could hear a crowd of people laughing, cheering, and applauding. Deejay music pumped a heavy beat, and part of the crowd was dancing. Everyone was in twenty-first century bathing suits. The three men dog paddled to the edge of the pool and climbed out. The people around the pool all hooted and hollered at what they thought was some kind of strange entertainment.

"Damen!" A familiar angry voice snapped, "what's ya doin' in the President's pool?"

Damen recognized the incensed man as his father, Big Lew. Good! He'd made it. He climbed from the pool and stood proudly, happy to be back where his old man was boss and he was heir to the Cypher throne.

"Sorry, father," Damen panted. "Considering you're the boss, I didn't think you cared. But that's not important. The good news is I got Matthew back for you. When I hopped on that old horse-stage, and it disappeared, I know where it went! I was there! If you can believe this, we went back to the past. And it looks like I saved our ranch for you. You should be pleased with me, my exalted father. Look, I have your gold lighter."

Damen turned his pocket inside out, but, to his surprise and confusion, the lighter was gone.

Some of the partiers around the pool laughed.

What's this? Damen thought. *Who dares laugh at a Cypher!* He stopped and listened. The peasants were freely laughing at them and having fun, and that was unthinkable. He looked around. Things were different. The pool area was filled with flowers and well kept. People weren't afraid of him, the lord-to-be, and his old man.

"Father, I thought you hated flowery landscaping. When did you do all these sissy upgrades? And-and why are you dressed like-like a servant?"

Big Lew Cypher's bark caused the hair on the back of Matt's neck to raise. He remembered that his father's time finished just as they fell free from the coach. They would have been successful, but his selfish actions caused them to fail.

His head became fuzzy as he tried to wipe the water from his eyes and focus. He closed his eyes and cautiously re-opened them. Then like the focused lens on a camera, everything was crystal clear. He looked toward Cypher's screeching voice, and for the first time in years he could clearly see his long-time adversary. Still something had changed. Cypher sounded uneducated and looked like a servant. His voice was brittle and his demeanor different. Matt watched clearly as Cypher extracted a cheap lighter and lit up a stenchy cigarette.

"Kicker," Matt whispered to Juan. "A miracle has happened! I can see clearly again."

Juan's eyes went wide with wonder. "You can see again? That's good, because Big Lew is coming our way. So get your feet ready."

Matt stood side by side with his buddy, both ready to face their foe.

RE-DEAL

"Damen," Lew Cypher yelled with the cigarette dangling between his lips. "Ya worthless kid. Gets yer butt over here, now! Ya's suppose ta be helping serve the appetizers to these fine peoples. Not talkin foolish nonsense." He bent down and grabbed a fist full of grass. "I'm gonna teach ya to respect yer elders." He reached between Matt and Juan and grabbed Damen by the ear, then stuffed the hand full of grass into his mouth.

Surprised at the assault, Damen let out a short yelp. Lew shoved the boy to the ground and kicked him in the butt. "Get movin'. And shut yer flapping trap!" He lowered his eyes. "Sorry Mr. McCain, Mr. Bowen, sirs. I think my son needs a good lickin'!"

Matt and Juan watched in stunned silence as Cypher, dressed in caterer's clothing, kicked his stunned son. "Ya worthless piece a crap! Does ya wants ta get us fired? It's not every day we gets hired to work at a fine job like this party!"

Everyone hooted as Lew herded Damen away, booting him in the butt. The party-goers assumed the scene was part of the entertainment.

Juan remembered how Nebuchadnezzar gobbled grass like a heifer, and now the Cyphers were doing the same. Kicker said a quick prayer that Lew Cypher would turn from Satan to the open arms of his compassionate Creator.

Matt was surprised to see Big Lew was no longer the powerful person he had left in the present. Matt blinked and massaged his eyes. He wanted to find out how far he could see. He was amazed to realize he could even see the blades of grass in the elegant gardens lining the lavish pool. He looked around and saw Big Lew's huge mansion.

Matt grabbed Kicker by the shoulders. "Everything is so beautiful!"

"Cool, Mano." Kicker looked into Matt's normal-appearing eyes. "I suppose that attack with the magnifying glass never happened."

The crowd laughed—they thought the young men were putting on a show.

"But Kicker, where is Miss Guided?" Then Matt remembered Damen had shoved her out the coach right before they fell. "Juan, she didn't make it."

Matt turned back to the swimming pool and searched side to side. To his chagrin, he saw nothing. "She's gone."

Kicker quietly pulled Matt away from the pool. He knew the angelic woman was fine, but he couldn't tell his friend. "I'm sure Miss Guided is just fine! You know how she is, like the wind, she comes and goes."

"Yes, yes," Matt agreed. "I'm sure you're right." He lifted his head and said, "Thank you, my Lord, for the marvelous moments you gave me with Miss Guided. I trust she is in your merciful hands."

"You're the one that's misguided!" a Texas Ranger cried out as he laughed and played along with all the joking.

A retired actor raised a glass. "Way to go, guys! Did you jump from a helicopter or what?"

"Are you sane, my silly brother?" Debra declared as she drew near. "Swimming in your clothes now, huh?"

Matt did a double take. It took him a second to recognize his dead sister Debra—now breathing, well-dressed, and business-like. "Debra!" He grabbed the girl and held her tight. "Sis, you're alive!"

"I'm alive." She pushed him away. "But you're going to be dead if you don't shut this party down and start getting ready for Daddy's special guests tonight." She turned to Juan. "You too, young Mr. Bowen. You also better start getting busy. Your father isn't the Pope, but he is important."

She quickly rushed away.

The boys looked around at the curious crowd in confusion.

"Kicker," Matt whispered to Juan, "let's get!"

They slowly backed away with a bow. Everyone laughed as if they were performing a comedy act.

"Um, excuse us, please," Matt said as they turned and trotted toward the mansion.

"I don't get the skit," Sensei said to Steve. "Do you?"

RE-DEAL

Once inside, the pair slipped past several people and sprinted up the staircase. Topside, Kicker peeked around the corner of the library. He saw no one, and even though they were still soaking, they slipped inside. But nothing seemed the same. Then Juan spotted a collection of framed photos, paintings, and memorabilia.

"Mano," Juan said. "I never saw any of this before."

Over the fireplace Matt noticed a large portrait of his great grandpa. They moved closer and Matt found another frame that held an old newspaper under glass. For the first time in years, Matt could read the faded headline. 'Cypher Scheme Stopped by Phantom of the Card Table.' He turned to Kicker. "Wow, it's a miracle. I can see this small print."

"Yeah," Juan said, "the Big Man is merciful."

"Despite my screw-up, our trip must have been a success! However, I have to admit the loss of Michala was the horrible price I paid for my sin." He faced the floor. "And the loss of her leaves a large hole in my heart."

"'Ey Mano, you know she's all right. And you and me, two bachelors to the rapture. Like the Tarsus dude, ready to take on the evil forces for the Big Man!"

Matt realized his feelings for Miss Guided were those of an immature schoolboy infatuated with his teacher. He might be twenty-nine, but his life was just beginning. And like Kicker said, they had a mission for the Big Man, and he had to be ready.

"Yeah," Matt agreed. "Maybe things won't be so tough with Big Lew out of the way." Just then Matt's eyes went wide with worry. "But Kicker, like you and me, Damen knows how this change happened."

"There you go again. Worrying about the unknown and not trusting the Big Man." Kicker pointed to another old portrait, "Now give it a break, and look over here. That's me and my great grandfather Raul with the Texas Governor."

Matt tapped the photo. "Which one is you?"

"That's me on the right."

"Amazing." Matt nodded. "Can't tell you apart. Kicker, I am so glad that we didn't leave you dead at Andrews House."

Kicker grinned. "Yeah, dead is not good. I'm sure gonna miss Asa and Raul."

"Kicker, my clever fighting friend. There are still some pieces missing from this puzzle. Please tell me what happened after we left you for dead back in Virginia City."

"First of all, Damen's bullet only grazed my head, and Asa got me right to a doctor. When I was strong enough, he took me to Texas. I knew that I had one year to convince Governor Turner to help me, then catch up with you in 1882. I also found my real family, and my true name, which believe it or not, is Bowen. The owners of the place we just came from are, or were, my great grandparents."

Matt stepped under the large portrait of Lucas McCain. "Look what it says under the painting." He read the inscription, "I cried to God and He saved me from all my enemies. – Psalm 34."

Wow! Juan thought. *The Almighty provided an actual angel to answer that prayer.*

They heard sirens off in the distance coming their way. The boys stopped to listen. "Something's wrong!" Matt cried.

They ran to the window and watched mesmerized as motorcycles with lights flashing and two large helicopters escorted a presidential motorcade. On the fenders of the lead limo, foreign flags flapped as they came down the driveway. The choppers landed and the center limo stopped at the entrance below. A valet came to the presidential limo door and opened it.

"No way!" Matt gasped in shock. "Let's get downstairs fast!"

The two rapidly bolted down the mansion's grand staircase, then stopped and stared. Inside the entrance, helpers and advisors surrounded a well-groomed man with the bearing of a world leader. The man turned and Matt saw that it was his father, Jim McCain.

Jim stopped and stared in shock when he spotted his soggy son. "What in the name of Moses? Matthew! Do you know what time it is?"

RE-DEAL

Matt and Juan froze in the midst of the staircase. They stared uneasily at each other.

"Boys!" Jim scolded. "I told you that pool party was gonna conflict with the state dinner tonight."

Matt smiled at the sight of his healthy, dignified father and a peaceful feeling folded around him. "Dad! You look just great!"

Jim grinned, then stifled the smile. "Don't you try sweet talking the ol' man." He stepped up the stairs towards his son. "Look at you, Matthew. You have got just one hour to be ready to entertain the gathering at our new little billion dollar outhouse."

"Billion dollar outhouse?" Matt mimicked, mystified. "Sounds interesting. I imagine there will be some important people there?"

"Mr. Bowen." Jim rolled his eyes and addressed Juan. "Would you introduce my son to your parents tonight, okay?"

"Yes, sir," Juan answered, wishing he knew what in the world was going on.

Matt and Juan stared at each other with their mouths hanging open as Jim passed between them and sped up the staircase.

"'Ey Mano, when you find out who my parents are, tell me and I'll introduce them to you."

"So there you are!" Debra walked up with an armload of formal Western wear. "I told you both to shut down that pool party. I'm tired of being your babysitter. Now, take these and get dressed fast. I want you both ready and out front in five minutes. Now get!"

Matt wondered where to go when Kicker grabbed him and shoved him into the nearest bathroom. "Wow!" Juan said. "Your dad sure looks important."

"Yeah," Matt said with a sigh. "And can you believe these changes are all from a single reversal of a winner in a poker pot?"

"Now," Juan asked, "the big question is, have you figured out what's going down?"

"No," Matt said as he slipped into his suit. "And if we stop and ask what's going on, they'll think we're crazy or playing games like my sister thought. Let's just get dressed and hope we figure it out as we go."

They changed and stepped from the bathroom in their Western tuxedoes.

"Let's hurry." Debra grabbed the guys and turned them toward the door. "Move it; we're late!"

"Um, Deb, um," Matt stammered. "That lady called Dad Mr. President. Well, president of, like, a big outhouse cleaning service or something?"

"Matty," Debra said, playing along with the constant kidding, "you are so goofy today. Daddy is not into royal flushes."

"Come on, sis," Matt said playfully. "Just tell me. Our dad is president of what?"

"Now I know you've lost it." Debra sighed. "Everyone knows Daddy is the President of New Mexico, my silly brother. Now move! Your chopper awaits."

Debra rushed them outward where a long, shiny, red whirlybird with a large rack of Texas longhorns affixed to the front was waiting.

"Hey, ya'll," a voice from inside hollered. "Stop lollygagging and get in. The President doesn't take lightly to being late."

"Wow!" Kicker said with a grin. "What a cool chopper."

Matt and Kicker climbed into the back while Debra moved forward with the pilot.

"Try this one on," Matt whispered to Juan. "My sister said my dad is the President of New Mexico."

"Yeah, right. You got your sight back and lost your hearing. She must have said resident, not President."

The two friends sat in quiet contemplation for about forty minutes when Debra finally broke the silence. "There it is, our new 3000-room Asa Spades Hotel."

They looked down on a spectacular forty-story palace. They saw magnificent mountains, tall trees, and a maze of stone walkways and staircases. In front of the imposing building they spied a prism-colored fifty-foot fountain. Now that Matt saw color for the first time in years, he especially appreciated the flower gardens that lined the pathways and pools.

Across the face of the resort were four aces with the ace of spades in front. Below in large illuminated red letters was the name—The Asa Spades.

The chopper sat down on the heliport. The door flew open and Matt's father forced his head in and grinned. "Wow, son, I like your duds. Deb must have picked them out. You look like the pictures of my grandpappy, Lucas. Now come see our latest Asa Spades Palace."

The stunned pair stepped down from the chopper. They held their heads low as the blades whipped. They cleared the pausing propellers and accompanied Jim over to the edge.

"It's beautiful, isn't it?" Jim said, scanning the side. "The Lord from above has blessed our country again. This place will provide many new jobs." He turned from the edge and said, "Come on, follow me, and I'll show you the insides of our little billion dollar outhouse."

The perplexed time travelers followed Matt's father to the elevator where they descended to the ground floor. They followed Jim through rows of lofty Corinthian columns with wide marble archways, astounded at the grandeur.

"I forgot to congratulate you, Matthew." Jim smacked his son on the shoulder. "Your trip was a big success."

"Excuse me, Mr. McCain," Kicker inquired. "But how did you know about our trip?"

"Mr. Bowen, where do you think I've been all week. Sitting on the ol' crapper? Why your visit to the White House is in every newspaper and on every TV channel."

Jim led them into the full foyer of the spacious Asa Spades Palace where Matt's mother Mary moved to meet them. "Welcome home, my handsome blond-haired boy." She fingered a fine piece of set gems. "Oh, and thanks for the cross. I love it!"

Matt's stomach skipped with excitement. "Oh, Mom." He grabbed her and held her close. "I can't tell you how good it is to see you again."

Matt kept his arm wrapped tightly around his mom as they all moved inside. As he followed his father through the hotel, scores of folks from everywhere on the planet milled around, chattering in their native languages. As the McCain group worked their way through the throng, boys bowed, women waved, and others scurried to shake Jim's hand and say, "Nice to see you, Mr. President."

It was no longer misconstrued hearing. Matt knew for sure he heard folks refer to his father as Mr. President.

A television monitor in the lounge caught Kicker's attention. He pointed to the TV. "Matt, listen!"

"... The President of our Southern neighbor, Jim McCain, has again decided to open discussions with President Bowen about possibly joining the US and becoming our fiftieth state. These discussions have been going on since the land patriarch, Lucas McCain, multiplied his land holdings back in 1882, when the disgraced New Mexico Governor allowed his territory to be wagered in a poker game. This set up the opportunity for one of the largest expansions in recent history. On the level of his contemporary, John D. Rockefeller, by the turn of the century, Lucas McCain had swallowed up all of the ranches in the New Mexico territory. This family is reported to be the owner of the world's largest privately-owned piece of land.

"In a related story, President McCain and Lori Turner, the heiress to Governor Asa Turner's hotel empire, have opened their fifteenth Card Phantom Palace at a cost of over 1,000,000,000 dollars. Even though gambling is not allowed at any of the Asa Spades Palaces, millions of rich tourists flock to these resorts annually. The McCain family receives none of the billions of dollars these palaces generate. The profits are used for the infrastructure and education for the ranch's 5.6 million citizens. The most unusual part of the McCain-Turner merger is how their partnership began. Back in 1882, a mysterious gambler known as the Phantom showed up at that infamous poker game just in time to expose a scam, which may have left Lucas McCain broke, and—"

RE-DEAL

"So there you are, Mr. President," an advisor interrupted. "I've been looking all over for you. Your guests have arrived."

"You're right." Jim checked his watch. "We're late! Come on, fellows. It's time to meet our guests and fill our bellies with some of the hotel's fine grub."

Jim led them to a circular staircase. As they spiraled up to the President's private banquet floor, they experienced an explosion of crystals and light, rich colors and mouth-watering smells. In the warm room, about forty people admired the archeological treasures, European furniture, and oil paintings set in gold-leaf frames. A portrait of Governor Asa Turner hung over an immense rosewood fireplace. Two women stood warming themselves in front of the crackling fire. A grandfather clock in the corner ticked away pieces of the present. In the opposite corner a pianist played "The Yellow Rose of Texas." And in the center of the room, a royally-laid-out, Chippendale table pressed down on a plush, maroon rug.

"Kicker, I can't believe Lucas kept the deed, and our family owns the whole state of New Mexico."

"Yeah," Kicker asked, "now that you're so rich, will you still talk to a poor little Mexican boy like me?"

The two ladies standing by the fire spotted the boys and stepped over. "Hello, little brother. Lori's place is beautiful, isn't it?"

"Rosemary?" Juan asked wide-eyed. "Is it really you?"

"My hermanito." Rosemary shrugged and shook her head. "Debra warned us you both were acting loco in la cabeza."

"Excuse me, everyone!" The conversation stopped as Debra tapped her champagne glass. "May I have your attention please?"

A set of double doors opened and two men in black suits with dark sunglasses took up their posts on either side of the doors.

"Please," Debra cleared her throat, "welcome the President of the United States, Raul Bowen the Third, and the First Lady, Maria!"

There were cheers and applause for America's first family.

"Juan, you little devil," Maria said as she slid over and clamped her hands on her sweet baby's cheeks and kissed him. "Fraternizing with the enemy, I see." She touched his head. "Look at this mop! You need a haircut. Who do you think you are, Samson?"

Matt's eyes went wide, and his mind whirled.

"Mr. Matthew McCain," Maria said. "You look like you're in shock." She fluffed her hair. "My new wig is not that bad, is it?" She gave Matt a kiss and moved on.

Wow, Juan thought, *in a mere forty-eight hours, the favor of the Father can turn a forgotten orphan into a famous figure.* Kicker recalled how the thankful Pharaoh overnight made Joseph the prime minister of Egypt. The approved-by-the-Almighty brings the riches of the amoral into the hands of the hallowed. Juan had never believed it could happen to him, however it had. *Thank You!* he prayed.

Juan and Matt looked at each other.

"Matt, my friend, it looks like the Lord has smiled on both of us. And if you're not too uppity yet, I'll introduce you to my father, the President of the United States."

Matt flicked a foot up the side of Juan's head and playfully tapped him on the ear. "Just remember who's the better fighter here!"

The two state leaders stepped over and joined their sons as a third man moved in among them. "Pastor Hagee," Jim stretched out his arm. "Glad you could make it. Caught your sermon online, good message. You're right, the days are numbered. How many folks heard you? Your broadcast goes ta what, fifty countries now?"

"Over one hundred," Pastor Hagee said heartily. "And we're growing everyday."

"Raul," Jim asked, "have you ever heard how Pastor's foregoing kin built his first church?"

"Of course," President Bowen replied. "Who hasn't heard the story about Haggai and manna falling from Heaven wrapped around a rock?"

RE-DEAL

Wow! Juan thought. *What a harvest.*

"Son," President McCain asked, "don't you have a date? Aren't you tired of hanging around with that foreign President's kid?"

The mention of a date made the sadness from the loss of Michala swarm over Matt like a mass of harassed hornets. He already missed her. "Um, no Dad, I don't," Matt said. "I had a date, but she disappeared."

"Well, my shy son," President McCain gestured with his glass, "have you met my new Secretary of Education? That's her over there coming in late."

The lovely blonde lady was dressed in a floor length white gown with a single strand of pearls and matching earrings.

"Michala," Jim called out. "What took you so long?"

"Sorry, Mr. President," Michala answered as she moved over. "I had a hard time findin' a place ta hitch my horse."

"Wow, Kicker," Matt whispered wide-eyed. "I have never really seen Miss Guided clearly except in my dreams. Is it her?"

"Could be, but I'm not sure."

"Kicker, I can hardly believe all this. It's as though we each have angels watching over our lives."

Michala shook his hand and said, "Thanks, Mr. President, for inviting me."

"Happy to have you, Madam Secretary," Jim replied. "Have I introduced you to my son Matt?"

"No, not this century." She looked back at Juan and winked.

RICHARD TURNER

About the Author

Richard Turner is a card mechanic. He does not do card tricks. He demonstrates the most difficult moves ever devised for cheating with cards.

His unparalleled touch with a pack of 52 has been written about and featured on dozens of TV specials around the globe, such as *That's Incredible, Ripley's Believe it or not, The 700 Club. The Paul Daniels Show* on the BBC, and *World Geniuses* in Japan.

Publications across the country, including the *Los Angeles Times*, the *Dallas Times Herald*, the *Orlando Sentinel*, and a cover story in *Genii Magazine,* have profiled Mr. Turner.

He has performed for hundreds of CEOs of large corporations: AT&T, IBM, ARCO Chemical, USAA, Southwest Airlines, and many more. He has entertained legends like Muhammad Ali, Johnny Carson, Gene Kelly, and Bob Hope. He cheated Brad Pitt in the 2009 movie *Tree of Life*.

Events at which Richard has spoken include the 42nd Annual National Security Forum at the Air War College. Defense Intelligence Agency (DIA), and Bolen Air force Base in Washington DC. He has also appeared before many excited students with Secretary of State General Colin Powell.

Mr. Turner has received numerous acknowledgements, including the FBI Director's Community Leadership Award, Rotary Leadership Award, Honorary Commander in the US Air Force, and Honorary Naval Flight Officer. He has won the Golden Lion Award given by Siegfried and Roy and is in

The Magic Castle's Hall of Fame. He is also listed in Believe the Unbelievable Book of World Records for his eight-coin roll.

Richard Turner is a Master in the martial arts, holding a fifth degree black belt in karate. His black belt test, ten rounds of three minutes each, was so grueling it was televised and appeared on the front page of the sports section of the *Los Angeles Times*.

He has designed and created a series of board and puzzle games including Batty and Texas Showdown. Richard has produced a bestselling DVD series on advance card table technique that is used by casinos and card men around the globe.

Due to the uncanny feel he has in his fingers, for years Richard has worked as the touch analyst for the largest card manufacturer in the world.

His latest venture is writing. *Re-Deal: A Time-Travel Thriller* is his first novel.

He co-stars in a stage show, *Hoodwinked*, the cast of which features four of the most renowned international con artists.

Richard has accomplished all this with vision four times lower than what is considered legally blind. A biography telling Richard's unbelievable life story is soon to be released.

For further information check Richard Turner on the Web at www.richardturner52.com or actually view many of Richard's skills at www.Youtube.com/Asa52.